Heart
OF THE
Mirage

BY GLENDA LARKE

The Mirage Makers
Heart of the Mirage
The Shadow of Tyr
Song of the Shiver Barrens

The Stormlord Trilogy
The Last Stormlord
Stormlord Rising
Stormlord's Exile

The Forsaken Lands
The Lascar's Dagger
The Dagger's Path
The Fall of the Dagger

GLENDA LARKE

Heart OF THE Mirage

BOOK ONE
THE MIRAGE
MAKERS

www.orbitbooks.net

ORBIT

First published in Australia in 2006 by Voyager,
HarperCollins*Publishers* Pty Limited
First published in Great Britain in 2007 by Orbit

7 9 11 12 10 8 6

Copyright © Glenda Larke 2006
Map by Perdita Phillips

The moral right of the author has been asserted.

A CIP catalogue record for this book
is available from the British Library.

ISBN 978-1-84149-609-2

Typeset in Minion by Palimpsest Book Production Ltd,
Grangemouth, Stirlingshire
Printed and bound by CPI Group (UK) Ltd, Croydon, CR0 4YY

Papers used by Orbit are from well-managed forests
and other responsible sources.

MIX
Paper from
responsible sources
FSC
www.fsc.org   FSC® C104740

Orbit
An imprint of
Little, Brown Book Group
Carmelite House
50 Victoria Embankment
London EC4Y 0DZ

An Hachette UK Company
www.hachette.co.uk

www.orbitbooks.net

For Mark and Mads
two people I wish I had known sooner,
with love and thanks

Acknowledgements

No one gets to this point in writing a book without help, and I have been lucky enough to have had enthusiastic people supporting me all the way. Top of the list is always my agent, Dorothy Lumley, who has read this particular book so many times without ever losing her enthusiasm for it. My editor Stephanie Smith at HarperCollins Australia, and Kim Swivel, my copy editor, have helped to make it better, even when I thought I was done. And many thanks to my first readers whose appreciation kept me going, and whose criticism and eye for holes is so much appreciated: in this case my fellow Voyager authors Russell Kirkpatrick and Karen Miller; Alena S., Fiona McL., bookseller Mark T. And lastly, thanks to Perdy Phillips for the wonderful map.

Many years ago, when my own children were very young, I heard for the first time two stories, from opposite sides of the globe. One told the tragedy of stolen babies raised by those who had murdered their mothers, inevitably indoctrinated with the very beliefs their true parents had died resisting. The second story, equally tragic and just as true, told how several generations of children were forcibly taken from their loving, caring families to be raised by strangers. They were told to forget who they had been and where they had come from, to forget their language, their culture and their people; indeed to denigrate their very origins.

Ligea's story is my way of saying sorry to all those mothers and their children; my way of paying homage to *los desaparecidos*, the Disappeared Ones of Argentina, and to the Stolen Generations of Aboriginal Australia. As a mother, I have wept for you.

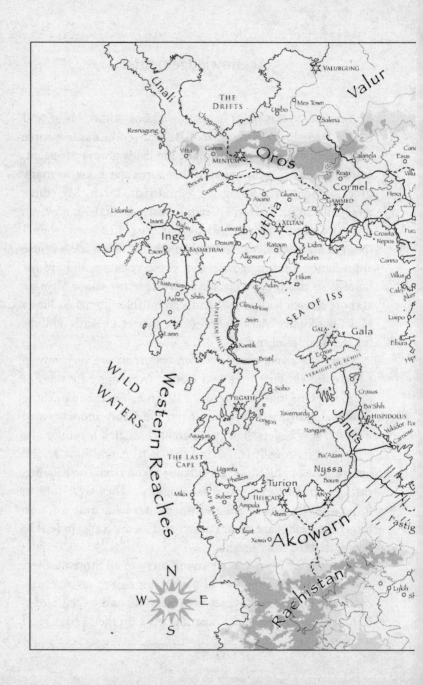

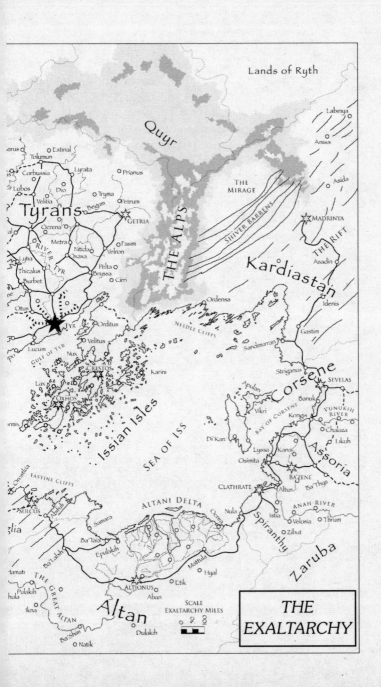

THE
EXALTARCHY

SCALE
EXALTARCHY MILES

Lands of Ryth

Quyr

THE ALPS

THE MIRAGE

SHIVER BARRENS

Labinya

Amisa

Asida

MADRINYA

THE RIFT

Kardiastan

Asadin

Idenis

Ordensa

NEEDLE CLIFFS

Gastim

Corsene

SEVELAS

Striganus

Apulan

Banuk

VUNUKIH RIVER

Sandimurran

Vikri

Kongs

Chalaza

Likuh

Di'Kan

Lyssa

Kanac

Assoria

Osimita

BAZENE

Altus

Ba'Thys

CLATHRATE

Nula

Istia

ANAH RIVER

Spiranthy

Ochen

Velosia

Thrum

Zibut

Zaruba

ALTANI DELTA

Samara

Ba'Taia

Epulakih

Mattula

Hyal

Etik

ALTIONUS

Aban

Dulakih

Natik

Ba'Shim

THE GREAT ALTAN

Altan

Pulakih

Ikna

Hamati

hula

SUICUS

FASTINE CLIFFS

Croalzia

Abdulu

Bo'Labih

zlia

ormis

Lax

OXHOS

CRESTOS

Karini

Issian Isles

SEA OF ISS

Velitus

Orditus

GULF OF TYR

Lucum

Nux

TYR

Otus

po

Thicalus

Burbet

Lytha

RIVER TYR

Metra

Nitida Oxaxa

Velron

Fasim

Pelta

Bryssa

Cirri

Ocrena

GETRIA

Begim

Petrum

Tryma

Prianus

Lyrata

Dio

Velitia

Corbussia

Tolumun

Esthnal

erus

Lobos

is

al

Tyrans

From my early childhood, my life was paved with the mosaics of illusion, each piece another tale of deceit – or delusion. A history of betrayal . . .

Betrayal of a child, and of children.

Betrayal of family, by those who thought they knew what was right.

Betrayal of their nation, by those who loved their country.

Betrayal by fathers, of those they fathered.

Betrayal by friends, of those they loved.

Betrayal by rulers, of those they ruled.

This is a story of treachery: my treachery, and the treachery of those who betrayed me.

It is the story of mirages, and of those who made them.

It is my story.

PART ONE

LİGEA

CHAPTER ONE

When an emperor laughs about you behind your back, you *know* you are in trouble.

When the person speaking to the emperor at the time of his self-satisfied and smug amusement is the Magister Officii, your immediate superior and a man with a cruel sense of humour, well, then you know you ought to find a way to melt into the floor and disappear. If you can't do that, you stride up and down the anteroom to the royal audience hall instead. The carpet, fifteen paces long, showed signs of wear down the centre, so I knew I wasn't the first person to pace while waiting to be called into the august presence of Bator Korbus, Lord of Tyr, High General of Tyrans and Exaltarch of the Tyranian Empire.

If I concentrated, I could feel the Exaltarch's presence in the next room. If I focused my concentration, I could determine his emotions, although once I became aware of them, I wondered if I hadn't been happier ignorant. He exuded a ruthless confidence, like a wily feral dog delighting in its position as leader of the pack. And I knew the topic of his conversation with Magister Rathrox Ligatan was me: why else would I have been called here to wait while the two men chatted? Rathrox headed the civil service, everyone knew that. Not so widely known was his interest in personally directing the Exaltarch's Brotherhood Compeers, of which I was a female agent.

Although I knew Rathrox well, his emotions were harder to divine through the walls of the audience hall. I thought I detected a certain watchfulness, and perhaps an amused tolerance towards his emperor, stopping just short of lese-majesty. Even a civil servant as powerful as the Magister Officii knew better than to ridicule a ruler whose power was absolute.

It was easy to imagine Rathrox, a thin grey man with yellow teeth, using his caustic wit to amuse his emperor. Easy to imagine the sixty-year-old Exaltarch, his handsome face marred by the cynicism of his eyes, being amused by Rathrox's brand of cruel humour. What I couldn't imagine was what they found so entertaining about me.

Even as I speculated, the Exaltarch gave a belly laugh loud enough to carry through to the anteroom. The two imperial guards outside the door affected not to hear; I frowned. I was still pacing up and down, irritably because of the unfamiliar feel of carpet beneath my bare feet, but the laugh halted me. It was the kind of guffaw a person might make if they saw a slave spill soup in a rival's lap. Under the circumstances it was hardly encouraging, although I couldn't imagine what I'd ever done to warrant the mockery of the Exaltarch.

One of the guards gave me a sympathetic look. He had been more appreciative when I'd first arrived, eyeing my bare right shoulder, long legs and the swell of my breasts with a connoisseur's eye, but his appreciation had died once he noticed the graceless way I walked and sat. Not even wearing a fine silk wrap threaded through with gold could make me feminine enough to please a man like that guard; the stylish wrap of the highborn lacked allure when it was worn as if it were a large, hastily donned bath towel. I had no pretensions to elegance, or even moderately good looks. I'm taller than most women, long-limbed and muscular. My skin is an unfashionable brown, and my hair the burnt-sienna colour of desert earth, although I did keep it curled and highlighted gold, more in keeping with Tyranian notions of beauty and fashion.

I felt someone approach the door and prepared myself for its opening. A slave appeared in the doorway and motioned me inside; I obeyed wordlessly and, eyes discreetly downcast, went to kneel at the feet of my monarch, just managing to suppress my distaste for the feel of carpet beneath my knees. The slave slipped away through a side door and I was left alone with the Exaltarch and Magister Rathrox. 'My service is yours,' I said formally, and touched my hand to the hem of the Exaltarch's robe in symbolic submission. The gold trimming was knobbed with seed pearls and felt stiff and harsh beneath my fingers. I kept my eyes lowered.

There was a long silence and then an 'Ah' that was little more than an expelled breath. 'So you are Ligea, the late General Gayed's daughter. Look up, girl, and let me see you properly.'

I raised my head and ventured to return the gaze of the Exaltarch's assessing eyes. I had seen him at close quarters once before, years ago. At the time he'd been returning to the city of Tyr at the head of his victorious troops and in those days he was lean and hard and arrogant, a politician-soldier about to wrest the last vestiges of political power from the hands of his senile predecessor and a divided Advisory Council. The arrogance was still present, but the hardness had gone from the body into his face. His physique was showing signs of easy living – sagging chest, raddled cheeks, a belly large enough to move independently of the rest of him – but his face said this was a man used to being obeyed, a man who knew how to be ruthless. No overindulgence would ever eradicate the brutal shrewdness of those cold eyes, or the harsh lines around his mouth.

He was lounging on a red velvet divan, at ease, the fingers of one hand playing idly with the gold rings on the other. His nails were manicured and polished, and he smelled of moon-flowers and musk. Suspended over his head, a long reed fan swayed to and fro to stir the warm air. There was no sign of the slaves who operated it; doubtless some mechanism enabled them to perform the task from an adjacent room.

When he looked away for a moment to glance at Rathrox, I risked a quick look myself. The Magister leant against the cushions of another divan but his thin, stiff body made no indent on the upholstery, his hands were rigidly still. I was unused to seeing him in the role of a subordinate, unused to seeing him tense. He seemed out of place, like an ugly, foul-smelling insect that had flown into the perfumed boudoir of some highborn lady and didn't know how to escape. Behind him, a marble fireplace dominated the other end of the room, flanked by a clutter of gilded furniture, painted amphorae and too many exotic ornaments. Lion skins, the glass eyes of their heads powerless to express outrage at the ignominy of their fate, were scattered here and there on the carpet. A full-sized statue had its own wall recess, two figures entwined in grotesque embrace: a reminder of the sibling founders of Tyr whose relationship had so repulsed the gods they'd punished the city with the plague.

I wanted to let my gaze wander around the room, to mock the luxury of it, but the one brief glance was all etiquette allowed me. I had to give my full attention to the Exaltarch.

His shrewd eyes lingered on me, speculating. I continued to kneel, awaiting permission to rise, or to speak, but the only sound was the murmur of running water all around us. Tiled fountains set into the walls, or so I guessed. I had them in my own villa. They helped to regulate temperature, cooling the hot air of the desert-season or, once heated, warming the cold air of the snow-season – but I'd heard that in the palace they were thought to perform another function as well. They made it hard for slaves to eavesdrop.

A minute crawled by in silence while we stared at one another.

What the Vortex was so damned interesting about me?

I didn't dare let my eyes drop.

'You are not what I expected,' he said finally, in the smooth-accented speech of the highborn. 'You may stand if you wish.'

I scrambled to my feet. 'I was only the General's adopted daughter,' I said. 'If you look for signs of General Gayed in me, you won't find them, Exalted.'

'No,' he agreed. 'And Gayed was ever a man of action. I'm told you have more of a talent for deviousness, and are well suited to the machinations of the Brotherhood. Rathrox tells me you have an uncanny instinct for the truth – or a lie – on the tongue of a prisoner. He says torture is almost obsolete in the Cages since you took on the important interrogations.'

'Lies come easily to the tongues of the tortured, Exalted. They will say anything to ease their pain. My way is better.'

'What is your way?'

'To assess each reply and use, what? A woman's intuition? I do not know, Exalted. It is just a knack I have. And if a man does not tell the truth – well, a lie can sometimes be equally revealing.'

He looked at me curiously, his attention finely focused. 'How long have you had this ability?'

'Since I was a child.' It had always been there, but I'd learned young to hide it. Adults didn't take kindly to having their untruths pointed out to them by a girl not even old enough to wear a wrap.

'A useful ability, I imagine. And we have a mission for you where your skills may be invaluable, Compeer Ligea. You are

Kardiastan-born, I believe. Do you remember anything of that land?'

'Nothing, Exalted. I was barely three when my parents were killed in the Kardiastan Uprising and General Gayed took a liking to me and brought me here, to Tyr.'

'Yet I'm told you speak the language.'

'There was a Kardi slave-nurse in the General's household when I arrived. It pleased her to have me speak her tongue.' I thought, without knowing why I was so certain, *And you already knew that.*

He gave the faintest of cynical smiles and glanced briefly at Rathrox. The exchange was worrying, and contained a meaning from which I was deliberately excluded. Once again I sensed their shared amusement. Suspicion stiffened me. The Exaltarch sat up, reaching over to a side table to pour himself a drink from a carafe of green onyx. The heady scent of moonflowers and musk was overpowering, catching in the back of my throat, and I had to subdue a desire to cough. The room was cool enough, yet sweat trickled down my neck and soaked the top edge of my wrap.

As the Exaltarch sipped his wine, I thought, *Now.* Now comes the whole point of this charade.

'We wish you to go to this land of your birth, Compeer Ligea,' he said. 'There is trouble there neither our Governor nor his Prefects nor our Military Commanders seem able to stem. It has its origins in rumour; we wish you to show this rumour to be a lie, trace it to its source and eradicate it.'

'And if it is true?' I asked mildly.

He snorted and reverted to the rougher speech of the soldier he had once been. 'It can hardly be true. Not unless the burned can rise from the ashes of the fire that consumed them. A man died at the stake in the port of Sandmurram, for treason. There is now a rebellious movement led by yet another traitorous bastard, who the superstitious say is the same man. He is known as Mir Ager. Some say that is his name, others believe it to be a title meaning lord, or leader. Still others think it has something to do with the area of Kardiastan called the Mirage. Perhaps he was born there.'

I inclined my head to indicate I was absorbing all this.

'As is so often the case where Kardiastan is concerned, there is confusion,' he added, his tone biting. 'I want you to find this – this sodding son of a bitch, bring him to justice, and discredit any claim that he is the same bastard as was executed in Sandmurram.'

I risked a puzzled glance in Rathrox's direction. All this was hardly a matter for my attention; still less something the Exaltarch would involve himself in personally. I said, 'But surely, our intelligence in Kardiastan—?'

There was venom in the Exaltarch's eyes, whether for me or his incompetent underlings or the whole conquered land of Kardiastan I couldn't tell, but it was unmistakable. 'If it was possible for them to find this man, or to squash these rumours, they would have done so. This is a job needing a special person with special abilities. Magister Ligatan tells me you are that person. I bow to his judgement, although—' He allowed his glance to sweep over me, disparaging what he saw. 'Are you up to such a task, Compeer?'

His scepticism did not worry me; the thought of leaving Tyrans did, but I knew better than to allow any sign of my consternation to show on my face. 'I shall do my best to serve the Exaltarchy, as ever, Exalted.'

'Rathrox will tell you the details. You are both dismissed.'

A minute later, still blinking from the abrupt end to the audience, I was tying on my sandals at the entrance to the ante-room and wondering just what it was the Exaltarch had not told me. There was much that had been withheld, I felt sure.

I looked across at Rathrox who was just straightening from fastening his own sandal straps. In the muted light of the hall he appeared all grey; a grey, long-limbed, mantis-thin man, waiting for me. A man of prey. I said, 'Suppose you tell me what all this is about, Magister?'

'What is there to say? The Exaltarch asked me to choose someone to send to Kardiastan. When I mentioned you, he was a little surprised at my choice, and wished to meet you before giving his approval. He found it difficult to believe a woman could possess the – the necessary toughness for the job, even though I did tell him you have killed on Brotherhood business, just as all Brotherhood Compeers must at one time or another.' His face was immobile, as ever. As a mantis is without expression while it awaits its victim. Dedicated, pitiless, patient . . . so very patient, waiting for the right moment to strike. I did not like him, but he was my mentor and I admired and respected him for his commitment and cunning.

Honesty was not, however, one of his virtues. He was skirting the truth, reluctant to utter an outright lie, knowing I would identify it as such, but equally reluctant to be completely honest. There was something lacking in his explanation. I asked quietly, 'Why me? Why anyone? Why cannot those already in Kardiastan deal with this?'

He looked around. We had moved away from the imperial guards in the anteroom, but apparently not far enough for Rathrox. He took me by the elbow and guided me through an archway into the deserted hallway beyond. Even so, he dropped his voice. 'Ligea, the Exaltarchy is only as solid as the soil it is built on. The situation in Kardiastan is far worse than the public here is given to believe. There we have built on a cracked foundation and, unless something is done soon, those cracks will become canyons large enough to swallow both the legions and the civil administration. Worse still, cracks can spread.'

It was unlike Rathrox to be so frank, and even stranger for him to be so grim about the state of the Exaltarchy. I said, carefully picking my way through the conversational pitfalls of a chat with the Magister, who could be vicious when tetchy, 'I would hardly have thought Kardiastan mattered enough to arouse the personal concern of the Exaltarch. The place produces nothing of essential commercial value to us. The only reason we ever felt the need to invade in the first place was because we feared Assoria might beat us to it, in order to gain ports along the Sea of Iss within striking distance of Tyrans. But we've tamed Assoria since then; it has been our vassal for, what? Twenty years?'

He interrupted. 'If a desert land inhabited by shabby, ill-trained peasants can make a mockery of our legions, how long will it be before other subject nations – such as Assoria – sharpen their spears? We must make an example of these Kardi insurgents.'

'Make a *mockery* of our legions? A few peasant rebels?' It all seemed rather unlikely. I recalled the Exaltarch's bitterness when he had spoken of Kardiastan. Rathrox's reason for involving me might be valid as far as it went, but it wasn't all; there was something I was not being told. 'And what about the Brotherhood?'

'There is no Brotherhood in Kardiastan.'

I stared at him in amazement. '*No* Brotherhood?' I'd never had much to do directly with either the vassal states or the provinces, but every Brother knew we were responsible for security throughout the Exaltarchy, not just in Tyrans. It had never occurred to me there was any place where Tyr ruled that was free from the mandibles of the Brotherhood. 'Why ever not?'

'You can't have a Brotherhood where there are no inform-ants, where no one will spy on his neighbour, where no one can be bought, or cowed, or blackmailed.' He gave a thin smile. 'A point the public elsewhere tends to overlook, Ligea. They hate us, but it is they themselves who supply us with our power over them. Apparently the point is not overlooked in Kardiastan. They are . . . different. A strange people we seem to have been unable to fathom even in twenty-five years of occupation.' The cold, speculative look of the mantis staring at its prey. 'Every single agent of the Brotherhood I have sent there has been dead within a year.'

I was chilled by a depth of fear I had not felt in years. Chilled – and stirred by the enticing whisper of danger. I said, 'You think I might have a better chance because I was born a Kardi, because I speak the language, because I could pass for one of them. Because I once *was* one of them.'

'Perhaps.'

His feelings rasped my consciousness, as tangible as grit in the eye. I thought, *Goddess! How he distrusts me* . . . Even after all the years of my service, he could still wonder about my loyalty to him.

We stood in the middle of the marbled hall, both motionless, both wary. Nearby, the life of the palace went on. An anxious-eyed slave scurried past carrying a basket of fruit; a small contingent of imperial guards marched by, their sandals squeaking on the highly polished floor. They escorted a royal courtesan, as thickly painted as a backstreet whore, on her way to the Exaltarch's quarters. She giggled when she caught sight of me, her lack of manners as blatant as the trail of perfume she left behind. Neither Rathrox nor I took any notice.

I asked, 'So I am to be sent to a land said to be so hellish it's akin to the realm of the dead? Without anyone asking if that was what I wished.'

'It is unwise to disobey the order of the Exaltarch.'

'It was your idea.'

'It is only a temporary thing. You will soon be back in Tyrans.'

I stared at him, hearing the lie. 'You don't intend me ever to return,' I said flatly. 'You think I will be too invaluable there.' *You wish to be rid of me . . .*

'Those in service to the Exaltarchy must serve where they are of greatest value.'

I interrupted. 'And that is not the only reason which motivates you, Magister Officii. I think you have come to fear me. I am too good at my job. It worries you that you cannot lie to me, that I know the feelings seething behind that expressionless face of yours. So now it comes to this: a posting without hope of recall. What is it they say of Kardiastan? *A land so dry the dust is in the wind instead of underfoot and the only water is in one's tears.*' I gave a bitter smile. 'Is that how my service to you, to the Brotherhood, to the Exaltarchy, is to be repaid? You wouldn't do this, Magister Rathrox, if Gayed were alive. My father would never have allowed it.' It was five years since his death, yet I felt the pang of loss still.

'General Gayed put his Exaltarch and his nation before all else, as you must. The Exaltarchy has given you all that you own, all that you are. Now you must pay the reckoning.' He shrugged. 'Supply the information that will quell the Exaltarch's rebellious subjects in Kardiastan and he will not forget you. Even now your salary is to be raised to six thousand sestus a year, while you remain in Kardiastan, and you go as a Legata, with the equivalent status of a Legatus.'

My eyes widened. A Legatus was someone with a special mission and they carried much of the status of the official who sent them. If my papers were signed by Rathrox, my power in Kardiastan would be extensive. It was telling that I'd never heard of the feminine form of the word. Such power was not normally given to a woman. 'You must be very afraid of me to have obtained those terms, Magister Officii. They are generous indeed. *If* I can stay alive, of course. Nonetheless, I think I would have preferred to resign the Brotherhood, had you given me the option.'

'No one leaves the Brotherhood,' he said, the words as curt as his tone. 'Not ever. You know that. Besides, what would you do without the intrigue, without the power, without the challenge, Legata Ligea? The Brotherhood is your drug; you cannot survive without it. You would never make a pampered wife, and what other alternative is there for you?' His voice softened a little. 'I'm twice your age, Ligea. One day I'll no longer head the Brotherhood. Take comfort from that thought.'

I hated knowing how well he read me. I turned abruptly, leaving him, and made my way to the palace entrance. The sentries swung open the massive carved doors, then sprang to attention and saluted as I passed. I'd identified myself as one of the Brotherhood on the way in, and they knew it paid to be respectful to a compeer.

Out once more in the dazzling sun, I looked around in relief. I'd never liked needless luxury and the extravagance of the Exaltarch's palace was stifling, especially when coupled with the emotions still warring inside me even now: anger, bitterness, pride, frustration. I thought I knew now why the Exaltarch had been amused. The idea of sending a Kardi to deal with Kardi insurgents was not without irony, and when the Kardi in question was a woman raised as a highborn Tyranian – oh yes, the situation was amusing. Unless you were the one being banished to a desert hell. The muscles of my stomach tightened in rebellion.

Tyr, capital and hub of Tyrans – of the whole Exaltarchy – was my home; the only home I remembered. It was the centre of the civilised world, the place where everything began, where all decisions that counted were made, where things happened. How could I bear to leave it?

I stood at the top of the stairs leading down from the palace doors and looked out over the Forum Publicum, the heart of Tyr. It was the hour before siesta and the Forum, a mile in length, was crowded in spite of the midday heat. The usual mixed throng: slaves and ambling highborn, merchants and work-stained artisans, strolling scholars debating a theory. Fountains jetted spray into the air in the centre of the marbled concourse and water channels bordered the edges. They even warmed the water when the weather turned cold . . .

Damn you, Rathrox Ligatan. I am to lose all of this.

I thrust back the rising bubble of anger and made instead a conscious effort to absorb all I could see, as if by carving a bas-relief of images into my memory, I could ensure that at some time in the future I would be able to recall them to assuage the emptiness of loss.

On the far side of the square, the massive Hall of Justice brooded, its white columns catching the sun. White-robed lawyers were just emerging from a morning session with their lictors, arms full of ribboned scrolls, hurrying behind. Only two days before, I'd stood in the Praetor's chambers there to give evidence in camera at a treason trial; the accused had led a rebellion against tax collection in one of the outliers of Tyrans. Two hundred people had died as a result of his ill-considered revolt. He'd been condemned, as he deserved, and I'd felt the satisfaction of a job well done. Our court system, where even a common man could argue his case, was one of the finest achievements of the Exaltarchy.

The next building along was the Public Library, separated from the Public Baths by the tree-lined Marketwalk. If I entered the quietness of the library reading room, doubtless I'd find Crispin the poet or Valetian the historian working on their latest creations; if I decided to bathe in the building opposite instead, I would be bound to meet my childhood friends, most of them now idle young matrons more inclined to eye the legionnaire officers in the massage room than to spend their time at the baths swimming, as I did. If I wandered down the Marketwalk, I could buy fruit from Altan, or ice from the Alps, or a talking bird from Pythia to the west. Jasper or jade, silk or sackcloth, peppercorns or pheasant livers: there was a saying in Tyr that the stalls of Marketwalk sold everything worth buying in the known world.

On my right, across the square opposite the baths, was the arched entrance of the Advisory Council Chambers, used as gaming rooms ever since the Exaltarch had dismissed his recalcitrant Councillors, never to recall them; and beyond that was the paveway to the Desert-Season Theatre, where two weeks previously I'd seen Merius immortalise himself with his powerful portrayal of the manipulative Cestuous, whose tainted love for his sister Caprice had almost doomed the fledgling Tyr, and whose name was now synonymous with the despised perversion of incest.

I shifted my gaze to the Academy of Learning on my left, where, as a citizen of Tyrans, I had often enjoyed the privilege of listening to the scholars' debates. It had been an Academy scholar who'd been in charge of my education from my seventh anniversary day until I'd turned sixteen, a privilege not often granted to girls. I sometimes wondered why my father, a man much given to talking disparagingly of 'a woman's place', had allowed – no, had *encouraged* – my formal education. 'You have a mind, Ligea,' he was fond of saying. 'Use it. Rely on it. Your emotions are those of a woman: foolish, unreliable and ruled from the heart. Ignore such stupidities. The heart is the foundation of ill-made decisions; the mind is where victories are forged.' I smiled to myself: I could hear him still, stern tones deliberately softening when he spoke to me. Others may have feared General Gayed, the man they called the Winter Leopard after his snow-season victories quelling the fractious tribes of the Forests of Valur to the northwest, but I never did. To me he may have been firm and intolerant of nonsense, but he was always kind.

I lingered on the steps, remembering him. The pang of grief I felt was a weakness, inappropriate for a compeer, but I didn't care. I decided I would head for his tomb at the other end of the Forum and pay homage to his memory. A long walk, although one I wanted to make. Masochism, in a way, I suppose; not because of the destination, but because all I passed en route would remind me of what I was about to miss. But I wanted those memories. I wanted to absorb the essence of these symbols of Tyr. For they weren't just buildings; they were also the commerce, the learning, the law, the sport, the religion, the arts: they were all the things Tyr stood for. We were a cultured, refined people who respected both the human intellect and the human body.

And Kardiastan? In Kardiastan, the soil was as barren as its cultural heritage.

How would I be able to bear it?

Damn you, Rathrox.

The Temple of the Forum Publicum was built to honour the deity Melete. Other public buildings were imposing, graceful even, but the temple was surely one of the loveliest structures ever built by mankind. The roof floated above lines of graceful caryatids, each supposedly a likeness of the Goddess in a different mood. The pediments and fascia were decorated with coloured friezes and statuary, the work of several centuries of the Exaltarchy's finest artists. Marbled columns glowed rosy in both the dawn light and the last rays of dusk or, as now, gleamed white with painful intensity in the midday sun.

General Gayed's tomb was not in the temple proper, but along the pilgrim's way leading up to the main steps. There was nothing ornate about it; I had insisted on that. A flat oblong of marble marked his burial spot. A life-sized statue on a plinth engraved with his name was the only adornment. Not a man who liked frivolities, he would have approved of the tomb's austerity. I knelt and prayed there, although my prayer was unorthodox. I spoke to him, not to any god, thanking him for the compassion that had prompted him to take a war orphan under his wing in the heat of battle, for all the kindnesses he had extended to me as his adopted daughter. I blessed him, as I had so often done before. Without him, I would have been a Kardi barbarian, and the thought was the subject of a recurring nightmare I'd had in my younger years. I'd had a narrow escape, and it was all due to him.

After I left Gayed's tomb, I walked on up into the public concourse of the Meletian Temple.

Melete was the city's patroness, the Goddess of Wisdom, Contemplation and Introspection. I always thought her a strange deity for a city ruling all the lands around the Sea of Iss by virtue of armed power. There were over a hundred deities in the pantheon, many more appropriate: Ocrastes, the many-headed God of War, for example. Or Selede, Goddess of Cunning. But no, our founders had chosen Melete. People said the Goddess was the reason Tyr became a centre of learning and scholarship; some even maintained the caryatids wept each time Tyr conquered another nation with bloodshed rather than negotiation. I was not given to such fancies, myself.

I bought some perfumed oil from the stalls littering the forecourt of the temple and went on into the sanctum. I gave the oil to the priestess on duty, and she used it to fill one of the votary lamps for me. I lit it and knelt in prayer before the statue of Melete, and then, as countless thousands before me, kissed the cold marble of her feet. My prayers were for the success of my endeavours, and even more for my own safety. I'd long ago decided it was not much use being a hero if you were also dead.

Yet even as I prayed, I wondered if it were any use. The statue appeared lifeless, and so very manmade. A man's vision of the perfect woman: mother, whore, temptress. If deities were so powerful, why did they not visit us in person, as legend told us they had once done? The old tales were full of stories of people who spoke to the gods, but I'd never met anyone who admitted he'd seen a deity face to face. I had a sneaking suspicion the gods had vanished. Or that they were man's invention in the first place. Sacrilege, I knew, for the temple told us we were all the creation of the gods, not the other way around . . .

'Domina Ligea?'

Startled, I turned my drifting thoughts to the woman who stood before me: Antonia, the temple's High Priestess. I had never spoken to her before, and she did not normally chat to devotees. I remained kneeling and inclined my head. 'Reverence?'

I'd heard she was brought to the temple as a young girl, selected because of her great beauty and virtue. Now she was more matronly than beautiful, but regal nonetheless. And powerful. Had she withdrawn the support of the Cult of Melete from the Exaltarch, she could have threatened his power base – although, knowing what I did of Exaltarch Bator Korbus, he would have had her assassinated first.

'The Oracle requests your presence.'

She could not have astonished me more. The *Oracle*? The Oracle did not speak to Ligea Gayed. In fact, the Oracle rarely spoke, and when it did, it was to kings and emperors or the very rich, not Compeers of the Brotherhood or even a general's daughter. For one mad moment, I even wondered if the High Priestess had mistaken me for someone else.

I stood, still puzzled. 'I am deeply honoured, Reverence.'

'You are indeed,' she said. Her voice was as dry as grape leaves in autumn.

She found my summons hard to believe too.

CHAPTER TWO

High Priestess Antonia took me behind the altar to the sanctum, that area of the temple not open to the public. Deep inside the building, we entered a small unoccupied room. 'I must blindfold you,' she said, taking a cloth from a hook. She meant me no harm, I could sense that much, so I acquiesced. However, with the blindfold on, I could see nothing and began to feel uneasy.

There was an odd noise, like the turning of a millstone grinding wheat. I thought, *Some kind of opening mechanism for a hidden entrance*, and filed the information away. Then she spoke again. 'There are stairs.' She hooked her arm into mine to guide me. I resented her touch, disliking my dependency on her, loathing my sudden sense of vulnerability.

A strong scent tickled my nostrils, redolent of some kind of incense, and after that I lost time, and touch. I floated, weightless. I saw colours – all shades of red, orange or yellow, each shade with its own smell: essence of poppies, wine, sulphur, wet earth, fermenting yeast. I think I laughed, although what was funny I could not have said. I heard the Goddess herself whisper, chiding me for my lack of reverence. I was chastened, but resentful nonetheless. The next moment that had any clarity was when Antonia removed the blindfold.

I was somewhere else. I must have walked there, but had no recollection of having moved, no memory of time passing. *Vortexdamn the conniving vixen*, I thought, as a semblance of rationality seeped back. The blindfold must have been soaked with something. *She drugged me.* There was an irony in that, of course; we of the Brotherhood were not unfamiliar with such tricks, but I was not in the mood to appreciate the parallels. *Goddess*, I thought, *if they expose everyone who comes here to an elixir like that, no wonder there's never been a coherent description of the Oracle.*

I was assailed by more pungent smells, a mix of odours of the kind that might drift from an alchemist's shop along the Marketwalk. I looked around. I was in an underground cavern. Light came only from flames burning in a bronze container – a bowl as wide as I was tall – set in the stone of the floor. 'The Eternal Flame,' Antonia murmured in my ear, 'lit by the Goddess herself at the founding of Tyr and never extinguished since. It burns without fuel.' She believed it, too. I nodded, but wondered if it weren't fuelled from below, subterranean gases, perhaps. I always was a sceptical bitch.

She waved a hand at the wall of the cavern directly in front of us. 'That is the Oracle.' She gestured again, this time at a pale young woman seated in front of the wall. 'The words of the Oracle will be interpreted for you by Esme, the Selected of the Oracle.'

Esme, as beautiful as a caryatid and almost as lifeless, did not look at me. Her eyes were wide and expressionless; her body swayed slightly. Behind her something crouched and murmured, but whether it was a living creature or just a strange rock formation, I was not certain. The drug had left my mind fuddled and my senses blurred. My head was beginning to ache, irritated by the vapours. My eyes watered. The flickering of the Eternal Flame made shadows dance and writhe. The

natural indents of the rough stone of the cavern wall behind
Esme appeared to ripple. I saw in them a figure, huge, forbidding, lion-like, maned – yet with a man's features centred in
the otherwise feline head. Eyes and nostrils and mouth were
depthless slits boring back into the rock, to viscera beyond. I
shook my head to clear my thoughts. Vapours wafted through
the creature's orifices, smelling of brimstone and pitch, the
breath of Acheron, from the netherworld beyond the Vortex,
surely. And the being – if such it was – muttered. No language
I had ever heard before issued from its throat.

I stared at Esme. She was young, though her skin had the
unhealthy pallor of the chronically ill, and her eyes remained
unfocused. Her voice, when she started to speak, was a mono-
tone, but it oozed truth. She believed all she said.

I assumed she was supposed to be interpreting the mumble
of the Oracle behind her as she intoned:

'Ligea will travel by land and sea and beast
To places new and far,
She will hunt the fierce hunter to the east
Who seeks our world to mar
And kills our noble emperor's time of peace.'

I blinked. One part of me hoped – with sardonic scepticism
– that the Oracle's poetry was better than Esme's translation.
The rest of me was appalled by the content of her lines. *How
could she know what I had only just learned myself?* I moved,
attempting to obtain a better view of the Oracle, but Antonia
had a firm grip on my arm and jerked me back.

Undeterred by my grunt of exasperation, Esme continued:

'With powers to see behind the face,
With ears to hear a lie,

Ligea shall bring victory to this chase,
And deal death to traitors sly.
All power in her wide embrace,
None will again deny
Ligea Gayed her rightful place.'

I was aghast. How could she – or the Oracle – possibly know of my talents? Acheron's mists, the Oracle couldn't *really* be percipient, could it?

Legend said so. History gave us records of prophetic verses, written in far more memorable poetry than this. The religious maintained that the Oracle was our conduit to the advice of the gods.

I felt sick. Damn it, Antonia was listening as my secrets were spilled from this silly girl's lips in infantile rhymes . . .

She droned on, the poetry even more execrable.

'A Legata shall journey back to Tyr,
To lay tribute at her ruler's feet;
Wreath'd, feted, granted gifts of gold,
Honoured at her nation's desire,
Her tale by poets shall be retold.'

Fortunately, that seemed to be all. Esme stared blankly at the opposite wall in silence. The Oracle's murmuring continued, but there was no more translation.

Antonia shook my arm. 'That must be all that is for your ears,' she said. 'Allow me to blindfold you again—'

I jerked my arm away and snapped at her. 'No. No more dulling of my senses. Show me the way out.'

Her eyes flashed, anger roiling with unexpected intensity. 'The Brotherhood has no power here that we do not freely concede,' she hissed. 'All who come before the Oracle are blindfolded. This cavern is part of the Sacred Way, not a path for the undedicated to know.'

'Very well.' I freed the end of my wrap from my waist and wound it around my head to cover my eyes. 'Now lead me out.'

She was silent for a moment, then grabbed my elbow and pulled me after her. I stumbled blindly in her wake for what felt like an age, but was probably no more than five minutes. As far as I could tell, we traversed the cavern of the Eternal Flame to some kind of tunnel which ended in steps. We ascended these, then I heard the scraping sound once more and we were back in the room behind the sanctum.

I unwound the end of my wrap. Antonia stood before me, glaring. 'With the Brotherhood behind you, you think you are untouchable. But before the Goddess, you are no more than each intake of mortal breath. All you are is easily snatched away, Compeer Ligea.' Her use of my title confirmed her knowledge of my Brotherhood status, something I preferred to hide from Tyr's highborn. She added, 'Don't mock the Goddess, or you will live to regret it.'

'I wouldn't dream of it,' I replied, schooling my tone to a careful neutrality. There was no point in upsetting the Temple High Priestess if it were avoidable. 'Nor would I mock the Oracle. It has given me, er, food for thought.' In truth, it had been worryingly accurate, but I wasn't going to tell her that. 'I trust that what you and Esme learned today remains unsaid to others.'

'We are servants of the Goddess. We keep many secrets.'

Not quite the promise I hoped for, but obviously all I was going to get. I nodded to her and left the temple.

Outside, I had to narrow my eyes against the glare of midday light. My mind seethed with all I had seen as I descended the stairs to the Forum Publicum. The crowd there was thinning now that the heat was so intense. Most of the well-to-do had headed home, leaving the streets to the slaves and the poor, but I had something I needed to do.

Noting the fineness of my clothing, litter carriers hurried up to offer their services, but I waved them away and started to walk. I wanted to be alone while I digested all that had happened. I slipped into the labyrinth of streets and alleys leading to the poorer sections of the central city, the area called the Snarls. The change from wide, well-kept public spaces to the closed-in squalor of poverty was rapid; the stink of open drains and rotting rubbish cloyed as the crowds disappeared. Beneath my feet, the smoothness of well-swept pavements gave way to the hard-packed earth of potholed lanes. No marble façades here, no creeper-shaded courtyards. The buildings were of crumbling rough-hewn stone, the rooms cramped, the windows and doorways narrow and mean, the occupants lean and tough. This was the other, more regrettable face of Tyr; but then, I supposed any centre as great as this city had to attract the scavengers as well as the cultured. Most who eked out an inadequate living in the Snarls were not citizens, but a mix of nationalities attracted to the capital of the Exaltarchy, thinking they would make their fortunes. Some of them were even right.

I halted for a moment, my head aching and the taste in my mouth foul. I couldn't even think straight. The Oracle had spoken to me, Ligea Gayed, and prophesied my future. Not many were so privileged. Why, then, did I feel so . . . besmirched?

I pushed the feeling away and directed my thoughts instead to assimilating the reality of my coming departure from Tyr. No more desert-season evenings spent at the open-air theatre to hear a new comedy from Crispin; no more sitting around a fire on a snow-season night with the Academy scholars, drinking punch and discussing Asculi's latest treatise or arguing about why the seasons change; no more pleasant hours spent at one of Nereus's musical evenings.

Kardiastan. Desert hell. Uncultured land of assassins and evil numina, of windstorms and rainless skies. May the wind of Acheron's Vortex take that *bastard* Rathrox!

I had no time, though, to dwell on the pleasant fantasy of an unpleasant end for my Brotherhood mentor, because my thoughts were jerked back to the present. Away from the safety of frequented streets, my senses had subconsciously roamed outwards to become aware of what was happening around me. It seemed my foolishness in crossing the Snarls while so richly dressed was going to bring me trouble: I was being followed. It served me right; I ought to have known better. I should have taken a litter.

I focused my attention. The people in the houses I ignored; those in the surrounding streets I allowed my senses to touch, taking note of their proximity, checking if they were a potential threat by testing their emotions. I found an irate woman and several sulky children, a man consumed with an as-yet-unsatisfied lust in the company of a woman who seemed unenthusiastic – a whore perhaps? – and, out of sight down a parallel street, a crowd of young people exuding drunken amusement. No one I need worry about.

My follower was another matter. I flicked my senses behind and felt his emotions as a black cloud of violence and avarice, too full of malevolent anticipation to be ignored. Damn the man. Around the next corner, I stepped into the nearest recessed doorway of the lane to wait, and felt for my knife. It wasn't there, of course. No one carried a knife into an audience with the Exaltarch.

With growing bad temper and exasperation, I tracked the progress of my pursuer. When he rounded the corner into the lane and found I was no longer in sight, he hesitated a moment, then began to run. I hitched up my wrap and stuck out a foot at the precise moment he drew level; predictably, he sprawled face down in the dirt. I was on him before he had even determined what had happened, pinning him down with a knee in the middle of his back, immobilising him still further by twisting his right arm up behind him. I assessed him quickly: an ill-dressed individual, foul-smelling, not all that young, with neither the strength nor the skill to resist. His clothes were ragged, but I saw some embroidery on what was left of the collar: Quyr beadwork, unless I was much mistaken. Rebellion within the Quyr region and legionnaire attempts to subdue the insurgents had forced many Quyriots out of their mountain homes. Some had made their way to Tyr in search of a living – honest or otherwise; doubtless this man was one such.

'What did you want, helot?' I asked.

'N-nothin',' he stuttered in shock. 'Was just walkin'—'

I tightened my grip. 'Your first lie,' I said. 'The next earns you a broken bone. Why were you following me?'

'I wasn't, Domina—'

I shifted my hold slightly and broke his little finger. He yelped in pain and disbelief.

'Why were you following me?'

He was silent, so I began to apply pressure on his next finger.

'Don't—!' he yelled, too late.

'Were you after my purse? Shall I add a third finger to the tally?'

He howled briefly, but increased pressure soon brought a more comprehensible mumble of admission. His disbelief had melted into fear, his outrage vanished into a numbed acceptance, a common enough emotion of the underprivileged when faced with their superiors.

'Any other reason?'

'No – I swear in the name of the Goddess! Lady, *please*—'

I felt the truth of his answer and released the pressure a little. Ordinarily I would have continued to question him until I found a way I could use him; I'd have held the threat of imprisonment over him and enlisted him in my army of informants, but now – what was the use? I was off to Kardiastan and had no further need of informants ... 'That could earn you a spell in the Cages, my friend,' I said. 'But you're lucky. I'm in a merciful mood today. Get going.'

I released him abruptly, and stood up. He scrambled to his feet, nursing his injured fingers. He opened his mouth to curse me, saw the look on my face and changed his mind, then scuttled away down a side alley without a word.

I walked on, rubbing my aching head, wondering why my distaste for what had happened was so pronounced. Usually that sort of incident didn't worry me. This time, though, as the man's acidic hate for mé lingered in the air after he had gone, I found myself wondering if my talents, especially those that gave me an awareness of other people's emotions, were worth having.

As a child I had been hurt again and again by my uninvited knowledge, until I'd learned to build a wall around my too-soft core. When I'd been very young, I'd thought everyone felt things the same way I did, and I'd gone on thinking so, until Aemid, my Kardi slave-nurse, had disabused me. She had drawn me aside one day, making sure no one overheard us, to say, 'You feel things others don't. You know things you shouldn't. And until you learn to control those feelings, to push aside that knowledge, to ignore all that comes to you unbidden, to squash it – until then, you will continue to be hurt. None of this inner knowledge of yours will do you any good, Ligea; don't listen to it. That way it will eventually stop coming to you.'

At first I'd tried to follow her advice. Then, one day I'd been saved from unpleasantness by knowing beforehand that some bullying young playmates of mine were waiting in ambush for me in our villa garden. Aemid, I decided, was wrong. The knowledge coming to me unbidden might often have hurt, but it also provided invaluable insights. Instead of crushing it, I nurtured it. I practised, I *trained* myself to listen, to be aware, to feel things others couldn't feel, to know what should have been unknowable. Slowly I learned to coax more nebulous intuitions into a coherent form of awareness, to recognise vague feelings about the emotions of others as information to be read and interpreted. The extent of my abilities was my secret, and one I kept well. Aemid may have guessed I hadn't taken her advice, but she never said. Gayed, and later Rathrox, sensed I was different, that I was more perceptive than others, but I never explained my gift to them; I never let them know just how good I was.

Even so, it seemed Rathrox knew too much, and now, because of my abilities, I was being sent to Kardiastan. Worse, the Oracle was aware of my abilities too. What was it Esme had said about me? *With powers to see behind the face.* And with her blurting that out, the temple authorities – Antonia and her ilk – would know there was something odd about me too, blast them. The fewer people who knew what I could do, the more valuable my power was.

I sighed. No matter what, exile was far too high a price to pay for my talent.

The tangle of alleyways I followed led me into the heart of the Snarls, to what passed for a prison in Tyr: the Cages. Lesser criminals were sold into slavery and usually never found themselves here. The Cages were for the more violent felons, for those awaiting execution, for traitors and insurgents.

The place had a stink all its own: sweat, excreta, disease,

dirt and hopelessness combined in a sour foulness permeating the air, a gangrenous stench that always clung to my clothes and hair even after I'd left the place. I should have been used to it – my job took me there often enough – but I wasn't. It was never easy to accustom oneself to a place like that.

Stacked like chicken coops in Tyr's fowl market, two high and two deep, the cages lined a rutted alleyway always sodden with the muck washed from cage floors. Scum-covered puddles of stagnant slime made walking a hazard; vermin lurked in every crevice. At night, and during the day too sometimes, some of them emerged to feed on the caged.

Each cage differed in size from the next: some were so cramped they could barely contain a grown man bent double; others were large enough to house ten or twelve adults – and did. Each had iron bars on all four sides, a slab floor below and a slab roof above. Each contained nothing but prisoners and blankets rotted with urine. They were sluiced once a day, but there was no privacy, no real shelter from the weather or fellow prisoners, no protection from a sometimes hostile public. In this, the desert-season, the place crawled with flies and maggots, and reeked with fever. In the snow-season, only the generosity of people who donated blankets saved the incarcerated from freezing to death.

To condemn a man – or woman – to a year in the Cages was as good as telling them they had an appointment with the Vortex of Death, a passage to Acheron. The law courts of Tyr might have been fair and just, but the punishment system was run by demoted military men, disgraced legionnaires. It was an irony Rathrox delighted in. 'True justice is to be found in the Cages,' he told me once, 'not in the verdicts handed out in pristine courtrooms. I loathe men who know the theory of law, yet never sully their lily-white feet by walking into the Snarls.'

I ignored the Cages for the time being and went straight to

the Warden's office, which was in a solid stone building nearby. Inside the door, burning incense pebbles did their best to conquer the less attractive smells and the miasma of disease wafting in from outside. The Warden himself was out and it was the Sub-warden I saw, a man called Hargen Bivius. He was seated behind the Warden's desk when I entered, his feet on the desktop and a jug of wine in his hand. His eyes slitted with sullen dislike the moment he saw me, but he didn't move. 'Ligea,' he drawled, 'and dressed in all her finery, too. We *are* honoured. But careful, m'dear, around here you could dirty the hem of your oh-so-*pretty* wrap.'

I refused to be drawn to anger. 'Dorus the Jeweller's son – Markis, I believe his name is – what cage is he in?'

It took him a while to decide to move. Finally he placed the jug on the desk with careful deliberation and swung his feet to the floor so he could consult a wax tablet in front of him. A wisp of incense smoke drifted between us, swirling delicately as it was caught on his breath. With infuriating slowness, he ran a dirty finger down the column of names impressed on the tablet and at last gave me the information I wanted. 'Number twenty-eight. One of our more luxurious accommodations – it's high enough to stand up in, is number twenty-eight. At your request, I believe. A lover of yours, perhaps? Hard up these days are you, Compeer?'

I suppressed a sigh. 'He's well?'

'As can be expected.' The sourness of his breath drowned the aroma of the incense stones.

'He is to be kept in good health.'

He gave an exaggerated bow. 'Anything to oblige the Magister Officii's pet.'

'Think of it as obliging the Brotherhood, Hargen. And if you should torment Markis for some petty reasons of your own, I'll see you face Brotherhood wrath.'

He gripped the edge of the desk as if that was the only way he could keep his hands under control. 'Ligea, m'dear, do you have any concept of how much I hate you?'

I could feel his loathing without even trying. 'I have a fair idea. Just remember, if anything happens to Markis, it will be Rathrox's wrath you face, not mine.'

Hargen Bivius had been a fellow compeer once, as well as a legionnaire, until I'd decided the Brotherhood would be better off without him. A gratuitously cruel and petty-minded man who'd crossed me again and again for no reason other than sheer malice, I'd had no compunction about ruining his career. He hadn't deserved the privilege of being a compeer, and his behaviour had been damaging the effectiveness of the Brotherhood. I'd enjoyed nudging him along to his own self-destruction. Apparently, he had finally figured out the part I'd played in what had happened to him: his emotions raged at me.

'One day,' he promised, 'I'll have my revenge.'

I heard the lie and smiled inwardly. Hargen had about as much resolution as a snail without its shell. 'I doubt it,' I said. 'Wine loosens the tongue, but it seldom sharpens the wits and never stiffens the spine. Or anything else for that matter.' I nodded to him pleasantly and went out into the street once more.

Assailed by the stench of the Cages again, I almost gagged. It was an effort to turn to one of the duty guards and ask to be shown cage number twenty-eight, an effort to breathe normally and ignore the rats slinking in the gutters, their fur stiff with filth. I could almost feel compassion for Markis Dorus, even though he had played at treason. He was eighteen years old, a pampered lad with an overzealous tongue who'd suddenly found out the world could be a vicious and unfriendly place to the unwise.

He sat alone, hunched up at one end of his cage, his hair matted, his clothing filthied, his skin scabbed with dirt. Flies buzzed around his head. He looked well enough in spite of the grime, and there was food and water in covered containers at his feet. His family evidently kept him well supplied, which was more than could be said for some of the other lowlife incarcerated around him.

I didn't bother to speak to him. My business was not with Markis, but with his father, and gloating over the lawless I'd brought to justice held no attraction for me. The majority of those imprisoned here were murderers, rapists, kidnappers, traitors – men and women warped with cruelty, dissipation and greed. I knew the hideousness of their crimes better than most, but I took no pleasure, as some highborn did, in seeing them mired in misery. I wanted to check that Markis was well, and that done, I turned my back on them all and set off through the Snarls once more.

It was a relief to emerge at last into the Artisan Quarter. The laneways of this part of the city may have been narrow, but at least they were paved and clean, the stone walls kept repaired and whitewashed. Doors and windows were shuttered and barred at this time of the day as shop-owners and house-holders dozed somewhere behind them: it was the siesta hour.

When I reached my destination, Dorus the Jeweller's, I paused until I was sure I was unobserved. I tugged at the bellpull, but it was a while before the door was unbarred and opened. The man in the doorway stared at me, his expression blank as he failed to recognise me dressed as I was. Then his plump face paled. 'Compeer . . . Holy Goddess—!' He gestured me inside, but not before giving a swift glance into the street in an agony of terror. 'Compeer, if someone were to recognise you—'

'No one saw me, Dorus. Do you have the information?'

'Yes, yes! Upstairs. But it's more than my life is worth to be seen talking to you!' He indicated a chair in the darkest corner of his workroom. 'Stay here, Lady Compeer, please. I'll get it.'

I ignored the chair and wandered about the shop while he was gone, looking at some of the silver pieces he had been crafting. I wasn't particularly interested in jewellery, although I had a lot, inherited from my adoptive mother. I never used any of it. The only piece I habitually wore was my own personal-seal ring. Still, I could appreciate the fine filigree done by Dorus. He worked mainly in silver, and many of his pieces were set with polished stones. I recognised the smoky topaz of northern Tyrans, red and black corals from the Sea of Iss, golden amber from the Island of Inge – and agates from Kardiastan. I ran a finger over the cut surface of a large piece of pink and white agate, and tried to remember why its geometric patterns seemed familiar.

A moment or two later, Dorus was back with a clay tablet. A pronounced tremor in his hands prompted me to take it from him before he dropped it. 'The names of everyone involved,' he whispered. He made an effort to control the shaking. 'They'll kill me if ever they find out.'

'They won't hear it from me.' I glanced at the list. 'You've done a good job.' I extracted a coin from the purse hidden in the folds of my wrap.

'I don't want your tainted money,' he said in revulsion. 'Some of them are my friends!'

'They are traitors, plotting the overthrow of their monarch. They will get the justice they deserve.'

'My – my son?'

'He is well, as I am sure you know. I doubt this sojourn in the Cages will do him any harm; I hope it will do him some good. If this list is as comprehensive as it looks, he will be released by nightfall tomorrow. I keep my promises, Dorus.' I started towards the door, but a quixotic impulse made me turn back to say, 'Markis is a young fool who let his silly ideals get him into trouble once, and may do so again. But he does love you. If you are wise, you will tell him what you had to do to gain his freedom. He will keep your secret, and his fear of putting you in a similar position again will keep him out of trouble.' I had intended to keep in reserve the propensity of Dorus's son to do foolish things, a lever I would be able to use against the jeweller in the future, but what was the point when I wouldn't be here to exert pressure on the handle? I flipped the gold coin in Dorus's direction. 'Use it to buy him a new set of clothes. He'll need them after three weeks in the Cages.'

I emerged into the deserted street, indifferent to the hatred that followed me.

I was used to it.

CHAPTER THREE

The moment I entered the front hall of my villa on the fashionable side of town, I was greeted, as usual, by a slave. This time it was Aemid, once my nurse and now my personal handmaiden. Glad to be out of the desiccating heat of the desert-season, I sat on the entry stool in the cool while she undid my sandals and knelt to wash the dust from my feet with water smelling of lemon blossom.

I tried to relax and let the tensions of the day slip away along with the grime. It wasn't easy. When I gazed around it was to look on something I was about to lose. I loved this house; I had been brought up here. I had played my first games on the terrace, read my first books in the library, ridden my first horse in the garden, taken my first lover in one of the bedrooms. After the death of my adoptive parents, I rid the rooms of much of the ostentation that had irked me as a child, so now it was all I desired. I liked to think I had chosen the best of Tyranian style and rejected the more florid embellishment that Salacia, my adoptive mother, had so admired.

The cool marbled hall, the elegant statuary decorating the wall niches, the great fireplaces that burned whole logs in the snow-season, the way rooms opened out on to fountained courtyards – I loved it all. If I listened, I could hear the splash of water mingling with the soft murmur of pink and grey mellowbirds. If I glanced through the archways to my right, I would see the vines, now rich with fruit, that covered the atrium. If I drew breath, it was to smell the trumpet flowers and lemon blossom, and just a wisp of freshly baked bread from my own kitchen ovens. If I reached out my hand, I would touch the soft velvet of the cold-weather drapes we drew closed to keep the room warm when the fires were lit and the wall fountains were heated.

This was the only home I could ever remember having.

And I had to leave it.

I looked back at Aemid and waved a hand at the foot basin. 'Since when has this been your job?' I asked, using the Kardi language, as I always did when talking to her. 'Where is Foressa – or Dini?'

She gave a grunt. 'They're busy.' It was a lie and both of us knew it. Before I could chide her, she blurted, 'What did the Exaltarch want with you?'

I smiled softly, touched that she had been worried. 'Something I never expected: he wants me to go to Kardiastan. With the rank of Legata, what's more.'

I was totally unprepared for the effect of this news on her. She jumped to her feet, dropping the sponge she had been using, and stood swaying, her fists clenched, her breath loud and rough. The normal olive-brown tint of her skin blotched unevenly, the lines on her face burrowed deeper.

'Aemid! Are you all right? What in Vortex has come over you?' I was awash in her emotions: joy and fear and panic in equal parts.

She didn't answer. Her eyes dropped to the sponge, but she didn't pick it up. Water ran in rivulets over the marble tiles. 'When?' she asked at last, the word a strangled sound in the back of her throat.

Seeing she was not going to fall, I released the supporting hold I had taken on her arm. 'I don't know; as soon as I can wind up my affairs here and obtain a sea passage. A week perhaps. I will have priority on any coastal vessel.'

'Wind up your affairs—?'

'It's very doubtful I shall be coming back for a while. What's upset you so, Aemid? Are you worried I'll leave you behind, or that I'll take you with me?' I looked at her uncertainly.

'Could I – *is it possible*? That I can go with you?'

'Well, of course, if that's what you want.' I was puzzled. 'I had no idea you felt so strongly about Kardiastan. All I've ever heard about the place seems to indicate it's damned inhospitable; a hellhole with a climate worthy of the Vortex of Death. Melete's heart, why would you want to return there? You belong here by now, surely.'

Aemid did not reply. She knelt and began to towel my feet dry with trembling hands, her grey head bent.

I went on, 'I shall take Brand as well, and I shall keep a skeleton staff here to maintain the house and gardens, but the other slaves will have to be sold. I can always buy another household in Kardiastan. You may tell the others. Tell them I shall see that they go to good homes.'

Aemid's head swung up in shock. 'There's no slavery in Kardiastan!'

I stared at her. 'What in the world are you thinking of? Weren't you yourself enslaved there? And what of all the newly arrived Kardi thralls you see here in Tyr from time to time? Of course there is slavery in Kardiastan!'

'Oh – yes. Yes, of course,' she muttered, flushing. 'I was just— For a moment, I was remembering how it once was.'

'Aemid, you haven't been there for, what? More than twenty-five years? You were taken while the Kardiastan Uprising was still in progress, I know, but that was a long time ago. Those wars are long over; Kardiastan has long been a province of the Exaltarchy, and where the Exaltarch rules, there is always slavery. It is the natural order of things that the conquered should serve their masters. Now go and tell Brand I want to see him after I bathe. I have the stink of the Cages on my skin and I won't feel clean until I've washed. You can send Dini in to do my hair.' She nodded, apparently in control of herself again, but as she left the room, I noticed her hands trembled.

When I emerged from my bedroom a while later, clean at last and dressed more comfortably in loose trousers and a long loose top, it was to find Brand waiting for me.

Like Aemid, Brand was a house slave. The red flecks in the brown of his irises and the red flash over his forehead in his otherwise brown hair proclaimed his blood to be Altani. Altan Province was one of the conquered nations to the south of the Sea of Iss – but Brand never spoke of his home any more than Aemid did. He had been a gift from General Gayed to me on my tenth anniversary day. Twelve years old then, a defiant boy, skinny and undersized. Now he was a large man, taller by a head than I was, with a width to match his height and a strength to match his width.

'Ah, there you are,' I said. 'Did Aemid tell you what the Exaltarch wanted?'

He nodded. 'Yes, Domina. Or should I say, um, *Legata*?'

A slave's existence had so instilled caution in him that his expression always had about as much animation as the standing stones of northern Tyrans. Right then, though, I suspected he was mocking me, but I couldn't tell for certain. Of all the people I had ever known, he alone was unreadable to me. I said, 'I think you know damned well that I don't care what you call me, although a little *respect* from time to time would be nice.'

'Of course, Domina.' The tiniest of pauses, then, '*Legata*.'

I resisted an impulse to throttle him. 'I do want to know what you think about the posting to Kardiastan, however.'

'Ah.' Serious now, he considered a moment before replying. 'I think the Magister Officii fears you.'

I nodded. 'And I fear you are right. I'll be a long time away. How do you feel about it, Brand?'

'Slaves don't have opinions on matters like that, er, Ligea. Where you go, I go, unless you will it otherwise.'

I gave him a sharp look, but I could not penetrate the mask he wore. He ignored my glance with unruffled urbanity. *Gods above*, I thought, *twenty years as a slave, eighteen of them as my guard-servant, and none of it has destroyed either your dignity or your bloody pride, has it?* Brand still knew his own worth, and he showed the world he valued himself. It often came as a shock to strangers when they noted his bronze slave collar. My friends warned me of the dangers of allowing helots too many liberties; I took no notice. My less charitable acquaintances spread the rumour I was besotted with my own thrall.

I was far from besotted. In fact, at moments like this, I felt more inclined to strangle the man. 'I should sell you before I go, preferably to the Domina Aurelia,' I growled, naming the highborn wife of the Prefect Urbis of Tyr, a woman as stupid as she was frivolous. Her male slaves dressed in pink, had their hair curled and their faces plastered with cosmetics. She'd made me an offer for Brand once, after I visited her villa with him in attendance. I'd enjoyed telling him that, just for the rare joy of seeing his expression change.

He pretended to consider the suggestion. 'No, I don't think so, if you don't mind. However, a position as a guard in that whorehouse for the highborn in Via Dolce, now . . .'

I rolled my eyes. All I had heard from the slave quarters of the Villa Gayed over the years suggested Brand didn't much like to sleep alone. 'Sorry to thwart your amorous tendencies, Brand, but you are coming with me to Kardiastan. Naturally.'

'Naturally.' His tone was as dry as crumbled brick dust.

More veiled mockery, I supposed. I sighed inwardly and changed the subject. 'Something else, um, interesting happened today.'

He raised an eyebrow and waited, alert to my altered tone.

'The Oracle asked to see me.'

Everything about him stilled. When I didn't immediately explain, he said, 'As you say, interesting. From what I have heard, it is more normal for people to beg to see the Oracle, than the other way around.'

I nodded again. 'Indeed. And as I understand it, there is quite often a considerable . . . donation to the temple involved before the Oracle obliges.'

He gave a half-smile. 'And you are not known for your generosity to religious cults.'

'No.'

'There was a deputation from the Meletian Temple at the door today, asking for donations for the Moon Festival. A coincidence, do you think?'

'Probably. They come every year. And are disappointed every year. They take enough from me at normal service collections.' Even as I spoke, though, I was wondering. Was this all a trick to increase my donation? Show the power of prophecy to the unbeliever in order to extract some of her wealth? I heard tales of unscrupulous temple priestesses from time to time. It was no more mad than the thought that the Oracle had the ability to predict the future. *No*, I thought, *I won't believe that.* If the gods did indeed intervene in our everyday life, if the Oracle always spoke the truth, then there would never be disasters such as the Kardiastan Uprising, or the earthquake deaths just last year in Getria, our sister city in the mountains. We would have been warned.

'So, what message was it the Oracle wanted to impart?' Brand's question abruptly grounded my thoughts once more.

'That's just it. Nothing much at all. Merely that I was going to take a journey to look for a traitor and I would be successful and rewarded as a consequence. Substantially rewarded.'

'And is that true?'

'As far as I know it, yes.'

'No details as to how you were to catch your prey? No helpful hints?'

'None.'

He had put his finger on the real puzzle of what had taken place, of course. There had been nothing in what I was told that was useful – so why was the message necessary?

I detailed exactly what I had seen and heard, marshalling my own recollections into coherent order, dismissing the more outlandish of my hallucinations. As I recited Esme's actual words, his smile broadened into a grin. When I was a child, Brand had accompanied me to all my school lessons; these days he stood behind me at every poetry reading, musical evening, theatre performance, Academy debate. He knew execrable verse when he heard it. He said, 'So, the Oracle is a bad poet?'

'The worst. Or else Esme is a poor translator.'

'They paint a rosy future for you. A little, um, *fulsome* in the promises, though, don't you think?'

'Somewhat.' I frowned. 'The whole thing is odd.'

'You know what it sounds like to me? All that talk of "rightful place" and being wreathed, feted, honoured and celebrated in epic poetry? It's as if they are saying: "You're not getting what you deserve. Go to Kardiastan and you will get that, and more." They are appealing to your sense of injustice.'

My frown deepened. 'I don't feel hardly done by!'

'They might think you do. Do you believe in the Oracle, Domina?'

'In its connection to the divine? Or in the truth of its predictions?'

'Both.'

'Well, the temple priestesses maintain that if any of the gods want to communicate, they do so through the Oracle. But if a god is divine and powerful, then why the need for an intermediary? If we are to believe the myths, in the past they spoke to people directly. So, do I believe in the connection to the divine? Probably not. I am more inclined to think none of it is true, or ever was true.'

He remained silent, so I went on to the second part of his question. 'Nowadays, people go to the Oracle because they want to know the future. They want advice on the outcome of their more momentous decisions: whether to invest money, invade a neighbouring country, marry into a certain family. From what I've heard, the advice is often couched in such obscure language it is ambiguous and therefore easily moulded afterwards to what happens. You know the sort of thing: "Marry that woman and a great commercial dynasty will be founded." No one actually says *whose* dynasty. The more ambiguous it is, the greater the chances the prediction will come true.'

He nodded. 'Clever. But your prediction was not ambiguous. It clearly foretold your success and rewards.'

I stirred uneasily. 'Up until today I would have said it was all a temple scam. To make money out of the gullible. Now I'm not so sure . . .'

'You've not become a believer, have you?' His mockery mingled with amusement.

'No,' I snapped. *Vortexdamn*, I thought, *why is it he always has the power to needle me?* I took a deep breath. 'Brand, they knew too much. About me, about my latest orders. How could they possibly have known?'

'Without supernatural means? Could be any one of a dozen ways. Magister Rathrox told them. The Exaltarch told them. Someone else who knows told them. Perhaps they have spies in the palace. More to the point, *why* the whole rigmarole anyway?'

'Why do *you* think?' I asked.

Being Brand, he considered thoughtfully before answering. 'Someone wants you to go to Kardiastan, but is afraid you will refuse. This is a way to entice you by appealing to your sense of justice and your love of a challenge. By predicting a rosy future if you go haring off to do the Exaltarch's bidding.' He chuckled. 'Whoever it is, they don't know you very well if they think you would be influenced by the muttering of a stone wall.'

I thought about that. The Exaltarch might believe I needed an incentive . . . and he had direct access to the Meletian Priestesses. I shivered. Was my presence in Kardiastan so important the Exaltarch would ask the priestesses to fake a prediction from the Oracle? Terror flickered, more tangible this time. And, keeping pace, that pleasurable frisson of excitement.

But there was a weakness in Brand's argument. 'I'm hardly likely to refuse a direct order from the Exaltarch,' I pointed out. 'Rathrox and Bator Korbus knew from the very beginning that I would go.'

'Maybe they just want you to go willingly, believing you have a spectacular future ahead. Rathrox knows exactly how ambitious you are. He must guess you would like to fill his shoes if he ever retires.'

I thought back to the meeting with the Exaltarch. To the feeling I'd had that I was missing something, that they weren't telling me the whole truth. Bator Korbus had implied Rathrox was keen to send me, but that he, Korbus, was dubious. Perhaps that wasn't quite the case. Oh, Korbus had been dubious of my abilities, true, but perhaps the Exaltarch was the one who wanted me in Kardiastan so badly he would stoop to anything to have me enthusiastic about it.

I frowned again. It all seemed so unlikely.

I felt a moment's intense nostalgia for my father, the man I had called Pater; I still missed his advice. He'd possessed such a talent for seeing ramifications, for visualising consequences. And always, always, his firm reassurance had given me faith in my own judgement.

'There were a number of messages for you today,' Brand said, changing the subject. 'Domina Curia has sent an invitation to a poetry evening in ten days' time – Segilus has apparently completed a new epic he wants to read to you all. Scholar Menet Senna wants to know if you'd like a seat at the debate on the validity of barbarian folk myths. A cloth merchant sent some samples of tie-dyed silk newly imported from Corsene. That rather unsavoury fellow who calls himself Bodran of Iss says he has some more information to sell about gold-smuggling, but he wouldn't deal with me so I told him to come back early tomorrow morning. Mazentius the Trademaster wants to know if you want to order anything from the Western Reaches. He has a caravan leaving for Pilgath in a day or two and said you might be interested in the papyrus they produce there. It's supposed to be much better quality than what we usually get from Altan. Um, I think that was all.'

Every word he said reminded me of the life I would leave.

I suppressed the sick feeling in my gut. 'I want you to take a message to Rathrox. A note from me, together with this list of names. The so-called Orsini conspirators.' I handed him Dorus's clay tablet.

He glanced at it and said, 'The fat jeweller came good, then, to save his son?'

'Yes. Damn it, Brand, it took me weeks to uncover that plot and now I have the names, someone else is going to round up the plotters and reap the praise for a job well done, because I won't be here.'

'Ah well, you've done similar things to others often enough, and planned it that way, too,' he said unsympathetically. 'Crabs shouldn't expect their fellow crabs to walk straight.'

I opened my mouth to give an irate retort, then closed it again. There was much truth in what he said. I'd a reputation for taking advantage of my fellow Compeer Brothers to further my own career – and yes, sometimes I'd prompted them into the mistakes in the first place, as Hargen Bivius could testify. 'Huh,' I said, a noncommittal grunt that could have meant anything.

I gave a wave of dismissal, but before he left he asked, politely enough, 'Are you going to issue a release request for the son?'

My friends were right: Brand could overstep the line. It wasn't his place to query things like that. Still, with Brand I preferred honesty to a dialogue based on intimidation, so I let it ride, and answered him. 'After Rathrox has someone check the authenticity of the list of names.'

He bowed his way out, passing Aemid on the way in.

'The Tribune Favonius Kyranon to see you,' she said. Her tone was neutral, but her face was pinched, accentuating the lines of middle age. Aemid did not approve of the legionnaire.

I pretended not to notice.

I hurried through into the entry hall where one of the lesser slaves was beginning to unbuckle the leather and metal battle cuirass of the soldier who stood there. 'Never mind, Dini,' I said. 'I'll do that.' I smiled up at the legionnaire and took his hands in mine. 'Favonius – well met. I didn't know you were back in Tyr. Welcome.'

He tapped his dusty cuirass. 'As you can see, I came straight here from the barracks. We got in late this morning.' He was a large man, of a size to match Brand, but his colouring was pure Tyranian: blond hair, blue eyes and a skin that tanned easily to smooth honey-gold. His nose had been broken once and was now twisted to one side; it gave his looks a toughness to match the furrows and crinkles carved on his face by the sun and wind. He was thirty-five years old, and he looked it. He added, 'I have missed you, Ligea.'

I smiled with genuine pleasure and started to work on the buckles of his cuirass. 'I'm flattered, Tribune. How was the patrol?'

'Routine. Boring. Just the way we like it.'

'Liar. You much prefer being attacked by barbarians or bandits or rebels so you can prove, yet again, that the Exaltarch's Stalwarts are the best legionnaires in the empire.'

He laughed. 'Perhaps.'

'Where were you?' I asked, curious.

'In the mountains beyond Getria.'

That didn't make much sense as the area was devoid of people, but I didn't bother to think about it just then. I laid aside his body armour and sword belt and said, 'Now if you'll be seated, I'll wash your feet.'

He grinned at me. It was an honour to have the lady of the house perform the welcoming ablutions herself. I knelt, undid his leather greaves and sandals, and began to wash away the dust with long caressing strokes of the sponge, each movement deliberately sensual, my lips slightly parted, my eyes on his face all the while. He stood it for a minute or two, then made a sound that was almost a groan. 'You *witch*!' he whispered, and pulled me up onto his lap. I knocked the water bowl over, but neither of us cared. I just had time to laugh before his mouth clamped over mine with a need born of long abstinence.

An hour later, as he half-drowsed in my arms on my divan, I said, 'Ah, Favonius, I could almost imagine you haven't had another woman in the two months you've been gone.'

'I haven't,' he said, nibbling my ear.

'Come now, a legionnaire of the Exaltarch's Stalwarts, one Favonius Kyranon, without a woman? You'd be the laughing stock of your fellow officers!'

He grinned lazily. 'It takes a brave man to laugh at a Kyranon. You have spoiled me for other women. It's you I want and only you. Other women suddenly seem – insipid.'

'Then doubtless you availed yourself of the camp youths,' I said lightly. Many of the legion's slaves were chosen for their comeliness, and it was common enough for legionnaires to help themselves to what was available, even if their preference was otherwise.

'No,' he said. 'Not once. They hold no attraction for me.' He raised himself on an elbow. 'Ah, Ligea, you think I'm joking, but it's true. There's only one person I want on my pallet. I wish you'd think about making this union of ours legal.'

I felt a pang of regret. He'd asked before, and my answer had always been the same. And yet, sometimes I wondered if it might not be pleasant to be married. He came from a good provincial family and such a marriage would have added yet another layer to the legitimacy of my Tyranian citizenship. And, of course, it would have helped his career to be married to a general's adopted daughter. I smothered a sigh. 'It wouldn't work, Favo. And if you were honest, you'd admit it. I have all the attributes of your ideal lover, but none of your ideal wife. The very things you admire in me now would be the snags that put holes in a marriage.'

'How so?'

'You admire my independence, you like my fire and passion and lust for life – but you would want to tame me if I were your wife. You wouldn't want me to be part of the Brotherhood for a start, would you?' Favonius was one of the few people who was fully aware of the extent of my Brotherhood connections.

He gave a quick frown. 'How can I feel happy with it? It's dangerous. It's not work for a woman. It's—'

I interrupted. 'It's what keeps me alive, Favonius. I *need* excitement and challenge. But because I'm a woman I'm not allowed to be a legionnaire or a seamaster or a trademaster or anything else adventurous or challenging. So I work for the Brotherhood. You would take that away from me if I were your wife – and then wonder why I was no longer the woman you had fallen in love with.'

'As my wife you could follow the legion, I suppose,' he said doubtfully. 'Would that be excitement enough?'

'It would be eating the dust of the Stalwarts without being able to participate in their battles. Could you do it?'

He looked astounded. '*I*? A camp follower?'

'It's what you just asked of me.'

He thought about that and then started to laugh. 'Now that's one of the reasons I love you: your conversation has all the spice of a new dish; you are never predictably boring like other highborn women.'

'Try thinking of me as a man and you may find me more predictable.'

He shook his head, still smiling. 'I could *never* think of you as a man. Ligea, I have something to tell you – which I shouldn't tell anyone, but I shall anyway. If a Brother can't be trusted with a secret, then who can, eh? The Stalwarts are being sent to Kardiastan.'

I sat up, slack-jawed, feeling as if someone had pummelled me with a fist in the midriff. It couldn't be true. This had to be a joke. Or fate playing a trick? *Both* of us being sent to Kardiastan at the same time?

Finally I managed a stifled, '*Kardiastan?* The Stalwarts on *garrison* duty?'

Favonius, never the most observant of men, didn't notice just how staggered I was. 'No. Active duty, as usual. We are to invade from the west.'

My astonishment grew. 'Across the *Alps?* Riding?' And then, 'Invade? But *why?* Kardiastan is already ours!' Inwardly, I fumed. Why hadn't the Exaltarch told me of this?

'That's what I always thought too, but it seems not all of it is.' He rolled over onto his back and put his hands behind his head. He was frowning slightly, as if he didn't quite believe what he was saying. 'The Exaltarchy invaded Kardiastan, what, twenty-six years ago?'

'About that,' I agreed.

'It seems we invaded from the coast inwards, bringing troops by ship. But there's one part of Kardiastan, in the west, bordering the Alps, where no Exaltarchy troops have ever been. The Kardis call the area the Mirage. An impassable desert separates this Mirage and the rest of Kardiastan.'

I began to take an even keener interest in what he was saying.

'The Mirage is a rebels' cauldron of intrigue and insurrection, with leaders there constantly stirring up trouble elsewhere. So we are to cross the Alps and take it.'

I stared at him in puzzlement. 'I don't understand. If the desert is impassable, then how can this Mirage be part of Kardiastan?'

'That's what I asked. Apparently it's only impassable to Tyranians. The Kardis don't have any trouble crossing it. And don't ask me how that can be, because I don't know.'

'Surely it's a simple matter to find a guide who would show us the secret.'

'You'd think so, wouldn't you? Offer enough money, and someone would oblige. Or torture someone into explaining the trick.' A worried note crept into his voice. 'It has been tried, of course. More than once. Those who did set off with a guide – whether paid or coerced – never came back.'

I rolled off the divan and began to pace the floor, forgetting I was naked. 'It seems there's a lot I don't know about Kardiastan. Which is strange when you consider it's where I was born. When do you leave, Favo? And how many of you go?'

'A legion under Legate Kilmar, and as soon as we're fitted out. We'll leave from Getria in about two months, I s'pose. Less perhaps.' His eyes followed me, appreciative. 'Keep this quiet. With such a small force, surprise is essential for success.'

'Oh, it'll be a surprise all right. Mounted on gorclaks across the Alps? You'll be lucky if you make it alive.' At least I knew now why he'd been in the mountains beyond Getria – they had been reconnoitring the route.

'Don't underestimate the Stalwarts. We'll be there. I just wish I didn't have to leave Tyr again so soon. You and I see far too little of each other.'

That at least was true. The Stalwarts, for all that their permanent garrison was in Tyr, were liable to be ordered away at any time if the situation in any of the provinces or tributary states warranted it, which often seemed to happen. I had known Favonius for six years, but in all that time he'd spent less than two years in Tyr.

I said, 'We have less time than you think, Favo. I'll be leaving Tyrans even before you do.' Briefly, I summarised my meeting with the Exaltarch. By the time I'd finished, the mellowbirds outside had quietened and gone to roost in the bushes around the fishpond as dusk darkened the garden.

Favonius sat up, his forehead wrinkled in dismay. A klip-klip flew into the room, the rhythmic flashing on its head still dim in the half-light, and he swatted irritably at it. 'But that sounds as though it's unlikely you'll be returning to Tyr for – for Ocrastes *knows* how long! That bastard of a Ligatan. How can you bear to work for a snake-eyed, ungrateful turd like that?'

'I work for the Exaltarchy, Favo. Not for Rathrox, or for the Brotherhood or even for the Exaltarch.'

'What d'you mean? They're all the same thing in the end.'

'No, they're not.' The klip-klip landed on the back of my hand and I stared at the perfection of its delicate winged body and its tiny flashing light as I tried to put what I felt into words. 'I work for the *idea* of the Exaltarchy – for what it symbolises. An empire where everyone speaks the same tongue, an empire without war or border disputes, where nations pay tribute to Tyrans or become provinces, and have peace in return. Where a man can travel along the tradeways and the seaways from one land to another in safety.

'That is why I despise people like these Kardis, even though I myself was born one of them. They stir up rebellion and bring trouble and death and fear. They deal in terror. They destroy. They are the reason I am glad to work for the Brotherhood. The public fear us but, believe me, the prosperity of the Exaltarchy is as much due to us as to you legionnaires. It's a pity people forget that.'

Only half listening and uninterested in my philosophy, he said mulishly, 'Damn it, Ligea, we're unlikely to meet in Kardiastan. You won't be going anywhere near the Mirage. And what if Rathrox won't ever recall you to Tyrans?'

The klip-klip flew from my hand, its light brighter now. This time Favonius caught it and crushed it in his fingers.

I said, 'I shall face that scorpion when it raises its tail. For now, I'll try to do what I'm being sent to do. And who knows, we might meet there. After all, you surely won't return to Tyr across the Alps. Once you've conquered the Mirage, you should be able to solve the problem of crossing the desert and be able to return through Kardiastan proper.'

'You are scratching your left palm,' he accused.

I looked down at my hand guiltily. It was a joke between us that whenever I was worried I itched the lump – the size and shape of half a pigeon's egg cut lengthways – in the middle of my palm. He stood up and came to take me in his arms. 'I don't like this, Ligea. You are right to be worried. Kardiastan is a strange place. I've heard strange tales. They are an odd people.'

I looked at him, deliberately arch. '*I* am Kardi.'

He lifted my hand and kissed the deformity on the palm. It was hard and solid beneath his lips. 'And look how different you are!'

'I am *not* odd!' I was careful not to be whenever I moved in highborn circles. I kept my work for the Brotherhood as quiet as I could, and tried to appear as Tyranian as possible. I kept out of the sun and powdered my face to lighten my skin, I had my hair highlighted to make it more blonde than brown. I was accepted as Tyranian. It was, after all, what I felt myself to be.

He asked, 'Do you remember Kardiastan?'

'No, not really. Except—'

'Except what?'

'Oh, sometimes I have the faintest recollections. About a woman; my mother, I suppose. My real mother. Sometimes, something will remind me of her. A whiff of perfume, a partic-ular laugh, a certain colour. And then there's this.' I indicated the swelling on my hand. 'I seem to remember her telling me not to show it to anyone. Goddess only knows why. I remember it as being . . . different then . . . somehow. Oh, I don't really recall, but my mother – my adoptive mother, Salacia – told me before she died that when the General first brought me home I was so sensitive about the lump I would not unfold my fingers, not even when I was asleep. They couldn't understand why. They were going to force my fingers up to see what it was I hid there, but Aemid persuaded them it was better not to upset me. She made me a glove to wear. And in a couple of months I opened my hand of my own accord, I suppose when I'd decided no one was going to worry about the lump there.' I gave a wry smile. 'I must have been a funny little thing then. I couldn't have been three years old, but I was obviously as stubborn as a closed mussel.'

'You still are,' he said with a laugh. 'Ligea, I am dirty with the dust of my journey. I've spent most of the day with my backside plonked in the saddle of a gorclak. I smell of sex and sweat and animal hide – how about a soak in that sunken bath of yours?'

I tilted my head. 'With me?'

His eyes twinkled. 'I thought you'd never ask.'

CHAPTER FOUR

I stood on the deck of the *Flying Windhover* and reflected that, for all the flying this ship did, it would have been better named the *Wallowing Pig*. I had taken the first convenient sailing, and I was beginning to regret it. It wasn't that I was so eager to reach Kardiastan; it was just that being cooped up for so long in such a small space gave me an intimate understanding of why a lion paces up and down in his cage. Four weeks, and we still weren't in Sandmurram. The seamaster blamed the weather and the cargo; the first because the winds were contrary, the second because the weight of the Tyranian marble we carried made the ship unwieldy. So he said. I was inclined to think the *Flying Windhover* probably always moved like a pregnant sow.

'Why on earth are we taking marble to Kardiastan anyway?' I asked Aemid idly. She was standing beside me, leaning over the rail watching the bow wave curl back like fruit-peel before a knife.

She snorted. 'Let me guess: so that your soldiers and administrators can build houses and public buildings to match their status. You people don't like to live in homes made of our Kardi adobe – not good enough for you. And we Kardis are taxed to pay for the marble and the construction of course, because you say the Exaltarchy's soldiers and civil servants are serving the Kardi people.'

'And so they are,' I said, nettled both by Aemid's criticism and her deliberate use of the words 'you' and 'we'. I gave her a sharp look. I didn't like the change I'd noted in her ever since the first mention of going to Kardiastan. I liked neither the overt realignment of loyalties nor the suppressed anger I had detected once or twice. But it puzzled me too. Aemid was not in the habit of being provoking and I'd never had to question her loyalties before. What in all Acheron's mists was wrong with the woman?

I tried to explain. 'Tyrans provides the soldiers for security and the administrators for efficiency, all paid out of Tyranian public coffers; so why shouldn't Kardiastan pay for their housing and for the public buildings, buildings that will belong to Kardi Province when they are completed? There is always a price for peace, Aemid.' I reached out – as I had often done lately – to touch her emotions, and felt her confusion. Just then the predominant feeling was one of bitterness.

'Aemid,' I asked softly, 'what is the matter? You are not happy. Do you regret coming with me?'

'Never.' The word was uncompromisingly definite and I needed no special intuition to know it was the truth.

'Then what is it?'

'Memories. Just memories. The closer we come—' She looked away from the sea to my face. 'I have a son there somewhere, if he survived. All these years . . . I have tried not to remember. Now I think of nothing else.'

I felt as though one of the waves had just slapped cold water across my face. 'A *son*? You left a child behind in Kardiastan? But you were – what, twenty? – when you came to Tyr, so he could have hardly been more than a baby! Why did you leave him?'

'*Leave* him? I didn't leave, I was stolen! I was made a slave, *sold*, because I kicked a legionnaire who put his hand between my legs. Sentenced to the slave block for kicking a man's knobs.'

I was immeasurably shocked, not so much by the severity of the sentence as by its unlawful consequence. I protested, 'But it is not permitted for slaves to be separated from their young children!'

'Perhaps that's what the law *says*, but who cares about the words of the law in the chaos following a conquest? A woman sells better without encumbrances.'

'Oh, Aemid – I did not know . . .'

'You never asked.'

The words were stark, summing up a lifetime of attitudes, and they stung. 'I'm sorry,' I said at last, not sure just why I was apologising. For my ignorance? For Tyr? Even to my own ears the words sounded weak. Inadequate. 'As you say, in times of conquest . . . Aemid, do you have any way of finding out what happened to him?'

'None. I do not know who took him – or, in fact, if anyone did. He may have died of neglect within days. He is lost to me.'

I felt an irrational guilt and did not know what to say. Finally I asked, sounding more abrupt than I intended, if she would tell me more about Kardiastan. I added, 'After all, it is my land too. Why did you never tell me about it?'

'The General forbade me. The only thing he allowed was that I taught you the tongue. *That*, he wanted. Don't you remember how he used to question you about all I said to you? He checked up on me whenever he could.'

'He was interested in all I learned.'

'Oh yes. Indeed.' The bitterness was there again. 'He made sure you were brought up Tyranian, every thought in your head.'

'He adopted me legally so that I could be a citizen of Tyrans.

It is natural he wanted me to be loyal to his country, the country he made mine.' Tyrans was the hub of the world, filled with people of every hue and varied customs, a place where my skin tone and the place of my birth could be rendered irrelevant by my citizenship – but only if I was seen to be Tyranian in every other way. And I was. I was *proud* that every thought in my head was Tyranian.

I hid my exasperation with Aemid and said, 'But tell me about Kardiastan.'

'Like what? As you yourself were quick to remind me, the place I knew twenty-five or thirty years ago is not going to be what's there now, is it? We were free then! *I* was free . . .'

I was still casting about for a way to answer that, to give her some speech about the benefits of Tyranian rule, when she poured out more of her bile: 'Tyrans may have conquered our bodies, but there are two things the legions can never kill.' She beat the side of her fist against her chest. 'What's in here. Our essensa.'

I didn't know the word, so she added, 'The life-force in every Kardi heart.'

'And the second thing?'

She pushed herself away from the railing and looked me straight in the eye. 'The Magor.'

'The Magor? What is that?'

'The day you understand the Magor will be the day you renounce Tyrans, Legata.' Without waiting to be dismissed, she walked away across the deck to the companionway. I frowned at her back as she disappeared below. Aemid was becoming much too forward; I hoped I wouldn't have to discipline her. I wasn't even sure how to go about it. Anyway, Aemid, like Brand, was almost family. Bought in a slave mart about the same time as I had arrived in Tyr, she was the only mother-figure I could remember with any clarity. I ran to Aemid when in trouble as a child; it was Aemid who dried my tears. My adoptive mother, Salacia, had mostly ignored me.

I sighed and was glad when Brand, who had been sitting on a nearby cargo hatch, moved across to me, unbothered by the ship's roll. He'd spent most of the voyage out on the open deck and his skin had darkened; it was now a match to my natural colouring. His hair, on the other hand, had lightened. The red streak had become a flash of copperish gold.

'Aemid been upsetting you, Legata?' he inquired.

'Oh, shut up, Brand. I sometimes wonder if the two of you are worth the trouble!'

'Ah. Well, I do know of a remedy for that, of course,' he drawled, fingering his slave collar.

I ignored that and changed the subject. 'Brand, has Aemid ever spoken to you about Kardiastan?'

He dropped the pose and was serious. 'Never, Legata. I wish she would. I'm curious about the place myself. It's funny, that; I've met a number of Kardi slaves over the years and there's not one who's ever told me a thing about their homeland. Still, it shouldn't worry you; the Brotherhood must have been able to tell you anything you wanted to know.'

'You'd be surprised,' I said gloomily. 'All I received from my esteemed Brothers was a history lesson about the conquest. As remarkable as it may seem, they know nothing about the Kardis. They don't even seem to understand much about the situation there now, and yet we purport to rule the place.' Even as I said the words, I wondered if they were true. Perhaps it was simply that the Brotherhood had not been honest with me. Rathrox, for example, must surely have known about the coming Stalwart invasion, yet he had not mentioned it, any more than I was going to mention it to Brand now.

Distrustful old bastard, I thought, thinking of the Magister Officii.

I continued, confirming my thoughts with my own words, 'And this even though Rathrox Ligatan was actually there for a time. Years ago, though. He was assistant to General Gayed. Although Pater wasn't in charge of the original invasion; Bator Korbus was.' I nodded at Brand's startled expression. 'Yes, the Exaltarch himself, in the days when he was High General and nothing else. But I'm not surprised you didn't know; believe me, taking part in that first Kardiastan campaign is not something any of them boast about.'

Intrigued by the Exaltarch's personal interest in my mission to Kardiastan, I had done some research. As a result, I thought I now knew just what had prompted result, I thought I now knew just what had prompted the bitterness in Korbus's voice when he spoke of the land of my birth. More than twenty-five years ago he'd had his pride wounded and time had not effected a cure; on the contrary, the original injury had festered. The Exaltarch hated Kardiastan.

The thought of a Tyranian defeat apparently amused Brand. He smiled as he asked, 'The campaign wasn't successful?'

'Tyrans was thoroughly routed at a place called the Rift. I gather it's a huge valley gashing the country from side to side. Rathrox described it to me as a place of howling winds and inhospitable terrain. When our legionnaires tried to cross it, fearful windstorms maddened their gorclaks and swept away their stores and camps. And all the while the Kardis harried them. So many soldiers were never seen again, and those who did manage to retreat told strange tales.' I snorted in disparagement as I recalled Rathrox's account. 'Such silly stories: warriors – both men and women – glowing with an eerie light, whirling winds that whipped swords out of hands, legionnaires who suddenly dropped dead with burn marks scorched through their cuirasses . . . Silliness to explain an inexplicable defeat. What is true, and almost as hard to believe, is that the legions involved were nearly wiped out. That first campaign was a dismal failure, the only time Bator Korbus ever personally lost a battle. He returned to Tyr immediately afterwards. He left the problems to Gayed and Rathrox and went back to begin his bid for the Exaltarch's seat.'

'So how did Tyrans win in the end?'

An unexpected gust of wind hit the *Flying Windhover* and we were dappled with spray as she heeled. I said, 'There were other campaigns in the years that followed, some equally disastrous. Eventually the legions changed their tactics. They used small groups of legionnaires in quick attacks and ambushes and then they were more successful. In the end, though, it was treachery of one of the Kardi nobility that brought Kardi noses down into the dirt at the feet of Tyrans.'

'One of the nobility? They had a royal line? A king?'

'As far as I could find out from Brotherhood records, there used to be a kind of royal oligarchy with a hereditary leader. All administration was in the hands of this ruling group.'

'It must surely have been quite large,' Brand remarked, shifting stance with easy grace as the ship changed tack.

'Yes. The nobles were scattered all over the country, but the highest rank lived mainly in Madrinya, the capital. It was impossible for an ordinary Kardi to move into the ruling class.'

'The Exaltarchy has changed all that since, naturally,' he said, his voice as bland as his expression. 'Now anyone who proves his loyalty to Tyr can serve in a position of importance.'

Although there was nothing to indicate he was mocking the Exaltarchy, I knew he was. The normal method of rewarding loyalty wasn't successful in Kardiastan: no one there *wanted* to serve Tyrans. And Brand must have found that out. He smiled, a lazy smile in my direction. 'Sailors,' he explained, weaving a hand in the direction of one of the crew. 'They gossip.'

'What else have they told you?'

'They say the ordinary Kardi was not even part of the army back before the Tyranian invasion. That it was only the high-born who fought. Is that true?'

'Rathrox said as much, yes. He told me there were rumours saying the nobility possessed special powers that made them invincible, but that was all superstitious nonsense, of course. Still, the nobles must have been fine fighters, otherwise how could they have put whole legions on the run? Especially those led by a soldier like the Exaltarch? And later by my father, Gayed?'

'What happened to this highborn traitor?'

I shrugged. 'I don't know.' I frowned again, remembering. It had been Rathrox who told me about the treachery leading to Kardiastan's fall and he had been deliberately vague. 'The details don't matter,' he'd said. For once, I'd been puzzled by his reticence. I was going to be working alone, so I would need all the information I could get. Instead of giving it to me, Rathrox had been evasive, even contradictory. The idea of a traitor did not seem to fit with what he had earlier told me about the Kardis never betraying their own, thus making the work of the Brotherhood impossible in Kardiastan. I sighed and rubbed at my left palm with my thumb tip. 'He probably committed suicide,' I said, in answer to Brand's question. 'I've noticed such people often do. They can't live with what they've done. And this man had done a lot – because of him, almost all the top stratum of nobility was slaughtered while they were unarmed, attending a feast.

'Another full legion was sent from Tyrans after that, and General Gayed became High Commander for Kardiastan. A major battle took place, which Tyrans won this time. You see, with the death of so many of their highest nobility, the Kardis lost most of their military commanders and civil leadership. The war wasn't entirely over, but Gayed and Rathrox went home to Tyr anyway. Fighting continued in Kardiastan for a further five years. Just skirmishes mainly.' I turned to look out over the stern. A few seabirds with huge wingspans cruised effortlessly in our wake, clipping the wave crests with their wingtips. 'You know, it's strange – I hadn't realised both Rathrox and my father spent so long in Kardiastan. They must have been there all of four years. Neither of them ever told me that.'

Brand leant beside me as a small flotilla of fishing dhows dipped and wallowed their way out from the coast we had been following, their hide sails taut with the wind. The seabirds left us to follow them instead. 'Where do you fit into all this anyway?' he asked.

'I don't know the details. I was never told. I was just an orphaned Kardi child Gayed came across somewhere. As I said, he and Rathrox were recalled to Tyrans soon after the victory following the betrayal, and I went with them.'

'You are probably the child of one of those noble families.' He snorted. 'The Magister Officii and the General would have loved the irony of that.'

'I don't suppose for a minute my father knew who I was, or cared. In a war, children get separated from their parents all the time. They get orphaned and abandoned. And it certainly doesn't matter now. I am Tyranian, and glad of it.'

Brand looked back at me, expressionless. 'And now the Magister Officii wants you to put down the beginnings of a rebellion against Tyrans. One would almost think the ordinary people of Kardiastan are not grateful at being freed from the oppressive rule of their nobility.'

There was no inflection of mockery in his voice, but I stirred uneasily nonetheless. Suddenly nothing was as it had been; I was questioning things I had never questioned before: Aemid's love, Brand's loyalty, Tyrans's strength . . . I shivered and rubbed still harder at my palm.

'Legata!'

I turned to see the *Flying Windhover*'s seamaster trying to draw my attention to something from where he stood inside the wheelhouse.

'Sandmurram!'

I followed the line of his pointing finger and saw the brown blotches of a town against the dusky blue of the coastline. With an unexpected feeling of wonder, I realised this might have been the port I had sailed from some twenty-five years earlier. Perhaps I had stood on the deck of a ship similar to this one and had seen this same scene recede just as I would now watch it approach.

In theory, I was coming home – but to Ligea Gayed, this had never been home, and never would be. Why then did I feel fear: not of Kardiastan, but of what it would tell me about myself?

CHAPTER FIVE

Sandmurram: the main port of Kardiastan. A bay that was a natural harbour, with the port buildings tiered from its edge; a town on flatter land beyond. Flat-roofed, two-storeyed houses of brown adobe, unplastered, unpainted, squatting along the streets like cattle dozing in the sun.

I saw it all with the eyes of a stranger; I had no recollection of ever having seen it before. Beside me, Aemid gripped the rail and stared, her emotions and the avid hunger of her gaze so intense they startled me.

The seamaster flag-signalled my presence on his ship as soon as we approached the port, so I was met at the dockside by a legionnaire escort. The officer in charge offered me a litter ride to the Prefect's house, but I preferred to walk. I wanted to survey this land, not because it was the place of my birth, but because the hunter needed to know the haunts of her prey.

'See to the luggage,' I told Brand. 'And keep an eye on Aemid.'

He nodded, and I set off on foot with the officer.

My first impression was one of monotony. The streets were unpaved and narrow, the brown of their earth a mirror reflection of the plain brown walls of the houses. Burnt-sienna brown everywhere, unrelieved by any other colour. No paint, no ornamentation; no grass even. Trees were misshapen gnomes with thick gnarled trunks, arthritic limbs and spindled leaves, growing only where the lanes swelled to become public well-squares – where, greedy for water, they could nestle up to the well itself.

The only flashes of colour were in the clothing of the local people, people who were always walking away, turning their backs, retreating into houses, closing doors. The brown streets with their brown houses were unnaturally quiet. There was no noise of hawkers, no whine of beggars, no litter carriers jostling for custom. Even the pack animals – strange, dull-brown creatures – padded along on soft unshod feet. Once or twice I did catch a glimpse of an inner courtyard, and had a brief impression of flowers, of laughter, of animation, of *life* – but then the view would be cut off, the life killed by the closing of a gate.

It was a while before I noticed the snakes. Then, once I'd seen one, I saw them all the time. They were also brown, blending into the ground as if they were made of the soil. They coiled themselves on house steps, draped themselves along gate tops, dozed lethargically in the sun at the edge of the wells. If we approached, they slid lazily away to the next patch of sunlight.

Goddess, I thought, *what sort of place is this?*

And even while I saw its strangeness with my eyes, I also *felt* its strangeness. The air brooded; malevolent, expectant. Never before had I been so aware of atmosphere. A confusion of overwhelming emotion rendered every breath an effort. I was made uneasy, troubled, tense, as though at any moment something terrible was going to happen. Yet, when I tried to pinpoint the source of my unease, it slid away from me, as slippery as a half-remembered dream.

I even became accustomed to it. By the time I reached the

Tyranian Prefect's house – built of white marble, thanks be! – and was received by the Prefect and his wife, I'd pushed the feeling of oppression into the background and was able to ignore it.

I'd read the Brotherhood intelligence report on the Prefect Martrinus, before I'd left Tyr. He'd risen through the ranks of the military magistrates, from a lowly position as a law court lictor to his present position, a change of status made possible by his judicious marriage into a highborn family from Getria. His first reaction on seeing me was predictable: he was taken aback to find I was a woman. I didn't blame him for that. I'd never heard of a legata before, either.

Once he recovered from his initial surprise, he bowed low over my hand in greeting, evidently deeming it prudent to show extravagant respect for a Brotherhood Legata even though he did outrank me. When he asked about my first impressions, I gave a casual answer. 'It's a strange land,' I said. 'Everything is so different. This is the first time I have been so far from Tyrans, you know. I am filled with wonder. The mud-brick houses with such thick walls, all the flat roofs – and what are those animals the Kardis use for carrying their goods?'

'They call them shleths,' the Prefect said. He was a thin man with shrewd watery eyes and a nervous habit of tapping his bent forefinger against whatever was to hand. 'A difficult word.'

His stylishly attired wife, the Prefecta Fabia, shuddered. I suspected she did a lot of shuddering in Kardiastan. 'An unpronounceable name for impossible beasts,' she said, her distaste thick about her. 'There are three kinds, you know. The little ones that carry small packs, larger ones that people ride and the huge ones that are found further inland. On those, five or six people can ride in a howdah – but we are content with horses and gorclaks. These shleths are heathen beasts, vicious things of uncertain temper.'

'And the snakes?'

Another theatrical shudder. 'Ugh! They come into the house, you know. They are *everywhere*! The Kardis *feed* them.'

'Are they poisonous?' I asked Fabia, glancing at the Prefect. He was busy reading the letter-scroll I had brought him from Rathrox.

She shuddered. 'Praise the Goddess, no! I've tried to get the slaves to kill them, but they won't. These stupid thralls think serpents bring prosperity to a household.' She paused to indicate the spread on the low table in front of me. 'Legata, will you not eat a little of what we have prepared for you?' As one of the waiting Kardi slave girls hurried over to pour water for me to wash my hands, she added, as if it were a self-evident virtue, 'We do not eat Kardi food in this house.'

I held out my hands over the washbowl but, as the girl poured the water, she suddenly gasped and dropped the ewer. It knocked the washbowl flying, splashing water everywhere. I jumped up in surprise and chagrin, my wrap soaked. I was wet and the water was cold. And then the girl's emotions hit me: shock, wonder, fear . . .

Domina Fabia was both furious and humiliated. She slapped the girl and fussed over me. By the time the mess had been cleaned up and I had convinced her it was a minor matter, the Prefect was impatient. 'The Legata and I have business to discuss, Fabia.' Ignoring the angry flush on his wife's face, he waved her out of the room, together with the slaves.

'I abhor fuss,' he told me irritably, then reverted to a more formal tone to say, 'It is time to discuss this letter you have brought.' He tapped his forefinger on the letter-scroll. 'The Magister Officii indicates I should give you every assistance. But I do not understand, Legata, why it has been thought necessary for you to come in the first place. This matter is already closed. The man in question, this Mir Ager, was executed by fire, as is customary for insurgents. Hundreds of people saw him die. There are rumours, it's true, and unrest. However, that is nothing new for Kardiastan. He died, and there was certainly no resurrection of the dead, I assure you!'

He added unhappily, 'Do you know we still have the same number of garrisoned troops here as we had in the years immediately following the conquest? And every single one of them necessary. We can do nothing unless we are backed by legionnaires. The Kardis never cooperate willingly. Not ever.' He leant forward to put some food on my plate. 'That incident with the slave just now – it was probably deliberate. The girl will be beaten, but it will make no difference. *Nothing* makes a difference to these people. Sometimes I think they are here to plague us, sent by the God of Acheron himself.' His forefinger beat a dismal rhythm against his knee.

'Perhaps if you were to tell me all you know about this Mir Ager?' I prompted.

'Rumours say he came from the quarter of Kardiastan that's on the other side of the desert they call the Shiver Barrens, to the west. We never did find out whether that was true. The first we knew of him was at a slave sale here in Sandmurram. There were slavers from Tyrans wanting stock, so we cleaned out the prisons and brought others down from Madrinya and similar inland towns, but there still weren't enough. Well, you know how it is at times like that – the legionnaires become a little stricter and a little more provocative, the number of lawbreakers increases, and so you get enough stock.'

I blinked, wondering if I had heard him correctly. They tailored their law enforcement to their need for slaves? The civil law courts didn't behave like that in Tyr!

Oblivious to my reaction, he continued, 'It looked like being a good sale. The Exaltarch would get his sales fee, the administration here would get its slice, and everyone would be happy. But there was a disturbance during the sale.' He took a deep breath but his tapping finger, now thrumming on the table, never paused. I tried not to stare at it. 'This man, this Mir Ager, appeared and posed as a bidder. Well, we were all surprised because he was a Kardi. There's nothing to say Kardis can't own slaves, but it had never happened before. They don't hold with slavery. However, he had money so no one questioned his right to be there.

'Anyway, to cut the story short, suddenly the auction square was – well, I know it sounds unlikely, but it was full of smoke and fire and colours and wind and noise . . . it's hard to describe. I've never seen anything like it. And this man was at the centre of it.' Martrinus shook his head in disbelief at the memory. 'Everything was so confusing; it was so hard to see what was happening. The women were shrieking, gorclaks went berserk, people ran in all directions, screaming. Even the legionnaires were spooked. Somehow the slaves got free. The only thing most of us knew for sure was that this Mir Ager fellow was at the middle of it all. He seemed to – well, *glow*.' Martrinus was embarrassed, but ploughed on anyway. 'And he had some sort of weapon in his hand, a gigantic thing that shot sparks. Well, one of the legionnaires, who had a little bit more sense than the others, managed to render him unconscious with a shot from a whirlsling. Mir Ager was packed off to the dungeons, but we lost the slaves – by then, they'd just melted away into the crowd. Worse still, the slavers took fright. They said they weren't going to trade in slaves who could escape from chains in the middle of a public sale. There was muttering about them being numina, or some such supernatural beings. Needless to say, we've had trouble selling Kardi slaves on markets throughout the Exaltarchy ever since.

'Mir Ager was tortured, but we couldn't get a thing out of him. Not a thing. He was sentenced to death by burning for inciting rebellion, which is high treason, as I am sure you know. He was taken out to the main square and chained to the stake. The fire was lit, but unfortunately the idiots who supplied the wood must have sent damp stuff. Instead of getting a lot of flame, there was enough smoke for a smokehouse. By the time it cleared, the flames were too fierce to see a damn thing. So that's when people began to say Mir Ager didn't burn at all, that somehow or other he escaped in the smoke.' At the memory, his eyes watered even more copiously and he produced a square of silk to dab away the moisture. 'Sorry about the eyes. It's the dust, you know. Irritates. There's always dust here in Kardiastan.'

'Weren't there bones? Some human remains?'

'I suppose so, although I don't know that anyone checked at the time. You must understand: we were hardly expecting a public execution to be questioned! The rumours didn't start until much later. Felons executed by burning are not entitled to a marked grave, you know. So any remains would have been thrown away.' He sniffed and used the silk to wipe his dripping nose.

'Is that all you can tell me about this Mir Ager?'

'Well, not quite,' he admitted. 'There have been reports from other places since, some of them true. Prisoners miraculously escaping, whole patrols of legionnaires disappearing, officers being assassinated. That sort of thing. And everywhere people whisper about how this Mir Ager out of the Shiver Barrens is behind it all. Sometimes I think the whole of Kardiastan is one big calabash of whispered rumours. It's so damned hard to find out the truth about *anything* – no two Kardis will ever tell you the same story, no matter what you do to them.' He'd lost his initial exaggerated respect for me and, formal tone forgotten, was treating me more like a confidante. His patrician accent faded into the roughness of a man who spent his days with military officers rather than politicians. I felt sure his wife would not have approved. 'Ocrastes' balls,' he complained, 'how I *hate* this place. Legata, I'm not giving away any secrets when I say there's not a Tyranian citizen, from the Governor in Madrinya to the lowest legionnaire cook-boy, who doesn't wish his tour of duty here was up.'

I kept my face and voice expressionless. 'Did you know that the land beyond the Shiver Barrens is sometimes referred to as the Mirage?'

'I've heard the term, yes.'

'Mirage, Mir Ager. Mirager.'

'It has occurred to us, naturally. That's why I don't think it was his real name. He took it as a way of making people think of this mysterious place beyond the desert. It's a symbol of hope to the ordinary Kardi – and a place that scares the crap out of legionnaires. Over the years, various military commanders have sent Goddess knows how many patrols into the Shiver Barrens in search of the Mirage – on foot, with horses, with gorclaks, with shleths. Every way you can think of. *And no one has ever returned.* Yet Kardis are seen riding off on their shleths in that direction, and back again, too.'

I nodded and changed the subject. 'This weapon you mentioned of Mir's; what happened to it? You *do* have it, I assume?'

Martrinus looked uncomfortable. In his agitation, his fore-finger was rattling the edge of his plate. 'It's kept in the military barracks, I believe.'

'I would like to see it. And I would like to interview the legionnaires who tortured him and those who were responsible for his execution. In fact, I'd like to speak to anyone who saw him at close quarters, or who spoke to him.'

'The Sandmurram Military Commander is away in one of the eastern towns. Some trouble or other. I shall arrange for his next-in-command to help you. Some of those you want to see may not be here any more. This all happened some twelve months ago, you know.'

I rose, fighting the feeling that the floor was a moving deck beneath my feet. 'All the more reason why no more time should be wasted. Prefect Martrinus, I thank you for your help and I would like to see the weapon and these people without further delay.'

'*Today?*'

'Certainly. I have been idle long enough getting here.'

He swallowed his surprise. 'Yes, of course.' He rang for a slave and a lad appeared, an Assorian if his curly hair was anything to go by. 'Agamin here will show you to your apartments,' he said formally. My tone had evidently made him wonder if he had been too casual. 'As soon as I have made arrangements, I will send someone to fetch you.'

I rarely bothered to read the emotions of slaves. They were either a seething mass of sullen resentment and fatigued indifference, or they were vague dreamers, escaping reality into thoughts of no importance to me. If they did their jobs well, they were like any other tool, easily ignored and irrelevant until something went wrong, and I took no more notice of them than I would a comfortable chair or a sharp knife. But now, my complacency rattled by the slave girl, I reached out to absorb the Assorian boy's feelings as I mounted the stairs behind him. And was immediately intrigued.

He could not have been more than twelve, yet he possessed the calm self-assurance of someone much older. He kept glancing behind to look at me, ostensibly to see if I were still following, but his fervid emotions told their own tale. He wanted to remember everything about me. Every detail. His passion startled me, yet also struck a distant chord of childhood memory. *Oh, goddess*, I thought. *That's me. The way I was once, aching to be an agent of the Brotherhood* . . . And then: *I wonder who the sweet hells he wants to spy for?*

On the next floor he opened a door, saying, 'Your rooms, Domina.' He had cast his eyes downwards, which was proper, but still his fascination to know me spilled out, enthusiastic, intrusive. It was an effort to ignore it. I wondered if he were already spying for someone. Martrinus? Fabia? The Tyranian Governor of Kardiastan in Madrinya? Or perhaps something more nefarious? Too many political intricacies to be considered, and it was dangerous to tread where the ground was unknown. Reluctantly, I let it ride and did not question him. 'Agamin,' I said, 'I wish to speak with the Kardi slave girl. The one who spilled water on me – I do not know her name. Tell her to come here.'

He bowed and left wordlessly; on the surface, the perfect slave.

While I waited, I looked around with approval. The Prefect's house was not unlike my own villa in Tyr, and the rooms given to me, overlooking a garden courtyard, were cool and spacious. The furniture and carved statuary were obviously imported from Tyrans, all of good quality. There was even a head of a youth by Mattias, one of the finest sculptors of Tyr.

I was running admiring fingers over the perfection of the piece when the slave, a frightened girl of about eighteen, arrived at my door. Her face, swollen where Fabia had slapped her, was also red and blotched from a recent bout of crying. She entered the room and stood with her eyes downcast. She wore an anoudain, the form of dress the Kardi women seem to prefer – loose trousers and a long top. The bodice was fitted, attached to skirting split into back and front panels.

'What is your name?' I asked, careful to sound neutral.

'Othenid, Legata.'

'Have you been beaten for spilling the water, Othenid?'

Her face tightened. 'Yes, Legata.'

'Where?'

'On – on my back.'

I walked across to her, turned her around and touched her back lightly with my left hand, trailing gentle fingertips over the thin blouse in an attempt to express my concern and win her trust. As far as I could see, she had been bruised but not badly hurt. Still, it must have been sore.

The girl turned surprised eyes to me. 'The pain – it's gone!'

While I was still trying to make sense of that, she knelt to seize my left hand and press her lips to the swelling there. It was all the confirmation I needed to tell me what had startled her into dropping the ewer. 'Theura—?' she asked, questioning. It was not a word I knew. And Goddess above, why did she think I had taken away her pain? For that was what she appeared to believe.

'Othenid, I need your help,' I said. 'Why did you get such a shock when you saw this?' I pointed to the lump on my palm.

'Why, Theura—' she began.

'*Silence*, girl!' The words cut across the room like a sword slash. We both looked around to see Aemid in the doorway, her eyes blazing with the intensity of rage. Her emotion was so tangible to me it was almost a physical assault.

'Keep out of this, Aemid,' I said, furious. 'Leave us.'

But Aemid didn't go. She continued to address the girl, not

me. 'Can't you see she is not Kardi? She is Tyranian to her very essensa! Go—'

Othenid whirled and was gone, without waiting for permission.

I turned the full swell of my fury on Aemid. 'How *dare* you!' I raised my hand to strike her, more angry than I had ever been before with any of my slaves. But Aemid did not move, nor did her eyes drop; it was my hand that fell away. 'You stretch your luck, Aemid,' I said, breathing hard. 'I *own* you; don't you forget it.'

'I never forget it,' she said. 'Not for a minute.'

'If I'm wholly Tyranian, whose fault is it anyway? You were the one person who could have taught me what it was to be Kardi, who could have told me what the meaning of this is' – I indicated the swelling on my hand – 'but you kept silent. You *still* keep silent.'

Her eyes fell and a slow flush coloured her face. 'Yes. I admit it. But I thought if I told you, you might tell the General and he would use what he learned to harm Kardiastan. Later I feared *you* would be the one to turn the knowledge against us. I couldn't risk it.' Her eyes begged for understanding. 'You don't want to know what it is to be Kardi; you want to know our weaknesses so you know how to defeat us.'

'You are already defeated.' I took a deep breath to calm myself. 'Tell me what Theura means.'

'Nothing. It means nothing!' And then, knowing I would hear the lie, she amended her words. 'It's a – a word designating rank. She was just being polite, that's all. Legata, if you show your hand to any more Kardis and probe their knowledge, you won't live long enough to use the knowledge you gain. There're people out there who would kill you, rather than have a Tyranian learn our secrets.'

My jaw dropped. 'You *threaten* me?'

She winced. 'No! I – I warn. And you know the truth when you hear it. Be warned.'

'*I'll have you whipped! And sold!*'

I couldn't have said anything worse. I saw her resolve harden before my eyes, as though I had cast her spirit in stone with the power of my words.

She nodded. 'That is within your rights. But I will see to it that any Kardi slave you buy to serve you in my place will watch you and report what you do. Legata, if you pose as a Kardi and show that hand of yours as proof, you are in danger. You will learn too much, and no Tyranian who knows too much can be allowed to live.'

I shook with shock and outrage. 'You want me dead!'

'No, child. I love you. I have always loved you. You are right; it is my fault you never became Kardi, and it is a decision I have had to live with all these years. I could have deceived General Gayed and taught you all I knew, but I didn't. I will never know if it was the right decision, because I can never know what would have happened had I followed the other road.'

I felt the love and pity and grief of the woman who had been my nurse, but turned from it. Right then, I wanted to believe the worst of her, not the best, and her resolve had not wavered. Vortexdamn her, she had as good as admitted she was now spying on me. It sounded as if she were contemplating passing on information to the very Kardi rebels I was hunting.

Her tone softened subtly, imploring. 'I beg you, Ligea, don't make your death necessary. Hide your hand. Hide your knowledge of our language. Walk the streets of Kardiastan as a Tyranian, one of the dreaded Brotherhood. Because if you dupe Kardis into betraying secrets by using your knowledge of our language and your Kardi looks, there will be a hundred thousand people ready to fling a knife into your back.'

'You're going to tell them!' I accused. 'You are going to tell them I am a Kardi who speaks the language and is intent on betraying their leader.'

She shook her head and her distress was filling the air. 'I don't want to tell them. They would kill you the moment you stepped out of the door! Just promise me you won't disguise yourself as a Kardi and I won't say a word, I swear. And I'll stop Othenid from mentioning what she saw in your hand. I can't tell them,' she added in a whisper. 'How can I? You are like a daughter to me. But I need your promise!'

I stared at her. She meant what she said; her truth was blatant. But did *she* know *me* so little? 'All right,' I said, my voice gravelled with genuine anger. 'You keep quiet and keep Othenid quiet, and I will do my work as a Tyranian. I'm proud of my citizenship, and I don't need to hide behind a Kardi skin. Now leave me. And be glad I'm not ordering your whipping.'

She left, her back proud and straight.

'Goddess,' I muttered. 'What *is* this Kardiastan?'

I looked down at my palm and rubbed the lump. A childhood memory surfaced: an old slave woman with aching joints and gnarled fingers telling me, after I'd held her hand, that I had 'the healing touch'. And a much later adult recollection: a tortured prisoner of the Brotherhood spilling out his secrets to me in gratitude because he thought I'd alleviated his agony, when all I had done was pat him on the arm in sympathy.

I shivered. It was all nonsense . . . surely?

A knock at the door prompted me to pull myself together. It was Brand, to tell me a legionnaire had arrived to take me to the Military Headquarters. 'Come with me,' I said, suddenly in need of company. I laid a hand on his arm, feeling the hardness of his muscle, taking strength from his solid reality. 'This is a mad land, Brand.'

He smiled slightly. 'I can't say I much like the idea of snakes on the portico. Does it have a certain symbolism, do you think?'

I tried to smile back. 'I hope not. Come, let us begin to make the acquaintance of this fellow, this Mir Ager.'

CHAPTER SIX

I braced myself to face the street again. I was back among those seething emotions that filled the air. Hatred dominated. Hatred for Tyrans, solid in its unity. The Kardis refused even to look at the legionnaire who was escorting us. Brand they stared at, intrigued. They considered me with initial interest, because of the darkness of my skin, but once they'd taken in my Tyranian wrap, my bare shoulder, my hair highlighted and styled in the Tyranian fashion, the glances would fall away, filled with contempt.

Brand bent to whisper in my ear. 'They look at us as though they wish us dead,' he said.

'They do,' I replied, with certainty.

I felt uncomfortable. Had fate thrown my destiny into another wind, I might have been one of these people. They looked so much like me with their tan skins, earth-coloured hair, brown eyes. A desert people who would have blended into the brown soil and the burnt-sienna adobe of their buildings if it hadn't been for the bright patches of colour in their clothing. The men wore loose brown trousers, plain light-coloured shirts with full sleeves, sleeveless boleros, cloth belts – and the boleros and belts were always in vivid, unpatterned primary colours. The women were all clad in the anoudain, and often the tops were brightly coloured, or adorned with a spray of embroidery from the shoulder across the slope of a breast.

I eyed them with envy. I liked to wear trousers, but Tyranian custom frowned on such informality outside the home. I wondered if the highborn of Tyr would approve of the anoudain. The long thin overskirt, slit almost to the waist on either side, did lend a graceful femininity to the trousers underneath, yet the wearer still had the freedom of movement trousers provided.

Anoudain . . .

The harsh light of the square flicked out and memory swamped my senses.

I was in a tiny room, being rocked with hypnotic rhythm. I was drowsing, lying back in cushioned comfort, a woman's arm round my shoulders, and the perfume I associated with happiness was in my nostrils . . . until the noise began. The room lurched. Screams, terrible screams of agony and anger. The woman became another person, a frightening person, ripping away the filmy skirting of her anoudain to reveal the more substantial trousers underneath; grabbing up a sword—

I cried out in my panic. The woman turned to me, tenderness briefly returning. 'Hush, little one,' she said. 'Remember, you are of the Magor. You must be brave.' She took my hand in hers and curled the fingers closed over the palm. 'But from them – from them you must always hide it. Do you understand, my precious? Always.' She hugged me and looked over my head to the woman who was the third occupant of that tiny room. 'I leave her in your care, Theura. Do what you can.'

And then she was gone, jumping out with a ferocious cry.

When I moved to follow, the other woman held me back and drew the curtains so that I could not see – but not before I had glimpsed hell first. My mother bathed in golden light, surrounded by evil, her sword cutting a swathe of red blood ... gold and crimson, light and blood.

And I began to scream.

The memory was abruptly, painfully, cut off. I tried to seize it again, to bring it into focus, but it blurred away.

I knew part of me did not want to remember.

'Are you all right?' Brand asked, puzzled.

I took a breath, forcing myself to nod. We were on the other side of the square from the Prefect's house and I had no recollection of crossing the open space to reach the white stone edifice dazzling in the sunshine in front of me.

Theura. That other woman in the room of my memory had been called Theura. And just this morning, the slave Othenid had called me Theura ...

'The barracks,' the legionnaire explained unnecessarily. The number of gorclaks tethered outside, all wearing military saddles, made it clear what the building was. The animals did not seem to mind the heat of the street; their thick grey hides protected them from both sun and cold. I could never look at them without thinking of war. With their small mean eyes, their single razor-sharp horn, the folds of thick skin they wore like armour, the cruel spurs on muscled legs built for endurance rather than speed, they looked as if they had been created to be mobile battering rams. Machines of war, of death. I thought of Favonius. He rode a gorclak.

The legionnaire took us to meet Deltos Forgra, the centurion in charge, and Deltos took us, with obvious reluctance, to see the weapon Mir Ager had used. Deltos was a tall, sad-eyed man with a slow, measured way of speaking, and he did not like the whole subject of Mir Ager, or his weapon, a fact he made clear. 'The sword is dangerous,' he said. 'We would destroy it if we knew how to.'

'Dangerous? Then why not learn to use it?' I asked.

He gave a hollow laugh. 'We don't even know how to pick it up.' He lit a torch and led us down into the cellars under the barracks, then still deeper down another flight of steps.

'Sweet Melete, wherever do you keep it?' I asked. 'In the sewers?'

'In the furthest dungeon cell. There are eight locked doors between it and daylight. Here we are.' He unlocked the last door and swung it open. In the windowless cell, a bundle lay on a table. Deltos remained standing by the door. 'That's it. It had to be pushed with staves onto the skin that wraps it now. Don't put your hand to it, Legata.' He nodded at Brand. 'You unwrap it, slave, but be careful not to touch it.'

I held Brand back as he moved to obey. 'No. I will.'

'Legata, if anything were to happen to you—' Deltos began to protest, but I was already unrolling the skin, spilling what it contained onto the table. At first I thought it was just a sword. It was far from gigantic; the Prefect's memory was faulty on that point. It was, if anything, abnormally short. The hilt and the hand-guard were ordinary enough, patterned but not jewelled. Then I realised the blade was not forged metal as I had at first thought, but translucent like frosted glass – and it was hollow. The tip was open, the edges razor-sharp. I reached out my left hand to touch the hilt.

'Vortex, Legata, *don't*!' Deltos cried. 'It's a spirit thing. Protected by— Goddess knows what! Numina spells. I know it sounds ridiculous.'

'Quite ridiculous.' A numen was an amoral spirit of ancient beliefs, not part of our pantheon of deities. We weren't even supposed to believe in them any more. I turned to smile at him. 'It will not hurt me, Centurion.' Somewhere in my distant memories, something told me I had nothing to fear. My hand closed around the hilt and I lifted it from the table. It was as light as cork wood and slipped into my hold as though it belonged there. I uncurled my fingers and looked at the hilt again; there was a rounded hollow there into which the swelling on my palm fitted when I closed my hand. *And the sword recognised me.* Shock squeezed my heart painfully, but I tightened my grip on it once again.

Deltos gaped as I held it up. 'Goddess! It took six men to carry it here. Six men to lift it. And not one could touch it for the pain.'

I blinked at that extraordinary statement, but decided not to ridicule him. He believed every word he said, so I decided to make use of his credulity. 'Never underestimate the Brotherhood, Centurion.' I wanted him to think it was my Brotherhood associations that made me special, but I knew differently. It wasn't easy to quieten the fear – the fear of my past, of my blood, of what I was – that jerked my heart to such unevenness.

I turned my attention back to the weapon that was not quite a sword. I slashed it through the air, bringing it down on the table. Had it been glass, the blade would have broken; had it been an ordinary sword, it would barely have marked the wood, because the force I used was insufficient to do much damage. This weapon sliced through the planks like a gorclak horn through horseflesh.

'Goddess preserve us!' Deltos exclaimed.

'A formidable weapon,' I said, impressed in spite of myself. 'Tell me, Centurion, has anyone tried to steal this from you?'

He shook his head. 'We spread the rumour we'd thrown it into the sea. The Kardis don't know we have it. If I'd had my way, we *would* have thrown it into the sea from a ship on its way to the Wild Waters.'

I smiled. 'You don't have it any more. I'm taking it.' I wrapped it up once again and tucked it under my arm.

'But, Legata, I can't let you do that! I don't have the authority—'

'Perhaps not, but I do. The Brotherhood claims this weapon, Centurion Deltos. Would you question the Brotherhood?'

He was aghast. 'Of – of course not, Legata. But have a care.'

'That I will. Believe me, I haven't the slightest doubt of its potency. Now, I wish to speak with some of the legionnaires who actually saw this man, this Mir Ager.'

'I'll see to it.' He ushered me back upstairs. 'I have one of the men who was present during the torture sessions, as well as the officer who was in charge of the execution. I'm afraid they are the only two who are here in Sandmurram at the moment. Which one do you want to see first?'

'The torturer, I think.'

'A man by the name of Achates. A rankman legionnaire coming up to the end of his time in Kardiastan. Not a torturer really, just an old reprobate who can't keep out of trouble and is always given the jobs no one else wants. He was assisting only. The man in charge, Regius, died of blood-poisoning soon after.' He took us up onto the second floor of the main wing of the building and indicated a door carved with military motifs. 'You can use this office. I shall send Achates in to you immediately. Is there anything else you require, Legata?'

I shook my head and he left. I looked across at Brand as we entered the room. 'I don't want any word of this to come to Aemid's ears, Brand. Especially nothing about the weapon.'

'As you wish. Do you want me to stay now?'

'If you will.' I would want to talk about this afterwards with someone I trusted.

I went to the window to wait. The room overlooked the Commander's walled garden. Several unfamiliar fruit trees and a number of flowerbeds were a tangled mass of blossoms – scarlets and purples and oranges predominating. 'How bright the flowers are here!' I exclaimed. 'Have you noticed? Every garden I've seen seems to be overwhelmed with colour. It's as if the flowers want to compensate for the dullness of the trees and the lack of grass and all those brown buildings.'

'All that brown getting to you already, Legata?' Brand asked. He sounded as if he were secretly laughing at me.

'No, of course not. Why should it?' I looked at him sharply, but he was opening the door in answer to a knock and had his back to me.

The man who came in did not look like a soldier. He was a little too unkempt, a little too knowing. I knew his type, though; I had met it often enough during the course of my work for the Brotherhood. He was the sort of fellow who would always be on the lookout for a way to make an extra sestus, but who didn't like to take too many risks. He'd probably only joined the legions to escape trouble elsewhere. And he would have no compunction about uttering a lie or two if he thought it would benefit him.

'Legionnaire Achates?' I inquired. I sat down at the desk in front of the window and indicated he was to approach the other side of it.

He nodded, his glance roaming over me in unconcealed – but respectful – appreciation. I said, 'I am Legata Ligea of the Brotherhood.' His look abruptly changed. Now he was deferential, but it was the deference of fear, not respect. 'I wish to ask you questions about the Kardi known as Mir Ager.' The look changed again; there was an animal wariness in his eyes now, and the fear I sensed deepened.

'What do you want to know, Legata?' Reluctance and trepidation warred within.

'First, describe him to me.'

''Bout your height. Typical Kardi mud-colour skin and hair. Not overly muscular, not like the slave you've got there.' He nodded at Brand. 'But no weakling neither. More like an athlete than a soldier. Handsome sod, he was. Got a smile I'd walk a league or two to have: the sort of smile that charms the wraps off the ladies – begging your pardon, Legata.'

'Did he speak Tyranian?'

'Oh, yes. With an accent, but passable.'

'What sort of torture was used on him?'

Achates stirred uncomfortably. 'Oh, the usual. Branding irons, beating, hanging weights—'

I looked at him in surprise. 'You're lying. Why?'

The fear flared and he shuffled his feet.

'The truth, Achates.'

'That *is* the truth, so help me, Legata.'

'It is not the truth.' Intrigued, I asked, 'Do you mean to tell me the man wasn't tortured at all?'

He almost choked on his alarm. 'I didn't say that!'

'What did happen? Achates, I'm not here to punish you. Whatever you say to me will not be repeated to any military authority. That is not the way the Brotherhood works. We deal with information – the truth. Tell me exactly what happened as you remember it, and the only thing I'll tell your commanding officer is that you've been cooperative. Lie to me, and you earn the enmity of the Brotherhood. And I think you know what *that* means. We are not beyond using the torture iron ourselves.'

He nodded with unhappy wariness. 'He was – Legata, he wasn't like no ordinary man. He was a kind of – of numen. Or worse.' He looked thoroughly miserable. 'If I do tell the truth, you'll call me a liar.'

'Try me.'

'Legata, I hardly believe it m'self.'

'Achates, just tell me what happened.'

He licked his lips nervously. 'Well, Rego – Regius, that is, he was in charge. He did *try* to torture the fellow. But this Mir Ager, he could do things other men can't. He could make things, um, happen. Things that should never be able to happen. I even – well, to tell the truth, I wondered if he could be a – well, an immortal.'

I just stopped myself from snorting. Immortals were the offspring of a god, or goddess, and an ordinary human. Supposedly, they could not die of illness or old age, although, as there were ways in which they could be killed, their claim to true immortality was suspect. They were reputed to have certain magical powers. There were hundreds of temple stories, religious-based myths, about how gods and goddesses came down from their heavenly home in Elysium to seduce mortal men or women, but oddly enough all such stories seemed to be about the past. From time to time someone would come forward to proclaim themselves an immortal, but they were always ultimately exposed as a fraud.

Once Achates started to talk, the story came pouring out of him as though he was glad to be able to tell someone. Mir Ager, he said, was brought into the prison cells unconscious, with a lump on the side of his head. The moment he showed signs of regaining consciousness he was chained to the inter-rogation table, in itself a form of torture because the table was covered with uneven protuberances that dug into a man's spine. He'd answered the first question, a request for his name, readily enough: they could call him Mir Ager, he said. But when they asked other questions, he refused to reply, or gave smart-tongued answers.

Regius then ordered Achates to take the cane and beat the soles of the man's feet, which he did. After a while Achates had the strange feeling he wasn't actually touching the man at all; that the cane was stopped just short of him, as though an invisible sheet of glass covered his feet. The beating certainly didn't seem to disturb Mir Ager. It didn't even seem to mark him.

Regius became irate at the lack of reaction from the prisoner. He ordered the irons heated and said he was going to put out one of Mir Ager's eyes to see how he would enjoy that. Mir Ager showed no signs of worry. Then, when Regius held the red-hot iron up and began to cross from the fire to the interrogation table, there was a flash of light and the iron suddenly melted, dripping molten metal all over Regius's hand. Mir Ager laughed and none of them doubted the Kardi had been responsible.

They left him on the table that night and returned the next morning. Regius was in terrible pain and ready to tear the Kardi apart. They walked into the cell to find Mir Ager had managed to free himself from the manacles that had held him. They were in pieces all over the floor, as if they had been cut. The wooden bar on the iron-reinforced door was almost broken through – and the bar was on the *outside*. True, there had been a crack between the door and the door jamb, but it was just that: a crack. Wide enough for a papyrus sheet to have slipped through, nothing more. Yet Mir Ager had been within a whisker of breaking out of the room.

None of them could discover how he had done any of it. After that, they doubled the number of chains he wore.

Regius wasn't about to try heated irons again after what had happened the day before. Instead, he ordered the Kardi to be suspended from the ceiling by his arms, with his feet off the floor. Then a weight was hooked onto his foot-manacles so that it, too, was off the floor. By this time, they were so rattled by the man's abilities none of them wanted to stay and watch. They left him like that, alone, for half an hour while they waited outside. When they re-entered, at the very least they hoped to find him subdued, if not begging for mercy. Instead, he was sitting on the floor, unhooking the weight. The chain they had hung him from had snapped in two.

Again Achates licked dry lips. 'We was real scared, Legata,' he said. 'Me and the other assistant was begging Rego to forget the whole thing, but Rego was as riled as a fly-blown gorclak. So we doubled the chains and hauled the bastard up again. We'd barely finished, when the whole room was filled with light, golden light. The pain of it was terrible, real bad. And Mir Ager told us – in a voice as calm as a woman nursing her babe – that he was taking his pain and giving it to us, for as long as he hung there. I sprang to the pulley chains to let him down, right quick, I can tell you, and not even Rego objected.'

They'd talked it over among themselves then, and decided they didn't want to try again. They chained the Kardi in a cell with every chain they could find, put a guard permanently outside and told the Commander that Mir Ager had been tortured and wasn't talking. A day or two later he was executed by burning. Rego died two weeks later, his hand all swelled up green and nasty.

'And that's the truth, Legata,' Achates said, 'so help me. It's not my fault if it sounds like one of them folk myths 'bout numina. You asked for the truth, and you got it.'

'I believe you, Achates. I can't explain what happened, but I haven't the slightest doubt you have told me what you think you saw.' I looked across at Brand to see his reaction, but his face was impassive. 'Is there anything else I should know? What conclusions did you come to about his character?'

'His character? Ah, he was used to being the cock on the midden heap, that one. Looked at us as though we were dirt specks on the floor.'

'Highborn?'

'I would say. Proud bastard. Brave, I'll give him that. He was heaped about with chains, lying in his own muck, given no food, but he could still laugh at us as though we were the bastards in trouble.' He gave a wary glance in Brand's direction. 'Legata, if I could have a word with you in private, like—'

I nodded at Brand, who rose and left the room. 'Yes, what is it, Achates?'

'If you want to know more, ask the Prefect's wife.'

I blinked. 'The Prefecta? Why would the Domina Fabia know more?'

Achates gave a sly smile. 'She's a whore, Legata, begging your pardon. One of them women who can't get what they need from their man. She pretends she's as pure as a virgin, but she likes to lay with the dirt. She pays me to bring her down into the cells when the need is on her – wraps herself in one of them Kardi travelling cloaks – and she wants the condemned men, no less. The worse they are, the better she likes it.'

I gave no sign of surprise. I'd heard stranger stories about even more unlikely people; it was the kind of thing those of the Brotherhood often learned about others. 'She came and asked for Mir Ager?'

Achates nodded. 'She'd already seen him. She was at the slave auction and he took her fancy then. Couldn't have suited her better when he ended up in the cells, condemned to death. She came down the day before the burning. I didn't want her to go to him, not after all that had happened, but she can be a nasty bitch.' He shrugged. 'So I let her have her way. After all, he had enough chains on him for a whole coffle of slaves and I checked to make sure they was tight. I let her into the cell and waited outside, like I always do. Usually she comes out looking like a legionnaire that's just had the free run of a brothel, but not this time. She was as white as fruit-pith. Reckon he'd just about scared the piss out of her. She hasn't been back since. Ask her about him, and see what you get. But don't say I was the one as told.'

'The Brotherhood never reveals its informants,' I said. 'All right, Achates. That will be all. See that the other man I want to talk to is sent in, will you?'

Brand ushered the second legionnaire in a moment later. His name was Ciceron, a centurion nearing retirement who obviously resented having his competence called into question by a member of the Brotherhood – or, for that matter, by anyone. 'That Mir Ager died,' he said flatly. 'He was burnt to death. This man who's wandering around creating problems for us elsewhere is someone else. I reckon Mir Ager is just a title. When the first one died, another took it over. There's no mystery, no fantastical escape, still less the resurrection of a dead man.'

'Why was there so much smoke at his execution?' I asked neutrally.

'I checked the wood beforehand,' came the defensive reply. 'It was dry. The only thing I can think of is someone sprinkled something on it for its nuisance value. The smoke was awful: horrible choking black stuff. I tell you, Mir Ager was burnt to a cinder, but he probably suffocated to death in that smoke first.'

'Were any of the crowd near the fire?'

'No. The pyre was ringed with legionnaires, at least until the smoke started – then they just ran. They couldn't do anything else. But it was Kardi slaves who collected the wood and brought it to the square in the first place. They could have tampered with it.'

'How was Mir Ager tied?'

'His hands were manacled to one another behind the stake. What else was necessary?'

'He seemed to have a knack of freeing himself from locked manacles,' I said mildly. 'Did you search the ashes afterwards for bones?'

He exploded. 'No, we did not! Why should we? The man was dead. It is customary just to shovel up whatever is left, ashes and all, and throw it into the sea so no one can gather the remains for burial. We don't want these people to make martyrs out of their criminals. Come to think of it, though, I did see a legionnaire retrieve the manacles, what was left of them. They had cracked and bent, the fire was so hot once it got going.'

'Who did the shovelling? Legionnaires?'

'Hardly. Slaves, naturally.'

Slaves, who might not have mentioned an absence of bones for reasons of their own. I almost sighed in exasperation; it was going to be hard to prove what had really happened, one way or the other. Had he died . . . or not? I said, 'Describe Mir Ager for me.'

'Tall, brown hair and eyes, your colouring, Legata – and fit – he had an athlete's body. He looked surprisingly alert for someone who had been tortured. Smelled as high as a rotting midden, of course. Everyone does after being in the torture cells. But he wasn't as weak as they usually are.'

'Did he speak?'

'I asked him if he wanted the prayers of a priestess, and he laughed.'

'Anything else?'

He hesitated. 'Well, when I ordered a legionnaire to light the fire at his feet, he said, "You'll be hearing of me, Centurion. Don't think to rid the Exaltarchy of me so easily."'

'What did you take that to mean?'

Ciceron grimaced. 'That the Kardis would use his name to rally support for their damned insurgency. There was an unusually big crowd at his execution, and the crowd was resentful. The place bubbled like water on the boil – it was almost frightening. To be quite frank, I was glad of all that smoke. It cleared people out of there.'

'Did you actually see the man burning? Be careful how you answer.'

'Well, no,' he said reluctantly. 'I can't say I did. When the smoke started I had to step back along with everyone else. My eyes were streaming, I was doubled up with coughing. By the time the smoke was gone, the flames were fierce and you couldn't see anything in there.'

'You don't think he could have been an immortal?'

He gave me a look as if I had taken leave of my senses.

I nodded. 'Thank you. That will be all.'

The man left, his resentment drifting after him, and Brand looked across at me. 'Was he telling the truth, Legata?'

I picked up the weapon, still wrapped in the pelt. 'Oh yes, as far as he knew it. But if by some miracle this Mir Ager freed himself, neither Ciceron nor anyone else would have noticed. Or so it seems to me.'

'Do you think he did escape?'

'I doubt it. I suspect Ciceron is right. Mir Ager is merely a hereditary title, and we have to look for whoever has inherited it. Let's go back to the Prefect's house. I want to have a word with the Prefect's wife next.'

'What are you going to do with the sword?'

'Nothing for the time being, except keep it hidden. But it's apparently a formidable weapon. Imagine if we could discover how to use it and make others like it. If we can't, well, it might serve a purpose as bait. If Mir Ager did escape, if he's still alive, then I rather think he would give a lot to have it back. If he died, well, perhaps the new leader will want it just as badly.'

'If he's still alive, then he's to be feared,' Brand warned. He eyed the wrapped sword uneasily.

'So am I,' I said grimly. 'So am I.'

'You wanted to see me?' Domina Fabia was reclining on the divan in her private quarters and, although polite, she did not bother to rise when I was ushered in. She was highborn, after all, and I was merely adopted. It was a subtle distinction some people loved to make.

I said, 'If I may.'

'Of course.' She waved a languid hand at another divan. 'This heat is *so* debilitating, I think. Would you like me to call a slave to fan you?'

'No. I would prefer this conversation to be private.'

She raised a surprised eyebrow, her highborn arrogance quick to flare. 'What *can* you have to say?'

'You know I hold rank in the Brotherhood?'

'Yes.' She began to cool herself gently with a scented fan.

'The Brotherhood keeps its secrets. Our job is to hear of trouble before it happens, to trap traitors before they have a chance to damage the Exaltarchy. We do not judge. We merely pursue the truth. We keep many secrets.'

'So?' she drawled.

'So, I want to know what happened when you went to see Mir Ager in his cell before his execution.'

There was the faintest of pauses in the fanning motion of Fabia's hand, but no other reaction. 'I did no such thing.'

'I know you did, Domina. You asked this man to service your need, and I believe he turned you down. I wish merely to know what he said. It may be of use to me.'

'How *dare* you insinuate something so, so disgusting!' Her indignation was false; she was all anxiety.

She reached for the silver bell on a side table, but I was there first, closing my hand over hers. 'No, Domina. You don't want anyone else to know of this. This is between you and me. Do you know what it is to defy the Brotherhood? Have you any idea what it would do to your husband's career? I can see to it that you *never* leave Kardiastan. Or I could tell your husband – all of Tyrans, in fact – that you visited the lowest scum of the prison cells.'

'You're hurting me!'

I released her hand. 'You have only one chance, Domina. I will not wait. What happened between you and Mir Ager?'

She rubbed her hand. 'You bitch,' she said. 'I know you people. You'll have this inscribed on a tablet for the rest of my life. And every time you need something from me you will get it. There's no escape once the Brotherhood has you! All right, all right, I'll tell you. The bastard looked me up and down as though I were the one who was lying in the dirt of my own waste and said he wouldn't fuck me if it was his last day on earth. Which it was, of course. Sarcastic bastard.'

'So then you tried to seduce him.'

A slow flush started on Fabia's throat and moved up to her face. 'How do you know that?'

I know you. 'A guess merely. It would be what I would do.' *If I had your kind of perverted needs.*

'Well, yes, I did. I slipped out of my wrap and put my hands on him – where it counts, you know. And he was as flaccid as a wilted flower. He *laughed.* He *dared* to laugh at me and said I was as sexless as a neutered gorclak.'

I gave the faintest of smiles. 'I don't suppose you let him get away with that?'

'I went to claw him. There was nothing he could have done; he was chained up like a bale of shleth pelts. I would have made *him* as sexless as a neutered gorclak—'

'But?'

'I couldn't. He stopped me somehow. There was a sort of barrier – I couldn't *see* anything, but it was there nonetheless. I couldn't get out of there fast enough. He was a Kardi numen. There are numina here, you know. Strange things happen all the time, you'll see.' She shivered. 'Well, I guess I always knew if you play with fire you get burnt. Goddess, how I *hate* this country.'

I rose to my feet. 'Thank you, Domina. I don't think I will need to put any of this on file.' I smiled blandly and left the room.

CHAPTER SEVEN

After dinner that night, I waited until the whole house was quiet and the last of the slaves had gone to bed before reaching under my divan to take out the weapon I had hidden there. I examined it again, running my hand over the hilt, touching the smoothness of the glass-like material in the short blade. It had a – a *perfection* about it, a flawless essence to it, and I began to wonder if it had not been crafted by mortal man. I considered the myriad stories about gifts from the gods: arrows from the Goddess of the Hunt, books from the God of Wisdom, dream powder from the Goddess of Sleep.

Swords from . . . Melete? Ocrastes? Ridiculous!

I prayed to Melete, on occasion, I gave money to her temples, but that was more habit or expediency than conviction. In my heart of hearts, I was dubious about the existence of any of the pantheon of gods and goddesses who supposedly governed the different aspects of Exaltarchy life. Yet, as I sat there with that sword in my hand, I felt it was somehow god-given. The idea was so outlandish it confused me, a confusion overlaid with the memory of that golden woman tearing away her anoudain and snatching up a similar weapon . . .

Vortex, I couldn't have been born of a goddess, surely?

My whole body rebelled at the thought. I was no immortal. I was just me, Ligea of Tyr . . .

And then the inner doubt spoke again: *You are a woman who knows when others lie. Who senses emotions on the air as easily as pungent scents or evocative sounds, who has a touch that apparently sometimes takes away pain. Is that normal?*

I had faced death in Brotherhood service, but I'd never felt the fear I felt right then. *Immortal.* Doomed never to age and die, to be condemned to watch all I knew vanish into old age and death and dust, waiting for an end that never came . . . I could think of nothing worse. Better to be insane. Perhaps I was. I sank down on my knees beside the divan and rested my forehead on the sword hilt. I took calming breaths and tried to clear the tendrils of doubt before they could permeate deeper. I was Ligea. Brotherhood Compeer. I was better than this.

Unbidden, my mind ranged outwards until it touched the familiar. Brand, sleeping somewhere below in the slave quarters. I calmed, and began to think again.

Silently, I took up the sword and left my apartments. If the Prefect posted guards, they must have all been outside in the gardens or beyond the walls, because I met no one. My bare feet made no sound on the marble floors as I made my way, after several wrong turns, to Brand. I paused outside his door, checking with my senses that I did indeed have the right place. Then I took a night lamp out of its niche in the passage and let myself in, glad I had insisted on a single room for him, a privilege of a favoured slave. I shut the door behind me.

The room was not much bigger than a cupboard. A low table and a raised platform for the sleeping pallet were the only two items of furniture. I put the lamp and the still-wrapped sword on the table, next to an empty jug, and looked around. Brand, clad only in a loin cloth and half covered in a blanket, was sound asleep and gently snoring. His clothes hung on a hook behind the door, his personal pack was on the floor – all he owned, if a slave could ever be said to own anything. It seemed pitifully little after thirty years of life.

'Brand?' I asked quietly. He didn't stir. I sat on the edge of his pallet and shook his arm. Even then it took several rough shakes before I elicited a response. At a guess, that jug had contained wine, and the Prefect's Tyranian slaves had been more than hospitable to an Altani freshly arrived with news of Tyr. Brand had been feted that evening.

He struggled awake, befuddled with wine and sleep and still not opening his eyes. 'Who's tha'?'

'It's only me, Brand. Legata Ligea.'

He opened one eye. And spoke, a tentative 'Ligea?' The eye stared at me, puzzled, and then I felt the other emotion in him. When he reached out a hand to touch my bare shoulder, I was – in my astonishment – unable to move. He murmured, 'Sweet Goddess . . . I have dreamed of this, but never thought—'

'No,' I said in a rush, aghast, and leapt to my feet. I wanted to unhear the words, to have them unsaid. 'No. You misunderstand. I brought the weapon down. I wanted you to hide it. I thought if I kept it in my room, Aemid would find it, and it's important she doesn't know about it.'

He scrambled up, fully awake now, and coldly sober, hope dead in his eyes at my rush of words. He cut off his emotions from me as he said, 'My apologies, Legata. I was half asleep, and I fear I had too much to drink this evening.' But even as he said the words, we both knew it was too late to take back what had just happened.

'Oh, Brand,' I said, trying to hide how appalled I was. 'I'm sorry. I never guessed. You – you hid it so well.' But then, he always had kept his emotions hidden. Ever since we were children together. Damn, damn, *damn*.

'What was the point? I'm just a slave and you had Tribune Favonius.' He glanced across at me with a calculating look. 'He's not here now. You must be missing him.'

'Yes, but – Oh, Brand. Oh damn it, you are – you are like a brother to me. I don't think of you that way.' My thoughts were more shocked: *Acheron's mists! You're my slave!* I couldn't be having this conversation. I didn't *want* to have this conversation!

'A *brother*?' he said bitterly and then, echoing my thought, 'I'm your *slave*.' He raised a hesitant hand to touch my hair. 'I've never been your brother. And a slave you could bed, for all that custom dictates otherwise.'

'But we were brought up together.' *Don't say it, Brand. Don't say it.*

'That doesn't make us siblings. And it's not love of Favonius that stops you, either. You don't love him.' He said that with utter certainty.

'No – no, I suppose not. He's a friend and he fulfils a need.'

'I could also be that. And I wouldn't ask for more than I could have.' He trailed his fingers from my hair to my face. 'I have loved you since I was a boy; in all those years, I've learned to be content with very little.' He bent to kiss me, gently brushing my mouth with his lips and moving his hand to cup my breast, but before he could deepen the kiss I pulled back. His hand remained where it was; the shining flecks in his eyes flickered.

'I can't, Brand.' For once, I could read his emotions, and I rather wished I couldn't. I was aware of a deep bitter grief filling the room and knew how much I'd hurt him. He must have guessed it was more my disdain for a slave-lover, rather than any sisterly affection, that stopped me from desiring him. I felt shamed, and didn't understand why.

His hand slipped away and his eyes dropped. 'I'll take care of the sword, Legata,' he said, voice neutral. He went to pick up the wrapped weapon from where I had placed it on the table – and found he couldn't move it. Startled, he withdrew his hand. 'Ocrastes' balls – it's so *heavy*! How can you lift it?'

I was glad to change the subject and said, 'It is not heavy to me. Where shall I put it?'

He hesitated.

I quirked an eyebrow at him. 'Ah, you too, Brand? What are you afraid of? Numina?'

He looked at me, amused. 'If it *is* a numen's plaything, what does that make you?'

I made a wry face. 'What indeed?' Inwardly I just felt sick. I heard myself silently repeating the words, *I am no immortal.* Nor a numen. There are no such beings. Probably never have been . . .

He tried to diminish his unease with a laugh. 'Put it under the pallet against the wall. It will be safe there. No one will find it.'

I did as he suggested and turned to go. 'Thank you. Goodnight, Brand.'

'Goodnight, Legata.' There was a familiar trace of mockery in his voice and his emotions were once more veiled.

Soft-footed, I started back to the main sleeping quarters of the household. Oil lamps flickered in wall niches, the smell of the burning muted by the perfumes added to the fuel. The halls were dim and silent. My thoughts were a chaos of swearing. *What in all Acheron's damnable mists was the bloody man thinking of? How could he possibly think I would respond to his lovemaking?*

I embarked on another of those silly, futile conversations I sometimes conducted with myself: Your fault, Legata. It was you who insisted on treating him as a friend.

The reply: He *is* a friend, damn it. That's the way I wanted it. The way I still want it. I *need* a friend . . .

You wanted him in your bed. You wanted to say yes just then.

I am not going to bed my slave.

You could go back.

Shut up!

I entered the corridor leading to my apartments. A single flame still burned at my doorway, unmoving, as if pasted onto its lamp. Others had guttered, dimming the passage. I walked on, preoccupied, towards my door, passing the silent row of statues with their marble faces made grim by the lack of light. And then that final lamp flame fluttered, dancing the shadows of those carved watchers.

Something had created a current of air at my door.

I stopped, uncertain of what I was seeing. The form of a man, yet he had no solidity. A transparent and ethereal man, a painting done on glass. No painting though. He moved.

I did two things at once, both instinctive. I stepped out of sight behind a statue, and I drew my knife. And stood there, immobile, while all the hairs on my arms rose up . . . The man walked through my door and into my bedroom. I had closed my door – *and it was still closed.* The man had walked through the polished planks of wood. And disappeared.

I didn't believe in shades of the dead. I was neither superstitious, nor given to hallucinations, nor easily deceived by tricks of the light or sleight of hand. I wanted a logical explanation. Yet, as I stood there in silence, peering out from under the arm of a life-sized statue of Bator Korbus mounted on a plinth, a shudder skidded up my spine. I took a deep breath and tried to remember exactly what I had seen.

A naked man about my height or a shade taller. Muscular, as well sculpted as a statue of a naked competitor in the annual games. I hadn't seen his face, but a fluidity to his movement spoke of a man still young in years. Hair too long for a

Tyranian. He'd worn it, Kardi-style, tied back at the nape with a thong. His skin could have been Kardi brown, although it was hard to be sure when he had been so . . . ethereal. I had seen through him, I was sure of it, the way one could see through a glass of white wine held up to the light.

A shade had just entered my room. A shade from Acheron? Or a god perhaps, in some . . . otherworldly form?

I couldn't believe I was thinking this. It was madness. *What was happening to me?*

I stayed where I was, still motionless. I thought of rousing the household, but quelled that thought immediately. I was a compeer, not some moondaft madwoman. I couldn't admit to being scared of a shade. And if I said I'd seen one, and no one else did, then I was going to make myself an object of ridicule. So I remained where I was, sweating even in the cool of the night air, waiting for Goddess knows what.

Five minutes later, the shade walked back through the door. No, not walked. He *seeped* through the door. And stopped. And hovered, then slowly turned his face in my direction, his features too transparent to be recognisable. There was a dark circle on the back of his hand, like a wound.

I held my breath. My skin prickled. It was dark where I was, and he was in the light of the lamp outside my door. If his eyesight was normal he would find it difficult to see me, hidden as I was. However, he was alert, poised, holding himself the way I did when I was sending my senses outwards. I tried to sense him in turn, but couldn't. Not unexpected, I suppose, seeing he was only a ghost. Or a shade. Or something else equally intangible.

I thought: *He can't see me, but he knows I'm here.*

For a breath-halting moment, we stood like that. And then he turned and vanished, gliding away like wind-wafted mist.

*　　*　　*

Back in my own room a few minutes later, I saw nothing to indicate someone had entered while I'd been gone. Nothing had been disturbed. The floor was spotless.

I shook, as if the foundations of my life were crumbling and I could find no security. Too many things had happened that day; piling on top of all that had preceded. The mother-figure of my childhood had threatened me with death; the slave-brother of my adolescence had proclaimed himself lover; the abilities I had were taking on new and frightening dimensions in this, the land of my birth. I was either flirting with madness, or someone had drugged me into seeing things that couldn't exist, at least not in the land of the living.

Perhaps this was connected to what had happened back at the Meletian Temple in Tyr. A conspiracy to make me believe in the gods of the pantheon? To have me consult the temple priestesses, to seek out the cult of Melete? Well, I wouldn't do it. I was the logical compeer. I was the Tyranian who bowed to a goddess more as a matter of conformity than belief. Who hoped there was an afterlife awaiting, in a not-too-daunting Acheron, after the Vortex had whisked her away from her body – but who was not wholly convinced of any of it.

Come on, Ligea. You are the cool-headed compeer. Think.

I turned to the more solid of my reservations. I started to make a list in my head of the things that bothered me most, trying – in vain – for dispassion.

Who had wanted me to go to Kardiastan so badly they had connived with the Meletian High Priestess and the Voice of the Oracle to make it seem like a good idea? If it had been the Exaltarch himself, Bator Korbus, then why? I was not so impor-tant in the overall scheme of things, was I?

Why had the Prefecta's Kardi slave called me Theura? Did I really remember that word from my childhood, but applied to someone else? I looked down at my palm, at the swelling there that had so startled Othenid she'd dropped a pitcher and earned herself a beating. It had been so important to me as a child that I had tried to keep it hidden. No other Kardi I'd ever met had such a lump. Was it a curse, a blessing, an accident of birth that the Kardis had some superstition about? What did it mean? *It had fitted so neatly into the hollow on the hilt of Mir Ager's sword* ... I should have asked if anyone had noticed a lump on his hand. No, perhaps that wouldn't have been a good idea. I didn't want to draw attention to my own.

I thought of the sword: how could it be so heavy to Brand that he could not lift it, yet so light to me I could pick it up with two fingers of one hand? *What was I?* The bastard child of a goddess? Immortal? Someone who could see the shades of the dead? Kardi nobility? *They say only the highborn fight in Kardiastan* ...

Remember – you are of the Magor ... but from them you must always hide it.

All that had once been solid was dissolving. I shivered.

I did not know myself.

CHAPTER EIGHT

Two days later, there was a report, which the Prefect immediately showed to me, from the city of Madrinya, capital of Kardiastan. A legionnaire, who had been present at both the slave auction in Sandmurram and at the execution, swore he had seen Mir Ager in the capital, very much alive.

There was other news from Madrinya as well, none of it good. Within the city itself, no less than four senior legionnaire officers, all men known for the severity of their treatment of local people, had been found slain. All had burn marks on their chests, and in each case there was no evidence to indicate who was to blame. In addition, there had been a steady stream of slave escapes from the city. The situation was so dire some Tyranians were reluctant to allow their slaves any freedom at all. Requests were being made for legionnaires to stand guard on the houses of high officials to stop further runaways.

Few of the escaped slaves had been found. Even worse, a military caravan carrying new supplies of weapons from Sandmurram to Madrinya was missing, gone with as little trace as water poured into desert sand. Forty legionnaires, their mounts and the carts of supplies they had been accompanying had simply vanished between one wayhouse and the next. The only clue was a report that a group of twenty or so shleth-mounted Kardis had been seen in the area. 'Terror riders,' Prefect Martrinus muttered.

The backstreets of every town whispered of how a man called Mir Ager, or possibly Mirager, was responsible, directly or indirectly, for all the deaths, slave escapes and legionnaire disappearances – but nothing was ever said openly.

As soon as I heard all this, I made arrangements to set off for Madrinya.

I was glad to go. I hadn't seen any more shades, but I had not been sleeping well in that bedroom, either.

When I spoke to Prefect Martrinus about my intended journey, he suggested we take horses, but I asked for shleth riding hacks. My request had sent legionnaires scurrying out all over the city searching for suitable mounts, because our army did not use them.

Unlike the Prefecta, I liked the look of the animals. The size of sturdy horses, they had coats of wool, large clawed paws rather than hoofs, and no tails or manes. Their main divergence from the horse, however, was their possession of a third set of limbs: long jointed feeding arms, usually kept tucked out of the way in grooves along the sides of the neck. To eat, they used the three digits at the end of these arms to pluck leaves or grass, which they then passed to the mouth.

When we all assembled at the army headquarters on the day of our departure, Brand contemplated the beasts with a jaundiced eye. 'Why did you decide on them rather than horses?' he asked.

'Because the Kardis ride them, even though they also have horses,' I said.

'Ah.' He nodded, following my reasoning. 'The local barbarians know best, eh?' He paused briefly to poke his riding crop at a snake trying to insinuate its way into one of our still-to-be loaded packs. 'Let's hope it's not the breeding season. I understand they – the shleths, not the barbarians – have a tendency to become irascible when the females are on heat. It is common then for a rider to complain of being pinched black and blue by the fingers of his mount.'

I glanced at him, but his face was bland as he watched the thwarted snake glide away through the dust, and I couldn't tell whether that last remark was a joke or not. Since the conversation we'd had in his room, he had reverted to his usual faintly amused, calm self. That night-time exchange might never have happened from all the signs he gave. Once again, I was left with the feeling that, for all we had grown up together, I scarcely knew him.

'What do you think about our audience?' he asked a moment later, jerking his head at a group of Kardi men and women who were standing across the square, watching the travel preparations with impassive faces.

I had become used to Kardis always turning away from us; suddenly to be the focus of Kardi attention was unsettling. The hostility of this particular group was obvious to me, as always, but this time I could also sense intense, urgent curiosity. These Kardis wanted to know what was happening. 'They're just interested,' I said, but I was thinking: *They are spying on us*. I didn't like the feeling.

Brand snorted, but didn't comment. He said instead, 'Tell me, Legata, how do we learn the trick of riding these beasts?'

'Aemid will teach us. She is familiar with them.' I looked across at the slave woman, who was standing patiently by the luggage, waiting to make sure it was correctly loaded. She was wearing an anoudain – which I certainly had not paid for – as she always did now. She delighted in emphasising her Kardi origins even as she discouraged me from publicly acknowledging my own.

I was still angry with her and had not solved the problem

posed by her disloyalty. No doubt if I did anything to threaten the Kardis, Aemid would warn them. I did consider having her jailed under a military guard, but the thought of incarcerating the woman who had raised me was ultimately unthinkable, just as it was impossible to consider selling her. In the end, as much as the situation galled, I decided it was better to let Aemid keep watch on me. After all, I was an expert at manipulating things to my own advantage, wasn't I?

I turned my attention back to the preparations for our journey. The mounted legionnaires accompanying the three of us to Madrinya milled around on their gorclaks. They were clad in their uniforms: short tunics leaving their knees bare, worn with the usual cuirasses, greaves, helmets and sandals. I myself had discarded my wrap for a tunic worn over loose trousers, a Tyranian outfit more commonly worn by artisans. I didn't care if it was unstylish; I was determined to ride rather than endure the discomforts of a litter or cart, and it was impossible to ride anything wearing a Tyranian wrap.

I caught the eye of the legionnaire officer and asked, 'I'm told the tradeway is paved the whole distance?'

'That's right,' he agreed. 'Designed by Tyranian military engineers, built by slaves. An easy journey now compared to what it used to be. Used to take four weeks in the old days.'

Although most of Sandmurram was wholly Kardi, the administrative and commercial quarters around the Prefect's residence had a distinctive Tyranian face and this was the area where I had spent most of my time. There was much that was familiar, toning down the strange. It was not until I left Sandmurram altogether that I appreciated just how different Kardiastan was from Tyrans.

Outside the town, even the Kardi sky had a character of its own: a vividness to the blue more intense than elsewhere, a clarity made more noticeable by the lack of clouds. When I remarked on the lack to Aemid, her reply was a terse: 'It never rains in Kardiastan.'

Indeed, numerous tracts of stony soil and sand made her assertion easy to believe. Nothing seemed to live in these desolate areas, although they had a kaleidoscopic beauty. The sands were multicoloured, often spread with intertwined swirls of colour as though the wind had sorted out grains of different weights or densities to create patterns. Sometimes windblasted rocks were heaped in the centre of such patterns, their tortured shapes struggling out of the sand like the petrified remains of long-dead monsters.

And then, just when it seemed Kardiastan was a dead world, we would come upon a wide, gentle-sided valley where it was hard to believe it never rained. In these lush vales, the soil was rich, the vegetation prolific and flocks of waterbirds skimmed azure pools and lakes. I liked the contrast, the abrupt change from the hot reds and oranges and browns of the desert sands and stones to the cool greens and blues of the low-lying areas between.

'But where does all the water come from?' Brand asked in wonderment. Aemid's explanation, begrudgingly given, was that in such low-lying areas water seeped up from under the ground to create havens for life; it was only the higher areas between that were dry.

Most of the valleys were settled by Kardis. Domestic animals grazed under the watchful eye of Kardi herders. Wild coppices separated fields planted with grain and other crops; fruit trees lined the meadows. Every so often, windmills with hide sails pumped water to irrigation systems. Villages and towns were never built in the centres of these dales as might have been expected, but on the edges where the soil was too dry and stony to be tilled. The houses were of adobe and blended unobtrusively into the desert landscape beyond them.

Curious to see the interiors, several times I stopped and asked an owner's permission to enter. The request was never refused, but we were never offered the hospitality of a seat or a drink, either.

Cool and dim inside, the rooms had stone-tiled floors and simple wicker furniture. I thought them spartan and was inclined to be disparaging – until I saw what Tyrans had wrought.

Where the Tyranian civil or military administration wanted wayhouses, they had erected vast stone and marble buildings, usually on a lakeside, marking the landscape – as Brand asserted – like gorclak turds in a flowerbed. For the first time I found my admiration for Tyranian progress was tinged with embarrassment. I had once regarded such monuments as magnificent, symbolic of the might and grandeur of Tyrans; now I looked and saw an oppressive lack of imagination, a desire to dominate rather than to belong. What was Tyranian suddenly seemed to lack grace and subtlety.

The Tyranian architecture out of a Tyranian context might have irked me, but my reaction to it appalled me. I couldn't understand how I, who had always loved all that was Tyranian, could feel that way. This strange land with its mystic beauty was shredding the solidness of the foundations on which I had built my life, and I didn't want to look inside myself to find out why.

Still, ugly buildings or not, I was glad enough to accept the comforts of a wayhouse after a day in the saddle. To sink into a perfumed marble bath, to have clean clothes and a choice of seven or eight dishes at the evening meal, to lounge against the cushions of a divan and listen to a slave play the songs of Tyr – that was paradise, even if it meant putting up with the sullen service of Kardi slaves, slaves who became even less helpful than normal after they had spoken to Aemid.

The worst part of the journey was the crossing of the valley that furrowed through Kardiastan like a gorclak trail through snow. Kardis called it the Rift and it had a grandeur that was magnificent when seen from its southern lip: red walls sliced downwards in columns and pleats to a flat valley floor strung with lakes, far below. In the distance, two days' ride away, was the north wall, just as steep and formidable. It took us a day to descend to the valley on a zigzag path, and once we were there, we were buffeted by fierce gales barrelling up the Rift. It may not have rained in Kardiastan, but it emulated it in that place. The wind swept up water from the lakes, mixed it with red dust and whipped it at us in stinging slashes; by the time we reached the north wall, everything we had was damply pink, including the shleths.

At least the shleths were stoic; the gorclaks were not nearly so composed. Even when the wind was at its worst, the shleths shielded their eyes with their feeding arms and plodded on; the gorclaks tended to go berserk, baulking at every movement, bellowing their displeasure and distress, swinging their great heads to and fro as if they could shred the wind with their nose horns. Every legionnaire had trouble; several were thrown and others had their mounts bolt.

There were two wayhouses in the Rift, one clinging to the foot of the south wall, the other huddled up to the north face, neither with any permanent staff. The continuous whine of the wind would have crazed anyone forced to live there. None of our party slept much during the nights we stayed in them. I suppose we all spent time thinking about the legionnaire caravan that had vanished somewhere along the paveway to Madrinya . . .

The arduous day's climb out of the valley seemed a pleasurable stroll after the hell of the floor of the Rift, and by comparison the rest of the journey was almost a carefree holiday.

Aemid cried when she saw Madrinya. She had been born there, raised there, but this was no longer the city of her childhood. That old adobe town with its brown buildings and quiet well-squares had largely disintegrated in war and conquest. White Tyranian marble and pink stone edifices now glowered like ungainly monsters along what had been a wooded lakeshore, while the once-fashionable Kardi buildings had begun to crumble into a semblance of the Snarls, complete with scum-covered drains, vermin and the stink of poverty. Even I, viewing the city first from the back of my shleth, felt a moment's pang. It seemed alien, an excrescence on the face of the land.

'The Pavilions have gone,' Aemid whispered as we rode in through the outskirts.

'What were they?' I asked.

'The palace . . . and other buildings. They used to stand over there . . .' She pointed to where the city's stadium, built of local stone, now stood. There were tears on her cheeks. 'That's where the Magoroth died,' she added in a whisper. 'In the Pavilions.'

I looked across at her and felt a twinge of anxiety. She had not stood up to the journey well and now the shock of seeing the Madrinya of the Exaltarchy rather than the Kardi city of her youth appeared to have shrunk both her body and her spirit, as if by growing smaller, by being less aggressive, she could avoid further pain. She was diminished. I felt her depression like a black cloud hovering about her, darkening her spirit.

'We'll be at the Governor's residence soon,' I said, trying not to show my alarm. 'Then you can rest. I shall make sure someone attends to you.' I glanced at Brand, reassuring myself that he, at least, had not changed. He'd enjoyed most of the journey just as I had and now rode his shleth with the same easy grace he possessed on horseback.

Still, since that night in his room, there had been a subtle shift in our relationship. He might have been the same, but I was finding it harder to see him as a slave first, and a man second. A man with a man's desires and needs; a man who saw me as a desirable woman before he saw me as his owner. I pushed that unsettling idea away in a hurry. It was a complication I didn't want to deal with right then, not when I had a job to do in difficult circumstances.

Instead, I reached behind to touch the weapon I had stowed across the back of my saddle. It vibrated slightly at my touch as though it were a living thing. On the journey I had been very much aware of its presence, but oddly enough, the shleth did not seem to notice its weight any more than I had. I felt an intense desire to meet this Mir Ager face to face, to find out what sort of man carried such a weapon. If he were still alive. It occurred to me that if he were, then he might present the greatest challenge of my career as a Brother.

I felt the familiar thrill of anticipation. The excitement of a hunt, the challenge of a cunning opponent, the false trails and wrong turnings, the sudden inspiration that solved a problem, the unravelling of a plot: those things I understood and loved. Especially that final moment when everything came together, when the enemy fell into a trap of my devising – it was as satisfying as the climax of lovemaking. It made life worth living.

I was suddenly glad Rathrox had sent me to Kardiastan.

Two hours later, the Governor was droning a bitter tirade about the country and its heathen people into my ears. Like most officials I had met in Kardiastan, he seemed to have succumbed to a feeling of hopelessness, the only bright point he could see in his future being the day he would return home. Kardiastan had defeated him.

'We'll never change these people,' he said. 'Never. My wife died here, you know. They said it was a fever, but I know better. She died of a broken heart. She couldn't take being surrounded by hate every minute of every day. I try to explain to those back in Tyrans what it's like, but how can you put such things in writing so that others can feel it as we do? I felt myself to be still young when I came here. I was ambitious then.' He ran a hand over his balding head. 'Now I'm as old as the desert itself and fit only to sit in the sun by the sea in Tyrans and remember.'

I did not comment, saying instead, 'Tell me what you know of this Mir Ager.'

'Nothing. Except the Kardis still seem to think he's alive, and a legionnaire officer – a good man – says he saw him a few weeks back. Rumour has it he wasn't burnt to death and that he now runs a secret escape route for slaves, spiriting them away into the desert and so to this place called the Mirage. Some say he was the one who murdered the officers; others say he was responsible for the disappearance of the military caravan. That can't be true. At least, he certainly couldn't have done all those things by himself. We are not facing a single enemy, but a whole host of them – the whole Kardi nation, if you ask me. And they are slaughtering our men without mercy. The legions call them terror riders. They are no better than savage beasts.'

'How bad is this business of runaway slaves?'

'Terrible. Almost every household has lost someone; sometimes as many as half their slaves.' He kneaded the worry lines of his forehead with restless fingers. 'We hardly ever seem to catch those who escape. They just disappear like morning mist in the heat of the sun. We tried to replace them with paid servants, but the Kardis refused to work for us freely. They *have* to be forced. So now we seize people off the street for minor infringements and give them terms of limited enslavement. I thought perhaps if they could see an end to their slavery ahead in a year of two, they wouldn't want to escape. It does seem to help.' He heaved a noisy sigh. 'What else can I do? Legata, presumably this Mir Ager, Mirager, or whoever he is, is some kind of a leader. If you can catch this man, we will be eternally obliged to you. Without him, perhaps the Kardis will lose heart.' He spoke as though he thought such a happening was unlikely.

'I'll do my best.'

'Are your apartments, er, suitable?'

'Ideal. I notice they have separate access to the street.'

'I thought – you being a Brother – it might be best—' He trailed off, embarrassed.

'You were right. I do like to come and go unobtrusively. Should I disappear for a few days at any time, please do not concern yourself.'

He nodded tiredly. 'Is there any way I can help you? The orders you brought are explicit. You are to have every facility extended to you.'

'You have already very kindly arranged for a woman to attend my slave and for a physician to see her, but there is something else. I would like the services of a bronzesmith. Someone who is discreet and absolutely trustworthy.'

He nodded again, with a total lack of interest. 'I'll get a military man.'

His despair irritated me and I was relieved when I finally left his office and headed back across the gardens to the apartments where Aemid and Brand and I had been quartered.

Brand greeted me at the door. 'Guess what,' he said cheerfully. 'There are no brown snakes in Madrinya.'

'Don't tell me – they're yellow instead.'

He laughed. 'You spoiled my line. No, there really are no snakes. But wait till you see the beetles. They're the size of a man's fist, and they're everywhere! Be careful not to tread on them; they spit back.' He pointed to a blistered patch of skin on his ankle.

I grimaced. 'How's Aemid?'

'Worse. The Governor's physician has been. He says she's just worn out, emotionally as much as physically. She has to be kept quiet for a few days. He agreed she would be best sedated, just as you suggested.'

'Good. This whole trip has been more of a strain on her than I anticipated.' Still, I thought, this couldn't have happened at a better time from my point of view . . .

PART TWO

DERYA

CHAPTER NINE

The next morning, after the smith had left, I surveyed myself in the mirror with smug satisfaction and then showed myself to Brand. 'What do you think?' I asked and spun on my heel so he could see me from all sides.

His lips gave the faintest of quirks. 'Not particularly appropriate to your personality.'

'Hmph. Why do I have the feeling you mean that as an insult?'

'Slaves do not insult their owners. It is not wise.'

I turned to face the mirror again. The woman who stared back was not the one normally there. This woman was a slave, wearing a bronze slave collar around her neck, and she was wholly Kardi. I smiled, and felt no guilt at breaking my promise to Aemid. How could she have ever thought I would let her dictate the way in which I served Tyrans? She knew me not at all.

I turned my head to see myself better. My hair, instead of being caught up high on my head, was free about my shoulders. It was crimped because I had slept with it plaited, and it lacked its usual artificial gold highlighting. As a consequence, it appeared darker and thicker. The change made my face seem younger, but also more peasant-like. The anoudain I wore was typically Kardi: the bodice and the panels of the overskirt were pale green and embroidered, the trousers darker.

My satisfaction suddenly vanished. *This wasn't me. This was a Kardi woman.* Disgust crawled my skin. Or was it foreboding?

'You are unrecognisable, Legata,' Brand was saying, 'but it takes more than clothes and hair to fool people.'

'Are you worried about my command of the Kardi language? I *am* fluent, I assure you. Aemid taught me well. If I use outdated idioms I can explain it away by saying I have lived in Tyrans for years, as a slave to the Legata Ligea. Don't worry about me, Brand. I've gone in disguise often enough in Tyrans.'

'But never as a slave.' He reached out and touched my collar. 'This does more than encircle your neck. It turns you into a chattel. A thing. You can no longer behave as though you have any rights to anything. A slave *has* no rights. And don't forget, in Tyrans you had the Brotherhood behind you no matter what hellish hole you stepped into. The Brotherhood is a long way from here.' For a brief moment he deliberately unveiled his feelings so that I was swept with his concern, his fear for me.

I turned from the mirror, sobered, to stare at him in silence. 'Ah,' I said at last – a sigh of understanding and acceptance. 'Stupid of me. How long have you known I could read feelings as well as lies?'

'Since I was a lad. It took me a little longer to find ways to hide my emotions from you. What do you do, smell them?'

I shook my head. 'No. It's more like having another sense altogether. One that interprets the way people feel. I don't need to see the person, or hear them speak, and I certainly don't need to smell them.'

He wanted to ask me more, I could tell. I did not give him time to frame another question; I didn't want to have to explain the inexplicable. I said, 'You are much cleverer than I ever gave you credit for, Brand. I had no idea you hid yourself deliberately. I always thought my inability to read you was a flaw in my talent – that what you did was more, um, instinctive, rather than intentional.' I forced a smile. 'I will be careful. Moreover, you will be following me. Get me a water ewer from the kitchens, and then we'll go.'

Madrinya may have been a Tyranian city, but the area just beyond the Governor's residence managed to retain its Kardi appearance. The street leading to the well-square was of hard brown earth; the walls on either side were adobe, the plainness of their façades broken only by the house gates.

I had no intention of lingering, but when I heard music I came to an abrupt halt. The sounds of several stringed instruments being played in harmony drifted out from one of the houses through a gate left ajar: Kardi music, a plaintive, mournful tune with a complex counterpoint weaving through the melody. It was the first music I could remember hearing in Kardiastan and so it should have been alien to my ears – yet I was suddenly awash with longing, so moved I stood as still as a temple pillar, forgetting where I was going, oblivious to the presence of Brand behind me. The clothes I wore, the language I heard spoken around me, served to reinforce something the music awakened.

I had thought of Kardiastan as a cultureless, barbarian land. This music did more than give me the lie, it stirred the Kardi soul I hadn't even known I possessed. The wrench of that melody pulled me into another world, into memories of childhood I had tucked away out of reach.

Playing hopsquares. Being cuddled when I cried. Sitting on a man's knee hearing stories told. Paddling at a lakeside. Loving and being loved . . .

The thoughts I had then were of things that had never bothered me before. I'd never thought a brown skin made me a Kardi. I'd never thought an accident of birth ensured my allegiance. I was Tyranian by inclination, by upbringing, by desire, by citizenship. Yet now the mere sound of a few instruments made me question who I was.

Shaken, I blocked out the sound, quenched the memories and walked on. *Don't be stupid, Ligea. You are Gayed's daughter, educated to be a highborn woman of Tyr.*

The well-square was a wholly Kardi scene too, but at least it aroused nothing in me except a vague distaste. By the time I arrived, it was crowded. In contrast to Tyr, the market stalls along one side conducted their business without argumentative bargaining or noisy rivalry. I saw no beggars. In the middle of the square, in the scant shade of a deformed tree, slaves and free Kardis waited their turn to draw water. The stone well with its narrow steps was only wide enough for one person to go down to the water's edge at a time, but those in the queue were orderly, chatting among themselves, with no pushing or jostling for position. They came just for drinking water, I knew; professional water sellers transported water used for general household purposes up from the lake in amphorae on shlethback.

The use of such a primitive method of collecting water puzzled me. Surprising, too, were the large spitting beetles lurking around the lip of the well, their wings shining iridescent purple, their spit drying in dirty yellow pools on the brickwork. Why hadn't Tyranian culture prevailed here, as it had in most conquered cities? Why hadn't the administration replaced the well with a public fountain or channelled water to the city along aqueducts? Why hadn't they rooted out the pathetic excuse for a tree, planted parks, eradicated the beetles? How did the Kardis manage to maintain their identity so easily?

I thought I already knew the answer, even as I framed the

question. No Kardi ever cooperated on anything – and that made change difficult, especially when there was little labour other than what the Kardis cared to supply.

Even as I hesitated at the edge of the group waiting at the well, I heard the tail end of a conversation confirming my thoughts. A youth was saying, '– and so when he wasn't looking, I dropped the bag of grit into the mill mechanism. Chewed everything up beyond repair in five minutes. You should have heard what he had to say! He was as wild as a whirlwind.' The lad laughed. 'But the barracks has had to buy its flour from old Warblen ever since and I don't think they'll try to mill their own again—'

I noticed the difference in being a Kardi among Kardis immediately. The speaker had not bothered to lower his voice at my approach, none of these people turned from me, there was no hate hanging in the air around them.

'New here?' a voice asked in my ear. I turned to find a girl of eighteen or so, with large brown eyes and a pert, inquisitive manner, smiling at me. She was wearing an iron slave collar. 'I haven't seen you before,' she added.

I gave what I hoped was a shy smile.

'Put the jug down in the queue first,' she said, indicating my ewer. 'Someone will move it along for you. Come and sit on the wall with me.'

I did as she suggested. I glanced up the street as I settled down on the low wall bordering the steps to a house, to see Brand lounging beside a horse outside a shop, as though he were caring for the animal while waiting for his master.

'I'm Parvana,' the girl said. 'What's your name?'

'Derya.' It was a Kardi name, of course, one I had chosen for myself.

'Where are you from?'

'Sandmurram – once,' I said and added the story I hoped

would explain any gaps in my knowledge, 'but my mistress took me to Tyr some years ago. We've only just come back to Kardiastan.' I stopped, afraid of saying something inappropriate.

Luckily Parvana was happy to do most of the talking and before long I'd learned her father was a street sweeper, her mother carded shleth wool for a spinner, while Parvana herself had sold twine for a string-maker. She was newly enslaved, bonded for deliberately untethering a military gorclak which had been tied to the gatepost of her house. Her term was only six months and she was working for one of the military officers and his family. As she told her story, I realised there was one aspect of the Kardi language, at least among people of her class, that Aemid had failed to teach me. Parvana used swearwords with a flair and variety that spoke of much practice; unfortunately I didn't know what most of them meant.

'The (curse) work's not (curse) hard,' she was saying, 'but those (curse) sods think we poor (curse) bints are only (curse) here to be (curse) screwed.' I blinked. It was an impressive string of expletives for one short sentence, and Parvana hadn't repeated herself once.

However, I didn't need to know the meaning of the words to realise she was far from philosophical about her position; the only decent part of her day was when she had to fetch the water; the rest was torment. The officer's wife fondled her whenever she could and Parvana was sure it was only a matter of time before she insisted on more. Then, because they lived in military quarters, it was a constant battle to dodge randy soldiers, many of whom did not have their wives or families with them and ached to relieve their frustrations on any available female. And slaves were considered available.

Sitting there listening to this recital, I had a sense of unreality. The girl was describing a life that seemed more fable than truth; did the Exaltarchy really make slaves of people for so little? What could it possibly be like to be someone's toy, to be fondled at will? Did legionnaires really hunt down slave women to use as they pleased without fear of disciplinary action? This was not Tyranian law. This was not the kind of civilisation the Exaltarchy was supposed to extend to the conquered peoples of its provinces.

I must have let some of my distress show on my face, because Parvana said, with numerous more unidentifiable words in between, 'Ah, don't look so upset, Derya. I've more or less decided how to wriggle my backside out of this one – if I can't escape, that is. I'm going to let the cat think she can bed me eventually.' She grinned. 'Maybe she'll get me a pretty bronze necklace like yours, instead of this bloody big castration ring. And if I play it right, she'll at least keep the other pricks out of my trousers. What's the matter? You look as if you've got a beetle up your arse—'

I saw my opportunity. I made a show of looking around to make sure no one else was listening. 'I have a problem,' I whispered. 'I don't know what to do.'

As I had intended, my secretive, conspiratorial tone immediately had her interested. 'What is it?'

'Parvana, listen, my owner was sent here from Tyr by the Brotherhood. Have you heard of the Brotherhood?'

She shook her head, her eyes already wide with wonder. She wasn't quite as jaded as the rest of her conversation had suggested.

'It's a secret, um, cabal of men – well, mostly men, working directly for the Magister Officii. My owner was sent here by the Exaltarch himself to find a man the Tyranians know only as Mir Ager.'

I had worded the latter sentence carefully and was rewarded by her breathless, 'The Mirager!'

I nodded. 'Yes. Parvana, I've been in Tyr. I don't know what has been happening here. I heard the Mirager was burnt alive in Sandmurram . . .'

She snorted. 'You don't want to believe what Tyranian sods say! Of course he's still alive.'

I endeavoured to look relieved. Inside, I was perplexed. Could the man *really* have survived? I said, 'I have something of the Mirager's that must be returned to him. Something left behind at the slave auction in Sandmurram. And I have to warn him of danger from the Brotherhood. I must talk to him, but I don't know how to contact him. What can I do?'

Parvana's air of world-weary disenchantment vanished fast. 'Don't worry – I don't know any of those cold-arsed Magor bastards, but we all know how to pass a message – one that will get right to the balls at the top if need be. Will you be sent for water tomorrow?'

I both heard and felt her breathless awe and guessed she wasn't as disparaging of the Mirager as her vocabulary suggested. 'Yes,' I said, 'I will.'

'Then be here. I shall tell you what to do then.' She jumped down from the wall. 'It's my turn to get the water. I'll see you tomorrow.' She gave a happy smile and went to pick up her ewer, now at the head of the line because an obliging slave had been moving it along in front of his own.

That was easy, I thought. But the Mirager may well be a different matter . . . What sort of man survived his own execution?

My thoughts were abruptly interrupted by a thunder of hoofs. I turned my head to see two gorclaks being ridden at racing speed down a lane that disgorged into the square. The riders, both junior officers, were whipping their beasts and calling for a free way ahead. The people at the well scattered in fright as the animals ploughed into them. One older woman who wasn't quick enough was brushed aside, a child disappeared under churning legs, ewers were smashed. The first rider, laughing, brought his whip down on a Kardi man who shook his fist at the racing men. The other gave a whoop of delight and caught the awning over a fruit stall as he rode by, so that the whole stall collapsed in on itself, spilling produce.

Then they were gone and the silence they left behind them was deathly. The child, ripped open from throat to pelvis by a gorclak spur, lay in a widening pool of blood so thick it seemed black. A woman rose to her feet, looked around in a panic – and saw what she didn't want to see. She sank down again, onto her knees this time, twisting her hands over and over as if she were participating in some strange ritual of cleansing, of absolution. Her mouth caverned open, but no sound came out.

The square was filled with hate and I found myself part of it, hating with a black hate, despising those laughing men for their casual murder, dreaming revenge.

The crowd closed in on the body and the grieving mother. I slipped down from the wall and went to fill my ewer, but my thoughts were elsewhere.

'I've written a message for the Military Commander,' I said harshly. 'See that he gets it, Brand.' I had removed my slave collar – unlike other such collars it snapped open – and I'd changed my clothing, but the atmosphere of the square was still acid in my mind.

Brand took the scroll I handed him and, after a nod from me, read it. He raised a sardonic eyebrow. 'Harsh words, Legata.'

'Officers, Brand! Behaving like that! Fortunately the gorclaks had their numbers newly painted; it should be easy enough for the Commander to have them identified and punished.'

'But will he bother? They only killed a Kardi child, after all.'

'That's what's the matter with this place,' I snapped, even though I knew he was deliberately baiting me. 'The standards that apply back home don't seem to apply here. How can we earn the loyalty of the people we rule if we behave like lawless ravagers ourselves?'

He gave a cynical snort. 'You won't change anything with this note. Haven't you learned yet that any society practising slavery is innately unjust? When you have the power to make a free man a chattel to be bought and sold, then it is you – not the slave – who loses humanity; you who become a little less than what a man or a woman should be. The system is marginally less arbitrary in Tyrans simply because lesser men like those legionnaires are not at the top of the midden heap there; they are near the bottom.'

I wanted to deny what he was saying, to brush the words aside because I did not like them, but the scene in the well-square stayed with me. And I knew at least one part of what he was saying was true: the system here *was* arbitrary; it was too dependent on the whims of individuals. Back in Tyrans, power was divided up: the Exaltarch, the Brotherhood, the generals, the highborn, the moneymasters, the court praetors, the temple priestesses, the trademasters – everyone had his or her say. There were checks and balances even the Exaltarch had to obey. But here, in Kardiastan? The Governor, the Prefects – they relied on the legions to enforce the law and the only courts were military ones. It was a system that could be easily abused; and in my heart I knew military men were notoriously unwilling to discipline their own kind for crimes committed against civilians, especially subjects who were not even citizens of Tyrans.

'I am sure other outposts of the Exaltarchy don't have a similar, um, *anarchy* as here,' I said in protest. 'Besides, we only enslave those who have committed a crime. Some would say that slavery is a preferable punishment to other forms. In Assoria they used to cut off the right hands of thieves. In Corsene they used to blind them. Nowadays, in all the Exaltarchy, thieves and other petty criminals have a chance to lead useful lives as slaves, well fed, clothed and housed. Society is therefore more stable. Crime is reduced. The punishment is more tolerable. Which is better?'

'Legata, enslavement was just as arbitrary in Altan, where I was born, as it appears to be here. Do you know why I was made a slave? No, of course you don't. You never bothered to ask. Well, now perhaps is the time for you to learn – my parents died. I was ten years old.'

'And—?' I prompted when he did not go on.

'That's it. I was ten and parentless. There was no one to protect me. No one to protect the property that was my father's. It was stolen and I was sold into slavery, with the open connivance of the legionnaires stationed in Altan. Where was the crime that justified the sale of a grieving ten-year-old boy into a lifetime of slavery? That is the truth of your Tyranian civilisation, Legata. Certainly we have peace – but at what price?'

I didn't want to think about what he was saying. I looked away from him to pick up the slave collar again and fiddle with it. It felt weighty, cumbersome, awkward in a way I hadn't even noticed when I was wearing it. Brand stood quietly, waiting for some acknowledgement of the truths he uttered. I should have scolded him. Chided him for criticising the Exaltarchy that ruled him, but the Altani and I had a more complex relationship than that. I said finally, 'You've never spoken like this before, Brand. Why now?'

'You've only just started to listen.' He held up the scroll. 'I shall deliver this.' He turned and walked away, leaving me feeling upset and restless. It was all too easy to remember a pool of blood, black blood, seeping into a woman's clothing as she knelt, wringing her hands . . .

The next morning, I thought about having Brand follow me again, but I did not want anything to jeopardise my meeting with Mir Ager. The Mirager. I would risk going alone. Brand did not protest my decision; I would have been surprised if he had. We both knew being a member of the Brotherhood often involved danger. We both knew I revelled in risk and that nothing Brand said would ever change that.

Parvana was in the group of women waiting at the well. She nodded to me and drew me apart from the rest. 'Leave your ewer. I'll fill it and leave it over there, with the vegetable seller just behind us. You can pick it up any time. Now, see that neat-arsed hunk at the fruit stall on the other side of the square?'

I looked around. There was a man, a Kardi with no slave collar, idly poking at some fruit on display while he chatted to the stall owner. I put his age at about thirty, and took in his slim but muscular build and easy posture. I turned back to Parvana and nodded. 'I see him.'

'In a minute he will begin to walk away. You must follow him. He will take you to the person you want to see.'

Across the square, the man bought some of the fruit, placed it in his belt bag and, without glancing around, began to move off even as Parvana smiled encouragement and took my ewer. I crossed the square and entered the labyrinth of lanes on the other side, keeping the fellow in sight. I tried to probe ahead to see what his emotions were, but the alleys were full of Kardis doing their early morning shopping and it was impossible to separate one person's feelings from another's. I was jostled by the crowd and found myself pushing in an attempt to keep up with my guide.

It was my fault, of course; slaves did not jostle legionnaires. Slaves were submissive and polite, not pugnacious. But for a moment I forgot I was a slave and shoved a legionnaire out of my path. He grabbed at my arm and yanked me to a halt.

'Well, well,' he said, in Tyranian. 'What have we here? A willing slave wench throwing herself into my arms?'

I pulled away sharply and stepped backwards, only to find myself seized from behind. Another voice said, 'No, into mine I think, Xasus.' Laughter followed as this second man pulled me hard back against his chest, his intrusive hands fondling my breasts. I stood rigid with shock.

Two more legionnaires came up, grinning. 'Hey, what about us, Evander?' one of them asked the man who was holding me. 'I could do with a poke and she's not bad – for a Kardi.'

'Why not?' the one called Evander replied. 'Let's find a place.'

'I noticed some sacks of grain stacked in the alley back there,' Xasus said. 'Just the spot.'

Hardly able to credit I was hearing this conversation on a crowded city street, I twisted in my captor's arms and said – in Tyranian – 'How *dare* you! Let me go, *this instant* or you'll find yourself feeling Brotherhood justice.'

Evander did not release me, but the others looked stunned. 'Who the Vortex are you?' one of them asked.

'Ah, er, my mistress is Legata Ligea of the Brotherhood, at present residing with the Governor. She'll have you skinned alive and sold for slave meat if you touch me!'

Xasus backed off a little. 'Perhaps we ought to let her go,' he said to the others. 'I don't want any shit with the Brotherhood. And I've heard of that particular bitch. You don't cross her and get away with it. My cousin was a tax inspector in Tyr until he ran foul of her. Now he's a scribe in Gammed and his name is mud in Tyrans.'

'Since when has a slave told a legionnaire what he can and

cannot do?' Evander growled. 'Damn it, Xasus, you reckon any Brother is going to give a shit about a slave?'

'You'd better believe it,' I snapped. 'She's *very* fond of me.'

Xasus held up both hands in a gesture of defeat. 'I'm off,' he said.

But Evander was not going to give up his prize so easily, and one of the others was prepared to follow his lead. The crowd around had thinned out, giving us space; people were backing off, concerned, wary, not knowing what to do. The oppressive humidity of their hate for the legionnaires hung in the air, but no one actually moved to help me.

I caught sight of the man I had been following, as he came back to see what had happened. He was broadcasting his concern before him, as strong to my senses as incense is to the nose. With what I hoped was unexpected suddenness, I sagged in Evander's arms and he lost his grin. While he was off-balance, I whirled and jabbed him in the throat with stiffened fingers. It was a deceptively harmless-looking blow, but in the Brotherhood we called it the Vortex-strike for its ability to send the recipient to Acheron. The jab was hard, crushing his larynx and slamming into the blood vessel behind; the shock stopped his heart as effectively as an arrow in the chest would have done. I didn't wait to see what happened; I was already running. Behind me I heard an outraged cry of: 'The frigging helot has *killed* him. *Get* her.'

My guide saw me coming, turned and dodged into an alleyway, also running. I darted after him. The legionnaires, spurred by fury, were not far behind, but my guide knew what he was doing. We hurdled a low wall, dashed across a deserted courtyard and skidded through an archway into another crowded square. Back inside the crowd he dropped to a brisk walk to make our passage less obvious.

I risked a swift look behind. The legionnaires were shouting to someone in front of us: more legionnaires. My guide changed direction. He grabbed my hand and pulled me through another archway into a narrow lane hemmed in by adobe walls. The alley itself was a dead end, but several wooden doors set into the walls, intricately carved, hinted at an illustrious past for the Kardi homes behind them.

Without hesitation the Kardi opened a door and pulled me into the courtyard beyond. Once it had been a spacious garden for a wealthy man's home, now it was an untidy fowl-run surrounded by crumbling tenements. A number of curl-feathered hens scratched diligently in the dirt. There was washing hanging out to dry from almost every sagging balcony bordering the court, but there was no one around. I was pulled across the open space to the unkempt straggle of bushes against the wall on the other side. My guide forced his way into the heart of them, still drawing me with him. I was about to protest that the bushes weren't thick enough to hide both of us when he slipped sideways and disappeared.

I turned to follow and found myself squeezing through a narrow cleft in the wall and into a rectangular recess beyond. Its purpose I couldn't begin to guess at, except to wonder if it had once been some kind of storage space. There was barely room for us both. I was jammed up against my guide, my head squashed down to tuck in tight under his chin, my hips hard against his, my breasts flattened against his chest. The only place he could put his arms was around me. He smelled faintly of spice and sweat – and squashed fruit. His belt pouch, oozing peach juice, was flattened between us.

'Huh,' he said, amused, and continued in Kardi, 'It wasn't nearly so small when I was a kid hiding from my sister here.'

'You live here?'

'The whole building was my father's house once. Now I have a single room above. Can't say I've been in this cubbyhole for a few years, though.' He was almost laughing. 'Sorry about this – I'm afraid we're stuck here for a while. I think the legionnaires may have seen us disappear into the lane; they will have every house searched. We will have to wait until they are finished.'

He had barely stopped speaking when we heard voices shouting and the startled squawking of the hens in the court-yard.

'Pull the place apart if you have to,' someone said in Tyranian. 'If there's as much as a mouse hiding in the building I want to know about it! Bring everyone you find down here.' I didn't know the voice; it did not belong to any of the legion-naires who had assaulted me. However, it was clear one of those men was present because the next words, spoken in lower tones were, 'You, legionnaire – you stay here. I want you around to identify that murdering thrall if they turn her up.'

The Kardi bent to whisper in my ear, 'Not a sound.'

I nodded and resigned myself to waiting. The noise continued: voices raised in protest, the sound of breaking wood, running footsteps on stairs, children crying, hysterical hens clucking their distress.

It was uncomfortable squashed as we were. My back was pressed against rough adobe, my arms were pinioned by his. I twisted my head slightly to look out through the entrance crevice. The bushes grew thickly to block out much of the light, but I could just see movement on the other side. The same voice, now alarmingly close, was saying, 'Check these bushes, legionnaire.'

Tension stiffened us both, and the movement, as slight as it was, jammed us still tighter against one another. A rustle in the leaves was an explosion to my ears; someone was using their sword to poke into the branches. Sweat, mixed with dust, trickled down my neck, and my slave collar seemed unbear-ably tight. I felt no fear; I was hardly in any danger from

Tyranians. No one except the Brotherhood itself would dare to question the killing of a rankman legionnaire by a Brotherhood Legata. If I were caught, all I had to do was explain who I was and what had happened. It wasn't fear that built the tension in me; it was excitement, the provocation of the chase, the stimulation of pitting myself against another . . .

The tension was pleasurable. I moved my head slightly to relieve the crick in my neck and found my face almost on a level with the Kardi's, my mouth brushing his chin. His smell was pleasant, his hard muscularity tempting. No hint of his emotions now reached me; he had obscured himself, just as Brand did. I was intrigued.

He stirred against me in turn. At first, I thought it was merely discomfort at our cramped position. Then I felt the real reason for his unease pressing into my hips. I jerked my head sideways so that I could focus on his face. He was looking at a point somewhere above my head. The light was dim, but I thought I could see a flush colouring his cheeks. Indignation swelled inside me: how *dare* he!

Before I could do anything to indicate my displeasure, I felt him quivering. It took me a moment to identify the cause. Laughter. I had no way of expressing my anger; I couldn't move, and I certainly couldn't risk saying anything for fear of being heard. I stayed rigidly still while the cause of his amusement remained abundantly clear to us both. Then, reluctantly, my lips twitched. The situation *was* funny. Despite his laughter, he was embarrassed – but there wasn't anything either of us could do about it. I sucked in my cheeks and tried to suppress the chuckles threatening to erupt.

His head dipped and his lips brushed mine gently, tentatively. I wanted my anger to return, but it stayed obstinately away. His mouth closed over mine, tender, then demanding as his tongue probed and I responded.

The sounds of the search outside continued. Irate officers snarled their irritation, legionnaires vented their frustration in muttered asides to one another. Neither of us moved to break the kiss. Neither of us wanted it to end. I could no longer distinguish the tension of desire from the tension caused by fear of discovery. When the noises finally faded and disappeared, I was hardly aware they were gone. Wave after wave of desire rippled, touching mind and body. Pleasurable tightness travelled across the surface of my skin, an unfamiliar sensation matching the more recognisable pressure building in my loins. Tension-desire invaded every inch of me, subordinating mind to physical senses. Tissues swelled and warmed and throbbed. I'd never experienced anything so pervasive and thought I would disintegrate if there was no release. Alarm slipped into the cracks between passionate hunger and an overwhelming yearning for this man's body. *Goddess*, I thought, *I've been drugged. Again.* But I didn't want to listen to the warning. In that moment, I wanted nothing but to satisfy an all-encompassing lust.

He broke away and I heard wonder in his voice as he asked, 'Blessed cabochon – a Magor? Who would have thought it?'

The words meant nothing; I felt only annoyance that he had stopped kissing me when I was still almost incoherent with need. But he gave me no time to say anything. 'They've gone,' he said and eased himself out of our prison. Wordlessly, I followed, trying to dredge up the vestiges of my equanimity, hearing the whisper of warning in my mind, yet unwilling to listen. No sooner had I extricated myself from the bushes than he had grabbed my hand again and was pulling me up wooden steps to the balcony above. I did not protest – I did not want to protest. My whole body was throbbing.

I noticed nothing about the room we entered. I had already forgotten the legionnaires, I had forgotten who this man was, all I knew was I wanted him as I had never wanted anyone before in my life, that I had to have him or die with wanting.

Later, I had no recollection of how I came to be naked, but I was and so was he and he had entered me and my world would never be the same again. The tension, which I had already thought unbearable, grew still greater until I wanted to scream and scream and go on screaming. But just as I opened my mouth, he touched his left hand to mine and the world splintered around me, slivered into light and colour and sound and beauty and love and velvet touch and I wanted to die with the joy of it.

I floated in magic, in music, in perfume, in tangy peach sweetness, in soft silk, in golden light, in an overload of sensation. Reluctant to descend to reality, reluctant to question, reluctant to have answers. Sure I had been drugged. Not knowing how that was possible. Not caring. Horrified I had so lost all control over my actions. Appalled *that I didn't care*.

In the end, it was he who spoke first. He was lying beside me, his glistening naked body brown and muscular and perfect to my still-besotted eyes. He propped himself up on one arm and allowed his glance to roam over the curves of my nakedness. Then he touched a finger to the brown of my nipple and said, 'You are the most beautiful woman I have ever seen.'

I was accustomed to being considered too tall, too muscular, too swarthy; not even Favonius had ever said I was beautiful. Yet I believed this man. I saw the truth in his eyes even before he allowed me to feel it in my mind. I took up his left hand and touched the swelling there, the swelling that matched mine in shape and size. 'What did you do?' I asked in wonderment.

'Have you never loved one of your own kind before?'

My own kind! Shock shivered through me. I wasn't one of these people! I shook my head, trying to deny the truth. 'Who – who am I?'

'You do not *know*?'

'There was never anyone to tell me. I was brought up in Tyrans. What I told Parvana wasn't quite the truth; I was taken to Tyr as a very young child.' I shielded my emotions from him; I knew he had the same abilities I had. If I'd wanted, he could have read me as easily as a scroll. The talents I once called intuition were no such thing; I knew that now. They were all part of being born different, of having a swelling in the middle of the palm . . .

'You have a lot to learn,' he said.

'The first lesson was . . . unbelievable.'

He laughed. 'We shall take you to the Mirage.' He touched my slave collar. 'Soon you'll be free.'

I studied his face. He was handsome, with eyes like mine: brown and tilted at the corners. A wide mouth that constantly quirked up with amusement, and white even teeth. A nose that was just a shade crooked at the tip. Curly hair that escaped the thong at his nape to fall forward over his ears. I liked his looks. Very much. And I liked the laughter I felt in him.

And I was an agent of the Brotherhood. *Snap out of it, Ligea.*

I said, 'The Tyranians have something belonging to the Mirager.'

'So we heard.' He took a deep breath as though he were faced with a truth too much to bear. With sudden intuition, I knew he had so far delayed mention of it because he was afraid to hear my answer. 'His – his Magor sword?'

'I suppose so. It looks like a sword with a hollow, translucent blade.'

'It's here, in Madrinya?'

'Back at the Governor's residence. The Legata brought it from Sandmurram. The legionnaires said it was heavy, but the shleth carrying it didn't seem to notice the weight.'

He closed his eyes, gripped by emotions he found hard to

control. 'Ah. You don't know it, beautiful one, but you've just saved my life.' He gave a sigh and collapsed back into the pallet as though he had just shaken off a horror that had ridden him longer than he cared to acknowledge. 'Another few weeks and the story of the return of the Magor to their rightful place in Madrinya would have had another hero.' He was laughing at himself, but I didn't understand the ramifications of what he was saying. 'This Legata, tell me about her.'

'Ligea Gayed of Tyr. She's a Legata Compeer of the Brotherhood. We are quartered in the Governor's residence.'

'The sword – can you get it? It won't be heavy to you.'

I nodded, but I was bewildered. Why was he so trusting? He'd only just met me! 'Can I really go to the Mirage?' That was far more than I had dared hope.

'Yes, naturally. Do you think we would leave someone of the Magor to *them*?'

I had to play this carefully. Better, I thought, to forgo meeting the Mirager until we were fully prepared . . . Besides, I needed to know more of what was going on.

I said, 'If I go back I won't be able to get out again until tomorrow morning—' I gasped and sat up. 'Oh – the *time*! I shall be missed! And I have to pick up my ewer yet, too.'

He grinned at me as I began to throw on my clothes, but he, too, started to dress. 'I'll take you back through the alleys. You don't want to run into those legionnaires again. Did you really kill one of them?'

I knew I had, and didn't mind him knowing it; he would hardly be suspicious of someone who'd killed a legionnaire. However, I did not want him to think of me as a deliberate killer, so I shrugged carelessly and said, 'I hardly think so. I just hit him. Oh, Vortex, there are so many things I want to ask you!'

'And I you. Never mind. Tomorrow morning: are you sure it

will be possible for you to bring the sword out of the house? If there's any danger, we can send someone in after it instead—'

I froze. The shade in Sandmurram . . . Goddessdamn, had that thing been sent by the Mirager? I pictured it again. And thought: *It could have been this man's twin* . . . except that this man was all too alive. I took a calming breath and said, 'No, there's no problem. I'll meet you at the well. Will you really take me to meet the Mirager?'

'Tomorrow. I promise. If you have anything precious among your things, bring it with you. You won't be going back to the Governor's residence again. Sweet damn, I can hardly bear to let you out of my sight. Are you sure you'll be all right?'

I nodded, but I was distracted. I was staring at the floor, my mind chasing an elusive memory. The tiles beneath my feet were of brown and white agate, quite unlike the usual cheap flooring of the few Kardi homes I had entered on my way to Madrinya. I glanced up at the walls: the adobe had been panelled. The wood was cracked and splintered, the tiles chipped and dirty, but once this had been a room of simple beauty – a nobleman's house, perhaps, or some wealthy Kardi merchant. And somewhere, faint in the edges of my memory, I was feeling the cool smoothness of polished agate stone beneath my bare feet as I ran, laughing, with other children . . .

I finished dressing and looked back at him. 'There is one other thing I'd like to know now.'

'Anything.'

'What's your name?'

He started to laugh. 'Temellin,' he said, chuckling. 'Friends call me Temel. Lovers call me Tem.'

CHAPTER TEN

Brand was waiting for me at the door. He took the ewer and prepared to wash my feet, but I refused the service with sudden distaste and bathed them myself. Afterwards, as I undid my slave collar in front of the mirror in the main room of my apartments, I remembered Evander's arms around me and the legionnaires discussing my rape as if I hadn't been there ... Slave woman. Chattel. Less than human. Less even than a valued animal. My eyes met Brand's in the mirror and then fell to his collar.

I didn't think I had shown him anything on my face, but he gave the slightest of cynical smiles and said, 'So I guess something happened to show you what it is *really* like to be a slave.'

I put my collar down on the desk. 'Yes.'

'I knew you would realise one day. In fact, it's taken a little longer than I once thought it would.'

I sat down at my desk and pulled a blank piece of parchment and the ink towards me. 'You're a bastard, Brand,' I remarked and began to write. When I had finished I heated wax, dropped it onto the bottom of the document and imprinted it with my ring seal. Once the ink was dry I flung it across the desk to him.

He read it without expression. Then, raising his eyes to meet mine, he said, 'I'm not going to thank you for giving me what was my birthright. But I think you know that.'

I nodded. 'Yes, confound you. You know me far too well, you Altani barbarian. But don't expect me to like you for being right.'

'That's what older *brothers* are for. To help their little *sisters* grow up.'

'You're sodding lucky I don't throw the ink at you. I shall make arrangements for you to be paid a wage in the future.'

'*If* I decide I want to stay in your employ,' he pointed out.

I gritted my teeth. 'Yes. *If.* I shall also calculate what is owed you in back wages from the time you entered my service.' It was only while I was waiting for his reply that I knew how much I feared he would leave me.

He knew it too, of course, which is why the bastard didn't answer immediately. He was punishing me. 'Salving a guilty conscience, Ligea?'

I noted the lack of title, but didn't remark on it. 'Allow me that luxury.'

He grinned. 'So, apart from the fact someone treated you like a slave, what else happened today?'

What happened? A man made love to me and showed me paradise . . . 'I have promised to bring the sword tomorrow and they will take me to the Mirager. In fact, they have said they will take me to the Mirage. Free me from slavery.'

'They didn't doubt you?' Without asking for permission, he sat down on the divan opposite the desk and began picking at the fruit on a side table there. I knew he was deliberately indicating what he considered the only possible basis for any new working relationship: I must consider him my equal. I was disconcerted, stifled the feeling – but thought he sensed it anyway, and was amused by it.

Damn it, I'd just freed him, but he was still a servant, by all that was holy! He ought to have shown me more respect.

He asked, 'And are you going to go to the Mirage with them?'

I stood up. 'I don't know. To discover the secret of crossing the Shiver Barrens, to find out just what this Mirage is – that wasn't part of my mandate, but it may be even more important than trapping the Mirager.' I began to pace the floor, scratching my left palm. 'I think I will decide what to do once I see which way the die falls tomorrow. I'll see what happens.'

Brand waved the paper I had signed. 'I see this is dated three days from now. I am still yours to command.'

I felt a twinge of shame. 'I wasn't sure what you would do once you were free. I'm still not sure, and I may need your help in the next day or so.' I paused, but he was silent, so I went on, 'I shall talk to the Military Commander today. I want you to follow me tomorrow, and I want legionnaires stationed all around the city within easy call, no matter where I end up. I'll signal you to fetch them if I need them. No signal will mean I'm going on to the Mirage and the arrest of the Mirager can wait.'

'And if so, then what? What will you do? How will you get back? Who will help you?'

My lips twisted. 'What's the matter, Brand? Worried I won't be around to pay you what I've promised? Well, don't worry, I'll draw up all the papers tonight, and have them properly witnessed.'

His eyes narrowed. 'I may well be a bastard, but you can be even more of a bitch. Doesn't it occur to you I may just be a little worried about you? That I might just help you simply because you ask? You didn't have to postdate my freedom, Ligea. Vortex take it, what you are proposing is more than dangerous, it's suicidal.'

'I'll be all right. If there's a way in, there'll be a way back. You will wait here in Madrinya for me?'

'Yes, I'll wait, damn you. And if I haven't heard from you in, um, say, two months, I'll come after you.'

'Now that *would* be suicidal. What I really want you to do is keep Aemid off my back. If she gets a whisper of what I'm doing, she'll be screaming it to every Kardi in Madrinya and my life will be worth less than the contents of a begging bowl.'

He looked disbelieving. 'She wouldn't hurt you.'

'She'd have me killed rather than see anything happen to her precious Kardiastan. Keep an eye on her. If I disappear into the Mirage, tell her I've gone back to Sandmurram. Anything but the truth. I shall leave her manumission paper with you just in case anything happens to me, but don't tell her I'm freeing her too. Not yet. How is she, by the way?'

'Resting. She looks a shade better.'

'I'll get changed and go to see her. You go to the Military Commander's office and ask when it's convenient for me to call.'

'Please,' he said.

I stared at him, uncomprehending.

'You may as well get in the habit of saying it now,' he told me. 'I shan't be a slave much longer.'

I resisted another urge to pitch the inkpot at him.

When I went in to see Aemid, I made sure the lamp was unlit and the room was dim. I didn't want her to notice I'd rid my hair of its gold highlighting and its curls.

She still looked tired and old, but she was fighting back, a good sign. I suspected that her physical weakness was as much caused by her mental state as anything else. She had held a dream in her head for over twenty-five years, and the reality diverged so much from her vision that she couldn't cope with it.

We talked for a while, neutral topics, then I asked, 'Aemid, did you bring any xeta for me from Tyrans?'

She shook her head. 'There was no point. It has to be taken fresh or it doesn't work.'

'I shall buy some here then.'

'You'll be lucky. It doesn't grow here, Legata.'

'It doesn't? Then what do women use?'

'A drink prepared from a root extract. But it doesn't work quite the same way as xeta. You can't just take one dose whenever necessary; you have to take it every day, and it doesn't work well until you've been using it some time. It's called gameez.'

'Damn.'

'What have you been up to?' Aemid looked worried.

'Never mind. Just a passing fancy. I'll get some gameez.'

'You don't normally let your loins do your thinking, Legata.'

Abashed, I said, 'No, I don't suppose I do. He just took me by surprise, that's all, and his – his technique was very good.' So good I couldn't put him out of my mind. *Goddess*, I thought, *how can I have lost myself so easily, lost who I am, in this man's arms? Am I no better than those silly highborn matrons back in Tyr, giggling over legionnaire officers riding past on their gorclaks?*

I'd had time to think about what had happened by then. Surely something had enhanced normal desire – I flushed just thinking about my lack of restraint – but it hadn't been a drug. It had been something to do with the lump in the middle of my palm. Something to do with being Magor, whatever that was. I wanted to be angry with Temellin, furious he had taken advantage of my inability to resist the stimulus. Instead, I just remembered how good it had been.

After I left Aemid, I had to deal with an irate Legate of the legionnaires, outraged that one of his men had apparently been killed by a slave of mine. I thought of telling him I had done it myself while on Brotherhood business, but decided the fewer people who knew about that, the better. Instead, I told him, in freezing tones, that I had no such young slave girl, which a routine inquiry in the slave quarters would have confirmed, and how dare he accuse my household without making such a logical inquiry first? I then told him what I thought of his legionnaires and his discipline, making it clear I had heard about the incident with the gorclak race the day before, and that I'd also heard it said the slave girl was only defending herself against rape. By the time I'd finished, the officer was not only staggered by the extent and rapidity of Brotherhood intelligence, he was terrified that I was going to report him to his superiors for failure to maintain disciplined troops. He left apologising and humbled.

That night I tossed on my divan with the smell of another man still in my nostrils and his soft laugh in my ears. And I was honest enough to admit the reason I was thinking of not having the Mirager arrested the following day was that I was none too sure it would be possible to capture him without involving one of his underlings, a Kardi called Temellin.

CHAPTER ELEVEN

He waylaid me before I reached the well, grinning. He took the ewer from me, as well as the small bag of clothing I had brought along – but he was looking at the other item I carried. The sword, well wrapped to disguise its shape, was tucked under my arm. He touched it reverently, and the smile he gave was as joyful as a child's laughter. 'That's it!' he said, almost as if he were afraid to believe it. And then, awed, 'You just walked out of the Governor's residence with it under your arm?'

I nodded. 'Who was there to question me? The Legata went out herself this morning. Anyone else seeing me leave the villa would have assumed I was on her business. And believe me, no one would question her orders.' The evasions slipped off my tongue as easily as water rolls from a gorclak's hide. I had to be careful with my wording; this man had a lump on his palm. What if he could read lies the way I could? Temellin would know I hid my emotions from him, of course, but then he did that to me too. I had to assume that was normal behaviour for one of the Magor. For one of us. Goddess but that expression stuck in my craw, as unwelcome as a fishbone.

'You didn't have any problems getting it?'

'None. She didn't think any of the slaves could lift it, let alone steal it!'

He gave back the ewer and took the sword from me instead, his hands caressing the hide covering, but he didn't unwrap it. Tears glistened and his fingers shook.

Tears? What in all of hellish Acheron was it about this sword that was so damned special?

'I was worried about you,' he said. He was trying to change the subject, to give himself time to regain control of himself. I thought he was acting more as if he'd just had a reprieve from death, than a man who had just retrieved a weapon for his ruler; I could sense relief so deep, nothing less seemed to make sense. Maybe that's it, I thought. Maybe this Mirager was going to kill him if he didn't find it. Maybe it was Temellin's fault it was lost in the first place. He'd told me the day before that I'd saved his life, but I hadn't taken him seriously. Now, I wondered.

I said, 'I've looked after myself for quite a while.' I had to curb the desire to reach out and touch him, I had to hide the way I was ridiculously stirred by his smile, by his hair curling this way and that over his ears . . .

'So I noticed. You did kill that man yesterday, you know.'

'Did I? Are you sure? I mean – I guess I hit him really hard, then.' My eyes widened and I gave a slight shiver. It was meant for Temellin's benefit, but suddenly it seemed genuine; I had gone straight from a killing to this man's pallet.

'Don't think about it. Here, let's be on our way.' He took my arm and guided me down a narrow laneway I hadn't used before.

'Temel, I'm scared. I know so little about you, or about what I am—' My voice wavered. I could be quite a good actress when I put my mind to it. It was all true anyway; I *was* scared, but I was also exhilarated. I was a compeer on the hunt . . .

'What do you want to know?'

'Tell me about the Mirager. And about me – us. What are we?'

'We are Magor. And the Mirager is the, well, monarch, for want of a better word. The ruler of Kardiastan by right of his bloodline and his Magor rank. There is no need to fear *him*; he's very happy with you.'

'How can that be? Temel, I am from Tyrans. I don't remember any other kind of life. I am so – so *ignorant*.' And that was true too. Rathrox had not mentioned the word Magor to me. No one had, until Aemid used the term on the ship.

'Turn right here; down the steps.' There were two legionnaires coming up towards us, and he was silent until we had passed them. Then he said, 'Someone taught you the Kardi tongue.'

'A fellow slave. But she said nothing of what I am. She was afraid General Gayed would find out, I suppose.'

'You are returning the Mirager's sword; believe me, he is delighted with you.' He was laughing at me, and I laughed with him and slipped my hand into his. Acting ... or was I? In truth, I felt as though I was fifteen again and all those years of being a Compeer Brother had never been. The woman who had killed and maimed and plotted and connived on her way to the top? She didn't exist, not then. That woman would never have felt this way, so swayed by desire, by a sense of light-hearted self-discovery. I strove to remember what I was supposed to be doing.

An occasional backward mental glance told me Brand still followed; I hoped he had a better idea of where we were than I did. The lanes we followed twisted and turned and divided confusingly.

The house we finally entered was a simple adobe place of two storeys with a number of small rooms. 'This is one of our safe houses,' he said, 'and it has access to the escapeway, the route for freed slaves. Here you will meet some of the other Magor.'

I cast around and felt their presence: five people, two women and three men. All their emotions as unreadable as Temellin's – or my own. 'One of them is the Mirager?'

'He is here.'

'Temel, how many Magor are there?'

He knew I wasn't asking about the group in the room at the top of the stairs, and his face darkened subtly. 'Adults of all ranks? Not even five hundred.'

The question had upset him, but I had no way of guessing why. I had no time to think about it, either; he was already ushering me up the steps. I was still wearing my sandals and not only had no one come forward to wash our feet, but there hadn't been any water or bowls in the entrance hall so we could do it ourselves. My feet felt dirty and the unfamiliarity of wearing shoes indoors grated on me. Did these Kardis have no sense of even the most elementary hygiene? I couldn't understand why something as basic as welcoming ablutions and going barefoot inside the house had not become part of daily life under our rule. I had to hide a shudder of disgust and yet was glad of it. It enabled me to remember I was Tyranian, serving my Exaltarch and on a mission to cut into the heart of Kardi resistance.

A moment later, we joined the others. I knew without looking that they all had swellings on their palms; I could sense that kinship to me. In appearance there was a sameness about them: they were all under middle years – tall, brown-skinned, brown-eyed, brown-haired, handsome people with strength and health in their bodies. But their likenesses went deeper than that. Their facial structure, the tilt of their eyes – Temellin included, they could have been siblings. With shock, I was aware of my own physical similarity to all of them.

'Here she is,' Temellin said. 'Derya.' I set the ewer on the table and he laid the weapon, still in its covering, beside it. 'And here's the sword back safe and sound.'

The oldest of them, a tall, lean man with premature slashes of silver-grey through his hair, stared at it and whispered, 'Just like that? I can't believe it!' He touched the cover, biting his lip. 'I suppose they must have hidden it underground,' he added finally, 'which is why we could never trace it when we tried back in Sandmurram.' He carefully unrolled the hide. They all crowded around to look, expressions rapt, some of them even reaching out to touch the blade as though they could not accept it was real. If ever I had needed confirmation the sword was important to them, I had it then.

The older man appeared to be the most moved. He, too, had tears in his eyes as he touched the blade with his long fingers, the emotion oddly at divergence with the hard, aristocratic lines of his face. 'You always did say you had a feeling they hadn't thrown it into the sea,' he said to Temellin, his voice unsteady. 'You will never know how glad I am to see this. It would have been an ill day for me if my hand had ever had to close around the hilt of a new sword.' There was relief in his voice, but I thought I caught an odd furtiveness of guilt as well. There was something faintly skewed about him, as if two warring parts within never quite meshed into the perfect whole he wanted himself to be.

Temellin gave a gentle smile. 'At least you can stop worrying about that baby of yours,' he said cryptically, 'and Gretha can rest easy.'

The older man turned to me. 'We are indeed grateful to you. My name is Korden. You are welcome, for all that you were raised in Tyrans and know nothing of what it is to be Magor.'

'Well met,' I murmured, aware his verbal welcome wasn't quite reflected in his eyes.

'And this is Pinar,' Temellin said. He indicated the person standing next to Korden: a full-bodied woman of about thirty-five, wide in the shoulders and hips, with generous breasts and long lithe legs. Her face would have been beautiful had she been able to keep it serene; as it was, lines of discontent had tugged at the corners of her mouth and eyes so often they threatened to become permanent. She inclined her head to me, but didn't smile.

The next man – hardly more than a youth – was a fascinating mixture of adult muscle, boyish enthusiasm and virile charm. He did not wait for an introduction, but gave a broad smile and said, 'Well met indeed, Derya. I'm Garis.' He was startlingly handsome, with tawny-brown eyes of a lighter shade than most Kardis, and long curling eyelashes any woman would have coveted. He took my left hand in his and touched palms. A warm wash of welcome ebbed through me with the touch. I was moved, then suspicious. A trick, I thought. It could all be fakery. These people have powers you know nothing about . . .

The remaining couple were introduced as husband and wife: Jahan and Jessah. They, too, touched hands with me, and their welcome seemed genuine, if a little more restrained than Garis's. Jahan seemed familiar to me, but then, he looked a lot like Temellin. I certainly couldn't remember ever having seen him before.

I wanted to ask Temellin, *And which one is the Mirager?* but was reluctant to have my fears confirmed. From what had been said, it must be the serious-faced Korden, already turning his attention away from me and back to the sword. He picked it up by the base of the blade and handed it, hilt first, to Temellin. 'Let's see if it has been damaged,' he said.

Temellin fitted the hilt into his left hand. For a moment it stayed as it was, then the blade was filled with glowing gold light and was translucent no longer. A golden glow played along his skin, and memory awoke in me. That golden woman, my real mother . . . I tried to focus on that haunting recollection, but details remained elusive.

'Are you particularly attached to your ewer, Derya?' Temellin asked.

Blinking in surprise at the question, I shook my head.

He pointed the sword at the jug and a beam of yellow light shot across the room to burn a hole the size of a child's fist in its side. 'It works,' he said laconically. Then, before I could move, he touched the sword point to my slave collar. 'Let's get rid of this, shall we?' There was a flash of cold light and the collar fell away into pieces on the floor.

'Sweet Melete,' I blurted, and sat down abruptly on the only available stool. I raised my hands to my neck in unfeigned wonder.

'What rank are you, Derya?' Korden asked.

Shock froze my heart. *Surely they couldn't know!* I licked dry lips. 'Rank? In – in what?'

'What colour is your cabochon?'

I looked at him doubtfully and began to breathe again. 'I don't know what you mean. What's a cabochon?' I had come across the word before, but I couldn't think what it had to do with me. As far as I knew, it was an unfaceted, polished gemstone.

'The stone in your hand, the gem – what colour is it?'

'I – *stone*?'

'You don't *know*?'

I shook my head and looked down at my hand. 'There's a *gemstone* in there?'

He nodded. 'Yes. It would have been there since just after you were born.'

'I didn't know. Or I don't remember knowing. It was always

like this . . . I think. Or was it?' I raised my eyes, confused by tendrils of half-memory. 'There's very little I remember about the time before I left Kardiastan. I was only three or so when I was taken to Tyrans.'

Pinar interrupted, her voice harsh. 'That wasn't what you told the girl Parvana. You only changed your story when you spoke to Temellin. Why?'

I returned her stare, hoping an honest answer would vanquish the obvious doubts she had about me. 'I was afraid she wouldn't trust me if I said I had actually been raised in Tyr.' I looked down at my hand again and touched the lump. 'Apparently, for the first few months I was in Tyrans I refused to open my hand. I think someone – my mother? – had told me not to show it to anyone. Oh, Goddess, was that because the gemstone was *uncovered* then?' Memory fluttered once more. 'Was *that* why I kept my hand covered so long? Until the skin grew over the stone that was there?'

It was Temellin who replied. 'It could be. Until the invasion, everyone wore their cabochons openly. We kept the skin pushed back. Now we all keep them skin-covered, because we feel the less the Tyranians know about them, the better. It doesn't make any difference to their efficiency if they're covered or not. Can't you remember *anything* about your life here in Kardiastan?'

Efficiency? At what? I shook my head. 'Not really. There was a woman, some fighting, but it's all very vague now. What does the colour of the stone – cabochon – mean?'

'Anyone who has a gem is one of the Magor. But there are three colours. The most common is green. It is not as powerful as the others. Those who wear the green we term the Theuros. If you are a woman and of the Theuros, you are called Theura; a man, Theuri. The next most powerful is red, and that makes you of the Illusos: an Illusa or an Illuser. The highest rank is that of the Magoroth. A Magoroth woman is a Magoria, the man a Magori. Their cabochons are gold. It is the rarest power of all. It is from among the Magoroth that the ruler – whether Mirager or female Miragerin – comes.' He waved a hand around at the group. 'We here all have gold cabochons. We are all of the Magoroth.'

I tried to absorb all that at once, but there were too many blanks. Powerful? The gems had some power? Their hereditary ruler could be a *woman*? Acheron's hells, *what colour was my stone*? I itched to haul out my knife and cut the skin of my palm to take a look. I suppressed the desire. To start with, I didn't want to reveal I carried a knife, and, anyway, the action might not have been in keeping with the character of Derya. I preferred them to think of her as meek, not aggressive.

'Temel, should you be telling her this?' Pinar interrupted again, her face pulled into a frown. 'After all, we hardly know her. She could be a Tyranian spy. There's nothing to say someone brought up in Tyrans will be loyal to us simply because they are Magor. Especially not when they are untrained Magor.'

'Pinar is right,' Korden agreed. 'We should wait, Temel, until we've had time to question her and ascertain the honesty of her answers.'

Temellin laughed. 'I have already,' he said.

He smiled at me, but Korden maintained a stern façade, backed up with an underlying disapproval. 'Don't say anything else.'

Temellin capitulated. He shrugged, grinning at me.

All the time they were speaking, their emotions flicked around the room, subtly loosed and then curbed as they reinforced the spoken word and layered their conversation with tiers of unspoken meaning. It was too quick, too skilfully done for me to be able to follow in its entirety – a subliminal, foreign language. Its presence challenged me, and my hunter's soul stirred once more. They had picked the wrong person to play games with . . .

'We are being watched,' said Jessah suddenly. 'By a non-Kardi.'

They all fell silent, heads tilted as if listening. *Goddessdamn*, I thought, *they sense Brand!* Why didn't I think of that? Of course they can do all the things I can – and more besides. My heart sped up, my muscles tensed, but I was careful not to look interested.

'She's right,' said the youngest among them – Garis. 'What ought we to do?'

'He's alone. Kill him,' Korden said casually. 'Whoever it is, he is not Kardi.'

I bit my lip in chagrin. 'I know who it is. It's Brand. He means no harm to you. He's an Altani slave of the Legata's. He must have followed me.'

'So you have the positioning and recognising powers,' Jessah said in surprise. 'And without training. What else can you do?'

I thought of lying, of keeping something back, but decided not to risk it. 'Sense the truth or a lie. Read emotions. Help people not to feel pain. That's all.' *That's all?* Stated so boldly, it sounded astonishing. I felt sick.

Jessah's husband, Jahan, was excited. 'Why,' he said, 'she might just be an Illusa! We must have a look!'

'Magor take it, Jahan! Not now,' Korden growled. He turned to me. 'What do you mean he must have followed you?'

I was careful to tell the truth. 'He saw me take the sword. He must be following to make sure I am all right. He is very protective of me.'

'Oh, a lover,' Pinar said with contempt.

Korden frowned at Temellin. 'How did you manage to miss him on the way here? That was careless, Temel. That kind of mistake could be fatal.' He nodded at Garis. 'Bring him in, lad.'

'Shouldn't I go?' I asked. 'I don't want anyone hurt.'

Garis laughed as if that was a joke, and left.

'He won't hurt Brand, will he?' I asked, my anxiety real. These people had power I knew nothing about, and I began to wonder if I were out of my depth.

'He won't have to,' Temellin said easily. 'And we're not in the business of killing non-Tyranians, especially not those who have also suffered under the yoke of Tyranian slavery. Quite the contrary.'

It seemed he was right to be so little worried because a few minutes later Garis re-entered the room holding a dazed Brand by the arm. 'He shields his emotions,' he complained. 'I can't read him. How in the world did he learn to do that?'

'He taught himself,' I said, 'in order to protect his privacy from me. We grew up together. He is like a brother to me. He means no harm. Brand,' I added reproachfully, 'why did you follow me? The truth now. These people will know if you lie.' I continued to speak in Kardi, but he had sufficient knowledge of the language to understand. He had grown up around me and Aemid, after all, although he didn't usually try to speak it.

He answered in Tyranian, taking his cue from me, his tone heavy with reproach. 'You shouldn't be wandering around the streets of a strange city by yourself. I didn't want anything to happen to you. I thought I might be able to help if anything did. So I followed.' The truth, just not the whole truth.

Before he could say any more he was interrupted by Jessah saying, 'Ungar's coming, and she's upset about something.' A moment later, another Magor Kardi came in, a girl of about eighteen or so. 'There's some kind of trouble,' she said without preamble. 'There are legionnaires everywhere. Grouped in almost every square. I've never seen so many. They're all talking about waiting for some kind of a message to act—'

Pinar gave me a sharp look, but she didn't say anything. She didn't have to. Her suspicion was obvious; it flooded the room.

'We'd better play it safe and get out of here, into the escape-ways,' said Korden, looking at Temellin. 'We can't risk anything going wrong at this stage.' He allowed his suspicion to leak as well.

'I heard there was trouble yesterday,' Brand offered by way of explanation. 'A legionnaire was killed by a Kardi woman. They are looking for her.' He continued to speak in Tyranian, but it was obvious all of them understood what he said.

Temellin glanced at me thoughtfully. 'Perhaps someone recognised you on your way here,' he said. 'I think you're right, Korden. Let's move out now instead of later. All of us.' Intrigued, I noticed that once the decision was made, he was stimulated by the situation rather than worried. The smile he gave me was one of controlled excitement. *Goddessdamn*, I thought, *he's like me.*

Pinar was not so happy. 'There's another possible explana-tion,' she said, her voice harsh to match the turbulence of her suspicion. 'What have you done with your wits, Temel? And what do we intend to do with this Altani fellow?' She began to advance on Brand, and to my surprise he paled and flinched away.

'There's no need for that, Pinar,' Temellin said sharply. 'Brand comes.'

'You can't take a non-Kardi all the way to the Mirage,' she protested.

'We'll discuss it later. Let's go.' He touched my arm. 'Sorry about all this.' He grinned and sounded cheerfully nonchalant. Then he leant over and said something to Brand that I didn't hear. The others were already busy grabbing up Kardi travel-ling cloaks, collecting packs from other rooms and, as I noticed with increased unease, strapping on Magor swords. We all went downstairs again, where a portion of the floor tiles had been removed in one of the rooms to reveal a set of steps leading underground. A servant hovered, waiting to replace the tiles after us.

'Here, Derya, you take this; it's for you,' Jessah said, and gave me a cloak.

The steps led down into an underground passageway. It was pitch dark and I assumed someone would light a torch; instead, Korden and Garis pulled out their swords, and the way was illuminated by their uncanny glow.

We walked for a while through a labyrinth of underground passageways, some natural, others excavated, and all obviously once well used. I would have liked to investigate further, but we were hurrying and no one spoke. When we reached a cavern clammy with dribble on the walls and slickness underfoot, Korden called a halt.

'We'll all be meeting back here once we've picked up our passengers,' Temellin explained to Brand and me. 'You two can stay here and wait for us.'

'Not alone,' Pinar said, her tone sharp.

'Garis can stay,' Temellin said. He nodded at the youth. 'Look after them.'

'*Guard* them,' Pinar amended.

Once only the three of us were left, Brand said in heavily accented Kardi, 'I don't think I like her very much.'

Garis laughed and answered in the same language. 'She is a little abrasive, isn't she? Desert sand in a storm. You might as well make yourselves comfortable; it will be a while before they are back.'

Taking his advice, Brand and I found a dry spot and sat down with our backs against a rock to rest. Around us, drips of water play a syncopated tune as they hit pools and puddles.

Conversation was desultory because none of us knew quite what to talk about. Finally, a bored Garis wandered off to the other side of the cavern where he started examining some of the glistening rock formations by the light of his sword. Brand and I were left sitting in near darkness.

'I'm sorry,' he whispered.

'Not your fault. What did Temellin say to you back in the house?'

'That I was to behave myself or he'd carve out my balls. If I didn't give any trouble, he'd try to see that I kept both my head and my balls. He has a way with words, this Temellin.' He gave a twisted smile and changed the subject. 'I gather it was you who killed the legionnaire yesterday?'

'He had no manners.'

'Thought it sounded like your handiwork. What did he do? Tread on your toes?'

'A little more than that. Besides, I thought if I killed a legionnaire, none of the Kardi would question my loyalties.'

'Goddess, but you can be a hard-hearted bitch, Ligea!'

I dropped my voice still further. '*Derya*. And that's right. I'm a Legata Compeer of the Brotherhood, remember? Trained to kill when necessary.' But even as I said the words I felt uncomfortable. They reminded me too much of Rathrox Ligatan, and I no longer wanted to be equated with him. I stirred unhappily. I had infiltrated traitorous groups in disguise before, but this time something felt desperately wrong with what I was doing. I wondered why. Was it because I was Kardi too? Because I was Magor, as they were – whatever that meant? Because I had lain with one of their number and experienced something so sweet I would never be able to forget it?

'How do we get out of this one, Ligea?' Brand asked.

'Acheron take you, Brand, *Derya*! Call me Ligea in front of these people and you might just as well slit my throat.' I took a deep breath. 'Just behave yourself for the time being and hope Aemid keeps her mouth shut.' He was silent, so I asked, 'What did Garis do to you?'

'He put his left hand on my back, just a friendly clap in between the shoulder blades as though he was an old friend. And I could hardly breathe. I was so damn weak I thought I was going to die. They scare me, L— Derya. When that cat Pinar came at me, with her hand upraised, I thought she was going to do the same thing. What are we dealing with here? They can't be – well, they can't be *gods*, can they?' He sounded as if he doubted his own sanity. 'Or immortals?'

My heart skittered uncomfortably. If they were gods or immortals, then so was I.

He added, 'They are going to question us. About Ligea. What she is doing here.' I thought he was going to ask me what he ought to say, but he didn't. Instead, he said, 'I won't tell any lies, Derya. Not to these people.'

I stared at him, a churning mass of thoughts whirling in my head, striving to deal with the fundamental change in our relationship. Brand was about to be free of his collar. Free to choose his allegiance.

'Will you betray me?' I whispered. The thought hurt more than I would ever have considered possible.

'Do you know me so little?' he asked, and I heard his bitterness. 'I will say nothing that will put you in danger, but I'll tell no lies to save the Exaltarchy or the Brotherhood, either. I'm free now, Derya, and I'll choose my own friends and allies.'

I was silent.

He added, 'Anyway, they know a lie for what it is the moment it's uttered, don't they?'

'Probably.' I stared at my palm, and had to resist the temptation to reach for my knife yet again. I would find out soon enough.

Garis came back to join us then, and we spoke of other things. Apparently the passengers Temellin had referred to were escaping slaves, a mass exodus of some one hundred Kardis who had been hiding out in safe houses all over the city. We – the Magor – would lead them to safety in the Mirage.

'How long will it take?' I asked.

'A few days. And please don't ask me anything about the Mirage, because I don't know if I should tell you.'

I indicated the cavern. 'Can you tell us about this? Did you build these passages, this cavern?'

'A lot is natural. The rest was built by the people of Madrinya and the Magor. These were once underground cellars and cool-rooms, storage rooms. When Madrinya fell to Tyrans, the underground portion of the city was hidden by the Magor who survived. We have used it ever since.'

I tried to extract more details, but he smiled and didn't reply.

Gradually people began to arrive in the cavern in groups.

The ordinary Kardis were too caught up in their own fears to be interested in us, but there were more Magor with them; even in among so many people I could sense that much. They came across and introduced themselves. They were friendly, but distant. I saw Pinar talking to some of them, doubtless warning them not to trust either Brand or me.

And then they were all moving, a river of people flowing through the dimness towards a new life, and we were caught up in the current. Attuned to their emotions, I felt their subdued jubilation, their suppressed excitement. I said to Brand, 'They are so happy! I don't think I've ever felt such joy from so many people all at once. It's – it's almost contagious.'

Beside me, Garis laughingly swooped down on a toddler who was giving his mother problems. 'Eh, now, none of that, my lad,' he said, and hoisted the boy onto his back, where he eventually went to sleep, his head on Garis's shoulder.

His mother gave a sigh of relief. 'Many thanks, Magori,' she said. 'He's been a right proper handful with me since his Dad died, but he obeys smartly enough when the order comes from a man.' She was a short woman, her arms and legs balled with muscle, her torso thin. She was not wearing a slave collar, but then none of those around us were, either.

'Were you a slave?' I asked, curious.

'Oh, aye. Me and my man both.' She jerked a thumb at her son. 'He was born a slave. Don't seem *right*, do it, that someone can be *born* unfree? My man, he died a slave, and that don't seem right neither. He worked in the Master's stables, and a gorclak gored him. Took him three weeks to die, it did.' She looked at Garis with troubled eyes. 'My mother used to talk of the olden days when the Magor walked with us, and she said they were healers. Magori, could you have cured my man if we could have got him to you?'

Garis looked unhappy. 'I can't say. Perhaps not, if the injuries were very bad. All we have is the ability to hurry along the healing process. We can't work miracles, you know. But your man wouldn't have died in pain.'

The woman shook her head sadly. 'It will be good when the Magor rule our land once more. Don't let it be too long, Magori. We are tired of waiting.'

Brand bent to whisper in my ear. 'So much for all the things Tyrans offers: the peace, the trade, the stability, the prosperity. Take note, Derya: nothing is more important than being free. Free to choose one's own form of government, one's own way of living – or dying.'

Garis, who had caught the end of this, said with suppressed savagery, 'They will have it, and soon. We, too, are tired of waiting.'

I wanted to reply, to defend Tyrans. To defend a way of life. But I couldn't, not if I wanted to maintain my new identity. And I had an uncomfortable feeling that any argument I used would sound worn anyway. I thought sourly: *They'd rather have anarchy and war than stability. They don't know how to rule themselves. They don't know when they are better off.*

As if he'd heard me, Brand added in a whisper, 'Did you enjoy your own taste of slavery, Derya?'

We walked for two hours in the semi-darkness and then the passage disgorged us into that brilliant sunlight and blue sky of Kardiastan. I looked around for Temellin, to see him giving orders, organising, directing the crowd. The others of the Magor were equally busy, and there were still more of them I hadn't seen before. The bare earth in front of us was crowded with pack shleths, howdah shleths and shleth riding hacks. I marvelled at how all of this had been brought together in such a short time.

It seemed the escapeway emerged at the edge of the vale of Madrinya, because beyond the shleths a dry plateau stretched into the distance, the brown sands marbled through with red and gold, the wind-sculpted rocks standing guard over the patterning. When I glanced in the other direction, I could see the city already separated from us by the green of fields and trees.

'We came *that* far under the ground?' Brand asked in awe. 'And their organisation – Vortex take it, Derya, no wonder the legionnaires can't catch them.'

I didn't reply.

Someone handed me a waterskin and I drank deeply before passing it on; it was followed by some grain-cakes. Only when I bit into one did I know I had been hungry.

In a surprisingly short time we were all mounted, the children and the more elderly or infirm in howdahs, everyone else on shlethback. I saw Temellin cajoling an aged man up into a howdah and heard him say gently, 'Yes, I know you'd rather ride, but I need you to keep an eye on these children in the howdah. They need a strong hand.'

Several of the Magor stayed behind; others, including Korden, rode in the lead as guides. Garis remained with Brand and me, chatting cheerfully on inconsequential subjects as we rode, ignoring the fact that neither Brand nor I had much to say. Gradually Madrinya dropped out of sight behind us.

Just before nightfall we rode down into another valley and made camp not far from the edge of a lake. There were no signs of habitation, no farms, no tracks – nothing to indicate anyone had ever been that way before. On the valley slopes, thick forest alternated with scrubby meadow; along the lake edge, marsh-willows jostled reed beds for access to the water. By the time Garis, Brand and I rode in past the outermost guards, hobbled shleths were spreading out along the shore-line to drink and feed, fires had been lit and meals cooked, Men were collecting dried reeds to use as bedding. Four-winged fisherbirds trailing long legs wheeled over the water in their evening gathering flights, while tiny marsh monkeys, scampering along the reed tops, chattered warning.

Before dismounting, I paused a moment to watch Temellin. He was cutting reeds with his sword, his bare back glistening with sweat, the swinging movement of his arm fluid and strong. Desire tingled my skin unasked, and I clamped down on my straying thoughts. When a small girl toddled past on her way to the water, Temellin dropped his sword and scooped the child up; she was far too young to be heading for a lake by herself. As I swung down from my mount, his laugh rang out over the camp.

It was not until I was sitting by the fire eating the hot coal-baked bread stuffed with desert beans that I saw him again.

He was making his way across the camp, stopping first at one fire, then another. His voice reached me in snatches: 'Don't worry, it's only a small cut . . . No, you're not slowing us down . . . He's a real handful, isn't he? But lots of fun . . . Take care of that sprain of yours, Vessa . . .'

He had a cheerful word for everyone and people responded accordingly, their faces breaking into smiles as he approached, their eyes following him warmly as he left. I felt a pang of envy. He had something I did not: the ability to inspire trust and respect in the people he helped to lead. All I had ever done was make people fear me. In that, I was more like Korden. Stern-faced and more taciturn, he also moved among the assembled crowd. They listened carefully when he spoke, nodding their acquiescence, their acceptance of his leadership – but their eyes didn't shine.

When Temellin reached us he lifted a hand to Garis and Brand, then touched my shoulder in greeting, unstrapped his sword and sat down. Someone produced some food for him and he accepted gratefully.

'Everything all right?' he asked Garis, but didn't wait for an answer. 'Brand, you must be the only person here who is still wearing a slave collar; let's get rid of that, shall we?' He unsheathed his weapon, touched it to the collar and in a brief flash of light the bronze circlet dropped away just as mine had.

Brand picked up the pieces, held them in his hands for a moment, his knuckles white, then flung them into the heart of the fire. 'Thank you,' he said quietly. 'A little earlier than I anticipated, but why the turd not?' He looked up and grinned at us all. 'Goddess, that feels good. Can I assume I am going to be allowed to keep my head on my shoulders?'

'If Derya trusts you,' Temellin said between mouthfuls of bread and beans.

'I do. And I have known Brand since he was twelve.'

'Then that is good enough for me.' Temellin looked at me. 'Derya, I'm sorry I've had to neglect you; there has been much to do.'

I smiled at him, surprised by the amount of pleasure I took in knowing he felt there was a need to apologise. 'That's all right,' I said. 'But I do have a great many questions.'

He stood, brushing the last of the crumbs from his trousers. 'Come for a walk with me.' I jumped up with alacrity and he handed me my travelling cloak. 'Take this; it's always cold out here at night.'

We walked away from the campfires down towards the water's edge. In the darkness the lake was a purple sheet, the only noise the occasional burp of frogs. 'It's beautiful, isn't it?' he asked. 'These vales, they are all part of what we are. We don't believe in Tyranian gods. We believe that every living thing has a life-force we call the essensa, a sort of personal spirit, or person-ality. Therefore we must treat every living thing with respect.'

I almost snorted. 'You cut the reeds. You kill to eat. Is that respectful?'

He laughed. 'Maybe not. We are also very pragmatic in our faith. But it's a pleasing belief anyway, because it stops us from waste, or taking life unnecessarily. It's better than having a god of war in the pantheon, surely! And to be respectful to a living being seems better than kissing the feet of a marble statue and praying for selfish desires to be granted, doesn't it?' It crossed my mind that this man had been well schooled, and back in Tyr he would have made a fine orator.

'I suppose so. I've never been much of a one for worship-ping Melete. Or any other deity.'

Now that we were away from the light of the fires, he put his arm around my shoulders. 'It seems a year since yesterday,' he said. He touched his left palm to mine and I was awash with knowledge of his desire for me.

'Tem—' I tried to remain detached. 'Is it always like it was yesterday?'

'Between those of the Magor? Yes, it can be. But yesterday, yesterday was – I've never felt quite that way.' He ran a hand through his hair. 'I've never *behaved* quite like that before. I've never met anyone who had such an immediate physical effect on me.'

Neither had I. I was silent, aware of his bemused embarrassment seeping into the air around me.

'Derya,' he said finally. 'I think we were both taken by surprise. The Magor are drawn – physically drawn – to one another through the power of their cabochons. Usually we keep . . . well, we keep an almost unconscious rein on that kind of desire. But you knew nothing of that, and I responded to what I felt from you without thought. Next time, if there is a next time, I want it to be a conscious decision on your part, not just a gut reaction to a stimulus. Besides, there are some things you should know before you tie yourself to me, to any one of us, with those kind of ties.'

'What sort of things?'

The hesitation before he spoke was telling. 'I am a Magori. After the invasion, there were only ten of the Magoroth left – all children, of whom Korden was the oldest. It is imperative more such are born, but the only way we can be sure that will happen is for a Magoria to have children by a Magori. In any combination of ranks, the children are more likely to be of the lesser rank. But we need the golds, the Magoroth. We need them desperately, Derya, because they are the ones who have the real power.'

'And you think I am not a Magoria? How can you know that?'

'I don't think it's possible. There weren't all that many Magoroth children even at the time of the invasion. We know who they were, and how they died, if they did indeed die. As for those who lived, well, we know where they are, too.'

I was flooded with disappointment; it would have been advantageous to have as much power as they did. Then I woke up to the significance of what he'd said, and almost laughed. The man was worried about me forming an attachment to him. Me – a Compeer of the Brotherhood! The idea of losing my heart to him, to any of them, was ludicrous. I kept a straight face. 'So what you are saying is that our, um, union has no future. That sooner or later you will choose a life-mate from the Magorias.' As if I cared.

His lips twisted. 'There's not all that much *choice.* There's only one unmarried Magoria who's more than twenty years old.' He bent to pick up a stone and then flipped it away across the water, where it bounced several times before disappearing into the darkness. 'We – those of the Ten – we lead these people, Derya. One day we will lead this country. None of us get to have that many choices.' He turned towards me, his face shadowed and emotions concealed.

In spite of my amusement, I felt an unexpected lurch of regret at the loss of what might have been. What I had felt in his arms had been physically wondrous, and I was sorry I might never know it again. Still, I hardly knew this man, certainly wasn't contemplating a lifetime commitment, was even intending to betray all he held dear: so why did what he was telling me matter? 'Never mind. I can live for the present and face the future when it comes.' I looked down at my palm. 'We're not *born* with these things implanted, are we? You said something about mine having been in my palm since just after I was born.' *Tell me I am not a god, or an immortal. Tell me this is something done to me, by ordinary men.*

'Yes. Our powers are usually latent or hard to access; it is the implanting of the cabochon, the sooner the better, that allows the powers to reach their potential. Children are later trained to use those powers. I'm not going to tell you right now about how the cabochons are implanted, or how the colour of the cabochon is decided upon. The cabochons are what make the Magor what we are; without them, we would be mere shadows of what is possible.'

'At death, what happens to the cabochon?'

'It falls to powder. It can never be used again. And if it is removed while you live, your death follows. If it is accidentally cracked, then your powers leak away.'

I changed the subject. 'Korden doesn't like me. But you said he would be delighted to see me—'

He was puzzled. 'No, I don't remember saying that. Whatever gave you that idea?'

'You said the Mirager would—'

'The – oh!' He laughed. 'Korden is not the Mirager, Derya.'

'He's not? Then who is?' But I knew already. 'Oh, sweet Melete – *you*? You're the—?' The one they couldn't torture, the one they couldn't burn. He was the man I was sent to capture. I was so shocked at my error, my knees buckled and he had to put out a hand to hold me. How could I have made such an elementary mistake? *Stupidity like that could cost me my life.* I felt a numbing shame. Where in all the mists had I laid my commonsense? Between my legs, for me to have been so easily overwhelmed by my physical response to a handsome man?

'Derya, what's wrong? Does it matter that much?'

'I – No, I don't suppose so.' It was hard to speak, to put the coherent deception together without uttering a lie. 'It's – just that – yesterday I was just me. And now I find I've lain in a – a ruler's arms—' I gave a weak laugh. 'I'm such a fool.' You could say that again.

He took me in his arms once more and held me, brushing

my hair with kisses, crooning to me as though I were a child. I *felt* like a child. Where was the compeer of the Brotherhood now? Where was my strength, my objectivity, my wits? Not so long ago, I had been one of the most powerful women in the Exaltarchy, now I was just a stupid female so caught up in the net cast by an attractive man that I was no longer in command of my senses.

'Was it you they tried to burn in Sandmurram?' I asked finally. *Is it possible?*

He nodded briefly, dismissing the incident as unimportant. 'Don't blame Korden for his mistrust of you,' he said. 'Or Pinar, either. They are both old enough to remember the invasion, the parents they lost, the world that was destroyed. Korden is the oldest of the Magoroth, another nephew of the last Mirager, just as I am, yet I was the heir, not him, simply because my father was older than his. He finds that hard to remember sometimes. He thinks he could do a better job than me, you see. It is a situation that has made him more than my friend: he is my conscience. He feels it is his duty to keep me from making mistakes. And it is hard for him – for Pinar too – to trust you because they look at you and see Tyrans.'

I nodded. 'I think – I think I'll go back to the fire. I need to think things over.'

'Good idea. I, um, wasn't thinking of coming to you tonight, Derya. There are, er, complications.'

'You mean Pinar, of course.' The only unattached Magoria over twenty; I knew it with certainty. I'd seen the way she looked at him.

'We are not lovers, not yet, and for the time being we go our own ways, but she will be Miragerin-consort one day, and I would not insult her by lying in the arms of a lover so publicly. Perhaps elsewhere, if you accept or want a – a – temporary relationship. If that reeks of hypocrisy, well, I'm not in a position to be honest. I'm the Mirager. I'm sorry if that hurts you, but it is the way things are.'

It should have been amusing. Here was someone apologising for not taking me to bed, apologising because he was afraid he was about to hurt my feelings. How Rathrox Ligatan would have laughed. He trained his compeers to have no feelings, to use their bodies without compunction to further the interest of the task in hand. But I was more intrigued than amused. I thought, *How he hates himself for this!* Temellin was trapped in an impossible situation, and no matter which way he twisted he would not like what he did.

I shrugged my indifference. 'Who am I to object? I have no claims on you. You did not speak to me of permanence. I have known you for a little over a day. I found something special in your arms. I would like to find it again. I can wait.' They were the words of a compeer intending to use this man and wrench out the heart of the Kardi insurgents and their terrorism – but there was truth in them too. I wanted to feel his arms about me again; I wanted to know the secret of the way I had felt when I had lain in his arms. I had found something then that most people never know, and it was hard to turn my back on it deliberately.

He touched my face with gentle fingers. 'Don't talk to Brand about the cabochons or such matters. It is better he does not know too much of what we are.' He bent to kiss me, but the brush of his lips meant a return of the memory of what his lovemaking had wrought the day before. It was far too easy to be seduced by that recollection. I felt like a moth, blinded by the allure of the torch, risking the scorch of its heat. I strove to tear myself free of the attraction.

'Goodnight, Temellin,' I said, hoping I sounded coolly collected.

I walked away from him back towards the campfires, pulling

my cloak tight about me, feeling I'd just been spat out of a whirlwind. For the first time, my private life and my mission on behalf of the Brotherhood were at war and I didn't know what I was going to do. I was disgusted with myself, with my lack of control over my emotions. Damn them all to Acheron – how could I feel this way?

I battled to start thinking sensibly again, and when I did, my heart skidded somewhere down to stomach level. If Temellin was the Mirager, then his behaviour that day, and the day before, was strange. What else had been going on un-noticed by me because I was too busy thinking with my senses instead of my head? If I understood the situation correctly, Temellin was the leader of an insurgency. The man who would be ruler of the country, if they had their way.

But rulers did not normally go looking for lost property in person, not even precious property. They sent other people to do it for them. Nor did they risk their lives seeking out slave girls who could have been the bait in a rat trap. A ruler was too precious to risk.

And yet he was the Mirager; he hadn't been lying about that. So what was going on? What had I missed? Why had he risked himself to seek me out?

I was so engrossed in my private maelstrom I took no notice of the cloaked figure standing between me and the fires, until an arm shot out and clutched at me as I went to pass by. Startled out of my reverie I looked up. It was Pinar. 'Where's Temellin?' she asked harshly.

I gave a vague wave of my hand, knowing she could have sensed his whereabouts if she had really wanted to know. 'He went back that way.' I tried to move on, but Pinar's hand, resting now in between my breasts, stopped me.

'I know you for what you are,' she said. 'I can see what they are all blind to. You mean to betray us.'

I did not deign to answer. I attempted to brush past, but the hand stayed me. I was suddenly breathless, as if I had been running. 'Let me be, Pinar. You've no cause for jealousy tonight,' I said. But I could not pass. I felt her cabochon push against my heart, and the answering arrhythmia of the beat. I staggered and tried to push her away, but my arms felt weak. I wanted to scream, but no sound would come.

'I can't let you kill us all,' she said, her voice rough with dislike. 'You're just a Tyranian brute in Kardi disguise. You sold your birthright. It's better you die here, now, at my hand. I don't care what they all say; I *know* I'm right—'

I could not believe what was happening. I was *dying*. I knew half a dozen ways to kill using my bare hands – and I was helpless. I had just seconds before my heart stopped its beating. Goddess, *I couldn't end like this*, dead in this desert world, aged not yet thirty. Not *me*. My left hand crept upwards to Pinar's breast, each inch closer a desperate act of will and pain with no chance of ultimate success. This was power I knew nothing about. Magor magic. I was untrained, of a lesser rank—

I tried to send out my terror to alert the Magor, but I appeared to be cocooned within a barrier of her making. And she let nothing slip by. I tried to fight, but I knew nothing of the weapons – not hers, or mine.

I fell to my knees, incapable of resistance, so weak I couldn't even whisper a protest to the woman who was murdering me. My left hand was no longer part of me. It moved on without my knowledge; it had a feeble life of its own and I was aware of it with a curious detachment. I saw it travel across the edge of my vision, reaching out to touch her just as she was touching me. The fingers uncurled and the cabochon on the palm rested against Pinar's breastbone.

And she smiled, not even bothering to brush it away. 'What

can you do?' she whispered, her triumph foul in my senses. 'I am a trained Magoria.'

In the seconds before death I remembered my mother, my real mother, bathed in gold and blood, giving the battle cry of the Magor. Words I must have understood then, and remembered now. My lips formed the shape of that heartfelt cry: *Fah-Ke-Cabochon-rez!* Hail the power of the cabochon!

I fell face down in the sand, blood rushing through me to obey the renewed vigour of my heart. I lay there, gathering strength to me as if it were a tangible thing in the air, to be seized on and imbibed. Then warm strong hands were holding me, lifting me, hugging me to a muscled chest.

'Temellin?'

'*Brand*, damn you! Are you all right?'

'She wanted to kill me. She tried – what happened?'

'You flung her away from you.'

'I did? Where is she?'

'She picked herself up and ran. She saw me coming, I think. She was crying. Are you sure you're all right?'

I stood back from him. 'Yes, I think so.' *Crying? Pinar?* 'Thanks—' I took a deep breath. 'You followed me,' I accused, anything not to think about what had just happened.

He shook his head. 'Don't flatter yourself. I came out for a leak. And then I saw her, and wondered what she was up to. I saw you both, but I thought you were just talking. It was too dark – Goddessdamn, I almost let her kill you thinking you were having a conversation!'

'Never mind. I'm all right. Let's go back to the fire.' I leant against him, still weak. As we walked, I said, 'Brand, Temellin is the Mirager.'

'Yes, I know.'

'You *knew*?'

'Yes, of course. That was obvious.' He turned his face to

look at me in surprise. 'Li— Derya, you didn't *know*?'

I was silent, shamed by his surprise.

'You seem to have been uncharacteristically dense. And I'm surprised you let Pinar get within pissing distance of you, too. Couldn't you see the way she has been looking at you? She loathes everything you stand for and, unlike the rest of these gullible folk, she has a pretty good idea just what it is you represent. What worm has addled your wits?'

I did not answer. He was right to ask the question, though.

That night as I lay on my pallet of reeds, I tried to persuade myself that all I felt for Temellin was lust: easily satisfied, easily forgotten once satisfied – and knew I was fooling myself. When I looked at Temellin, I lusted – but I also saw, for the first time in my life, a man I recognised as being the mirror of myself. Temellin responded to power and responsibility and excitement the same way I did: he was stimulated. We fed on those things, the way most folk thrived on security and routine. Challenged, we came alive . . . We were two of a kind.

And that was, at best, intriguing, appealing, unsettling; at worst, worrying. A mirror image had the power to shatter a reflection.

Such a man had the means to bring me down.

CHAPTER TWELVE

The next day, I came face to face with Pinar as the morning meal was being doled out from the pots at the fire. She gazed at me, emotions safely corralled behind her eyes. Temellin and Garis and Korden were all within hearing, so she was scrupulously polite. 'Good morning, Derya,' she said. 'How are you feeling this morning? You looked as if you had some indigestion last night.'

'Indeed I did.' I held out my plate for my share of porridge. 'Must have come across something . . . rotten.'

'You should be more careful.'

'Oh, I will. In future.'

'Tell me, Derya, what sort of slave were you?'

I had been about to turn away, but her words halted me. All instincts alert, I wished I could feel through the barriers she erected. 'A reluctant one. Why?'

'Well, there are different kinds of slaves, are there not? Whores for the military brothels, for example. Pallet slaves for officers, that kind of thing. I couldn't help but notice your hair has been well cut, your hands are not roughened with hard work. So I wondered if you were the Legata Ligea's love-slave.'

Temellin's voice cut across her questioning like a sword slash. 'Pinar, that's enough. It's none of our business.'

She turned to him. 'You are too trusting, Temel. If she was a love-slave, then perhaps it is foolish to trust her at all. Lovers can have loyalties to one another, rather than to the land of their birth.'

'That's true,' Korden agreed. 'Anyway, I'd like to know why she has said so little about this Ligea woman. I'd have thought Derya would have told us all sorts of things by now, without prompting. A Legata of the Brotherhood is surely a danger to us. We need to know what sort of person she is.'

'Derya was no pallet slave,' Brand said. He sounded offhand, but they must have all felt his honesty. He continued, 'The Legata's taste is for handsome males. Her present lover is one of the Stalwarts, an officer.' He smiled at me. 'And believe me, I wouldn't be hankering after Derya here if she preferred women on her pallet.'

Several people laughed at that, but I'd also felt the flare of suspicion from others like a slap in the face. I glared at Brand as I sat down by the fire to eat. Pinar and Temellin remained standing and the look they exchanged was full of meaning, although only they knew what. 'Let it rest, Pinar,' he said. 'Please.'

She went to get her breakfast, but I knew nothing had been laid to rest. Pinar hated me and if at any time she thought she might be able to get away with it, she would try to kill me. The irony was that she was right. I was bent on betrayal and she was the only one with the sense to see it. Korden's naturally suspicious character made him wary and distrustful, but he wasn't sure in the way Pinar was. She *knew*, although I suspected jealousy was her foundation, not evidence. Poor Pinar. I could almost have felt sorry for her. At least I would never have my thinking clouded by that kind of love and jealousy. This, I thought, is a battle I can win in spite of my Magor weakness.

Brand, curious, sat beside me and asked in a whisper if I were going to let Pinar get away with the attempt on my life. 'That would be most unlike you, Li— er, Derya,' he remarked.

'If I try to deal with her myself, who's to say I would win? I almost died last night,' I said. 'And if I did do away with her, who would get the blame for her death or disappearance?'

'Why must you always think in such extreme terms? You could just tell everyone what happened.'

That was true, and they'd have to believe me, too. But I wouldn't win any friends among the Magor by unmasking the murderous intent of one of their revered and cherished Ten. Better to let her make a fool of herself, all on her own. I was alerted now, and perhaps I could use her weaknesses to further my own ends. I said to Brand, 'I will deal with her in my own time. The woman tried to kill me. *No one* gets away with that.'

That morning Temellin asked me to ride alongside him. 'I want to talk to you while we ride,' he said. 'Korden is right. You should be able to tell us more about this Legata. How important is she to us? We have had little experience with the Brotherhood here, except when they tortured ordinary people for information about the Magor. But that was years ago. I think they finally realised it never got them anywhere because we never tell the non-Magor anything about our movements or where we hide. The freed slaves we take to the Mirage – they never return, you know. It is our price for their freedom. Anyway, after the Brotherhood tired of their fruitless interrogations of the non-Magor, we didn't see too much of them for years. Until a couple of weeks back. That's when we heard the Tyranians were expecting a high-ranking compeer to arrive in Sandmurram from Tyr. That worried us. We sent someone to investigate, but they weren't able to find out much.'

I felt the familiar surge of intoxication. That piquant thrill that comes with playing a game of deception, pitting my wits against a worthy opponent. Even more delicious this time because he almost certainly had no idea there *was* a game . . . 'That would have been Legata Ligea,' I said. 'As far as I know there is no one else from the Brotherhood in Kardiastan at the moment. She has been complaining about that – about being on her own. Gossip in the slave quarters back in Tyr said her main value to the Brotherhood is her skill at interrogation.'

He may not have known much about the working of the Exaltarchy in Tyr, but he had sense, this man. Sense enough to see the weaknesses in a story. He continued, 'They say she is the daughter of a general. General Gayed the Baby Butcher. How did the daughter of a general get to be an agent of the Brotherhood? She is highborn! Her father was an honoured legionnaire commander, friend to the Exaltarch.'

Baby Butcher? I bristled, but kept a tight hold on my emotions. 'Well, people don't explain things like that to a slave, you know. But rumour in the household said Gayed sent her to the Brotherhood because he didn't have a son to give to the legionnaires. It was an odd thing to do, but the General was a proud man who put his patriotism first, always. He was – well, honourable would be the best word to describe him, I suppose. He believed he had a duty as a citizen of Tyr.'

He stared at me, leaking strong irritation. At a guess, he didn't like the word 'honourable', but I hadn't been about to let the calumny of 'Baby Butcher' pass unremarked. He took a deep breath and returned to the original question. 'Tell me more about Ligea. What is she like?'

My shleth reached out with one of its feeding arms and began to comb the wool of Temellin's mount, looking for blood-sucking lice, I supposed. I said, 'She's not yet thirty. She's tough. Hard even, but fair. She doesn't suffer fools gladly. She would never mistreat a slave, but people are afraid of her. She has a reputation. They say if you cross her, then you're doomed.' All true enough.

'Are you afraid of her?'

'She's never given me cause.' My shleth edged closer to his, and I had to pull it away. The two beasts were making interested noises at one another, and I was irritated. I wanted to focus on our conversation, not be diverted by the necessity of keeping overly amorous mounts separated.

He said, 'You've given her cause enough to be angry now.'

I gave a smile. 'But I am safe, aren't I? I'm sure you don't think she will find her way to the Mirage, do you?'

'No likelihood at all. Why is she here, in Kardiastan?'

'As I understand it, she is supposed to find you. They heard the rumours you survived being burnt at the stake. Her mandate is to find the Mirager and – eliminate him as a danger to the Exaltarchy.'

'Why send her, and not someone else?'

'Elysium's bliss! Is it likely a slave would know that?'

He grinned at me. 'Silly question. Sorry. I suppose I should be surprised you know as much as you do.'

'Ah, slave quarters are the best place to hear gossip, believe me. It's amazing how much does travel between households, and how accurate it is.'

He looked round and waved to Brand, beckoning him over. 'Brand,' he said as the Altani drew up at his side, 'how well do you know the Legata?'

Brand shrugged. 'How well does a slave ever get to know their master? I was bought for her when I was about twelve and she was ten. I was supposed to guard her, as well as be at her beck and call. She was a little brat, full of herself then. Rude, abrasive, spoiled, demanding. Used to get into one scrape after another, most of which I got blamed for. She improved with age.'

'How so?'

'Learned to be a shade more considerate. Learned that co-operation gains you more than belligerence. She's intelligent. Bit of a slow learner with respect to social relationships, but she gets there in the end. Gullible sometimes, though.'

I glared at him when Temellin wasn't looking. My mount, annoyed by the presence of Brand's beast, acted as if he was equally peeved.

'Really?' Temellin asked, disbelieving.

'She was used by her father to further his own grasping ends, but she could never see it. She worshipped the ground he walked on. Still does, for all that the bastard is dead.'

I gritted my teeth and slapped at the feeding arm of my mount.

'So he didn't push her into the Brotherhood out of the kindness of his heart, to give her a distinguished career?' Temellin asked.

Brand snorted.

'What *did* he want, then?'

'I'm not sure. Some said in the slave quarters that he did it because his wife, Salacia, didn't want her around,' Brand replied. 'That could have been true too, because Salacia didn't care a pebble for Ligea. But Gayed didn't care a rat's arse for her, either.'

'Brand exaggerates,' I said. 'He just didn't like the General.'

Brand nodded. 'That last is right. The man was cruel to the point of sadism. A bastard who was indifferent to the suffering of his underlings, even his own soldiers. He was vindictive and unscrupulous.'

It was just as well my mount took that moment to nip at Temellin's. It gave me an excuse to swear and drop back behind the two of them. I could have wrung Brand's neck. How *dare* he speak of my father that way?

*   *   *

The next two days were spent travelling through country much like that between Sandmurram and Madrinya: arid plains and plateaux, with lush shallow valleys hunkering low in between. We kept away from settlements; we saw no Tyranians, although I knew even this back country was regularly patrolled by legionnaires.

When I had an opportunity, I told Brand exactly what I thought of him. He retaliated with some remarks about purblind females, self-delusion and being ruled by the emotions. Which was – ironically – almost the same spiel Gayed had regularly dealt out to me when I was growing up. I called Brand a myopic crank, so blinded by the hatred of a system that he couldn't see the virtues of an upright man. After that, we mostly avoided each other.

Gradually the large group split up, Temellin evidently deeming it safer. Smaller groups were more manageable and left fewer signs behind in passing. It was with relief that I noticed Pinar disappear on the second day accompanied by a batch of ten or so Kardis.

I spent a lot of time watching Temellin for signs that would tell me this was a man who was more than just a man, that he was a being who could resist torture and his torturers, who could rise above his degradation to laugh in the face of a woman come to his death cell to use him, who could survive a conflagration lit to consume him. I watched, but I saw none of it.

I saw only a man with a great deal of energy, who always seemed to be on the move, cajoling, encouraging, urging those under his care. I envied the easy camaraderie he had both with the ordinary Kardis and with the Magor, especially when I noted he also had their respect. If he gave an order, it was obeyed instantly by the same people who might tease him around the campfire at night, or insult him with cheeky banter in their more relaxed moments.

Wherever the Mirager was, there was laughter, often his own. He laughed a lot; not with the cynicism that marked Brand's amusement, but with full-hearted humour of the kind that came from a love of life, a love of mankind. And in the back of my mind, I wondered about that laughter: how could he who must have seen so much that hurt him, still regard the world with such childlike joy?

'Is he always so good-humoured?' I asked Garis once as we rode side by side.

'Temellin? Most of the time, yes. That's the kind of fellow he is.' He looked across at the Mirager with an expression that was almost tender. 'But he's got a temper, too. Cabochon help you if he ever loses it. His tongue could sizzle a carcass over cold ashes, and he's not beyond lashing out physically, either, when he's really riled. Takes a lot to get him that mad, though,' he added. 'And his anger always has an understandable cause.'

'You look a lot like him. Are you related?'

'Only distantly. My parents were not Magoroth. I'm one of those odd cases where a higher rank emerges from marriage between lower; it happens occasionally. But the others – they are all related. Each rank tends to marry people of their own rank, you see, because no one likes to dilute the Magor blood they have, especially not now. Korden and Temellin and Pinar are all first cousins. Jessah and Jahan are brother and sister, Ungar is Korden's wife's cousi—'

'But Jessah and Jahan are married, surely!' I protested.

He nodded, unconcerned. 'Yes. That's common enough among the Magor. It makes for strong children, both in body and Magor abilities.'

I was shocked. Brothers *married* sisters? 'That's disgusting. It makes for idiots, too,' I said finally, my distaste as strong as bile on the tongue. In Tyranian mythology, our nation had been brought close to ruin by the incestuous love of Cestuous and Caprice, Tyr's early founders. Although repeatedly warned by the gods, they had been defiant, continuing their relationship until the gods had punished them – and Tyr too, for condoning their behaviour. Their children were born crippled and warped. They'd grown up to rule the fledgling nation, but their lives of corruption, heedless dissipation and final madness had brought the city to financial and military ruin. Plague and famine had followed. It had taken Tyrans generations to prosper after that.

'Idiots?' Garis smiled. 'Among common folk perhaps, but not with us. In fact, it is encouraged as a source of strength.'

'It's – unnatural. Horrible!' Some of my revulsion must have communicated itself to my mount because it shied nervously and flapped its feeding arms. It took me a moment to bring it under control again.

'Why unnatural?' Garis asked. 'You are judging Kardis by Tyranian laws, but such rules are meaningless to us. To be able to reinforce sibling love with sexual love is considered a blessing among the Magor.'

I was silent, unable to find the words to convince him how wrong he was.

'Derya, Temellin said I could explain to you anything to do with our customs or history, as long as I don't tell you about how Magor powers work for us. You tell me what you don't know, and I'll try to explain so you can understand us better.'

Wary, I thought: *Even Temellin has his reservations . . . there are some things he doesn't want me to know yet. Be careful, Ligea. The Mirager is no fool.* Aloud I said, 'Anything you tell me will be new. Perhaps – tell me why Temellin is the Mirager. What makes a Mirager?'

'His birth. The eldest child of the Mirager becomes the next Mirager or Miragerin when the Mirager dies. If there is no child, then it goes to the next in line, male or female. Temellin has been Mirager since he was a child, when the last Mirager, his uncle Solad, died during the Tyranian invasion. Naturally, a new Mirager has to be of the Magoroth.'

'What happened to Temellin's parents?'

'The same thing that happened to all Magoroth adults during the invasion. They were killed. By a treachery we don't really understand. Did you know the Tyranians like to call those times the "Kardi Uprising"? As if their invasion of our soil was legitimate, and our defence of it was illegal!'

'What happened?'

'Well, it started with several different invasions. The first was turned back at the Rift. It was followed by various skirmishes over the next couple of years or so, one of which killed the heir to the Mirager – Solad's only child. A cousin to both Temellin and Korden. But otherwise none of these small battles seemed particularly dangerous.' He frowned, angry emotion ripping through his barriers in a cresting wave, even as his ire broke through in his words. 'They were so stupid, our forebears, Derya! They were so sure of their powers that they failed to plan, failed to keep a proper watch on the coast, failed to train the ordinary Kardis as support troops and so on. Mirage be thanked, Temel has ten times the sense of his uncle, Mirager-solad. And he has learned by watching the legionnaires.

'Anyway, one night, at the height of the Shimmer Festival – that was our major yearly celebration in those days – someone led a small band of the enemy into the heart of the Pavilions in Madrinya. This was about, oh, twenty-five, twenty-six years ago now. The Magoroth were seated in the main hall for the Shimmer Feast, all of the Magoroth gathered from all over Kardiastan. Tyranian archers shot them down from the gallery. Every wearer of the gold cabochon over the age of ten was killed. Archers have a greater range than cabochon magic, you see.'

Damn it, I thought, *Rathrox must have known this! Why in all Acheron's layers of hell didn't he tell me?*

But no matter how hard I tried to think of a rational reason, none came to mind. Rathrox had always been secretive, but to send an agent out into the field with inadequate knowledge was foolhardy, and Rathrox was no fool. He'd done it deliberately . . . why? So that I'd fail? Be caught? Killed? Or did he think I'd succeed anyway, and the reason he hadn't told me had something to do with my past history?

Garis hadn't noticed my abstraction, and was still telling the story of the Shimmer Festival feast. 'And none of the Magor were armed with weapons: it was customary not to bring weapons into the feasting hall. With the Magoroth dead, including the Mirager, Solad that is, the Exaltarchy was able to claim the land as theirs.'

'And the younger Magoroth children?'

He counted them off on his fingers. 'Pinar, Temellin, Korden, Miasa, Jessah, Jahan, Selwith, Berrin, Markess and Gretha. Ten of them. They were all somewhere between three and ten years old. They had been sent to the Mirage just before the Festival – on, well, training I suppose you could call it. They went with their Theuros and Illusos teachers. It's strange they were away at the time of the Festival, and in retrospect no one can understand why Mirager-solad sent them. Some people think he must have had a premonition. Anyway, it saved their lives. And mine too, perhaps, because I am the son of two of those teachers, although I was born much later.

'Those wearers of the gold under three years old didn't escape the massacres. They weren't old enough to be sent away, so they were all in the palace for the festivities. They were killed in the nurseries by the legionnaires. They slaughtered all the babies,

Derya. Every one.' His rage whirled around him, unrestrained. 'Someone betrayed those who attended the Festival. We have never found out who. It has always seemed unbelievable, because the betrayer must have been one of the Magoroth. Only a Magoroth could have raised a ward around the feasting hall strong enough to hide the approach of legionnaires, only a Magoroth could have removed it to allow them entry.' He shook his head in a mix of distress and rage. 'I don't suppose we'll ever find out who now. By the time the legionnaires had finished, all the Magoroth in the Pavilions were dead.'

'What's a ward?' I asked.

'A kind of magical barrier. An invisible wall that can stop people, or even Magoroth power, from passing through.'

He stopped, obviously wondering if he'd said too much, so I changed the subject.

'Did any of the lower-ranking Magor – the Illusos and the Theuros – did they escape?'

'Oh, yes. Most of them. Most weren't at the feast. But they don't have Magoroth powers. They tried to resist Tyrans, but they weren't powerful enough. Sporadic fighting occurred for years, but once the tradeways were built and the legions could ride from one end of the land to the other in a matter of days, there was little hope. Worse still, until Temellin grew up a bit, no newborn Magor children received their cabochons. Oh. Um, I guess I can't explain about that just now, though.

'Gradually the lower-ranking Magor gave up the fight and came to the Mirage for safety and to offer their services to teach the Magoroth all they knew. We have been trying to strengthen ourselves ever since, to make our powers even greater than those of our parents, until the time when we are strong enough to sweep the legions into the sea. For some time there have been those who have thought we have sufficient power, but Temellin still won't allow a full-scale insurgency.

He says we have to ensure the next generation first, in case we are killed.'

'But it is beginning, isn't it, your rebellion?' I asked. 'Your aim is first to disrupt Tyranian society in Kardiastan. To make Tyranians uncertain, nervous.'

'Exactly. Temellin says it is important to free slaves for just that reason.'

Not to mention the murder of legionnaire officers, the terrorising of those who used the trade routes, the disappearance of caravans.

He continued, 'It brings the common folk to our side. After all, there is a whole generation of Kardis who have grown up having no first-hand knowledge of the people of the Magor. They had a right to feel abandoned by us. We have to dispel that feeling. Nothing Temellin does is without reason,' he added, and there was no mistaking his pride in his Mirager.

'But he hasn't done much towards ensuring the next Magoroth generation if he himself hasn't married,' I replied. 'Or has he been begetting bastards along the way?'

He laughed. 'Perhaps. But not Magoroth ones. Although, to be honest, I don't think that's likely, either. Temellin takes his duties as Mirager too seriously to flaunt himself like that. Anyway, he was married at eighteen, like many of us. His wife was Miasa, one of the original Ten. She was, um, barren for many years. Then, when she did conceive, she had a difficult time. She died, with the baby unborn, just last year. It was an awful time for Temellin, but now it seems he will marry Pinar once the mourning period is up.' Garis the romantic sighed, his eyes troubled. 'He doesn't have all that much choice. As Mirager, he should marry a Magoria and Pinar is the only one of age who is not spoken for. I don't think he likes her that much, although she is his cousin. It is sad.'

'And the others all have children?'

'Oh yes. Korden and Gretha have ten! And another on the way.'

'All Magoroth.'

'Of course. And we have been lucky, too, in the number of such children born to Theuras and Illusas. Altogether there are forty-eight Magoroth children in the Mirage. And many more of the lower ranks. So now Temellin feels the time has come to move against the Tyranian presence in our land.' His tawny eyes danced at the prospect. 'Temellin says the break-up of the whole Exaltarchy will start here, in Kardiastan.'

Goddess, the man had the gall of a gnat biting a gorclak! He didn't really think it was possible to bring about the down-fall of the greatest empire ever conceived, did he? The Exaltarchy stretched over half the known world . . . I decided to keep that thought to myself, and changed the subject. 'What is the Mirage like, Garis?'

He looked uncomfortable. 'Temellin says I shouldn't tell you that.'

I hid a sigh. I thought perhaps I was going to become quite tired of hearing Garis say, *Temellin says* . . .

He went on, 'He'll have time for you soon. The last of the other groups leaves us today. Then there will just be you and me and him and Brand. I think he wants to know you better before you see the secrets of the Shiver Barrens and the Mirage. We risk much to show you, if you are a traitor. Anyway, you'll see for yourself soon.'

I gave an involuntary look at Temellin where he sat on his shleth at the head of a group of Kardi ex-slaves. He was smiling and I felt my throat tighten just at the thought of him turning that smile on me. I forced my attention back to Garis, who was asking, 'But won't you tell me a little about Tyr? Does water really travel from the mountains along bridges? Do they really have public games where everyone is naked? Is it true the Exaltarch has orgies every night and has an insatiable appetite for slave women?'

'Well, I know he has an appetite for women, yes,' I said gravely, answering the last. 'And wine too. But he made the Exaltarchy what it is; he extended it from a few tributary neighbours to all the nations bordering the Sea of Iss. He couldn't have done that if he spent his time indulging in drunken orgies. The Exaltarch is an ex-soldier and he has a soldier's discipline.'

He gave me a puzzled glance. 'You sound almost admiring.'

'I am. Only a fool would not respect what the Exaltarch has achieved. *Approving* of it is another matter.'

'She's right, Garis,' a voice behind me said. I turned in the saddle to see Korden had ridden up. 'But what we have to decide,' he continued, addressing me, 'is whether you are one of those who approves, as well as admires.'

'Slaves do not usually approve of those who run the system that makes them slaves in the first place.'

'One would think it illogical, wouldn't one?' Korden was nothing if not urbane. 'And yet I have seen it happen with slaves who were raised in slavery. They know no other life. They are brought up to believe it is a just state of affairs. They may even love those who enslave them, giving up their lives for their owners if the situation arises.' He considered me thoughtfully. 'Sometimes people are irrational beings. I do not *distrust* you exactly, Derya, but you will have to prove your loyalty before I give you my trust. I do not have Temellin's faith in the blood running in your veins. Temellin is our Mirager, but he is not an absolute monarch. He rules by covenant and *must* listen to others of his kind. Be warned: there will be those who watch you and who will turn the power of the Magor on you if you prove faithless.' With that, he switched his attention to Garis. 'I came to say goodbye. This is where I leave with my group; I will see you on the other side of the Barrens.' He stretched forth his left hand and Garis touched palms with him.

He made no such gesture to me.

CHAPTER THIRTEEN

We slept at night wrapped in woollen blankets, under the shelter of waxed sheeting strung up on poles to keep the dew off. After Pinar had left on the second day, I kept wondering if Temellin would come to me at night, but he never did. During the day, if anything, he avoided me. He didn't have to try hard: there were always people claiming his attention, always problems to be solved concerning the ex-slaves. After Korden left on the fourth day, he didn't have that excuse. There were only four of us left – Brand and Garis being the other two – but he only came to me the next morning.

He woke me just at first light. 'Come,' he whispered, 'I have something to show you. A wild shleth.'

I rose and followed him, brushing the sleep from my eyes as I went. He led me out into the desert, using his sword for light, but keeping the glow of it subdued. 'I thought you might like to have a look at this,' he said, pointing to where a lone shleth was using its feeding arms and feet to excavate a deep hole in the sand. 'It's about to give birth.'

The beast finished its digging, and knelt down in the hole. Almost immediately it began to strain, and within minutes it had passed a blood-streaked leathery sac about the size of a cat, oval in shape, into the hole. The shleth proceeded to cover up its newborn with sand.

'What is it doing?' I asked in astonishment.

'They bury the sac in sand and promptly forget about it. It's like a large, half-developed egg. When the young is fully developed, it uses its feeding arms to dig out to the surface where it can fend for itself.'

'Shleths don't feed their young?'

'Kardis speak of shleth's milk the same way Tyranians refer to hen's teeth or Assorians talk about snake feathers. The young will grow up on the edges of the lake here, feeding on the grasses.'

He turned towards me. 'We have tried to raise the young from the time they dig themselves out, but we've never had success. They survive best by themselves for a year or two. Which has a disadvantage for us – we have to catch and tame them later on.' He reached out and drew me to him, kissing me gently on the lips. It wasn't the kind of kiss I wanted from him. 'It has been hard not to . . .' he said, and made a vague gesture with his hand. 'I want you so badly. Yet I shouldn't be here with you now. It has no future.'

'It doesn't have to have a future, Tem. In fact, I am not in the habit of considering a future for my relationships.'

'No, I don't suppose slaves can. I find it hard to imagine what it must be like to be enslaved. But now? You can have a future, Derya. You can plan to have a husband, a family, lots of children . . .'

'I can't say children have figured much in my plans either.' That was certainly true. I'd never considered having any, and had taken good care I wouldn't. 'What's the matter with just here and now?' At least this time I was well fortified with gameez to prevent conception.

He didn't need more of an invitation. The shleth had

wandered away, but we stayed there on the sands and found something in each other's arms as magical as the sword he carried.

And yet, later, lying in my blankets back in the camp, I wondered if it hadn't been a mistake. When he clasped his palm to mine and we joined for that moment in time, we gave something to each other and gained something from each other that changed us both. We forged connections – in Magor magic, in physical loving. We fashioned bonds that lingered on afterwards in a way I'd never experienced before in any lustful coupling.

We forgot bonds could also be fetters.

'That's it?' I asked Temellin. 'That's the Shiver Barrens?'

'That's it.'

The two of us pulled up our mounts on the top of a stony rise. A red-rock slope of a few hundred paces led down to an expanse of sand that appeared to stretch on forever. Beside us Garis and Brand also halted, and all conversation ceased.

After the initial question, I was speechless. Any words would have been too mundane to express the cascade of overwhelming emotions swamping me at that moment. Whatever I had expected, it wasn't what I saw then – there had never been a place in my logical world for anything like this.

From a sky of unforgiving blue, unblemished by cloud, the sun screamed full-voiced down on the desert sands, relentless, scorching – *and the sands responded*. The grains rose up to greet the heat of the day and gyrated for the sun god, as sensual as a semi-naked dancing girl discarding her veils.

The Shiver Barrens danced . . .

They moved in patterns that wove and unravelled, formed and disintegrated in shimmers of light and dark, and as they

danced they sang a whispering song of seduction. The whorls
and streams of sand grains reached twice the height of a man,
pouring through the air from the ground and back again like
wraiths of mist in a wind. But there was no wind. The sand
moved of its own volition, every particle self-propelled, yet
each obeying some cosmic law that orchestrated its movement
into this tidal dance.

I watched in wonderment, and remembered being a child
at our cliffside holiday villa on the Sea of Iss, watching schools
of fish swimming in the ocean far below – the annual run of
sardines along the coast. Sometimes the sharks would pierce
the shoals in vicious thrusting stabs, and the fish would whirl
away, turning and twisting in skeins of light and dark, each
with a mind of its own, yet performing its part in perfect
unison as the swarming mass split and rejoined.

Such were the dancing sands of the Shiver Barrens.

And as they flowed and re-formed, clustered and seethed,
they sang. Not in words, but in soft sound just out of range
of my understanding, half heard, like the far-off tinkle of wind
chimes, the patter of raindrops on water, the soughing of a
breeze through pine needles, the soft licking of a cat's tongue
on kitten fur.

In a dream, I urged my mount down to the edge of the
Barrens, where rock gave way to dancing sand. I dismounted
and leant forward to hold my hand out and catch up some of
the grains bouncing in the air – but they couldn't be captured.
They jiggled away from me, teasing.

'Try your left hand,' Temellin said at my elbow. This time I
caught them and they nestled in my cupped palm, twinkling
at me, purple and silver and gold and grey . . . slivers of colour.
They tickled my skin until I released them and they flew away,
humming their song of joy.

'What do you think?' Temellin asked softly. But I refused to be drawn; I still had no words. He stood close behind and put his arms around me. 'Can you hear it?'

'Oh yes.'

'Only the Magor can hear the song . . .'

'Does it mean anything? I keep thinking that if only I could listen a bit better, I'd be able to understand what it is saying.'

He was dismissive. 'There's nothing to understand. It's just a meaningless melody.'

He believed what he said, but I couldn't shake the feeling. I was also painfully aware of his body against mine. *Remember, Ligea, you are a compeer.* 'Why can't the legions cross?'

'They don't know the secret. They ride out, not knowing the further you ride, the deeper the dance becomes. At the edge, where we are now, the firm ground is just a pace down; the pain of the grains brushing your skin would be bearable.' He waved a hand towards the horizon. 'Out there the sand dances above your head. You breathe it into your nostrils, you gasp and it dances into your mouth. It fills your ears and abrades your skin. You start to bleed; just pinpricks to start with, then your mouth and nose and ears trickle blood and your skin is rasped raw and the pain maddens you and your mount. You try to return, but you cannot see which way safety lies. Your clothing is shredded and you yourself are flayed to a mass of bleeding, skinless flesh. When the sand finally chokes you and you cease to breathe, it is the mercy you have prayed for. The Barrens are cruel to those who trespass in ignorance. Even to us, the Magor. For some reason, our – our abilities are limited here. The sands do not obey our magic.'

'But there is a secret—'

'Yes, and tonight you will discover it.' His cheek rested against mine; his voice caressed, although his words were gravid with warning. 'The Shiver Barrens are the Mirage's protection from Kardiastan, just as the Alps are its protection on the western side, from Tyrans. And after today, you and Brand will both know the secret . . .'

He trailed fingers down the side of my neck to my breast, then swung me to face him. 'Don't betray us, Derya. Pinar and Korden think the legionnaires who were all around the safe house in Madrinya had something to do with either you or Brand.' His hand still cupped my breast, tantalising me through the cloth. 'I cannot believe that. Not when I have lain in your arms and felt your trueness, but I am not foolish enough to think I am always right. We all have the ability to hide our emotions from one another, although not our lies.' He looked back to the top of the slope, where Brand stood staring at us both with an expressionless face.

'I asked Brand about those legionnaries, and he refused to answer. He said if I doubt you, then I should talk to you, not him. He gave the same answer to Pinar. I wish he had been more . . . straightforward in his replies. Pinar and Korden are now convinced he won't answer such questions plainly because he knows we'll catch him out in a lie.'

'It was Legata Ligea who ordered the legionnaires out in force,' I said, with perfect truth. 'She wants to catch the Mirager. You. What else can either of us say? Ligea is not in the habit of talking to her handmaidens about the details of her plans. And as for Brand, he cares for me. He doesn't like to see others distrust me, or treat me like some kind of criminal. He is angry with Pinar.'

He looked up at Brand again.

'Is he your lover, Derya?'

'He is a brother to me.'

'That does not make any difference to a Magor.'

'So I've been told. It does to me. A wealth of difference.'

'He does not think of himself as your brother.'

'No.'

He put his left palm to mine, reinforcing his words with his flow of emotions. 'I have not had a woman other than you since the death of my wife. After she died, I desired no one until I put my arms around you and felt something so powerful it could not be resisted. I loved my wife, Derya. It hurts even now to think of her. And yet, she never made me feel the way you do. I wanted her, yet it never made me ache just to look at her, as I do when I look at you.' He released me and stood back a little. 'You have had time to think, Derya. Do you still want me on your pallet, knowing that's all we'll ever have?'

'Yes.' The word jerked out. I felt I was physically incapable of giving any other answer.

He nodded and leant forward to brush his lips against my forehead. 'Warn Brand that if he thinks to leave the Mirage before he has gained my trust, I will kill him before he reaches the edge of the Shiver Barrens as surely as the sun rises. As I would *anyone* who would betray Kardiastan to Tyrans. And now we will set up camp here for the remainder of the day. We will move only after sunset. We must rest; it will be a long ride tonight.' He turned away, calling to Garis, giving orders, smiling his friendship and goodwill.

I wondered what had happened to his laughter while he had been speaking to me.

I went over to Brand and gave him Temellin's warning.

'Charming fellow,' he said. 'And how long have you been bedding this scorpion, my sweet?'

I bristled. 'The slaking of my appetite is no business of yours, Brand.'

'No, more's the pity. But remember, scorpions have stings in the tail. It doesn't pay to play with them.' He grinned at me, but there was little humour in it.

I tried to sleep under the makeshift shelter they erected, but the heat was so intense it seemed to shrivel me, making my skin too small for my body, squeezing me into too small a space. The rock beneath my sleeping pelt seared as if I were meat basting over a fire. And the music from the Shiver Barrens teased, promising something just beyond my understanding. I still felt that if I could only concentrate, I would be able to comprehend the words and arrive at some eternal truth ... but I could never quite hear. I rolled over to watch the dance, the endless movement that was colour and sound as well, and was again a moth fascinated by a flame. Could such beauty be deadly? I felt I could walk into the dance, be part of its glory – and emerge unscathed. Yet Temellin could not have been lying; I would have known. And the legionnaires who had set out to cross the sands had never returned.

Gradually the dancing slowed, as if the grains grew too heavy for the air, sinking lower and lower until their movement was stilled and the ground was quiet and purple under the last rays of the sun.

I slept.

When I awoke, the ground sparkled with frost. Once the warmth of the day was gone, no longer enticing the sand to dance, the Barrens were calm and virginal, a white-clad bride breathlessly awaiting the sweet violation of the wedding night.

Temellin and Garis were dismantling the camp. Brand passed food to me and I ate hurriedly, infected by the eagerness of the others to be away. 'Why didn't we start to cross at sunset?' I asked Temellin. 'We'd have had more time.'

'There are patches of quicksand out there. Ride over one of those and our mounts would flounder and sink. We'd be mired. And once again the Barrens would have claimed the unwary. The ground has to be hard for us to cross.'

I understood then. We'd had to wait, wait until the temperature fell to freezing as it did each night under those cloudless Kardi skies. Until the sand grains were bound together with the sparkle of desert dew frost; until the ground was frozen beneath the feet of a mount.

Only then could we start our journey.

I rode with Temellin beside me, Garis and Brand and the pack shleth dropping away behind, each of us careful to make our own path across the crust. To have followed the tracks of another would have been to risk breaking through the surface. If I looked back, I could see the pawprints the shleths left behind, but when I looked ahead, Temellin and I could have been the only people ever to have crossed the Shiver Barrens, ever to have made a mark on that virgin white.

As we rode, I realised why a horse or a gorclak could never have made that journey and lived. Their small feet would have broken through the surface. Only a shleth could cross the Shiver Barrens. They spread out their pads to the size of serving plates and used a fast-walking gait that spread their weight evenly on three legs at a time. The constancy of the speed they maintained was impressive; a glance at the concentration on Temellin's face convinced me it was necessary. If we didn't reach the other side of the Barrens by dawn, we died.

We rode in silence. Temellin travelled in a world of his own as if he listened to voices only he could hear, yet I did not regret the lack of conversation. I, too, wanted to listen. I wanted to listen to the song of my own body, to the sound of the footbeats of my mount, to the now-stilled music of the sands, echoes of which I still seemed to hear. Above, the purple softness of the sky with its blue points of light and swirls of stardust; below, the sparkle of blue-frost and the crisp crunch of paws ... No, there was no need of words. I was beyond them.

We had no time for rest. Safety was a night's ride away; the pace had to be steady and relentless. Occasionally Temellin would draw his sword and swing it in an arc in front of him.

Each time, when it flamed briefly, he would make a slight adjustment to the direction of our ride.

When we passed a dozen silent frost-covered figures, half buried in the sand, half exposed in a naked tatter of bone and desiccated flesh, we did not stop. Temellin did not seem to notice them, but my heart clenched painfully as recognition came. There could be no mistaking the lance still clutched in a fleshless hand, the clasp from a military cloak lodged in leathered skin, or the metal links caught on the white curve of ribs, gleaming in the starlight – all that remained of a cuirass. And beyond the men, the skeletal remains of animals with pitted and pock-marked horns in the middle of bone-white skulls. Appalled, I averted my eyes.

In predawn light I had my first glimpse of the end of the Shiver Barrens: a dark silhouette across the horizon ahead, a continuous jagged line of a low ridge against the mauve of sky. Temellin spoke for the first time. 'That's the first Rake,' he said. 'That's safety.'

Dawn came: a shaft of light that shot across the plain from behind, sending our shadows racing ahead to touch the stone of the Rake, now coloured the ebony-red of newly shed blood. The shleths quickened pace, aware time was slipping away from them with the darkness.

'Don't worry,' Temellin said from beside me. 'We will make it.'

But soon I was doubting his words of reassurance. The crispness was gone from beneath the paws of our mounts. They were forced to slow as the crust broke slightly each time a foot landed. A little later, when I looked behind, I saw sand escaping from the confining surface wherever the crust had cracked. The grains weren't truly dancing as yet; the sand bubbled, broke and fell back only to bubble and burst again. Ahead, the white plain was white no longer; the frost had melted.

'Temellin—' I began. Fear and excitement mingled. I knew my eyes shone.

'Trust me.' He laughed and let loose his emotions. He was exhilarated, revelling in the race against time, the possibility of death, the joy he anticipated. 'I'll get you there. Believe me, there's no way I'll be cheated out of what I intend to have today.'

Yet by the time the Rake was within reach, the soft sound of the song of the Shiver Barrens murmured anew. The shleths were floundering, almost wallowing as the grains rose up to batter at their legs. On their last desperate run to the rock ahead, they even unfolded their feeding arms and used the balled fingers as an extra pair of feet, anything to give them added purchase on the restless sand. Behind, our tracks were a ploughed furrow through a barren field.

And then we were safe. The rock was beneath us and our mounts halted, heads hanging low with fatigue.

Garis whooped and laughed. 'Wow – that was terrific!'

Brand shook his head and muttered something about youth and idiocy.

I looked around. The lengthwise red crease of the Rake, slashing across the sands in a seemingly endless ripple, was no more than ten minutes' ride widthways in the flatter places. But it wasn't often flat. It was a naturally carved flounce of curves and caves and fissures accentuated by light and shade. In the sun, the red was almost blinding; shadows cooled it to mahogany and rust. Such were the tortured convolutions of the rock that some niches and corners were always shadowed, and in these places pools collected the run-off of dew and frost.

All this I hardly noticed just then. I was looking across one of those flatter areas and seeing what was on the other side of the flounce – and in my fatigue, my heart plunged. All I could see was sand and more sand. The Shiver Barrens began again on the far side of the Rake, stretching as far as the eye could see.

With a speaking glance at Brand, I slid from my shleth.

Temellin dismounted beside me and came over, his eyes sympathetic. 'It takes five nights to cross the Shiver Barrens, Derya,' he said. 'There are four stone ridges like this one, slicing through the desert from one side to the other. We must reach one before dawn of each day. As you can see, on a Rake there is shelter and water and shade and firm ground. Here we are safe. You can even bathe. There is no need to look so miserable.'

He grinned at me and suddenly I didn't feel so tired.

We found a shaded cave where we could water the animals and feed them the fodder cakes we had with us. Another recess carved into a cliff provided us with shade. However, after we'd eaten, Temellin disappeared. I sat waiting, and was not disappointed; when he returned it was to beckon me away from the others. I joined him out in the sun once more, wincing in the already savage heat. 'I have found a place,' he said. 'Come.'

He held out his left hand and instead of giving him my right in return, I reached across with my left. The touch of his cabochon to mine was the drug I needed to reassure myself that I was desirable – and desired.

He had found a cave for us, a hollow rounded and smoothed like a scooped-out melon half, just big enough for the sleeping pelts he had thrown down. A little lower, there was another rounded dip, also shaded, full of ice-cold water.

He took me in his arms and whispered, 'Your bath awaits, my lady.' But in the end, it was the bath that had to wait. Once we were naked and in each other's arms, we could not stop the flame of emotion demanding instant physical consummation. We were intoxicated with each other, drunk on the smell and taste and touch of each other; unbearably aroused by our desire, then inebriated with its satiation. At that moment, the idea any action of mine could lead to the death of this man was utterly unthinkable.

Afterwards, lying side by side, I found myself crying with the wonder of it all. He lay there, naked, perfect – sculpted thighs, hard buttocks, taut length of muscular leg. Our left palms were still clamped together so we could feel every nuance of each other's emotion, or at least those we cared to share, but when I wondered how I would ever be satisfied again with a lesser lover, when I remembered I was supposed to betray him, I shielded my guilt from him. And there was, even then, a part of my brain thinking through possibilities. Like: if Tyrans wanted to prevent the Kardis from crossing the Shiver Barrens, then all they had to do was kill all the shleths. Or: the Stalwarts need not cross the Alps; they could commandeer shleths and cross the Shiver Barrens just as the Kardis did. They could wrench the Mirage from Kardi control, and that would wreak havoc on the Kardi heart and soul.

But I had no way to get that message to the Stalwarts in time. They would cross through one of the world's most treacherous mountain ranges, enduring horrors I could hardly imagine, in order to serve their country and their Exaltarchy. To bring peace to a warring nation and a people who could not accept the natural order of subservience to a superior culture . . .

We drowsed, then bathed together and made love again, this time with a more leisurely passion, although the culmination was as intense as ever. I fell asleep naked in his arms and did not wake until it was dark.

Temellin had gone and I was already chilled.

It was Garis who had awoken me. He was shaking me by the foot, his voice full of laughter.

'Derya? Are you awake? Temellin says it's time to get up.'

I stirred and sat up. I was still naked.

'Now that's a sight I'd walk all night to see!' he exclaimed. He rolled his eyes and grinned. 'You are incomparable, Derya.'

I pulled the sleeping pelt up over my nakedness. 'Scat, Garis.'

'Killjoy,' he said, not moving.

'*Scram*, Garis!'

'I'm going, I'm going! Temellin wouldn't appreciate too much appreciation anyhow. But I'm glad for him, Derya. I really am.' This last was said without the banter, and then he was gone.

I was glad, too – for myself. For now.

CHAPTER FOURTEEN

We were on the fourth Rake.

I lay awake and watched the patterns of water reflections on the cave roof. A pretty dappling, a moving artwork. Beside me Temellin lay replete with lovemaking, his face young and contented in repose. I resisted the temptation to kiss him, and touched my cabochon to his instead. I felt his dreaming: pleasant dreams of contentment. I wished this journey could go on forever, that I would never have to face the decisions awaiting me on the other side of the Shiver Barrens, that I would never have to make a choice between desire and duty; between a man and an obligation; between Kardiastan and Tyrans, between the land of my birth and the land of my loyalties.

I turned my gaze back to the roof of the cave and tried not to listen to the song of the Barrens.

Something was moving the surface of the water outside to cause that dappling, and yet I'd felt no wind. Puzzled, I rose, dressed and stepped out into the blazing heat of the day. The tiny pool tucked away in among the rocks was as flat as oil in a lamp. I looked back at the cave roof: the dappling had vanished.

My skin prickled warning.

Come. I heard the voice singing in the dance, the invitation clear and unequivocal. And knew immediately this was not the voice of the Shiver Barrens; this was no melody of movement, beautiful but meaningless; this was something quite different.

It was we who woke you, we who ruffled the water. Come.

Appalled, I asked in a whisper, 'Who are you?'

We are the Mirage Makers. Come.

Mirage Makers? What in all Acheron's mists were Mirage Makers? 'Come where?'

Into the dance.

'You would kill me?'

You will not die. Come.

'I dare not.' In fact, I thought I was probably not having this conversation. I was dreaming. Or I had a bad case of sunstroke.

You do not dream. Nor are you ill. You listen to our song. As we listen to yours. Come. It is your time to receive what is yours to own, your time to hear what is yours to know, your time to hear the song of your birthright.

I felt an all-consuming terror and shook my head. I started to back away, thinking to wake Temellin. 'I will not listen.'

Come, you who call yourself Ligea.

The horror I felt then was stultifying. *Sweet Melete. It knows who I am! Temellin will kill me.* I thought those words in my head, but they answered, those voices, nonetheless.

Of course we know. Are we not the Mirage Makers? And are you not of the Magor?

The sun beat down at me, yet my horror was as cold as frost. I dared not wake Temellin. Instead, I gathered the tatters of my shredded courage, and walked to the edge of the Shiver Barrens to look into the dance. There were patterns within patterns, and somewhere I thought I saw shapes – wispy shapes in relief against the patterned background.

'No,' I said. 'You entice me to my death. I will not go.' Yet the fast beating of my heart was not just generated by fear; there was also that wretched love of danger urging me on, telling me: this could be the greatest adventure of your life . . .

You have a duty. You are the Miragerin.

'Turds. I am not Temellin's consort, nor ever will be.' And with those words came a pang of regret. But I had no time to think about that.

You are the Miragerin. We have no knowledge of what will be, only of what is. What is cannot be denied. Refuse to come to us now and tonight we shall break the frost beneath the feet of your mount and draw you under. Neither way will you come to harm, but this way is better. Come.

I looked back at the cave where Temellin slept, and I was torn.

What must be, must be, the voice said gently. *Come.* The tone contained no real hint of threat, in spite of the words. There was no menace, nor even seduction. It was more the reasoned tones of a teacher, gently admonishing a reluctant pupil.

And I went. I stepped away from the rock and began to walk into the dance.

I felt nothing. The sand did not batter me; the only thing that touched me was the caress of the song, the Shiver Barrens' song, rippling along my skin and into the weave of my being. The dancing sands rose higher and higher around me as I walked, yet parted before me as I moved. Waist-height, shoulder, chin – I gave one last look back at the safety of the Rake and was submerged.

The music of the sounds was almost unbearable in its beauty. I heard and saw and felt and smelt it. Purple light bathed me; I was looking through a mist of movement and somewhere beyond I could see the forms that were there, but not quite visible. When I stared at them they slipped away like elusive dreams, always just out of reach, just unknowable.

I did not hear the voice again; yet, surrounded by the music, I heard meaning being woven into the song of the Shiver Barrens, meaning coming from something, or things, that were not the Barrens. There was no need of words. I heard and understood.

When the music twisted I saw a Magor sword suspended before me. The song wove itself from these things calling themselves the Mirage Makers, to the sword, to me, and I knew it was mine; all I had to do was to fit my cabochon into the hollow on its grip and it would belong to me, could never be turned against me. I reached out and closed my left hand around the hilt. It melded to me, throbbing with a desire to be used.

This is your Magor sword. Still the music spoke to me, slotting knowledge wordlessly into my mind. *There is a responsibility that comes with this weapon. This is not the sword of Tyrans which drinks blood for the sake of power; it is the sword of the Magor, an instrument of service.*

'Service? To whom?' I asked.

To the Magor. To Kardiastan. To those others of this land, the non-Magor. Use it for personal gain, pursue corrupt goals, and you break the Covenant made by your forebears with those they called the Mirage Makers. Are you willing to accept this gift?

My hand tightened on the hilt. It was part of me . . . I could no more have refused it than I could have denied my hunger for Temellin. *Yes*, I whispered in my mind. *Yes, I accept.* The response was emotional, irrational even. It was not possible to serve Tyr and the Brotherhood at the same time as the Magor. Yet I accepted the sword and ignored the contradiction.

Inside my head, I sang my thanks for the gift and knew I was heard. I closed my eyes, strangely lulled, and felt myself drifting, bodiless.

And then came a vision. It was a message woven in music, yet it was not as sounds, but as images, that I knew it.

It was night-time and there was a Mirager. It was not Temellin, or any particular Mirager, but rather the essence of a Mirager, of all ruling Miragers and Miragerins that had ever been or ever would be, male or female. He knelt on a flagstone floor with his head bowed, and his hands held his Magor sword. I knew he had fasted. I knew he was praying, but not to any deity. He was not praying *to* anything; rather, he was praying for a newborn child, praying for its wisdom and its service. He was dedicating a baby to the Magor.

He chanted words that themselves had no meaning – and yet which contained a wealth of meaning. Gradually the sword he held began to glow with a gold light. He gave no sign he'd noticed, but held it lying across his hands with the hollow in the hilt uppermost. Then, after a time that seemed endless, the hollow was no longer empty, but was filled with a gem, a cabochon. Although I had no memory of ever having seen one, I knew it for what it was.

It was shaped like half a pigeon's egg, sliced lengthways.

It was rounded, without faceting. I strained to see its colour, but sometimes it looked gold, sometimes green, sometimes red. It was the essence of all cabochons that had ever been . . .

Then the night ended and the Mirager rose to his feet, still carrying the sword. He went into another room where the baby slept in his mother's arms and the father stood watching his wife and child with tenderness. The mother held out the child and the Mirager knelt before her and laid the hilt of the sword, cabochon down, onto the tiny left hand. There was a flash of light, a baby's cry, and pain, the Mirager's pain as the cabochon was ripped from his sword and became part of the child for all his life. Yet when the Mirager stood his face was calm and proud.

Knowledge came to me as I watched. Just as the swords were gifts from the Mirage Makers to the Magor, so were the cabochons, only they were bestowed through the medium of a Magor sword. The Magor had no say in the gem colour.

I looked down at my own left hand. Somewhere, some time, I had lain in my mother's arms and a Magor – a Mirager? Temellin's uncle Solad? – had pressed the hilt of a Magor sword to my palm . . .

The vision was gone.

There was another in its place, but less defined, more blurred, as though it was something that had never happened, may never happen. I saw a figure – a Kardi who could have been man or woman – holding a soft, rounded shape cupped in his or her hands, a shape that throbbed with a regular beat. I stared at it, puzzled, and was given the knowledge to understand what it was. A woman's womb with a living embryo, a womb and its contents ripped from its mother . . . Appalled, I drew back, putting a protective hand to my own abdomen as if I were denying to be identified with the woman who would supply that disembodied organ and its doomed child. I strained to see the person's face, but it was featureless. Whoever it was, he or she appeared to be offering the unborn child to the indistinct shapes inside the dancing sands, offering it to the Mirage Makers. And the Mirage Makers were accepting it, drawing it into the sands so it merged with them, so it became one with those shadowy beings who definitely weren't human. I thought, and knew it a truth: *The Mirage Makers want an unborn child.* And to supply it, a woman was going to have to die . . . Then, in shock: *Why is such a vision being shown to me?*

But I had no time to dwell on the horror, on the terror of that moment, or on the additional knowledge that was then slotted into my mind. Before I could assimilate all I now knew, there was another vision.

Two hands. Reaching out to one another. One was indubitably mine, the other was the personification of something that was not a person: the Mirage Makers. Then the vision split. In the first image the hands clasped and melted into one another in a symbol of unity. In the second, my hand took up my Magor sword and split the hand held out to me so its blood drained onto the sand below to become a black foulness that was death without redemption.

Then the vision was gone and I was standing under the dancing sands once more, the singing filling my ears, my eyes, my body. It was telling me the Mirage Makers knew who I was, knew I had the power to destroy both them and the Magor, that they had indeed *given* me that power with the bestowal of my sword, but that they'd had no choice. They were not free to make decisions, they could merely accede to the immutable rules laid down in antiquity, when Magor and Mirage Makers had settled their differences and made their pacts.

The singing took on the sound of tragedy, of grief, of a plea asking me to respect my birth-gift. It was a song filled with such a depth of sorrow, I felt every dancing sand grain was a teardrop to be shed at the moment of my betrayal. I wept then, wept for what I was: Kardi Magor-born, but bred to know there was a better way of life, a great civilisation offering so much more . . .

I turned and stumbled away, instinctively groping back to the safety of the Rake.

When I stood again in the desiccating sunlight with the hard red rock beneath my feet, I looked back at the dancing sands and knew they had become once again deadly for me. The Mirage Makers were gone from the Shiver Barrens. The song was there, still beautiful, but the melody now belonged only to the sands. And yet, I still thought that if only I could listen in the right way, I would understand. That it was *important* to understand.

It was hard to imagine I'd stood beneath the Shiver Barrens in the heat of the day and survived, yet I held the Magor sword in my hand as proof, its hilt fitted so comfortably into my palm . . . Right then, though, my thoughts were not of the sword. Nor did I think of the gift of an embryo, the bestowing of cabochons – I could think about all that later. It was something else that had me standing out there in the sun, unable to move in my shock.

There was one piece of information I had unwittingly gleaned along the way that tore me apart. *No. It couldn't be true . . .*

'Ligea!'

I looked up. Brand was looking down on me from the crest of the Rake. *Don't think about it.*

'What the world are you doing out in the sun?' He came down to me and looked at the sword in my hand with surprise. 'Temellin's?'

I shook my head. 'No. Mine.' *Concentrate.*

'Where in Vortex did you get it?'

'I think – from the place that all the Magor obtain their swords. Brand, there's no way I can explain.' I refused to meet his eyes as I added, 'And please – don't mention this to the others, either; I don't want them to know I have a Magor sword. Not yet, anyhow.' I looked down at the weapon. I wanted to know what it meant; I wanted to know what this Covenant was . . . and I wanted to know my own mind. Only then would

I know whether I should tell the Magor that these Mirager Makers had bestowed a sword on me.

Brand looked irritated. 'You expect me to take much on trust, Ligea. One of these days you will push me too far.'

I shrugged. 'You are free. You have only to tell me and I will ask nothing of you.'

'Ligea, Ligea, what are you doing?' The depth of his grief sliced into me, focusing my attention. He had deliberately bared himself. 'I feel I don't know you any more,' he said. 'This passion you have for Temellin, it's insane. Do you think you can bed a man one day and betray him the next? Not even you can do that and stay yourself.'

I gave a bitter laugh. I wanted to say, *but I have to do just that, Brand. I have to betray either Temellin or Favonius. And I have known and bedded Favonius for years. It is Temellin who is the stranger, the foreigner with foreign ways. Temellin is just a lust in my loins. Such lust won't last, it mustn't last – if it did, it would drive me insane because I can't have him forever . . .*

Instead, I said, searching for calm, for reason, 'What passion? It's just lust, Brand. No different to the needs I slake with Favonius. Or the others, over the years.' *Dear Goddess, what about that other thing they told you?*

He gave a disbelieving snort and said, still angry, still grieving, 'I don't understand you. These people – those who call themselves Magor, I mean – for all their strange customs, they are an improvement on those you served in Tyr. I don't know why, because they have terrible power. I'm not going to forget in a hurry what Garis did to me that first day! But somehow they are not corrupt, the way those of Tyrans are. And if they win here, they won't be basing the nation they build on slavery as Tyrans does. Tyrans is *sick*, Ligea. Don't you know that yet? And what loyalty do you owe to such as

Rathrox anyway?' He gave another snort of disgust. 'Vortex take it, how could someone who can see through a lie as easily as you can, let themselves be fooled the way you were? *Think, Ligea. Think.* Think about Gayed, about your childhood. Think about who it was who loved you. There's no more time for self-deception, not now. Now is the time for decisions, no matter how difficult they are to make.'

'And what's your decision to be?' I asked levelly. 'Will you leave me, to stay with these people, when I return to Madrinya?' I had deliberately emphasised the 'when'.

He winced, an expression of both pain and exasperation. 'Why are you so blind to the things and people that touch you closest, Ligea, when you see other, more distant things and people so clearly? I *love* you. I love you so much that I can stand here and watch your eyes hunger for another man, and listen to your cries of joy in his arms, and still take the pain rather than leave you. I make myself less than a man for you. I serve you, not Tyrans. I am so besotted, so *weak*, that I put you before what I know is right.'

His words cut at me, slashed me with their tragedy. Tears blurred my image of him, but were not shed. I reached out to touch his arm. 'Brand – oh Goddessdamn, Brand, this is not right. You will come to hate me. When we reach our destination, you must leave. For your own good. How can I ask any loyalty of you when I give so little; no, when I give you *nothing*, in return?'

His lips twisted bitterly. 'That would be my ultimate punishment. I would rather live in pain than in loss.'

He turned away, leaving me to return to my cave. I made a hole in my sleeping pallet and thrust the sword inside. I was responsible for the packing of my own things and stowing them on the pack shleth, so I had no fear anyone would find it. Then I crept back into Temellin's arms, trying not to think because thinking was painful. Because I didn't *want* to think about that other thing I knew.

An hour later, I knew the pain had to be faced because I couldn't sleep. Because I couldn't push away the sound of Brand's voice. *Think, Ligea. Think about who it was who loved you?*

Memories . . . the journey inside oneself can be the loneliest journey of all . . .

I loved the terrace of the Gayed villa; it had the best views in all of Tyr. From there I could see the Meletian Temple on a neighbouring hill, with the Desert-Season Theatre tiered beneath it; from there I could see the river and the life of the docks and the sea beyond; from there I could watch for visitors coming up to our house. I could be the first to know Pater was on his way home.

I loved the terrace best of all in the desert-season when it was heady with the smell of flowers and the warmth of the sun – as it was today, my sixteenth anniversary day.

The mellowbirds droned their somnolent call in the garden, mocking my impatience. I was waiting for Pater to come back from the city; I was waiting for his news concerning my future, and I wanted to thank him for his anniversary gift. I'd even put on my best wrap, the one with garnets sewn along the hem, just to please him, although I didn't like it much. It was too stiff and uncomfortable. Besides, it stopped me from doing what I most wanted to do right then: ride the big roan stallion stalking its proud way along the garden path just below the terrace.

I had to be content to lean against the balustrade and gaze instead. The roan coat shone in the sunlight, the muscles of his shoulders and neck and legs spoke to me of power and speed. I gave a slight shiver of excitement.

'Ah, Goddess, Brand,' I said. 'Isn't he magnificent? Can you

believe he's really mine? Isn't Pater wonderful to have bought him for me?'

Brand, who was walking the horse, halted and looked up, squinting against the light. 'The General doubtless had excellent reasons for buying you such an unsuitable mount,' he said.

I pouted, trying to decide exactly what he was telling me. Brand often said things that never meant quite what I thought they did at first; it was an annoying habit of his. 'I hope you are not criticising Pater,' I said severely and then, not wanting anything to spoil my day, turned my attention back to the horse. 'Oh mount him, for Goddess' sàke, Brand, although I shall be jealous – I just have to see how he moves.'

Brand smiled, an indulgent, teasing smile of the kind that usually infuriated me into throwing something at him, but today I refused to be even mildly irritated. He swung himself up onto the animal's back, apparently unconcerned by the lack of a saddle. His strong square hands gathered up the reins and held the roan in tight as it stamped a front foot in annoyance and tried to swing its head free. It occurred to me Brand looked almost as magnificent as the horse, but I pushed that thought away. That was not the kind of thing one should think about a slave.

He moved the roan from a walk to a trot to a canter, swinging it around through the garden in a wide figure of eight and then jumping it across the fishpond as a finale.

'Well, what do you think?' I asked as he reined in beneath the terrace. 'I think he's perfect.'

He patted the roan's neck and looked up at me. 'He's edgy. You'll need wrists of steel for this one, Miss Ligea. I don't think you should ride him until he's more schooled.'

'Oh, nonsense! My wrists are strong – don't I ride nearly every day? I shall school him myself.'

He slid down to the grass, frowning slightly. 'Well, I don't think you ought to ride him yet a while. He ought to be, um, cut. If *he gets a whiff of a mare, you'd never hold him. He's no mount for a sixteen-year-old girl—'*

A voice at my elbow said coldly, 'And I don't think you should say any more, thrall. It's not your place to pass judgement on the General's gift to his . . . his daughter.'

Salacia, my adoptive mother. One of the most beautiful women of Tyr, or so everyone told me. I knew she was fifty years old, but she looked fifteen years younger, mostly because her skin was white, kept from the sun and unblemished by wrinkles. She never frowned, never laughed and rarely smiled; a face so devoid of animation had no chance to develop creases. I could never look at her without thinking of a statue, perfectly polished but incapable of showing emotion. Perhaps that was why I invariably felt gauche in her presence, all arms and legs and ungainly height. I knew the emotions were there of course; I might not have seen them on that alabaster mask of hers, but I could feel them. Cold indifference usually predominated, occasionally laced with a strangely impersonal spite. I wasn't enough of an object in her life even to arouse her dislike.

'Take that animal away, Brand,' she ordered, 'and get on with your work.' She turned back to me, her malice momentarily satisfied.

As a child I had been constantly bewildered by her lack of interest, but I was older now. Sixteen . . . Old enough to understand and pity her. She'd wanted a child of her own; instead, I'd arrived in her household to mock her desire. Fortunately for me, she had been far too proud ever to allow herself to care overmuch, and even her verbal jibes were muted. Mostly she ignored me; only occasionally did she rouse herself enough to deprive me of something I enjoyed, such as admiring the stallion. They were the petty tyrannies of a petty woman and I was used to them.

I almost smiled. I felt very adult. What Salacia did didn't matter; Pater made up for everything . . .

He wasn't alone when he came back; he'd brought the Magister Officii with him. I knew Rathrox Ligatan by sight and I knew why Pater had brought him to the house: to meet me. Pater had promised to ask the Magister if I could train to be a Brotherhood Compeer. My heart beat uncomfortably fast. The Brotherhood did not usually accept women as trainees at the compeer level, or accept non-Tyranians at any level – and I'd been born a Kardi. Gayed had never made any secret of my origins.

I performed the welcoming ablutions myself, and tried to assess the Magister Officii's thoughts. His emotions were complex; a tangle of conflicting feelings that were hard to interpret. I could sense strong amusement, a touch of contempt – but mostly he was smug. I didn't think I liked him very much.

'Well,' Pater asked me, his dark blue eyes mocking gently, 'how do you like your horse?'

'He's wonderful! But Brand says he'll be too much for me.'

'For my Ligea? You must accept the challenge, child. There's no place for weaklings among the Brotherhood, is there, eh, Rathrox? Ocrastes' balls, what does an ignorant thrall know about horseflesh anyway? That beast is not too much for you!'

'Among the Brotherhood?' I stammered, seizing on the most significant thing he'd said. The roan suddenly seemed unimportant.

I turned to Rathrox Ligatan. 'Magister Officii? The – the Brotherhood will take me?'

He inclined his head, smiling faintly. 'I don't see that being Kardi-born will be a disadvantage, do you, Gayed?'

The two men exchanged glances. 'Why should it?' Pater asked. His voice was smooth, his features relaxed, yet I caught an undercurrent of something I didn't altogether like. I could have deliberately opened my mind to his emotions – I could have listened for a lie, but I didn't. I never did with him. It would have been disloyal, dishonourable even. He was my father and I loved him.

The rules were of my own making, but I kept them.

'Why indeed?' agreed the Magister Officii. 'I have nothing against the Kardis. In fact, I admire them. A fine people from an interesting land.'

That was a lie so blatant the blast of it almost made me choke, and it was followed by a churning blackness of rage and hate. For a moment I thought the emotion was directed at me, but once I gathered my wits together again, I realised it was not me he despised; on the contrary, he was quietly pleased with me in an amused, self-satisfied fashion. What then had aroused a rage so irrational in its intensity? Kardis? Kardiastan? Or had mention of the place just conjured up some unpleasant memory? I had no way of knowing. I sensed the emotion, never the cause.

I looked back at Pater, and he was now the one who was smiling, as if he were aware of the depth of the Magister Officii's sentiments and was amused by it. He said, 'You must work hard at this, Ligea. One day you'll be a compeer; make sure you're the best.' He was serious now, almost cold. 'You're my daughter; you bear my name. Live up to it. The Magister Officii is going to take a personal interest in your progress, and perhaps one day—' He gave a half-smile. 'Perhaps one day you will be a heroine of Tyr, and of inestimable service to us.'

I stood a little straighter, and felt the swell of pride.

That night I dreamed of the kind of services I could perform to make my father proud of me . . .

The scent of blossom was gone from my nostrils and I was lying back on the sleeping pelts, Temellin's arm flung carelessly over my body, his breathing even and peaceful. I rolled away slightly, unwilling to be distracted.

Think, Ligea, think. Think about who it was who loved you?

Not Salacia, certainly. I'd never believed that. It had been Aemid who had been mother to me and I'd never thought otherwise. Aemid – of Kardiastan. Aemid the slave. Aemid, who now put her love of her country before her affection for me. Who would rather see me dead than have me betray her people. (Hardly the kind of love Brand wanted me to think about!)

Who *had* loved me?

Brand? Yes, certainly. The slave boy – from Altan. The eighteen-year-old who had looked up at me in concern from the back of the roan, worried I wouldn't be able to control a half-broken stallion. (He'd been right, too, damn him; the animal had thrown me more than once and I'd been lucky to escape with no more than bruises and a broken collarbone.)

I thought of Rathrox Ligatan, mentor, but never friend.

About him, I'd never had any illusions. He'd used me, again and again, but then, I'd been willing enough to be used. Willing enough to learn from him and in return to use my abilities to bring him the traitors, the criminals and the enemies he sought. Until one day he'd learned to fear me and sent me to the one place where there was no Brotherhood to help me.

To Kardiastan.

To get rid of me? Perhaps. Or perhaps because he wanted me to exact revenge on the people he hated . . . With the sudden cold of realisation, I knew why I had been remembering that sixteenth anniversary day of mine – because that was the day Rathrox had shown me his intention. That was the day he'd told me I was nothing to him but the future instrument of his revenge on Kardiastan. Perhaps he hadn't used words to say it, but he'd told me nonetheless. I just hadn't listened.

And Gayed had been there that day. Gayed, General of Tyrans, the only father I could remember.

Perhaps one day you will be of inestimable service to us—

The cold tightened its grip in my chest. Those had been Gayed's words . . .

But Gayed had taken me into his home, given me his name,

made me a citizen of Tyrans, shared his wealth with me. He had raised me, educated me, given me everything he would have given a true daughter.

Would he have given a true daughter to the Brotherhood? An unbidden, unwanted thought, and suddenly it was impossible to think of any child of Gayed and Salacia's becoming a Compeer of the Brotherhood. *Gayed would never have allowed such a thing* . . . Would never have even *contemplated* it.

Had he loved me? That proud man who'd given a sixteen-year-old daughter a horse too tough for her to handle because he'd wanted her challenged? The man who'd urged that same sixteen-year-old into the Brotherhood, into the manipulative hands of Rathrox Ligatan, to be trained and hardened and taught how to kill? A proud man who had once been part of a defeated army, an army humiliated by Kardiastan. The only time he'd been on the losing side. The only time treachery rather than military might had provided the ultimate victory.

Would such a man have taken a three-year-old enemy child into his family for reasons of love or compassion?

Of course not. *Delusion.*

Then what was the truth?

A far-sighted man, he'd taken a child of Kardiastan and made her a woman of Tyrans. A man of vision, he'd taken one of the Magor and made her a Brotherhood Compeer. A man of foresight and planning, he had moulded me, the malleable, eager child; wrought me into his instrument of revenge. *One day you'll be of service to us* . . .

I'd mourned him when he died. I'd *wept* at his burial griefs.

I lay there, and my blood froze with the betrayal of memory.

I had been betrayed by a man I'd loved as my father. By the man who had *been* my father. Whom I had loved. Who had used me. Who had doubtless despised all I was . . .

Tears trickled unbidden down my cheeks. Tears from Ligea

Gayed? She never cried. But I'd never been so utterly bereft before. I'd never felt that choking in my throat, that crushing sense of betrayal turning my whole life into a lie.

Yet they'd forged their weapon well, those two brutal men of Tyr. I was still a woman of Tyrans . . . wasn't I?

CHAPTER FIFTEEN

My clothes weren't made for those nights. The still air was cold and the bitterness of it seeped into my bones. Under the feet of the shleths, the sands were hard with ice; ahead the last of the Rakes clawed at a purple sky pricked through with stars, stars as bright as sparkles of sunlight on the sea. The Shiver Barrens: a land that burned with vicious heat by day, and stole the warmth from our bodies by night, a land that killed so easily, yet possessed a beguiling beauty destined to linger on in memory.

A land frightening in its mysteries.

My head pounded. Yesterday's strangeness had been real; I had the sword to prove it. And those visions, they must have been real too. I had walked *under* these killer sands, and lived. Something non-human had spoken to me. Something had shown me a vision of unspeakable brutality. And something had told me that thing I didn't want to think about.

I felt sick. Confused. Afraid.

And then those memories Brand had coaxed out of me with his taunting words . . . Had he any idea of what he had done to me? He had scoured my life of its illusions. What did I have now to replace the mockery of destroyed childhood dreams? The love of a slave, perhaps? I thought not. Or the love of an enemy, a man destined to marry another? Hardly that either. No, all I had in that empty space was the blight left behind by the deepest of betrayals.

I shivered.

'Are you cold?' Temellin asked.

We were walking our mounts, because apparently this last band of the sands was narrow, and there was no need to hurry. Garis and Brand were ahead of us, leading the pack shleth, and having their own conversation. By the sound of it, Garis was being amusing.

'Cold? Yes, a little.' In the vast emptiness of that landscape, my voice seemed frail, the whimper of a worm before the might of a god.

He fumbled in one of his saddlebags, and tossed me a blanket woven of shleth wool. 'Put this around you.'

I smiled my thanks, draped it over my shoulders and asked the first thing that popped into my head. *Anything to stop thinking about what had happened the day before. Anything to be Ligea Gayed again.*

'Is slavery the only reason you fight Tyr?' I asked.

I had previously avoided talking about Kardi politics. I had been wary of doing anything out of keeping with the personality of a woman brought up as a slave, but the time for that kind of caution was over. I hoped that by now Temellin trusted me, and I needed to know a lot more than I did. A lot more than what I could find out from observation and judicious eavesdropping.

'Why do you ask?' Temellin countered.

'You risk so much,' I said, choosing my words with care. 'All of you. Have you any idea what can happen to you?'

He shrugged, apparently indifferent.

'I don't think you really understand,' I told him, and the urgency I felt was genuine. 'Listen, let me tell you about a place called Crestos. General Gayed's brother was the Governor there for some years, and the Gayed family used to holiday there. It's a large island in the Sea of Iss. The Crestians rebelled against Tyranian rule, oh, about ten years ago. They drove the legions out, slaughtered every Tyranian they could find on the island. They were left alone for a year or two, but the Exaltarch was just planning his revenge. He built a new fleet, landed legionnaires on every beach of Crestos, and killed every man between the ages of twelve and sixty. Then he repopulated the place with Tyranian soldiers who were retiring from military life. They were granted land or town properties. The only catch was that they weren't allowed to take any women with them. So you can imagine what happened. Every child born on Crestos thereafter was half-Tyranian.'

He nodded, his emotions sober. 'I've heard the story.'

'I was on Crestos once, with the Gayed family, when I was about thirteen, before all this happened. I remember a peaceful, prosperous nation with a thriving commercial centre and port, a fine theatre and some of the best sculptors in the Exaltarchy. They had a good life then. They ended up with nothing. Not even their bloodlines. Was it *worth* it, Tem? Is what you do here worth the risk?' To add a little verisimilitude to my anxiety, I added, 'I don't want to see you dead.'

He grinned at me. 'I hope you won't.'

'Then maybe you could negotiate. Have the Magor swear allegiance to the Exaltarch in exchange for making Kardiastan slave-free. Kardi slaves are not popular in Tyr, I do know that. It would be no great loss to the Exaltarchy, and they would save on the number of legionnaires they have to have quartered here.'

He raised an eyebrow. 'Is that your idea, or the Legata's?'

'I believe she was going to mention something along those lines to the Governor. She could arrange it.' Perhaps.

'You don't understand,' he said. 'How could you? You weren't brought up here! This is *our* land, Derya. Ours! It doesn't belong to Bator Korbus and his legions. It is our *right* to govern ourselves. To be free. To decide what sort of buildings to have, what sort of law, what sort of punishment for wrongdoers. To decide how to educate our children, and what language they should learn.'

I tightened my hold on the blanket over my shoulders, trying to keep out the cold. 'But hasn't Tyrans brought you many advantages? The Tyranian road system, for example.'

'Built with the blood and sweat of Kardi slaves.'

'The theatres. The stadia. The games. The schools. The baths. The libraries. I've seen all these things in Sandmurram and Madrinya. There would be more, if there was peace here.' I heard a hint of desperation in my voice, and wondered at myself.

'All built with slave labour, on the Tyranian model. The theatres perform works that have nothing to do with us, in a language which is not our own, playing music that is not ours. The games encourage a competitive culture foreign to us. The schools would teach our children to be Tyranian, if they could. They certainly try. Bathing naked in public and lying about afterwards being pandered to by a bevy of slaves – or even servants – is not our custom. And the libraries don't contain works written by us. In fact, if any book or scroll written in Kardi is ever found, it is destroyed. We have lost our literature by the promulgation of Tyranian law, Derya. So much has been taken from us – can't you understand that? Because if you can't, then you ought to return to Tyrans. All we want is to be left alone to rule ourselves. To be equal to Tyrans, not subjugated to it. Why is that too much to ask?'

'And yet, from what Garis and others have told me, the ordinary Kardi never did rule. Ruling was the prerogative of the Magor.' *That's right, Ligea. Slide the knife in, right where it hurts.*

He was silent for a moment. I glanced across at him, and he was staring straight ahead, his face grim. He didn't like the implied criticism. 'Yes,' he said. 'That's correct. And I'm not going to apologise for it. We at least are Kardi. We speak the same language, and live by the same code. We have special abilities that make us eminently suited to rule. And we ourselves are governed by laws of service to all.'

'That last is exactly what Legata Ligea would say about the Tyranian authorities.'

He almost spat his contempt. 'Can you really believe we have anything in common with their methods of governance and commerce? You've lived in Tyr! You've seen what happens there, surely.'

'Yes,' I said. 'And I know what slavery is.'

He was instantly contrite. 'Ah, by the Mirage, I'm sorry. Of course you do. Better by far than I.' He looked at me then, and smiled his apology. 'You are right to question, for only by questioning can we learn. You have come far for someone who was brought up a slave.'

Something unpleasant crawled across my skin to nibble at my soul. My own lies, perhaps, so cleverly worded to be sure he wouldn't sense the falsehoods. I said, 'Don't think of me as someone who emptied the chamberpots or scrubbed the dishpans. Ligea took her slave with her everywhere – to school as a child, and then later to the theatre and the debates and the poetry evenings. Her slave learned along with her.' True enough, although the slave had been Brand. I hoped Temellin would believe it of Derya.

He stopped and stared at me. Almost immediately, the ice beneath his mount began to melt, and the sands stirred. I halted alongside, wondering just what part of my statement had put that peculiar expression on his face. 'I've been a fool,' he said quietly. 'You have been her companion all your remembered life. You love her, don't you? She is as an older sister to you. You don't want to betray her.'

'Slaves don't find it so hard to betray their owners,' I said woodenly. My mount shuffled uneasily as sand grains bubbled around its feet.

'Nonetheless. If you had to choose between the two of us, Ligea or me, who would it be?'

'I already have chosen.'

'No. You chose between freedom and slavery.'

'I would not willingly see anything happen to Ligea. But then – I wouldn't want anything to happen to you, either.' And that was true enough. Derya had vanquished Ligea in that particular battle.

He nodded, accepting I could go no further than that, and we continued on.

CHAPTER SIXTEEN

Brand and I looked upon the Mirage and did not believe what we saw.

'It is not real,' I said flatly. 'How can anything like this be real?'

'You are right,' Temellin replied. 'In one sense it is not real. Why else would it be called the Mirage? What is a mirage if not an illusion, a dream that is not there?'

'I don't understand.'

Temellin signalled Garis to ride on with Brand, leaving the two of us mounted on our shleths looking out over a land-scape that could not exist. He reached across and took my hand. 'It is the creation of entities we call the Mirage Makers. They have made a land including everything that pleases them, and because they are who they are, what they create has reality. I can eat the fruit and be sustained, drink the water and have my thirst slaked. But if the Mirage Makers decide they want a change, then the lake you see here today will be gone tomorrow; the leaves that are purple now might be white in an hour's time, the road that runs across this valley may not exist two seconds hence – or it may last a thousand years. If they want music, there will be music; if they want silence, they will have it. As a matter of courtesy, they do not usually remove the buildings from around us without warning, nor do they banish a chair that's in use, nor do they build a wall across a road just as we ride down it.'

I remembered the shapes I'd thought I had seen in the dancing sands. 'These entities – where do they live?'

'They *are* the Mirage, all that you see before you now. It is impossible to think of them as being creatures like us, Derya. They have none of our limitations, none of our frailties. They do not need a form to move, nor sustenance to survive, nor a mouth to speak, nor eyes to see. They do not give birth or die, they just are. They are as much found in every grain of the soil beneath us as they are found in every leaf of that tree over there, or every stone in that wall, in every feather of that bird you see.'

He spoke almost as if I weren't there, with a lyricism that spoke of his deep love for this place, the orator coming to the fore again. He continued, 'To our Kardi forebears, the Mirage Makers were enemies to be feared because they were so far beyond ordinary Kardis, so unknowable. In those days patches of the Mirage were found throughout Kardiastan. Those places were dangerous. The Mirage could kill us, and did, without even noticing we were gone. And then the first of the Magor was born. She passed on her skills to her children and her children's children. They were also mirage makers of a kind, people with the power to make what did not exist seem to have reality. Probably you and I also have that latent ability, although we do not know how to use it.

'The illusions our forebears made had none of the – the solidity of the Mirage you see around you, but they could create mirages on a vast scale. And did. They regarded them as an art form, and those who rendered them were revered, just as Tyrans reveres its sculptors. But for some reason, this Magor ability confused the true Mirage Makers, sending them mad with visions of a world that might or might not be. It became the weapon of the Magor, a weapon they turned against the Mirage Makers to punish them for their illusory world so treacherous to us. As more and more Magor were born, the Mirage Makers suffered immeasurable distress. And in their distress – no, in their madness – they damaged the land and its people still more. It was not a situation which benefited either side. Nor was it a conflict that could ever be won.

'It was then the first pact was made, between Mirage Makers and Magor, a pact that stands to this day. A covenant, if you like. One day soon you will be shown the Tablets of the Covenant and you will be asked to swear allegiance to the agreement. Until then, it's enough to say one result of the pact was that the true Mirage Makers withdrew behind the Shiver Barrens, and contact with them was restricted to what was necessary.'

He fell silent, his good humour in abeyance.

I prompted him to go on. 'But you came to live in the Mirage. First just you and the other children of the Ten with your teachers; now it seems every Magor who wants to come. Not to mention the Kardis you have freed from slavery. Why did these Mirage Makers allow that?'

'I wish I could tell you. None of us know what really happened, and the Mirage Makers choose not to tell us. After the invasion, Korden was the oldest of the Magoroth left alive: he was ten. I was only five. None of us knew what decisions were made by the Mirager, my uncle Solad, or why. The Illusos, the Theuros who went with us, did not know. Why did Solad send us to the Mirage when he did? Did he sense the Magoroth were about to be betrayed, and sent us away to save us? He told those who took us how to cross the Shiver Barrens: how did he find out? No one had ever done it before. No one had ever tried; it was forbidden for us to try. What bargain did Solad make with the Mirage Makers so we can now take refuge here? No one was told directly, although I think perhaps I was given an indication, when I received my sword.'

He stopped abruptly, biting his lip, but you can't pack words away again once they are spoken.

I prompted, 'Received your sword?'

He ran his hand through his hair, chagrined. 'Sorry. I shouldn't tell you anything about that, not yet. It's just, well, something I was told then indicated that there was a price, negotiated by Solad, which has not yet been paid and one day we will have to pay it. The Mirage has saved us for now; the Mirage Makers tolerate us and adjust the Mirage so we do not suffer too much from its unpredictability, but there will come a reckoning and perhaps the discharging of our obligation will be difficult for us. For me.'

'But you will pay?'

His face seemed grey as he replied. 'Yes. I believe we must pay, whatever the suffering it causes. If there was a bargain, made by my uncle, I must honour it. To do otherwise would be to flirt with a disaster of unimaginable proportions. The Magor must have the cooperation of the Mirage Makers, or there will be no more cabochons and therefore no Magor in the future.'

I stared at him. There was so much pain in his voice, I could only assume there was something he was not telling me, something so terrible he could not put it into words. I remembered my vision beneath the Shiver Barrens, and wondered if we both had more than an inkling of what the bargain was.

Infanticide.

No, don't think about it. Temellin is not like that. He would never kill children, anyone's children.

And yet when his eyes met mine, I saw only despair. I wanted to take him in my arms, I wanted to ease his torment, but instinct told me that would make things worse, not better. He was too used to bearing his burdens alone; perhaps no one had ever taught him to share them. Perhaps Miasa hadn't been a particularly perceptive wife, or perhaps it was just that once she was gone, he no longer had anyone who would share his cares. He was hardly going to confide in me anyway, not when some of the Ten regarded me with such suspicion. Not when he couldn't be absolutely certain of my loyalty.

I turned back to face the land ahead. I couldn't decide whether it was beautiful or mad. Nothing was as it should be. Blue feathers grew in place of grass and they tinkled metallically in the breeze. The sky was pink and splintered with lines like cracked glass. There was a charming stone bridge crossing nothing except some rosebushes, and a crazy-paving road that changed to a waterfall at its end. Animals grazing on the feathers in a nearby field had green fur, black whiskers and no feet; a bird flew past with a furry tail, tasselled at the end. A large red statue of an upside-down dragonfly dominated a field of cabbages. The plinth was built of bubbles. Something that looked suspiciously like a cow was curled up asleep on the roof of a house. The house itself was built of glass balls filled with fish and it leant at an impossible angle in insane, asymmetrical beauty. A sentry marched up and down outside playing a lute: he was made of wood, no more than an oversized children's toy with the ability to move.

'Nothing that leans so far off the true should be able to stand,' I murmured looking at the house. I felt I needed to say *something*.

'It will, unless the Mirage Makers want it otherwise. Are you ready for the rest of this land?'

'Where do we go?'

'There is a city the Mirage Makers built for us. It is just a little idiosyncratic in places, but not too traumatic. And it is bizarrely beautiful. Not more than two hours' ride from here. At least, that's what it was last time I rode this way. The time before that, a black lake blocked the route and it took me four days to ride around it. The Mirage can be tricky.'

I opened my mouth to reply, then closed it again. I couldn't think of anything sensible to say.

We rode for an hour in silence. I did not want to talk; there was too much to see, to marvel over. After we crossed a stream that flowed, impossibly, both uphill and downhill, I was prompted to comment on the one ugly thing I had seen: a patch of black and khaki green on a hillside. I wondered at first if it was some kind of bog, but the stink soon made it clear it was more than that. No swamp this, but rather a suppurating sore about the size of a town forum, an expanse of foul rottenness that looked and smelled corrupt. Black scum floated over clear greenish ooze dribbling in rivulets out from the core, as though spreading contagion.

'What happened there?' I asked, halting my mount.

Temellin refused to look at it. He said curtly, his voice once more edged with pain, 'We don't know. There have always been such patches, ever since we first came here as children. They grow larger with time, and new ones appear. We have tried to clear them away, but it's impossible. They are poisonous to everything. I cannot believe they have their origin in the Mirage Makers. They are too . . . evil. We call them the Ravage.'

I was about to ride on when I was submerged in a suffocating emotion so thick I could barely breathe. Someone was hating me. The feeling was so real, so personal, I gagged, choking. I looked around wildly for whoever was responsible for such an outpouring of malicious loathing, but the only people in sight were Garis and Brand riding ahead of us, and – closer at hand but equally innocuous – an old Kardi woman fishing in a pond, with a couple of children playing around in a shleth cart behind her. I took a hold of myself and made an effort to pinpoint the source.

'What is it?' Temellin asked in alarm.

'It's the Ravage. It hates me!' The words sounded ridiculous as soon as I gave voice to them.

'Oh.' He sighed and nodded. 'Yes, I know. I mean, it hates everyone. We've got used to it, I suppose. Try not to let it worry you; if you don't go near it, nothing can happen to you.'

'Let's get out of here,' I said. 'I – I don't like it.' I slapped my heels into my mount, desperate to leave that corrosive loathing.

A little later on, once we'd left the Ravage behind and had slowed to a walk once more, I asked Temellin if, when the Magor were free to live in Kardiastan again, they would leave the Mirage.

He nodded. 'Oh yes. This has never been more than a temporary haven; it does not belong to us. I am sure it was never part of my uncle's bargain with the Mirage Makers that our stay be permanent.' He glanced at me, his look soft, and I felt an answering surge of emotion. It occurred to me I had come to know Temellin surprisingly well in a short time. I knew how much pain he concealed behind that cheerful exterior of his; I sensed how much inner uncertainty, how much anger at injustice, there was inside him. One part of me wanted to help carry that load. Appalled, I tried to remember yet again that I had a duty to destroy him.

Neither thought brought me any joy.

A moment later, Temellin said, 'Look – the Mirage City is in sight.'

He was pointing, and I saw the buildings rising out of the plain like a pile of ill-stacked bowls and mugs. They leant against one another, occasionally meeting overhead, sometimes held apart by crooked covered bridges or walkways. It was a city of narrow curved streets and winding stairs, of back alleys that dipped and humped like loop caterpillars. The stonework of the walls bulged with eccentric lumps and nodules or was pitted with niches and hollows planted with ferns and flowers. There was no symmetry, no planning. It had the unexpectedness of nature.

'However do you find your way anywhere?' I asked later, as we wended our way into this mess of streets and drunken buildings.

'With luck, more than anything,' he said with a grin. 'And don't forget, things can change overnight. A straight street can suddenly develop as many corners as joints on a shleth feeding arm, or a main road can become a stream. There was one awful week when we had to go everywhere by boat on canals; luckily the Mirage Makers tired of that change fairly quickly.'

'Where are you taking me?'

'All the Magoroth live in one building we call the Maze, for want of a better name. It contains any number of apartments, as well as servant quarters, nurseries – everything we need. We'll find a place for you for the time being. Korden and Pinar will demand both you and Brand be under supervision, I'm afraid.'

I reined in my mount. 'Will I – will I see you at all?' It was an act. A touch of pleading, to show my trustworthiness. To give him a hint that perhaps Derya was falling in love with him. And yet, it was also not entirely a deception. Even as I spoke the words, I knew I wanted to see him again. *Vortex*, I thought, *why the Goddess is he so blamed attractive?*

He stopped alongside me. 'I – cabochon help me, Derya – I don't think I can stay away. But I have promised Pinar she wouldn't have to wait much longer; she is almost thirty-five. If she is to have children, we ought to get together soon and she wants marriage.'

His face was so drawn, his voice so stressed, I couldn't bear to look at him. I knew, without him saying it, that once married he would be faithful to his wife, no matter that she was a murderous bitch. I said, 'Perhaps it would be better if you and I did not live in the same building.'

'Perhaps – later. Not now, not yet. Please, Derya, not yet.'

'It is not a weakness to feel this way,' I told him, nettled by the shame I sensed in him.

'No. No, to feel this way is wondrous. But to give in to it? It will hurt Pinar, it will anger Korden and some of the others. And yet I can't help myself. I don't even want to try.'

I heard his ache and shuddered, hurting. The huntress shouldn't love the prey.

Such a love disarms you.

We were cheered as we rode towards the Maze. People poured out of the houses, welcoming their Mirager, clapping and waving and smiling. Far from accepting the adulation as his due, Temellin appeared profoundly moved and not a little embarrassed. Yet there was a natural regality about him too. He unsheathed his sword and raised it over his head for everyone to see, and the cheering redoubled. There were tears in his eyes as we rode into the courtyard of the Maze.

He was busy then, greeting people, organising, talking. He asked Garis to look after me, and Brand as well, which the youth was happy enough to do. It was Garis who led us into the building, saying, 'You won't see much of Temellin in the next few days, Derya. Now that he has his sword back,' he glanced at Brand and lowered his voice, 'he has to attend to some babies.'

He was being indiscreet, to say the least, reminding me that he was little more than a youth, capable of a rash lack of caution when he wanted to impress. However, I was too pre-occupied to think about what he said. I was trying to make sense of the building and its furnishings, a difficult task when there was so much absurdity.

'A drunken architect?' Brand suggested.

'And a blind mason as well, I think,' I said. Stairways ended in blank walls, passages led nowhere, bridges were strung across the top of tall rooms. Some rooms had no furniture, while in others even the wooden chairs were so solid it would have taken four strong men to lift just one. I saw empty bookshelves floating in the air, and fires that burned without consuming anything – in fireplaces built of anything from fish skeletons to blacksmiths' hammers.

There were plenty of people about: ordinary Kardis to undertake all the menial chores, as well as Magor of all ranks. And underfoot, everywhere, Magoroth children, laughing, playing or being marched to lessons by their Magor tutors. One passageway we passed along had an intricate game of hopsquares chalked out on the floor, although no one was using it just then.

At first the informality grated on me. This was the building that housed the man who claimed to be the rightful ruler of all Kardiastan; why then did it have more of the atmosphere of a country market fair than a monarch's residence? I thought of the Exaltarch's palace in Tyr, with its rich ornamentation, its uniformed guards everywhere, its rigid rules of etiquette and protocol, all more appropriate for a ruler than this cheerful informality. And then I remembered, guiltily, that I'd found those marbled rooms in Tyr stifling. In fact, I had hated the palace. I'd hated the coldness of the atmosphere, the faint touch of unease pervading it like an invisible mist – the residue left by absolute power. I'd hated bending my knees to Bator Korbus and touching the hem of his robe.

Confound it, my thoughts were as muddled as my emotions.

I couldn't even be sure what I believed in any more. I was surrounded by too much that was bizarre. And I'd had insufficient time to consider all I had learned from my contact with the Mirage Makers.

After a confusing ten-minute walk, Garis found a room for Brand close to his own and another for me. 'The Mirager's apartments are just down that flight of steps,' he whispered, pointing. In ten minutes more he'd produced a maid for me, had a meal sent up, arranged for hot water for a bath and procured me some clean clothes. Then he left.

With infinite relief, I removed my sandals, reflecting I would never be able to accustom myself to wearing shoes inside a building. I still found the whole idea of tramping the outside dirt into one's living quarters disgusting.

An hour later, having bathed and eaten and changed, I lay down to rest.

It was four hours before I woke, when someone knocked on my door. It was Garis, with Brand behind him. 'You're wanted,' he said. 'Both of you.'

I glanced out of the window; the sun was just setting in a patchwork sky. 'Who wants us?' I asked.

'Well, Temellin sent for you,' he replied as I tied on my sandals to go with them, 'but it's really a meeting of all the Magoroth.' As the three of us hurried over a rope bridge a moment or two later, he filled us in on what had been happening. 'Pinar's been earbashing everyone with her suspicions. Her party got back yesterday, you know, because our route was longer than hers, and she's had plenty of time to spread her poison. We were the last to arrive, more's the pity.'

Before I could reply, a male voice echoed up from the room below. 'Hey, Garis, Tavia says to tell you if you don't get to her pallet soon, she'll straighten out your lovely eyelashes!'

Garis was young enough to blush rather than laugh. He

raised a hand in acknowledgement and gave me an embarrassed shrug. 'It might not be an easy meeting for you.'

'I'm sure I'll survive,' I said as we passed a group of small boys and girls coming the opposite way, all with that newly scrubbed look of children on their way to bed. The elderly Theura who was shepherding them along gave me a curious stare and a wide, toothless grin.

'Here we are.' Garis opened a door and ushered us in.

There were about thirty people in the room, too many, I thought, for them all to be of the highest rank. I guessed the sprinkling of older Magor were the respected lower-ranked teachers of the original ten Magoroth children. Brand and I were introduced to everyone we had not yet met. Pinar, full of confidence, with her malice carefully concealed, inclined her head in greeting. Jahan and Jessah, the married Magoroth siblings, came across to greet me. I still hadn't managed to work out why Jahan had looked so familiar to me on the day we had met in Madrinya.

Temellin smiled at me, but I sensed his tension. Whatever had happened in the room before our arrival had not pleased him. 'Derya,' he said. 'We have decided one of the first things we must do is to find out who you are. To help us, we must know your Magor rank. We would like to cut back the skin from your cabochon; do you mind?'

I smiled in return. 'No, of course not. Who will do the deed?' I held out my hand.

'I will.' It was Korden who stepped forward, drawing his sword from its scabbard.

I eyed the sharp blade with reluctance. 'Isn't that overly large for the job, Korden?'

He gave a faint smile. 'If I use my Magor sword it won't hurt; a knife would.' He took my left hand in his right and with a swift slice of his blade he drew a line across my palm.

Blood welled up, but I felt nothing. He laid the weapon aside, put both thumbs on either side of the cut and pulled the flesh so that it slipped away from the cabochon.

The flare of light took us all by surprise. It was as if it had been trapped in my hand and had ached to escape. It shot forth, showering us with its brilliance, and then settled back into a steady glow on the palm of my hand.

The silence around the room was as profound as death. No one moved, no one spoke for so long I wondered if they had been struck dumb by the light. Then an old woman, an Illusa who had introduced herself as Zerise, stepped forward to kneel at my feet. She took up my left hand, wiped away the blood and kissed the cabochon. 'One of the blessed has been returned to us,' she said. 'Welcome home, Magoria.'

The light from my cabochon bathed the woman with a warm gold radiance.

PART THREE
SHIRIN

CHAPTER SEVENTEEN

The silence splintered into babble and movement and emotional turmoil. Pinar's angry 'But that's impossible!' was lost in expressions of delight from others. The Magoroth came up to hug me, touching my cabochon to theirs, showing me the warmth of their welcome to their ranks.

Across the room, Brand's shock segued into cynicism, but I refused to return his gaze. The glow in my cabochon subsided. All I saw now was a translucent yellow gem set into my palm. A cabochon that could kill. What did that make me? More than human? Or less? I shivered.

Then, as the excitement died away a little, Korden bent to murmur in my ear. 'I am glad, for you, and for us. But – are you truly with us, Derya? Or do you think with a Tyranian heart, as Pinar would have us believe?'

I smiled ruefully to cover my anxiety. 'I can't change overnight, Korden. I will admit that. There are things which are strange, distasteful even. And things have happened too quickly for me to adjust.' I took his left hand and pressed my cabochon to his. 'Perhaps this will convince you; do you feel anything but happiness there?' I knew he would be able to detect nothing suspicious. Not even Temellin had noticed the slightest sign of disloyalty within me, although he had often held my hand; I was a Brotherhood Compeer, and the masking of emotion was a Brotherhood skill as much as it was a Magor one. I was confident I could hide myself even better than they did.

But Korden wasn't convinced, and his 'Welcome to the Magoroth, Magoria-derya,' was as welcoming as the stare of a guard dog.

Temellin laid a hand on Korden's arm. 'My turn, I think,' he said, and then drew me aside. He held my hand and I was shot with his delight. He was *transformed*.

I stared at him, wondering what I was missing.

He laughed at me, whispering in my ear as he drew me into a congratulatory hug. 'Don't you know what this means, Derya? *You* can be Miragerin-consort! I do not have to turn to Pinar.'

My heart leapt, absurdly, then cracked. What was I thinking of? I was not going to stay long. I was an agent of Tyrans. I was going to betray them all, put down this damned insurgency of theirs. Bring back peace of their land. *Marry* a Kardi barbarian? The idea was ludicrous.

Marry *Temellin*? I gazed at him, and those eyes of his were full of humour, of anticipation. His delight washed over me in waves. *Goddess*, I thought, *the idiot is in love with me.* And then: *This is what love ought to be.* And then: *But not for me. I'm a compeer.*

I thought of Favonius, remembered all that his emotions had said. Favonius had lusted after me. He'd been proud of his possession of a general's daughter. He'd loved me as much as he was capable of loving anyone, but there had been nothing like this in him. The memories of all the time we had spent together withered like sun-seared leaves.

I remembered the way Brand had felt when he had – oh, so briefly – allowed me to touch his emotions. He loved me the way Temellin did, too.

My thoughts, unbidden, took another leap. I remembered the time Temellin and I had spent together. I remembered his body, his tenderness. The way he laughed. His intelligence. The way his voice softened when he spoke of things he loved. The way his language became poetry. I remembered how the children of the freed slaves adored him. *Sweet Elysium*, I thought, *stop me from being so – so witless. Just because no one has ever loved me before is no reason to fall apart like – like a broken amphora spilling its contents. I cannot crack simply because I find a man attractive and his love flattering.*

'Derya—?' Temellin asked. 'Are you all right?' His concern was palpable. I was far too aware of his unconcealed emotions.

My eyes searched for Pinar. The older Magoria was staring at me, hatred-filled, but with her emotions under tight control. 'Pinar will kill me,' I said involuntarily.

'Don't be silly! She and I don't love one another, not that way. It was to be a marriage of – of friendship. For children. She will be glad for me.'

I blinked at this extraordinary self-deception, but before I could comment, Korden was there again, saying, 'Temellin, shouldn't we continue with what we intended? We wanted to find out who Derya is; let's do so.'

'How?' I asked. 'Is it possible that I – that I have family here? That—?' I couldn't give voice to the words, but my mind was suddenly filled with my childhood memory of a woman with a mane of russet hair, a woman bathed in gold light and splattered with scarlet. Perhaps I had been loved before this, once. I felt I was choking on memories and emotion and sentiment.

Goddess, Rathrox would never believe his eyes if he saw me like this.

Temellin slid an arm around my shoulders. 'Illusazerise,' he said, indicating the woman who had kissed my cabochon, 'was the Magor in charge of the palace nursery in Madrinya at the time of the invasion. She knew all the children. Including, therefore, you. She was one of the few people who survived the massacre of the Shimmer Festival.' He led me across the room to the Illusa.

My immediate thought was that if I had indeed been one of Zerise's charges, she would have scared me out of my swaddling clothes. She was all sharp edges: face, body, hands, all honed to acute peaks and ridges with no softening flesh. One cheek was badly scarred by two deeply gouged holes and two flanking lesser marks, all in a straight line. Her eyes had a sharply focused intensity and she held her body as if it were a poised axe. She was aged about fifty, not quite as old as I had first thought; the sparseness of her iron-grey hair and the angular thinness of her body were deceptive.

'Zerise,' Temellin was saying, 'who can Derya be?'

The woman looked at me with those sharp eyes, searching my face as if to find the imprint of the child there. 'What do you know about yourself?' she asked finally. 'Your real name perhaps? There was no child called Derya. Anything at all might be helpful.'

Her voice was soft, at complete variance with her looks, but I was breathless with the tension of that moment; truth was suspended somewhere in the minutes ahead and I longed for it to be plucked and given to me. Yet when I spoke, my voice was calm; that, too, was a Brotherhood skill.

'I can't remember my real name. General Gayed renamed me.' True enough, although the name had been a good Tyranian one: Ligea. 'He found me and took me to Tyr when I was just a little less than three. That was in the tenth year of Senna Timonius's Exaltarchy, in the fourth month, I think. Before that – I remember the woman I think was my mother. A Magoria, I guess. She had a sword and there was gold light streaming out of her. There were people shouting and screaming. There were curtains. I wanted to look through the curtains, but someone wouldn't let me. Another woman. And then she disappeared too and I was horribly afraid and surrounded by strangers. There was a lot of fighting. And blood.' My left hand had curled up into a fist and it was an effort to relax it again. 'I can't remember much else.'

Zerise bit her lip, considering.

I stared at her face and thought, *I've seen that kind of scar somewhere before* . . . Then I remembered. It had been on the cheek of a man held in the Cages in Tyr, a rebel. I'd been told that a legionnaires' weapon, a circular piece of metal with jagged edges hurled from a whirlsling, left just such a mark. A rip-disc, the legions called it.

'Almost three in the fourth month of the tenth year of the previous Exaltarchy,' Zerise was saying. 'Let me see, that would mean you were born around the fifth or sixth month of the Kardi year Veshol-twenty-three. There were two Magorias born about then—'

'Mirageless soul!' The exclamation was Temellin's.

Zerise nodded. 'Yes. Shirin. Magoria-shirin was born in the fifth month. It's got to be her.'

'And the other?' Korden prompted.

She addressed Temellin. 'Your cousin Sarana, Mirager-temellin. Magoria-sarana was just a month younger than Magoria-shirin.'

The silence in the room developed an intensity so widely shared it could almost be touched. I darted glances from one person to another, not understanding why everyone was so tense, knowing something significant was not being said, hating my ignorance, but not sure I wanted to dispel it. They were all horrified – no, more than that – they were devastated by the idea I might be Sarana. Emotion skipped around the room in flurries.

Even Garis was aghast. 'Are you *sure* she is Shirin?' he asked.

'Oh, she couldn't be Sarana,' Zerise said. She dispensed a comforting calm in liberal waves that said even more than her words. 'The Mirager-solad himself brought Magoria-sarana's body back for burial. We all went to the burial griefs.'

'There can't be any doubt? A misidentification?' It was Temellin who asked, and his voice was unfamiliar to my ears; it was harsh and almost cruel.

'Oh no. Utterly impossible. The Mirager-solad himself identified her. And he was her father, after all. She was unmutilated, killed by an arrow through the heart. He was the one who found her shortly after the ambush. He'd ridden out to persuade her mother to come back, you see . . . He shroud-wrapped her, and her mother Wendia, and rode back to Madrinya with them both in his howdah. I saw them arrive. He was shattered. He worshipped that child. And he loved Wendia too. The tears were streaming down his cheeks. Do you think if there had been the slightest doubt the bodies he carried were not those of Sarana and Wendia, he would not have seized on it? I have rarely seen a man as broken as he was by the death of his daughter. He fought like a whirlwind during the Shimmer Feast attack, though.' She looked at me and explained. 'I was there, you understand, one of the few to survive. I saw Solad kill more Tyranians than anyone else that day, even though he was stuck through with arrows like a roast on a spit. It was sheer burning rage that kept him alive long enough to kill so many.' She wiped away tears with the back of a hand and turned to Temellin. 'No, the Magoria here cannot possibly be Sarana.'

'Are you sure the only other possibility is Shirin?' Once again the question came from Temellin. This time he was smiling, his eyes sparkling with a partially suppressed joy.

'Yes, if the Magoria is right about how old she is. And even if she's not—' Zerise thought for a while. 'No. Reneta was about a year younger and I saw her body myself. The other girls were little more than babies and they were all accounted for, murdered in their cradles. But Shirin's body was never found. And she was the only Magoria missing. The part of the palace she was in was devastated by fire; there was little left to find. We thought she'd burned. I suppose it is possible she was saved by a Tyranian soldier.' She touched her scar and added bitterly, 'There were enough of *them* about.'

But Temellin was already reaching for me, whirling me in his arms, holding me tightly, hurting me in his joy. 'Shirin . . . Shirin, my Shirin – don't you remember me? I gave you my wooden shleth when you cried after I broke your toy sword. Don't you remember?'

I shook my head, laughing. 'Temellin, put me down—! Who am I? Tell me, who is this Shirin?'

'*You* are Shirin, my love! I thought you were dead! I remember crying when they told me—'

Over Temellin's shoulder I caught a glimpse of Garis's face. He wasn't rejoicing. He was filled with consternation, as though he were waiting for a calamity he knew was inevitable. I thought, *He realises something Temellin doesn't.* I pushed Temellin away. 'Garis,' I asked, 'who is Shirin?'

He blurted out the answer, knowing how I would feel, remembering as apparently Temellin did not. 'Shirin was – is – you are Temellin's little sister,' he said. 'You had the same parents.'

My world died in a crashing roar in my ears. I saw people opening and closing their mouths, speaking to me, but I could not hear them. I saw their joy become uncertainty as my shock registered with them. My revulsion spilled out all over the room. I saw Temellin's grin become a horrified mouthing. I destroyed his happiness with my unbridled reaction, with the warding-off gesture of my hands. I turned from him to Brand, walking into his arms, clutching at him, burying my face in his chest. I couldn't speak. I was choking on the bile and vomit rising in me.

Oh, Goddess, I thought. *I have bedded my own brother.*
Oh, Goddess, forgive me.

Oh, Goddess, now I knew – I *loved* this man. Ligea Gayed gave her heart without even knowing it. The Brotherhood Compeer fell in love with the enemy.

Goddess forgive me. I did not know. *Bedded my brother.* Fitting punishment for thinking myself immune to sentiment.
You stupid fool, Ligea.

Brand knew. He swung me away from Temellin's imploring hands, herded me out of that room, somehow found his way through the labyrinth to the quietness of my own bedroom. When I lay down on my pallet, he chafed the coldness of my fingers, covered my shivering body with a blanket, gently stroked my face and hair. There was no triumph in him, no satisfaction. When I could not cry, when I shrivelled and froze inside, it was Brand who had tears in his eyes.

'Don't let him near me,' I whispered. 'I don't want to see him.'

'He won't come in here,' he promised, and he was as good as his word. Temellin came and was turned away.

When my trembling died, it was Brand who tried to offer consolation. 'It's not so bad, Ligea. You've never been one to worship the Goddess and her rules, so you *can't* think you have sinned—'

'Sinned? No. It's just – just the *thought* of doing such a thing,' I said finally. 'It's *unnatural.* And they think it so *normal.* Oh, Goddess, Brand. I wanted him so much. Just to look at him was enough to start the ache. And do you think I will feel any different now? I will always remember that; there will be part of me that will want him still . . . And yet the thought of his touch now – makes me *sick*. Physically ill.'

He looked at me, and heard what I didn't say. I had loved Temellin. He read it in my pain. 'Then let's go away from here,' he said at last. 'Back to Madrinya, if you must. Bring the legions here, raze the place to the ground, kill them all if that's the only way you can lay your ghosts.' He was pointing out what I couldn't do, of course, forcing me to clarity of thought.

I said, 'Damn you, Brand, you know I can't. Maybe that compeer bitch, Ligea of Tyr, could have done it, but she doesn't exist any more. He is my *brother*. My flesh and blood.' I turned my face to the wall. It was difficult to say the next words, to tell him what I had refused to think about since I had learned the truth of it under the Shiver Barrens. 'He is the father of my son.'

He was stilled with shock. 'You *can't* know that you—' he said after a long pause. 'You've known him only a matter of what, ten days? How could you know that you are—?'

'I know. Just as I know when people lie. I have a life growing in me, his son. His nephew.' I gave a bitter laugh. 'I shall be mother and aunt all in one.' I rolled off the pallet and went to stand at the window. I had known my pregnancy in one split second when I was inside the Shiver Barrens. The knowledge had suddenly been there in my body, in my mind. And more than just that, I'd known his gender. A boy, conceived the first day when I had been so overwhelmed by the attraction of a Magoria to a Magori that I had cast all sense and precautions away in exchange for pleasure. The Goddess Melete – or fate, or whatever you like to call it – had made me pay for that moment of fervid passion.

Doubtless the knowledge of the child, my son, should have been the source of joy, of wonderment. But what joy could there be when I learned of him just moments after I was shown a vile vision of death? A vision of a nameless baby ripped from his nameless mother's womb, to cause her demise – and for what? Some sick purpose of the Mirage Makers? What conclusion was I to derive from that, except the most obvious? And that was another thing I had spent days trying not to think about: I was being primed as a sacrifice, to supply an unborn child.

Yet now I wondered. Perhaps I had mistaken the meaning of the vision. Perhaps the Mirage Makers had been telling me something slightly different: that the child was an abomination, seeded by a man who was his uncle as well as his father. That he had to be destroyed, even if it meant my death. Perhaps they didn't like sibling pairing any more than I did. Yet if that was the case, why my child and not, say, Jahan and Jessah's? They had children, I knew. Several of them. Why mine? Why *me*?

I covered my face with my hands, to hide my horror from Brand.

'Let's go back to Tyr, then,' he said. For once, his calm had deserted him. His face was ashen with shock. 'Tell Rathrox you failed. Resign. Live your own life.'

'I cannot return to Tyrans. I would be accused of treason. No one leaves the Brotherhood without Rathrox's consent. No one walks away from an assignment without being punished for their dereliction of duty.'

He was disbelieving. 'Punished? *Treason?* You think they'd *burn* you?'

'Oh no. Burning is for non-citizens. Citizen traitors are crucified.'

'They wouldn't dare! You are Gayed's daughter. You are being melodramatic.'

Goddess, I wished I were. I could already feel the nails being driven into my hands, see the blood dribbling down my arms, hear the coarse mockery of men like Hargen Bivius. I said, 'But there are other factors involved here, aren't there?'

We stared at one another while he considered what I meant. 'They set you up,' he said softly. 'The three of them. Korbus, Rathrox and Gayed. Your whole life was aimed at this moment. The moment you would be in a position to be an instrument of their revenge on Kardiastan.'

I nodded, nausea seeping through me like poison. Gayed. *I'd thought he loved me* . . . I forced myself to sound rational, reasoned, calm. 'If I fail here, and go home with the task unfinished, their revenge will extend to my downfall. There would be some trumped-up charge, to make my dereliction seem truly traitorous. Would they stop short of crucifixion, do you think? I don't think so. Anyway, at the very least, they will strip me of all I own, including my reputation and my respectability. My life wouldn't be worth ten sestus.' *Tyr*, I thought. I had loved that city once.

'Vortex*damn* them.' His next words were said with an urgent passion. 'We can go somewhere else, then. Leave them all behind: Kardis, Tyranians, the Brotherhood, escape all of them. Build a life for yourself somewhere else. In Altan perhaps. Or even outside the boundaries of the Exaltarchy.'

'Yes. No. I don't know.'

'There's nothing here to hold you back.'

I was silent a long while, looking out of the window at the conglomeration of crazy buildings, now just curious shapes in the darkness. I said finally, 'It is his son too. He has a father's rights . . .'

I heard the faint expelling of his breath: a sigh, acknowledging his acceptance that there was no gain for him in my loss.

'Don't tell Temellin about this pregnancy, Brand. I'll tell him in my own way, in my own time.'

'I won't say anything to anyone. This is between the two of you.'

Oh, Goddess, I thought. *If only it was.* But there were the Mirage Makers . . . Did they want the child in order to destroy an abomination? Or for some other reason? Did they need a child to bring them new blood, to rejuvenate whatever it was they were? A new Mirage Maker to become one with them? I had never heard of a mother surviving the trauma of having a child and womb lifted from her body. The Magor had healing powers, I knew that, but I doubted they included the skill needed to save a woman from such a mutilation. What was it Garis had said? They were healers, not miracle workers.

And then there were the Magor. When it became known I was pregnant, and if it were true Solad had gained a sanctuary within the Mirage in exchange for a future unborn Magor child, then they might consider my life to be forfeit.

I wondered how many people knew about the required sacrifice. Temellin, certainly. I'd seen his face when he spoke of Solad's bargain and his own responsibility to fulfil it. What was it he had said? *I believe we must pay, whatever the suffering it causes.* He was probably the only one the Mirage Makers had told, although he could well have passed on the knowledge to others. To Korden. To Pinar? After all, she had a right to know. She was going to marry Temellin, and the logical sacrifice would be a child of the Mirager. And the woman who carried it.

I shuddered. I was the outsider, the expendable one. Who would care? Temellin, when he believed the sacrifice was necessary and others called for my death, as they most certainly would? Pinar would actively pursue my murder, I had no doubt of that. Quite apart from the prompting of her jealousy, sacrificing me and my child might save her own hide if ever she conceived Temellin's child.

I won't do it, I thought. *No one is going to kill me. I won't let them. And I am not going to run away, either.*

You are the Miragerin . . . Words whispered in the sand. 'There's something that doesn't quite—' I began, and then stopped. Could the Magoroth be wrong? Could I not be the other woman they had mentioned – Sarana? 'I want to talk to – to Zerise would be best, I think. Can you get her for me, Brand?'

'Certainly. If I don't get lost, that is. Damn place has more passageways than a fish has scales.'

I continued to stand at the window after he had gone, but I wasn't seeing the view. I was back in the Shiver Barrens, hearing the song of the Mirage Makers, trying to fan a spark of hope. Anything was better than the alternative.

An hour later, Brand entered with a heartfelt look at me indicating he had indeed managed to lose himself. He ushered Zerise in and then left us. The Illusa moved through the dimness of the room to the table and lit the candle there. I didn't see what she did, but she used her cabochon to do it. When she spoke, her voice was gentle. 'We didn't understand at first,' she said. 'We all thought you would be glad. To be the sister of the Mirager—'

'You knew he was also my lover?'

'We do now. We do not feel your revulsion. Such unions are usually blessed with a lasting love. The children of sibling unions are also much blessed. You and Temellin are the children of such a union—'

'Oh, sweet Melete help me! My *parents*?' I wanted to be sick. I warred with my body to halt the reflex, to keep the food in my stomach. Inbred! And my son . . . the grandchild of siblings, the child of siblings, inbred to a point of insanity.

'Temellin is the strongest Magori we have,' Zerise said. 'His powers are strong within him, as yours will be when you are taught how to use them. There is nothing wrong with such a union, Magoria-shirin. A marriage between you would be cause for great happiness, and your children would be very, very special. Perhaps the greatest Magoroth ever born. Healthy, intelligent and Magor-strong.'

But I didn't want to hear. I said, 'This other Magoria, this Sarana—'

'If she had lived she would be Miragerin, and Mirager-temellin would not hold the sword of the Mirager. She was your cousin, the only child of your oldest uncle, Mirager-solad. There were five siblings, you know: Solad who was the eldest, then a brother and a sister, Ebelar and Niloufar, who were Shirin's and Temellin's parents, then another brother who was Korden's father, and finally another sister, who was Pinar's mother. Sarana was the heir, but she died before the Madrinya Shimmer Festival massacre. The massacre was not the first attack on our people; it was just the worst.'

I was stilled, remembering the expression on Temellin's face when he had thought I might be Sarana; remembering the emotion that had twisted his voice. He had almost hated me then. Wryly, I thought to myself that here was something else we shared besides a love of power: a marked reluctance to relinquish the power we had. I asked, 'There is no possibility—?'

'None.' She shook her head sadly. 'It was a terrible time, Magoria. The Mirager worshipped his daughter from the moment of her birth. Some said she was his obsession. Her mother, Magoria-wendia, thought so. She thought the Mirager was ruining their daughter to the point of idiocy, and I must say I agreed with her. Sarana was fast becoming an unpleasant little brat. Wendia decided to take the child and leave Madrinya. She wasn't the Miragerin-consort – Solad wasn't married – so it wasn't all that hard for her to go. Unfortunately her howdah was ambushed and everyone in her party was killed. I thought the Mirager might die with grief when he realised Sarana had died.'

I interrupted. 'But if Wendia and Solad weren't married, how could Sarana be the heir?'

'The first-born child of the ruler is the heir, no matter who the other parent is, as long as the child is a Magoroth and as long as the ruling Mirager or Miragerin acknowledges the child as theirs. That is Magor law. We put no store by a child's legitimacy as Tyranian law does.' She snorted. 'They try to tell us their laws are better, but we will never acknowledge their ways. Why should a child be robbed of his birthright because his parents did not marry?'

'So if Sarana had lived, she would have become Miragerin. Is there anyone *else* who might use that title?'

'Well, the official consort of the ruling Mirager. If you were to marry Mirager-temellin, you would be Miragerin-shirin, the Miragerin-consort. And then there is the mother of the heir. Even if she is not the consort, she is honoured with the title of Miragerin. And then finally there's the mother of the Mirager. Your mother, yours and Temellin's, would have been termed Miragerin-niloufar, had she lived.'

The mother of the heir. *Oh, Acheron's hells*, I thought. *My son will be Mirager in this land.* I wasn't Sarana, but I truly was Miragerin anyway, just as the Mirage Makers said. I was the mother to the heir, the unborn heir. They had known that . . . Then a new thought blasted me. Until the baby was born, *I was Temellin's heir.* I was his younger sister, and the Kardis made no distinctions between the sexes where their ruler was concerned.

If Temellin died, Ligea Gayed, Legata Compeer of the Brotherhood, would be regarded by the Kardis as their rightful ruler. I gave an ironic laugh that hiccupped into a sob. I should kill him. Then, as the Miragerin-ruler, I could bring the Magor down in ways they could never have dreamed of . . . and reap such glory in Tyr there would be statues of me built in the Forum Publicum. My success would be a legend handed down to the next generations. Was *this* the triumph Rathrox and Bator Korbus had schemed to achieve? They'd wanted me to kill or capture the Mirager. And then perhaps they'd planned to tell me who I was – and plant me, obedient and loyal Ligea, on the Kardis as their rightful ruler. A grateful vassal, to do as I was told by Tyr.

Goddessdamn. The Oracle. Of course. They'd aimed to give my future an apparent spiritual dimension, to seed me with a sense of destiny by sending me to the Oracle. How had the poem run?

'All power in her wide embrace,
None will again deny
Ligea Gayed her rightful place.'

My rightful place. Miragerin of Kardiastan. Goddessdamn.

Zerise was watching me, mystified. 'My child – why do you cause yourself so much grief? Your love for the Mirager is blessed. Accept it. Go gladly to his arms. Bear his children. Why cling to the laws of a land that was never really yours? You are Kardi; you are Magor; rejoice in it!' Her voice had an edge to it now, an intensity matching the rest of her. She shot out a bony hand to grip my arm. 'You have a duty to the Magor. We all have! Look at me, Magoria – I was a nurse, a children's nurse – can you see that when you look at me now? I doubt it. I haven't been a nurse since I had to wade through children's blood, carrying the only two babies I could save, both Theuros children, my own face smashed beyond repair. Now I fight. My cabochon will burn a legionnaire to ashes one day

– I, who only wanted to care for my babies. Your duty comes before your wishes, Magoria.'

I swallowed bile and said, 'Ask Brand to come in, will you, Illusa-zerise?'

She heard the dismissal and the fire damped down. Yet, just as she was on her way out, she turned back. She wanted to say something, started to say it, but changed her mind. A most extraordinary expression skittered across her face. It was so fleeting I wasn't sure I'd seen it, yet I was left with the feeling I had glimpsed a dismay so profound it bordered on panic. Then she was gone.

I thought: *If I go back to the Brotherhood, I can rule this land. I can have whatever I want. Power. Wealth. Respect. The things I've always wanted. The Oracle's predictions, all come true. Goddessdamn.*

Once that knowledge would have set me dreaming. Once that would have brought a sparkle of triumph into my eyes. Instead, all I heard were questions. Nasty, provocative little questions demanding answers, refusing to go away. *The power to do what? The respect of whom? Why would you want more wealth than you already have? And would the puppeteer be any different this time around?*

When Brand returned, I said softly, 'I have decided. I will stay here. I will learn the ways of the Magor and be Kardi. If you are wise, you will leave. Make a life for yourself somewhere else. Go to Tyr, claim the money awaiting you from my estate, then go back to Altan. Lead your own people to freedom.'

'Just like that, eh?' He gave an unbelieving, sardonic chuckle. 'And am I still a brother to you, Ligea-Derya-Shirin?'

'No – no. That was a stupidity. Now I have felt the real thing, now I know the revulsion of real ... incest. You are a friend, Brand. The best friend I have ever had, or ever will have. That is why I ask you to leave. There is nothing I can offer you. You are better away from me, building your own life.'

'My answer is the same as always. I stay, at least for now. You need a friend, Ligea. Derya. Shirin. Whoever. Perhaps now more than ever. Have you given a thought to what Temellin and the others will do when you tell them you are the Legata Ligea Gayed?'

'What will that matter? It is past. I will tell them when the time is right.' I hardened myself. 'For the past week or so I have been thinking with my loins. You were right, Brand: it was insanity. But I'm back to my senses now. Power, that's what it's all about. That was why the Brotherhood fascinated me: it gave me the power of life and death over my fellow citizens, it made me feared, even to those who had money and position and political power. As compeer I used that power – yes, and sometimes *mis*used that power, on Tyrans' behalf.' I added, surprised at its truth, 'I couldn't do that any more. But I don't love power any less. It's what I am. And I will wield it.' *And no one's going to kill me for my child, either.*

I wandered over to the window again and looked down on the dark cobbled street below without really seeing it. 'I feel as if I used to walk around with my head under a pail. Why couldn't I see, long before this, that there are better ways to use power? Why couldn't I see the iniquity of slavery? The inherent injustice of Exaltarchy rule?' The shards of past possibilities scored furrows of sadness deep into my spirit. 'The Exaltarchy has many fine things to offer its tribute states, but the price is too high. Kardiastan would be – *will* be – better without Tyrans.'

'You're too hard on yourself,' Brand said. He came to stand by me, and the gentle touch of his hand on my arm told me more about his concern than his shrouded feelings did. 'Firstly, you were brought up to be Tyranian. You were *supposed* to believe those things. Secondly, there was always a part of you that fought the iniquities anyway. You tried to use your power to ensure that there was no injustice. That the innocent went free. That torture was not used.'

'I can't absolve myself of guilt so easily. You are too generous, my friend.'

'I don't happen to think I am,' he said and his certainty was comforting. 'And so, what next, Magoria?'

I took a deep breath. 'I am sister to the Mirager and mother of the heir. Pinar can be his wife and consort, but it is I who will have the greater power. Perhaps this time I'll use it better. We will make something of this Goddessforsaken land.' I straightened and turned to face him. 'I am ready to see Temellin.'

He shook his head, his dismay tinged with reluctant admiration. 'I might have known. You are rock-strong, Ligea.'

I was still standing by the window when Temellin entered and I didn't feel rock-strong. I felt empty, an outer shell of fragility that could be shattered by the wrong word, the wrong touch.

He entered and began to cross the room towards me.

'Don't touch me, Temellin,' I said. 'Not ever again.'

He stopped, his body rigid. 'Der— Shirin, don't think of it as wrong. How could anything so beautiful be wrong?'

'It wasn't wrong then. It is now. I'm sorry, Temellin, but it's over. I can't bed my brother, nor ever will be able to. Any desire I felt for you has vanished.' *Liar. Vortex take you, Ligea, even now your loins crawl with longing – and yet the touch of him would have you heaving up your stomach.* 'Forgive me.'

His hands hung loose at his sides as though he feared what they would do if he moved them. 'I love you, Derya.'

'Just lust, Temellin. Just lust.'

He shook his head. 'No. Don't tell me how I felt. Feel. It was more than that. *Is* more than that. Certainly I want you on my pallet, but I also want you by my side as my partner – my consort – my wife.'

'You will have me as your sister.'

'I don't feel brotherly. It takes a lifetime to feel brotherly. We haven't had a lifetime of growing up together; we've had a week of lying in each other's arms, of talking about things that matter—'

I cut him off brutally. 'We will be siblings or nothing, Tem. I'd leave Kardiastan rather than come back to your arms. *I can't.* Can you understand that? I can't love you that way any more. Just as something would have died in you, had I proved to be Sarana and usurped your position.'

He opened his mouth to deny it, but his inherent honesty wouldn't allow him to give voice to the words. He was human enough not to like having it pointed out to him, though. He said, his timing a petty cruelty I knew he would later regret, 'I shall have to marry Pinar.'

'Yes, I know.' *And I shall hate her.*

'Ravage hells, you really mean it, don't you?'

'I mean it.' I saw the slump of his shoulders and had to curb that treacherous desire to go to him. I opened my mouth to tell him about his son, and then changed my mind. It wasn't the time. It could wait. No point in adding another burden to him right then.

His eyes fell away from mine, and saw the sword I had put on the table. Confused, he touched the blade as if to identify it. He must have felt its power through his fingers because his head jerked up. '*Yours?* How—?'

'I walked beneath the Shiver Barrens.'

As I had suspected he would, he accepted this as being

within the bounds of possibility, but surprise flitted across his face nonetheless. His conclusion was not quite the one I had expected. 'Then you knew all along you were a Magoria?'

'No. Why should I know—?'

'Only the Magoroth have Magor swords.'

'No one told me that! I thought it must be something that happened to all Magor.' Only now did it occur to me I'd never seen an Illusos or Theuros wearing a Magor sword. I chided myself for missing the significance. Ligea the compeer was indeed slipping.

'Why didn't you tell me at the time?' He sounded more puzzled than suspicious.

'I—' There was no rational answer I could give him. I settled for a vague: 'It seemed such a private thing.'

He explained, talking for the sake of talking, because it was better than thinking, remembering. 'It happens to all Magoroth, usually around puberty. It has always been so, even before we came to live in the Mirage. We have walked the Shiver Barrens, just at the edge, for generations – long before we knew how to cross them. It is usually the only time any of us meet with the Mirage Makers. Except for the Mirager: he walks the Barrens a second time, when he inherits. There are certain things he has to be told—' He paused before adding, 'Not me, though. I inherited the job when I was five years old, long before I had my sword. I walked the Barrens only once, when I was ten. I was given my weapon and told what I had to know then.'

I nodded at the sword. 'I want to learn how to use it.'

'Yes, you should.' His voice was carefully neutral. 'Garis will teach you the elementary things.' He took a breath, grew taller, more in command. 'This ought to be the happiest day of my life – the day my sister is returned to me. I can remember you, you know. I can remember loving you. Grieving for you. I should be happy. It is wonderful to have you back, Shirin.'

'Thank you.' My voice was small, the thanks ridiculous. If there had ever been anything wonderful in my homecoming, it had all been lost.

CHAPTER EIGHTEEN

My room had a spartan but pleasing decor relying on natural wood and stone to achieve a warm attractiveness, or that was the way it was when I fell asleep that night. I woke the next morning to a riot of colour blazing forth from flounces and frills and preposterous ornamentation; a richness of absurdity and lunatic juxtapositions that brought forth a gasp of reluctant laughter from me.

I was still smiling when my maid, an ex-slave called Caleh, came in with my hot water and tea. The girl was so astounded she almost dropped the tray.

'I thought perhaps it wouldn't be such a surprise to you,' I said. 'Doesn't this sort of thing happen all the time?'

'Well, yes, sometimes. But not quite like this in someone's bedroom.' She looked around in bewilderment. 'I mean, this is wild.' She reached up to touch a tumble of glass wind chimes that glowed with colour. The music they played was tuneful, a delightful gaiety of notes. Indicating the mobile bouncing on the other side of the room, she added, 'I've never seen hanging chamberpots before.'

I waved my hand helplessly. 'Why, do you think?'

Caleh considered. 'I think it was to make you laugh, Magoria.' And that was perhaps the best explanation I was ever to receive.

I thought back to my time inside the sands of the Shiver Barrens. There, the Mirage Makers had not seemed to be entities given to humour, but the Mirage itself did seem to be a collection of the amusing, the absurd: the bridges that crossed nothing, the road that went nowhere, the street that became a river. Perhaps the Mirage Makers had been touched by my desolation, the bleakness of my lonely, dream-haunted night.

I dressed and readied myself to meet this new world, this new life.

It was Garis who told me, just after breakfast, that the first thing I had to do was to take part in a dedication ceremony, a ritual of allegiance all Magor had to undergo, usually around puberty. 'But you sort of missed out then,' he said cheerfully, 'so Temellin has arranged it for you this morning. That is—' He gave me a sharp look. 'You don't look so well. Would you rather wait till some other day?'

I was touched by his concern; he was only eighteen – still partly naive boy, still partly feckless adolescent and quixotic romantic – but partly responsible adult too, with an adult's understanding. I liked his exuberance and humour, his eagerness to make something of me.

'I'll be all right,' I said. 'What do I have to do?'

'Oh, nothing much,' he said vaguely. 'Just wait in your room for the time being. I'll fix it all.'

He must have spoken to Caleh, because fifteen minutes later she came in with five or six borrowed anoudain over her arm. 'You have to wear something nice for your dedication ceremony,' she said. 'It's a very important day for one of the Magor.'

Thankfully, I reflected that at least I wouldn't look as ridiculous in a ceremonial anoudain as I did in a ceremonial wrap. The green outfit I chose was plain, but it hung softly and, although the Mirage Makers had neglected to supply my room with a mirror, I suspected it made me appear more feminine than usual. I also wore my sword, in a borrowed scabbard sent around by Garis, for the first time. It felt strange hanging there at my hip and had a tendency to get in the way. As a compeer I'd always relied on a knife for protection, preferring the stealth possible in its use and disliking the cumbersome obviousness of a sword. Besides, Tyranian women did not wear swords, and the last thing I had wanted to do in Tyr was draw attention to my oddities.

Shortly afterwards, Garis escorted me down to the main meeting hall where all the Magoroth were waiting for me. The moment I entered the room, they drew their swords and held them aloft in salute so that the hall blazed, the light so bright I found myself blinking like a night bird in sunlight.

Temellin stepped forward out of the crowd to smile at me, a gentle smile of encouragement and support. 'We, the Magoroth of Kardiastan, have come to escort you to the Chamber of the Tablets of the Covenant,' he said formally. He indicated I should take his arm, but he was careful not to look at me as I did so.

We walked in procession, Temellin and I in front, the Magoroth behind, their swords still drawn and held aloft to light our way. No one spoke. In Tyr, at any ceremonial procession, there would have been rose petals strewn in our path and horn fanfares as we passed – but this was Kardiastan, and the emphasis was on the solemnity of the occasion rather than any grandiose display or pointless ritual.

Within minutes, I was lost. We proceeded along one passage after another, many of them sloping downwards, others passing through tunnels or crossing bridges or leading down steps – and still more steps – until I was sure we must be somewhere under the ground. I wanted to ask, but faced with the funereal silence around me, I didn't dare. Finally we halted in a large windowless hall. At one end there were massive wooden doors, now closed.

Temellin released my hand. 'Beyond those doors are the Tablets of the Covenant,' he explained. 'You are to read them all. Once you have done so, you will return here. We will not enter with you, but it is customary for whoever enters to select someone of the Magor to accompany him or her, someone who will testify you have read all the tablets and understood their meaning. Who would you like to accompany you?'

Over his shoulder I saw Pinar looking at me, eyes smouldering. 'Garis,' I said.

If Temellin thought I had slighted him by naming another, he did not let it show. He inclined his head and beckoned the youth forward. Garis stared at Temellin in consternation, then, as the Mirager did not react, looked in my direction with a pleased smile, before finally managing a more solemn demeanour as he remembered the seriousness of the occasion.

'Unbuckle your sword and leave it with me,' Temellin said. 'It will only be returned to you if you take the oath to obey the terms of the Covenant.' I did as he asked, and felt a pang as I surrendered up the weapon; I had felt it was already rightfully mine.

Then Garis and I turned towards the door at the other end of the hall. It swung open as we approached, although no one had touched it, to reveal an immense cavern beyond. Just over the threshold I paused, momentarily unable, in my awe, to move. While I stood rooted, the doors swung shut behind us.

The cavern itself appeared to be a natural chamber of rock and, although large, there was nothing spectacular about it; what caught my attention was what it contained. At its centre a number of shapes glowed with a gentle silver light, a glow as beautiful as starlight, and each of the shapes was as large as a man. Five of them rising up out of the sandy floor of the cavern like moonlit standing stones on a moor.

I walked forward, Garis beside me.

The shapes were tablets, not – as I had expected – of clay, but of light; of starlight if that were possible. And the texts on each of them were etched with the blackness of a lack of light, as if the letters had been written with the darkness of night.

'Holy shit,' Garis said at my side, with a distinct lack of reverence, 'the Mirage Makers have been mucking about with things again. When I came to read the Covenant a couple of years ago, it was carved on ordinary stone tablets – now look at it!'

'I'm sure this must be much prettier.' I peered at the first of the tablets. 'I'm not sure it's going to be easier, though. Garis, this is all written in Kardi.'

'Of course! What did you expect?'

'I didn't expect anything,' I confessed. 'But I don't read Kardi well, and this stuff is archaic—' Laboriously, I began to spell out the words, hesitating and stumbling over unfamiliar letters. '*And where is* – no, *whereas thou who shalt thine eyes* – It'll take me a week to read all this, and then I'm not sure I'll understand it.'

No sooner had I made the complaint than the language on the tablets changed, and I was reading good modern Tyranian. 'Ah, now that's more like it,' I said. '*And you who read this*—'

Garis looked taken aback. 'I hope the Mirage Makers remember to change it to Kardi again,' he said finally. 'Korden would have a fit if he ever found out the Covenant was written in Tyranian!'

I read silently on.

Part of what was there – the reasons for the necessity of such a covenant – I knew already because Temellin had told me. The first tablet related the story of how the Mirage Makers and the Magor had been hurting one another with their different forms of mirage-making, and how this Covenant had been drawn up to solve the problem.

It seemed to me, as I read the second, third and fourth tablets, that the Magor had been the recipients of the better end of the bargain: they'd acquired the Magor swords and, through the swords, the cabochons, which enhanced their power. At the same time, the Mirage Makers promised they'd take every care their mirage-making would not harm people, whether Magor or not. In order to ensure there were no accidental deaths as a result of their mirages, the Mirage Makers would withdraw to the land beyond the Shiver Barrens. In return, the Magor promised not to indulge in mirage-making anywhere in any form, and not to cross the Shiver Barrens. And they were to take a solemn oath, generation after generation, that their powers were not to be used for personal gain. They were to use their enhanced abilities to better the life of the non-Magor or to heal those in need; they could use their powers to protect their land, but never in the pursuit of wholly selfish motives. The Mirager was to be obliged to take an additional oath that he would always act with the consensus of the majority of his Magoroth peers.

The fifth tablet made it clear that if any of the rules mentioned on the preceding three tablets were broken by the Magor, then future generations would not receive their swords or cabochons – which raised an interesting conundrum: the Magor now not only lived in the Mirage, but had brought ordinary Kardis here. Why, then, were the newly born still receiving their cabochons; why were the adolescent Magoroth still receiving their swords? The Covenant had been broken from the moment Solad had sent the ten Magoroth children and their teachers across the Shiver Barrens – yet the Covenant was still in force.

I stood for a long while in front of that tablet, and the conclusion I came to was as unpalatable as it was inescapable. The Mirage Makers had needed something further from the Magor, something they knew the Magor would normally deny them, something they needed so badly they had struck a new covenant with Solad to get it. Paradoxically, in so doing, the old covenant had doubtless been broken a second time: Solad had acted without the consensus of his peers. And the Mirage Makers had done nothing about that, either . . .

I knew then that my reasoning had been right. Temellin knew what the new covenant was. And so did I. An unborn child in exchange for safety. Nothing else made sense.

I turned away from the tablet, afraid.

At least, I thought cynically, I could tell Brand that what kept the powerful Magor from the kind of corruption found among the rulers of the Exaltarchy wasn't entirely the kind of altruism he may have imagined. The Magor were scared that their children – that all future generations of Magor – would be denied cabochons and swords if they, the parents, misbehaved. Human nature being what it is, there would always be the odd individual who would misuse his or her powers, but the cost was high enough that others would soon unite against them. Not such a bad idea; the Mirage Makers had been deviously clever.

I turned to Garis. 'Let's go,' I said. 'I've read it all.'

'And do you understand it?'

'Yes, I think so. Seems fairly straightforward to me.' It wasn't the Covenant that was confusing; it was the events of recent years concerning it.

Back in the hall beyond the cavern, the Magoroth were waiting for us. When the doors swung open again, we faced Temellin once more. He looked not at me, but at Garis. 'Has the Magoria read and understood the Tablets of the Covenant?'

'She has,' he replied.

Temellin turned to me. 'Then do you solemnly swear not to indulge in mirage-making, and not to use your powers for personal gain or in pursuit of selfish motives? Do you solemnly swear to use your enhanced abilities to protect the land of Kardiastan and to better the life of the people you serve? Do you solemnly swear that once it is safe for us to leave the Mirage, you will do so, never to return, and you will do everything in your power to protect the Mirage from violation? Do you swear to uphold the decisions of your Mirager, as sanctioned by the majority of his peers?

'If you are prepared to swear these things, place your left hand on the hilt of your sword and say: I do so swear.'

It should have been easy to say. I'd made up my mind, hadn't I? I'd chosen Kardiastan over Tyrans, Temellin over Favonius, the Magor over the Brotherhood.

But now, faced with Temellin's love, the ache I saw and felt in him as he stretched out my sword to me, the words were hard to enunciate. There was an irrevocability about them – and I, who had once found it so easy to utter a falsehood or practise a deception, knew this time I could only speak the truth, although it might not have been quite the same truth everyone else in that hall envisioned.

I stretched out my hand and closed it about the hilt. My cabochon slipped into its place and the sword flamed; I could feel the power throbbing.

'Yes,' I said, and committed myself to a land, to a new way of life. 'I do so swear.'

And the Magoroth, as one, cried, '*Fah-Ke-Cabochon-rez*! Hail the power of the cabochon!'

I had thought it would be easy enough to tell Temellin the truth about my life in Tyrans.

It wasn't.

For a start, I never seemed to have the opportunity. I saw him often enough, that day and in the ones that followed. I usually ate in the dining hall with the other Magoroth; I attended all the Magor meetings held to discuss the strategies to be adopted against Tyrans and he was always there – but I never saw him alone. He was always surrounded by others, listening to what they had to say with his head cocked to one side in a way now so familiar to me; or talking, moving his hands to illustrate a point; or laughing and carrying others along on his amusement. He spoke to me often, asking my opinion, including me in the discussions, inquiring after my progress with my study of Magor skills.

But never alone.

When I went to him to let him know I wanted a private conversation, he turned from me and draped a friendly arm around Pinar's shoulders. 'Do you know Pinar is a cousin, Shirin?' he asked, not looking at me. 'Her mother and our parents were siblings. We intend to marry as soon as the necessary arrangements are made.'

Pinar smiled pleasantly. 'I hope we'll be friends, Shirin.'

'I'm sure we have no reason not to be,' I replied, my voice smooth with deliberate blandness. They both heard my lie, of course, just as Temellin and I had heard hers. And when I turned away a little later, with my intended request still unspoken, I caught the look in Temellin's eyes: pure, aching hunger – and I wondered how much Pinar would tolerate if she ever saw that look.

I knew my delay in telling Temellin the truth about myself was dangerous. The longer I left the telling of who I was and what I knew, the harder it would be to explain my delay in telling it. It wasn't that the Mirage was in imminent danger from the Stalwarts – it would surely still be several months

more before the legions arrived at the edge of the Mirage –
but people would wonder at my reluctance to have given the
information. How could I explain the truth: that I didn't want
Temellin to know of my past? When his eyes were on me, I
was ashamed of having been a compeer; the thought he might
despise me for what I had been was as unpleasant as his absence
from my pallet. And I dreaded the poison Pinar would spread
about the Legata Ligea; she might be able to turn Temellin's
trust into suspicion and contempt. Nor did I want to betray
Favonius and his friends. I had found satisfaction and compan-
ionship in Favonius's arms; the thought I might cause his death
was lacerating. He didn't deserve my betrayal.

Yet I also knew I must tell; if I didn't, the invasion of the
Stalwarts would come as a surprise with inevitably tragic
results; if I didn't, sooner or later someone would recognise
and name me. Already Aemid might be talking to other Kardis,
spreading a warning about Ligea Gayed. There would be other
slaves arriving from Madrinya or Sandmurram who might
know my face . . .

Unfortunately, with Temellin's deliberate unavailability, it
was so easy for me to keep postponing my confession. So easy
to rationalise the irrational, to say it would be better to put it
off until my fellow Magor had come to know and trust me
more. Easy, and stupid.

Perhaps love makes cowards of us all.

It wasn't easy to settle into my new life. I had thought that
as a Magoria, as Temellin's sister, I would have a position of
power. I was soon disabused of that notion. I was included in
the councils, but anything I said was largely disregarded; with
the exception of Temellin and a few others, I was considered
to be a pseudo-Kardi and therefore untrustworthy. I had
returned the Mirager's sword, and taken the oath of the
Covenant, yet neither helped. It wasn't hard to see Pinar behind

most of the distrust, but I couldn't counterattack without jeopardising my position and hurting Temellin.

Garis defended me every chance he got, even telling the Magoroth how the Mirage Makers had changed the Covenant tablets for me to make them both beautiful and more understandable. He'd thought that would help. Instead, it alarmed those who shared Pinar's distrust, prompting them into pressing for more restrictions on what I was made privy to, or what I was taught. 'We can't rely on the Mirage Makers to protect us against treachery,' they said. 'We have to do it ourselves.'

I was humiliated by my powerlessness, but trapped in my own deceit and woefully ignorant of all things Kardi, there wasn't much I could do about it. Temellin did try. He sensed my affinity for power and something in him recognised and sympathised with my need for challenge, but in the face of Pinar's intransigence and the general prejudice against me, it was hard for him to offer me much.

I was also lonely. I hadn't mastered the art of the two-level conversation the Magor took for granted. They spoke to one another as a matter of course in both words and quick flares of emotions. Sometimes they used words only as signposts, and conducted much of a conversation in cleverly differentiated displays of emotional reaction. They delighted in word plays where something was said, but immediately negated by the accompanying flash of a contrary sentiment, in a form of sardonic wit. In understanding their conversations, I was always a step or two behind, missing the nuances.

Worse, I was unable to utilise my emotions as speech. Having schooled myself always to hide the way I felt, I found it difficult to use deliberate emotional display in order to give another level of meaning to my words. In the end, the Magoroth spoke to me the way they did to the non-Magoroth:

in ordinary speech. They were polite enough, but the end result was a subtle exclusion from their ranks.

The person who kept me from going mad with frustration was Garis. If he did use emotion to speak to me, he slowed it down so that I could understand. He took his duties to me seriously and wanted no misunderstanding between us. He'd come to me in my room immediately after the oath-taking ceremony that first morning and told me it was time for my first lesson. 'We'll start with the art of building wards,' he'd said without preamble. 'Now the first thing you have to be aware of—'

There were two kinds of power available to a wearer of the gold cabochon, I discovered. The first was power that came through the sword, the second was power straight from the cabochon. 'All the most powerful wards are built with the aid of the sword,' he said. 'So these are not available to the two lower ranks of the Magor.' He unsheathed his sword and fitted it into his left palm. 'There's one thing you must never do, and that's put your cabochon into another's sword hilt.'

'Why not?' I asked, guiltily remembering I had done just that with Temellin's weapon.

'Once you have tuned a sword, any sword, to your cabochon, it can never be turned against you, even in the hands of an enemy. Nor can it be used to build a ward you could not break. Of course, none of the Magoroth would turn his sword on another Magor, but to deliberately tune another's sword to your cabochon is to show your distrust of a fellow Magor, and that would be a terrible insult. It is never done.'

'I'll remember that,' I said gravely, and he went on with the lesson. He showed me how to draw a square of protection around myself with sword and conjurations. Inside this, I – and anyone else – would be safe from intrusion. He also showed me how to achieve the converse: to confine a person, or people, within a warded area. 'They are not actually as much use as you'd think,' he warned. 'You can't make them too big, not much larger than this room, in fact. If you did, you'd be sick for a month. It takes health and strength to build wards. Moreover, protection wards for yourself only work if you stay within them, so you can't use them while travelling. They won't last forever, either; nor can you keep rebuilding them. You'd tire yourself out.' Nothing was done without a price. Each time something was warded, each time conjurations were uttered, personal strength and sword strength were depleted, a depletion only time and rest would cure. Use magic too much and you could end up prone to illness, dying of anything from pneumonia to apoplexy.

'Tell me about healing power,' I asked him. 'How effective is it?' *Can you save the life of someone who has a baby ripped from her?*

'It's not as effective as we'd like,' he admitted. 'My mother has made it her speciality. She says that all we can do is heal something that has a chance of healing anyway. We make the chance a certainty. And we speed up the healing process.'

'No miracles?'

'No miracles.'

As the days went by, Garis progressed to more active uses of the sword. He taught me how to use it in a more conventional way, then how to supplement fighting strokes with its power. I learned how to send forth a narrow beam of cold light that could sear or melt anything in its path for three or four paces beyond the tip of the weapon, and I began to learn how to control the power so that it could be used for delicate tasks – such as breaking open a slave collar.

I was determined to learn it all. One day, I would put it to good use. If Pinar and others of the Magoroth thought I was going to be some kind of wall decoration, never actually doing anything except exist, they would have to rethink; I was going to be a power in this land.

In the meantime, I was glad to tire myself out. It helped me to sleep. It helped me to forget that somewhere out there the Mirage Makers might have an interest in my death because they coveted a child; that somewhere out there was the Ravage, which apparently loathed us all; that right here within the Maze, the man I loved was about to marry a woman who had tried to kill me.

And so I was grateful for those nights when I was so tired I would collapse onto my pallet and drop into an exhausted sleep that kept me insensible till dawn.

Inevitably, when I awoke in the first light of the day, it was to find a new room waiting for me. The Mirage Makers were trying everything in their repertoire – a whole gamut of humorous idiocies – to find something to drive away the hollowness inside me. I knew there was nothing that would help, but they went on trying. Far from making me happy, however, their attention sent shivers of dark fear through me. I remembered walking the Shiver Barrens; I remembered the visions. I touched the place where my child grew, and wondered if the Mirage Makers worked to please me because they wanted him healthy – for them to take. I tried to take comfort from knowing the Covenant forbade them to kill. In my more optimistic moments I thought perhaps they just wanted to show their benevolence so that I would never use my powers against them, never use my Magor sword to spill their lifeblood as one vision had shown.

I remembered it vividly. My hand clasping another that was the representation of the Mirage Makers. Then two images: one where the hands melted into one another in unity, the other where I severed the Mirage Maker's hand in a way that suggested I killed him. Them. Killed them *all* . . .

The future wasn't sure. I had a choice. I just had to work out which choice was best for me. For my son. The trouble was, how could I tell?

I saw little of Brand during those days. He had elected to join the troops the Magor were training, troops to be used against Tyranian legions. The ordinary Kardis were enthusiastic soldiers, and Brand was an apt pupil even though he was coming to it relatively old. He was soon promoted to officer rank, and was a popular leader, inspiring loyalty in spite of his foreign blood.

He no longer had a problem with the language. Ever since we'd arrived in Kardiastan, he'd been building on what he'd already learned from Aemid and me over the years, improving every day until now he was fluent. He never lost his accent, but as far as I could see, most of the Kardi girls seemed to think that was part of his charm.

I wondered sometimes why he elected to become a soldier. Boredom? Or revenge? Perhaps a little of both. Tyrans had made him a slave, now here was a chance for him to fight the Exaltarchy and help bring about a nation's freedom. I wondered, too, why the Magor trusted him so much. I asked Garis that, and he laughed. 'Brand may be able to hide his feelings from you, Shirin, and sometimes from us too. But he can't hide lies. Temellin believes Brand is an honourable man.'

I watched the troops exercise one morning, and it was a revelation. Just to see his rapport with the men, the clever way he could manipulate the small squad under his command into doing better, and still have them admire him as a man. He wasn't like Temellin – he had none of Temellin's easy camaraderie – but he'd earned their respect and admiration in spite of being an outsider.

Yet as I watched, I felt sick inside. This man had been a slave for most of his life, deemed to be unworthy of my friendship, considered to be the property of others, with no recourse to the very laws that Tyrans considered its finest achievements. For twenty years he'd had the same rights as an animal: none. I could have had him whipped, or sold, or starved, or killed. I could have given him away to one of my friends to bed.

In Tyr, we referred to our slaves not as men or women, but as 'speaking tools'.

And as I watched Brand, that memory made me sick with shame. Twenty years. What a Vortexdamned *waste*. And then another thought came, so obvious; yet revelatory nonetheless: how much untapped potential there was in Tyrans's thousands of slaves . . .

Now, at least, Brand seemed content enough, and had taken up with my maid, Caleh: a vivacious girl with a kind heart. She had been badly abused during her time as a slave and had been man-shy, until Brand helped her, with infinite gentleness and complete lack of his usual cynicism, to forget.

Yet sometimes when he looked at me, even with his emotions shielded, I could tell his desire was as strong as ever.

The day before the scheduled wedding of the Mirager and his cousin, two incidents broke the routine of the previous days for me. The first occurred when I was alone in the training hall after Garis and I had been practising some swordplay. I put my weapon down on a bench and wiped my sweaty face and neck with a towel, thinking of a hot bath and a rest, trying *not* to think of the ceremony planned for the next day.

When I heard the sound of the door opening behind me I did not bother to turn, or even to reach out with my mind to see who it was – until a sudden pain shot into my hand from my cabochon.

I whirled to find Pinar standing there, smiling, her left hand fitting tight around the hilt of my sword. 'First rule of a wise Magor, Shirin. Keep your sword in its sheath at your belt.'

I felt like a lump of mountain ice on sale along Tyr's Marketwalk. She could have killed me, right then, and we both knew it. I said, 'I did not think I needed to do so here.'

'And I never thought I would need to protect myself by fitting my cabochon to another's hilt.'

'You have no need to fear me, Pinar. I would not hurt my brother's wife.' At least, I didn't *think* I would. Not if she behaved herself . . .

'You know the significance of what I have just done, I think. Your sword cannot harm me.'

'I am more concerned I cannot build a ward to keep you out,' I said and wrested the weapon from her hand. She didn't resist. I took a deep controlling breath and raised my eyes to her face, expecting to see her aglow with triumph at what she had done, but there was no exultation there. Only a wrenching anxiety.

'I can't make them see what you are—' she whispered. 'You're going to destroy us all, and I can't make them see it.' I think we both heard the unspoken words she could have added: *and I can't make him love me.* For a moment I was touched by her tragedy. Then she turned on her heel and walked out.

My anger died, but I still loathed the woman.

I made my way out of the practice room just as Selwith and his wife Markess, two of the original Ten, came in. They were followed by their students, an unruly group of Kardi youths about to have instruction in the art of swordplay. I brushed by them rudely, still feeling the warmth Pinar's hand had left on my sword hilt.

The second incident occurred that night, some time after I had fallen asleep. A sound awoke me and I opened my eyes, knowing someone had entered my room. My first thought was of Pinar, but an instant later I knew it was not the Magoria who stood just inside my door, no more than a black outline.

I did not speak and neither of us moved.

'All you have to do is say one word, Shirin,' he said finally. 'Give me hope.'

I wet my lips, but even so, my whisper was scarcely audible above the sound of my breathing. '*I can't.*'

He left without another word and the door closed silently behind him, yet the action was as final as the last breath of a dying man.

CHAPTER NINETEEN

The formal bonding of Mirager-temellin and his cousin Magoria-pinar was not unlike similar Tyranian ceremonies. It was brief, a recital of legal vows rather than emotional pledges. The celebration was more in the feasting that followed; a jubilant night of eating, drinking and entertainment that seemed to be endless. All the Magor were there, and many ordinary Kardis as well, and I – who would have liked to have avoided it altogether – found myself seated next to my brother at the head table, on display with all my pain. Once again I was grateful for my Brotherhood training; I was damned if I would show any of them how much I cared. I listened to the music but never heard it, I watched the dancing but never saw it, I drank steadily, ate little, and was sure I must still be cold sober because the pain grew worse, not better, as the night wore on. My only satisfaction stemmed from the sight of Temellin beside me matching me drink for drink with more obvious results. By the time the wedding couple finally left the hall I doubted if he were in much of a state to serve his bride.

When I myself rose with the idea of wending my own way to my pallet, I discovered I wasn't as sober as I'd thought; in the end, I needed both Brand and Garis to escort me to my room – via the earth closet and some moments there that I later did not want to recall.

Halfway through the next day, when I finally awoke, I was none too sure it had all been worth it. Brand's expressionless face and the remedy he offered, a foul-tasting Kardi herb brew, did nothing to convince me, either.

Later, having decided I was certainly incapable of undertaking more training when I felt like a piece of storm-tossed flotsam thrown up on a beach, I decided to go for a walk. Never mind that my head was pounding, never mind that my stomach heaved, it was better to walk free of the Maze, free of the city, than to stay and know that somewhere under the same roof Temellin lay with Pinar in his arms.

I walked for hours, leaving the roads and heading out across the wilder parts of the Mirage. That day it happened to be mostly moorland covered with blue and white flowering grasses as far as the eye could see. It was hard to remain so savagely depressed in such surroundings, and by the time I headed back towards the city, I was feeling more at peace. By then, though, the sun was setting and as I walked in the growing darkness, with only the lights of the buildings to guide me, I remembered the Ravage. After that, I wasn't nearly as insouciant about strolling along in the dark.

I was glad to hit a road again, and even more cheered to sense and then hear the soft pad of a trotting howdah-shleth behind me. I stopped and waited by the roadside.

A man sat on the driver's seat of the howdah and he halted his animal as he drew level, peering at me through the gloom. 'Well met, lass,' he said. 'Want a ride to the city?'

I couldn't see him properly, either, but I had already sensed his amiable ordinariness. 'Gladly,' I said, and a few moments later I was seated in the howdah on top of a load of something pale and soft. 'What is all this that you're carrying?' I asked. I was half buried under billows of white fluff.

'Pallet-cotton. Comes out of the seed pods of a tree. Someone told me they'd seen a grove of them growing back up the road a bit, so I went out to get some before it disappears. What with all the new people coming in, we can always do with more pallets. Sometimes the Mirage Makers supply 'em already made up just like that, but we can't rely on it, more's the pity. Were you here when there wasn't a cake of soap to be had anywhere? Until we'd made up a batch big enough to last us for months, which is when the Mirage Makers dumped five hundred bars, each as large as a roof beam, in the city's main square?' He gave a sigh. 'Ah, lass, this is a right queer place. I'll be glad to leave it behind. We don't belong here. It's back in Kardiastan proper we ought to be, living our own lives, with the Mirager to rule us.'

A little later, as we approached the city, he pointed off into the darkness with his driving prod. 'Did you see there's a new patch of the Ravage over there somewhere? That's the closest it's ever come to us.' He shook his head worriedly. 'One day we'll wake up to find a swathe of it destroying the Maze like legionnaires on the rampage.'

I didn't like that thought. I lay back in the pallet-cotton as we trotted into the city streets, and wondered if I were wise to think of staying in the Mirage.

Temellin and Pinar left the Maze several days later.

Accompanied by many other of the Magor, they were on their way to another slave-rescue mission, this time in Sandmurram and other southern towns. The city streets were lined with people to wish them luck as they rode out. 'Ah, fate willing,' I heard one woman say, 'next time the Mirager leaves, it will be at the head of an army, on its way to free our land, bless him.' Foolishly, I let him go without ever telling him who

I was. It was as though I wished to have my deception discovered and exposed, rather than have to confess.

By this time, I was learning to control my cabochon, finding it harder than the sword skills I had mastered. My ability to read emotions, to know a lie, to aid healing, to know the position of unseen people around me – all these skills stemmed from my cabochon magnifying inborn Magor talents.

'But there is much more you can learn,' Garis promised. He had stayed behind in order to tutor me, and we were walking back through the streets towards those strangely crumpled walls of the Maze after watching Temellin's departure. 'You must persevere with those exercises I showed you.'

'Just what more will I be able to do?' I asked, deftly sidestepping to avoid being sprayed with fresh chicken blood and green feathers as a woman strode by holding a headless but still flapping bird by the legs. 'I don't see much evidence of extraordinary abilities among the Magor here.'

'Oh, you'll see,' he said vaguely. 'Lots of things. You're already at Theuros level. But I can't teach you everything; I'm not advanced enough myself. And you don't see much happening because we don't have any reason to use our powers on the ordinary people here, and even less to use them among ourselves. It would be very bad manners, for a start.' He reached out and stealthily removed a bunch of small fruit from a loaded handcart without the owner noticing.

I shook my head as he offered me some and, following another train of thought that had been puzzling me, said, 'I still find it hard to understand how Tyrans was able to defeat you, er, us. If the Magor are so *capable*, a single act of treachery is hardly enough to explain such a devastating defeat. What did you say about it before—?'

'I said the Magor in those days were stupid,' he said with a snort of contempt and popped several of the fruit into his

mouth at once. 'They were so secure in their feelings of supe-
riority they didn't bother to practise, to hone their skills. You
can see how hard you've had to work to control your sword.
They were so *arrogant*, they didn't bother. They knew the
theory, but never put it into practice. They thought some of
the things they could do – control storms, for example – were
enough to keep them safe. Even so, most of the minor skirmishes with the legions were won by the Magor, you know.
The one where the heir, Magoria-sarana, was killed was an
exception. I suppose that's one reason why the Mirager-solad
took it so badly. It must have seemed unfair: of all the people
to die, it had to be the heir.'

He spat a fruit seed out with an accuracy that spoke of
expertise, hitting a young and pretty Illusa on the rump. She
whirled around indignantly, but Garis, straight-faced, walked
on, saying, 'They underestimated Tyranian persistence and
cunning and they died because they hadn't worked at all their
skills. When they were caught without their weapons, they just
didn't have enough control of their cabochons to defeat the
archers.'

He couldn't resist a backward glance at the Illusa, and
promptly received a rap on the nose from the same fruit seed.
'Illusa-jenka knows me too well, I think,' he said with a rueful
grin as he rubbed his nose. He gave the rest of his fruit to a
boy sitting on a wall banging his heels to the detriment of his
sandals, and continued, 'We will not make the same mistake
as our parents' generation. Temellin or Korden or Pinar, any
of the original Ten, there's no way they could be defeated like
that. Even you and I – we would have felt the presence of
intruders in the feasting hall.' He paused. 'Although we believe
the traitor used a ward to prevent that . . . To tell the truth,
we don't know too much about what happened there. The only
account we have is from Zerise. None of the Magoroth

survived. Anyway, you may not have known what you were doing back in Tyrans, but you must have been constantly prac-tising to improve those skills you were aware of. Now you must practise even more.'

I gave him a heartfelt look. 'Practice can be very boring.'

He laughed. 'Why don't you take a break sometimes? Go for a ride? You can borrow a shleth from the stables, you know, any time you want.'

I hadn't known, but from then on I rode out almost every day, sometimes with Garis, sometimes alone. During those rides I was close to happy, perhaps because it was then I felt an affinity to the land itself; to the Mirage Makers who were the land. At those times I certainly couldn't believe they would deliberately harm me in order to obtain my unborn child. Alone on my pallet at night, my thoughts tended to be less comforting.

The worst part of those rides was when I came across the sores of the Ravage eating away at the land, swallowing its beauty and its joyful absurdities in those creeping excrescences of foulness. I once made the mistake of dismounting near one of these abominations, gagging on its stench, to take a closer look. I shut out its hatred with a deliberate mind-block, but even so I could feel the hammer blows of vicious dislike against my mental shield. If it wanted to terrorise me, it succeeded. It took every particle of courage I had just to approach it close enough to look down into its depths.

As I stared into its green-black slime and saw past its surface to the horrors below, I wished I had not come. The dimness beneath was full of writhing, bestial forms exuding pus and other fluids, stinking of gangrenous flesh. At first I thought they were true animals, managing to survive in putrescence. Strange deformed things, but just creatures.

Then one of them rose up through the slime to poke its

head out into the air, to look at me. Its body resembled a bulging caterpillar, except it was the size of a hound. Its head had tearing feeding parts and large, voracious eyes. Its gaze enveloped me with gleeful, cruel hunger . . . and I was back in another time.

Tyr. Ligea on her first job for Rathrox. She wanted so much to please him because she knew he would be reporting to Gayed. She was sixteen years old, sitting in the Brotherhood's interrogation rooms, a bleak place inspiring fear even in the innocent.

It wasn't an important case. Rathrox was just testing her. He'd discovered she had a knack of identifying a lie, and he'd asked her to accompany him to interview a number of suspects. He asked the questions; all she had to do was listen, and make a sign when a lie was uttered. She didn't find it difficult, until the fourth man was brought in. He was arrogant, bumptious, sure of himself, confident no one would be able to find him guilty of anything, and indeed, the evidence was slim.

Ligea didn't like him. He could not hide his emotions from her, and they were vile. Outwardly, he was ordinary enough. He was a boat builder, neatly dressed, but when his eyes lingered on her, his thoughts were viciously predatory. Behind the bland exterior, behind his smile, there lurked the sentiments of a sadistic killer. His mind slavered, his emotions were raw and unrestrained. He told the truth when he protested his innocence of the minor treason Rathrox accused him of, but there were crimes far darker smouldering inside him. He terrified Ligea. She had never met someone so dark. She had never been so sure of someone's criminality.

Rathrox questioned him, and to each answer she had to give the sign that said he spoke the truth.

She thought: What if he goes free? *He smiled at her, his lips curling up to charm. His eyes twinkled. The blackness within darkened. She could not read his intentions, but the way he felt*

*about her was akin to the emotions of a starving dog offered red
meat. Given the chance, he would have devoured her.*

*And when the next question came, she turned her hand over,
palm up, to indicate a lie.*

*They sent him to the Cages on the strength of that, while they
hunted for evidence. He was dead of disease within a month,
and the case was closed. Ligea knew she'd murdered him as effectively as if she'd slid a knife into his heart. She'd lied and killed
her first man . . .*

Worst of all, perhaps, I never felt the slightest guilt. For
others that followed perhaps, dead for other reasons, but not
for that one.

I lay on the grass a few paces away from the Ravage with no
idea of how I had come to be there. One moment I had been
engulfed in those savage eyes, then I'd been back in my childhood reliving something as a spectator, in every detail. I'd had
to wrench myself away, as dreamers suffering nightmares pull
themselves by an effort of will from a treacherous sleep.

Shaken, I stood. Something had happened that I did not
understand. And I wanted to know. I had to know. If I didn't
understand the Mirage Makers, then the chances I was going
to die seemed high. Temellin could say the Ravage was too evil
to be a part of the Mirage, that it caused pain to the Mirage
Makers and therefore must be something else, but that was
spurious logic. The Ravage existed within the Mirage and
nowhere else.

Foolishly, I returned to the edge of the Ravage to seek
answers.

And the same thing happened again. I met the eyes of
another of the creatures and was once again caught up in the
past . . .

*A much older Ligea. Twenty-five, and making a name for
herself within the Brotherhood.*

In Tyr society, however, she was regarded as a little strange. She was too intellectual, too uninterested in temple, too masculine, too forthright, too independent. She was occasionally seen in odd places or in odd company. Rumours abounded. At her age, she should have been married, of course, but there hadn't been too many proposals, and now she had openly taken a legionnaire lover. It was one thing for a Tyranian matron – who had already presented her husband with sufficient progeny – to behave that way; it was quite another to see an unmarried woman be so shameless.

And then General Gayed and his wife Salacia both died, leaving their adopted daughter heir by default. Ligea suddenly became eminently eligible because she had money. The change both irritated and amused her, and she could be abrupt with those who so presumed to court her. One, charming and personably plausible, had been the most persistent and the most ardent, protesting his admiration for strong women and his affection for her. His name was Casmodius, and she might have believed him if she hadn't been able to read lies and sense emotions. In reality he despised her and inwardly he ridiculed her. He was not the wealthy man he professed to be, but a gambler trying to hide his losses from his creditors and society, with an eye on her fortune.

His hypocrisy was so profound, his lies so blatant, she determined to punish him. In public she played the affectionate friend, in private she teased and smiled and stroked his ego, even as she spoke of her feelings for Favonius, away in Quyr at the time. She tormented him with her unpredictable behaviour and fluctuating affections. At the same time, she used her position in the Brotherhood to gather information about his debts. When he finally lied once too often, and with promises of undying love implored her to marry him, she showed the extent of his debts to all his creditors and spread the tale all over Tyr. Within days, the whole of the city was despising Casmodius for his deceptions, ridiculing him for being so publicly mocked by the woman he had courted. Hounded by his creditors, he came in desperation to Ligea. She sent him away, laughing at his naivety. When he went to others he had considered friends, they turned away in contempt.

Within a week, he had taken poison and died . . .

I had felt no remorse then, either.

I tore myself back into the present. Once again I was lying on the grass, closer to the Ravage this time. Or was it that the Ravage had moved?

I stood up and looked at the patch of slime. Fingers of liquid oozed out of the main body of the Ravage, each rivulet crawling in my direction. It *was* coming closer. *Shit*, I thought. *This is personal. It's aiming at me.*

And then I felt the appalling pain of the Mirage Makers. They screamed with the agony of the cancer eating deep into them in a hundred different locations, dissolving, corrupting, devouring their living flesh. Aghast, I remembered what Temellin had said about these sores having been present even when he was a child. How long then had the Mirage Makers suffered? Only then did I understand the strain there had been in Temellin's voice when he had spoken of the diseased land. He, too, had felt their pain.

I began to shake. Sickened, I was careful not to look into the slime again, but just as I was about to turn away, a bony limb shot out in my direction, jabbing at me, drawing the attention of the others.

I stumbled backwards in shock, thumping down on my backside. In one flash of rage and energy they had all turned on me, all those nightmarish creatures, rushing up out of the shadows of the depths in a mass of claws and talons and teeth, snapping, hacking, slashing, frothing, clawing at the edges in an attempt to lever themselves out of the slime . . .

I scrabbled away, still on my rump, my screams raw with terror. They flung themselves upwards, bloodying their jaws on each other in their efforts to reach me. They grunted and shrilled their need to rip into my flesh, then plopped back into the fester, their hate shredding my mind-block and slamming into my thoughts.

I got up and ran, incoherent with terror.

It was some time before I could think enough to acknowledge I wasn't hurt. In spite of their rabid desire to devour me, those creatures hadn't been able to leave the confines of the Ravage.

I was unhurt, but I had to walk back to the Mirage City in urine-wet trousers.

My shleth had long since fled.

CHAPTER TWENTY

I spent the next few days thinking about the Ravage. That wasn't altogether a matter of choice: it impinged on my thoughts whether I wanted to think about it or not. I'd wake in the middle of the night, bathed in sweat, remembering those shapes, recalling their hunger. *Knowing I was their target.* Not just anyone. *Me.* I was sure of it.

I tried to make sense of what had happened. Why were they able to take me back and make me remember past incidents with such lucidity? What were they? When I asked others of the Magoroth, they didn't seem able to give me a satisfactory answer to explain my regression into the past. They dismissed my assertion that the hatred had been personal. 'Oh, the Ravage hates everyone,' they said. Perhaps it did, but it was me it wanted most.

I spoke to Brand, describing everything I could remember.

'What do those two past episodes have in common?' he asked.

'I have no idea, beyond the obvious,' I said. 'In one I was just sixteen. And I told a lie to punish someone. In the other I was an adult and told the truth to punish someone. The result was the same, I suppose. Both men died. Both were unpleasant men deserving of punishment.'

'Both incidents never gave you a sleepless night.'

'So?'

'I don't know. It just seems that maybe they should have. You don't appear in your best light, Ligea, either time.'

I thought about that, but came to no conclusions. 'They are foul, whatever they are, those Ravage creatures.'

'Perhaps that's it,' he suggested. 'They were looking for things in your past that are—'

'Foul? Are you telling me what I did was foul?'

'No, not exactly. But your lack of—' Once again he stopped, unwilling to speak his thoughts.

'Remorse?'

'No. Not lack of remorse. Lack of *thought* about what you did. In those days, you could walk away from all you did without wondering if it was right or wrong. Without *doubts*. Most people would worry about whether they could have done things differently. If their decisions were correct. You never did. It's very human to plague oneself with doubt after the fact.'

I stared at him. 'You think I was inhuman? And yet you loved me!'

'Yes. Because I know what was done to you. And by whom. And how. And I always knew what you could have been. What you still can be, and are becoming.'

'Weak,' I snapped.

'No. Human.'

I didn't want to think about that. I changed the subject. 'So why is the Ravage interested in that part of my past? Why would they be linked to my . . . inhumanity?'

But he had no answer to that.

I went to bed that night hearing a refrain of facts like a temple litany inside my head:

The Ravage hates you above all others.

There must be a reason for such a specific, virulent hate.

The Ravage and its beasts live inside the Mirage.

What the Ravage knows about you it can therefore only have learned from the Mirage Makers.

And what is special about you anyway?

A puzzle worthy of a one-time compeer. Reluctantly, I thought I was beginning to make sense of it all; the trouble was, I didn't like the answer, because whichever way I looked at it, I ended up dead.

When Temellin and the other Magoroth returned with the freed slaves, Pinar was not with them. She had, Temellin said, gone to Madrinya on a private matter, but would be back within a few days.

I was alarmed. That Pinar, already brittle with jealousy, should allow Temellin to return without her was odd, even sinister. It prompted me to action: I told Temellin I had an urgent need to talk to him; he nodded and said he was busy making arrangements about the ex-slaves, could it wait until the next day? I agreed one more day would make no difference and spent the time trying to think of the right words to say and despising the cowardice that had kept me silent so long.

But when the next day came, we had other things on our minds. An outbreak of disease among the newcomers from Sandmurram kept all the Magor fully occupied, trying to stop its spread and cure those who had it. I did not sleep for two days, and I doubted any of the others did, either. We were all exhausted and drained; my cabochon was colourless with a lack of power.

On the evening of the third day, although there had been several deaths among the elderly, the contagion was halted and the ill began to recover. Those Magoroth, myself included, who had been involved with the sick, now found time to gather for a meal. There were a few wan smiles of subdued triumph, but most of us were more interested in the food the servants had prepared.

Temellin, slipping into a vacant seat next to me, said, 'We never did get to have that talk. What did you want to see me about?'

'Myself. Who I am. And—' I stopped. Conversation had died at our table and people nearby were listening. 'It's waited this long, it can wait until after we've eaten,' I said, glad, I suppose, to have yet another excuse. 'We're both too hungry to give any serious topic full attention. But it had better be today, Temel. It is a matter of some . . . seriousness.' I dropped my voice. 'In private.'

He nodded wearily and began to eat. The conversation around the table remained desultory as most of us confined our attention to the food and thought of our pallets. When the door opened, it took a moment for it to register with me that it was Brand who stood there and something was wrong. I half rose to go to him, and then sat back down again as the reason for his agitation became obvious. Pinar had entered the room on his heels and she wasn't alone.

Aemid was with her.

Temellin rose, smiling, and went forward to greet his wife, but she hardly seemed to see him. She pointed to me and turned to Aemid. 'Is that her?'

Aemid, her face resolute, nodded. 'That's her, Magoria. That's the Legata Ligea, Compeer of the Brotherhood.'

Not even a troupe of the Exaltarch's nude dancers could have silenced the room as effectively as that statement did. Pinar turned to Temellin, her lips curling up in a smile of triumph. In her animation, she was both magnificent and beautiful. She said, 'I *knew* there was something wrong about her!' She came forward to take Temellin's hands. 'We have been terribly deceived by this woman, Tem. I have never trusted her. I didn't want to tell you this, but she tried to kill me once, when we were on our way to the Mirage. She knew I was suspicious and thought she could take my life.' There was just enough truth in that statement to make it credible. I met her eyes coldly and wondered at the woman's stupidity. Did she think to endear herself to Temellin by denigrating his sister? And if I chose to say she'd tried to murder me first, everyone would hear my truth just as they heard hers. She continued, 'This was my business in Madrinya. I went to see what I could find out.'

'And what *did* you find out?' Temellin asked. His tone was cool, but the bleakness in his eyes was searing.

'This woman with me is the Legata Ligea's slave, Aemid. She has been with the Legata since she – the Legata – was brought to General Gayed's household in Tyr as a child. The woman we knew as Derya *is* the Legata Ligea. She is not and has never been a slave. She may be Kardi, she may be your sister, but she was raised a Tyranian citizen, an adopted daughter of the General. At sixteen she joined the Brotherhood as a novice, and by dint of her talents and ruthlessness she has risen to the rank of Legata Compeer. Her Magor skills have been used to bring about the imprisonment and torture and enslavement of cabochon knows how many innocent people. Tem, she came here to betray us. She has Kardi blood but a Tyranian soul. The infamous Rathrox Ligatan sent her to Kardiastan specifically to bring about your death. Her full intention is to ensure our ruin, to ensure complete Tyranian control over all Kardiastan.'

The shock of those listening swept the room, buffeting us all. Magoria-jessah, Jahan's wife, started to cry.

Temellin stood motionless, his arms now limp by his sides.

There was no expression on his face. He turned to Aemid. 'Is this true?'

Aemid nodded. 'Magori, I am sorry,' she said. She looked at me. 'I raised this woman, but everything the Magoria-pinar says about her is true. She will destroy you all if you give her the opportunity.'

They felt Aemid's belief in her own words; so did I. It rolled over us as tangible as wind-ripples on a sand dune. A sigh of painful tension followed it. A split second later, I was blasted with the sentiments generated by a roomful of baleful Magor. My stomach roiled in response and I almost disposed of the meal I had just eaten.

The next words were Brand's. 'But Ligea has changed her mind,' he protested. He looked at Temellin. 'Surely you cannot doubt that! She's not the same person any more. She has told me the way she feels now; test *my* truth—'

'You guileless barbarian. Can't you see how she has fooled you?' Pinar asked, contemptuous of his apparent naivety. 'Your protestations are valueless.'

Temellin didn't appear to have heard Brand. He turned to walk to where I still sat motionless, and faced me across the table. 'Is this true?' he asked quietly. 'Are you the Legata Ligea?'

I stood up, meeting his gaze. 'I was. Once.' *It seems such a long time ago now . . .*

'You were sent here to kill me?'

'To capture the man who was organising the Kardis and causing problems for Tyrans. And note you are still free, Temel. And alive.'

'Did you come to the Mirage with the intention of betrayal?'

'Temellin—'

He drew his sword and it was already glowing with the gold of its summoning. 'Did you?'

I was silent, knowing there was nothing I could say to lessen his anger, or his grief. He was thinking my love had all been a sham, that every moment I had spent in his arms had been a lie. His lack of faith tore wounds in my soul, adding to the hurt caused by Aemid's willingness to believe the worst of me.

'*Did* you?'

'Yes,' I whispered. 'Yes, I did, at first.'

Then with a cry of rage and pain he flung his weapon at my chest, as if he could not bear to have contact with its hilt when it impaled me.

There was no way he could miss. He was only a pace or two away across the table and he hurled the sword with all the strength of his anger. Yet I did not move. I could not move, not when it was he who wanted me dead. Just knowing his intention was death itself to me.

Only one person made any move to help: Brand. As the sword left Temellin's hand, he threw himself across the room, a cry of pain wrenched from him as he realised he would never make it in time. But even he was driven to a halt by the unexpectedness – the impossibility – of the sword's trajectory.

One moment the blade was hurtling directly at me and I knew I was going to die, the next it was quivering, perpendicular, in the wood of the tabletop, its vibrations singing out over the room as it shivered there.

In shock, no one else moved or spoke.

Two tears slid down my cheeks.

In the end, I was the one who broke the uncomprehending silence to explain. 'I once fitted my cabochon to your sword hilt, Temellin. You will have to use someone else's blade.' I turned my head slightly to where Garis, his white face aghast, still sat with a half-filled spoon in his hand. 'Garis, give your weapon to the Mirager.'

Garis did not move.

Temellin still stood before me, his face now a mixture of

emotion: horror at what he had just done jostled with relief that he had not succeeded and guilt that he had tried – and it was all overlaid with biting, tearing anger. At me.

Pinar's voice spoke into the silence, adding yet another layer to the shock. 'Here – use my blade, Tem.'

But Temellin was already moving, brushing past his wife, thrusting Aemid aside to get to the door. He nodded to Korden as he went. 'Ward her,' he said. 'Him too,' he added, indicating Brand, and he was gone.

Garis looked up at me, his expression pleading to be told none of this had happened. I placed a hand on his shoulder and said softly, 'What Brand said was also true.' Then I started across the room towards Korden.

'Your sword,' he said.

I unsheathed it and handed it to him, hilt first. He took it, insolently placing his cabochon in the hollow of the hilt.

'Any cages here, Korden?' I asked wryly.

'Your room will do.' He was stiff with anger, but I had an idea not all of it was directed at me. At Pinar perhaps, for the crass, insensitive way she had broken her news and hurt her husband? Or at Temellin for having trusted me in the first place? 'We are not the Brotherhood,' he added.

I inclined my head and shifted my gaze to Pinar, standing beside him. Her face was a twist of misery and bitter rage; in her victory, she had lost everything she had ever wanted, and she knew it. The revelation that – although she had been right, although she had been more perceptive than anyone else – she could still lose was such a shock to her that, for one brief moment, faced with the person she judged to have been the cause of her loss, her mind was bared in a flash of naked emotion. The moment was so brief I doubted if anyone else noticed, but I saw – and was appalled, for my senses glimpsed a jagged red crack across the face of her mind.

It was an effort to turn away, to touch Aemid on the arm and say, 'Aemid, you are not well. You should not have made this journey.' And, in fact, she did look ill; her complexion was grey, her eyes sunken and the skin loose on the bones of her face.

'It was necessary.'

I shook my head. 'You should have had more faith in Magor blood. It was not necessary.'

I walked on to the door.

They warded me in my own room, encircling it with their sword-spells, using conjurations I had not yet learned and did not know how to break. Then they left me.

I was so tired I slept immediately. The pain would only begin the next day, when I would see Temellin's face again and again as he hurled his sword, intending to bring about my death.

CHAPTER TWENTY-ONE

I woke in the morning to a different room. Tucked away in a cabinet that had not been there before was a practical and welcome addition: a bathroom. The Mirage Makers had evidently noticed my discomfort at having to use a pail supplied the night before by my jailers; I was touched by this sign of pragmatic thoughtfulness.

The other changes were less useful. There was a large hole in the outside wall as if the Mirage Makers wanted me to feel I was not actually imprisoned at all. I knew differently. I could feel the warding and knew, hole or not, I was imprisoned as effectively as if I were chained. The other walls were now covered with drawings, all ridiculous: people with three eyes and lopsided faces, or with four arms and no legs, or who were half man, half insect. There were hundreds upon hundreds of them, all doing different things – standing on their heads, swimming in the sky, cutting their toenails with an axe, drinking soup from a sieve, birthing flowers from their breasts ... If I had been in the mood for absurdities, I could have spent hours examining them, hunting out their riddles, laughing over their delights.

Instead, I remained most of the day lying on my pallet, looking at a ceiling made of rippling waves of water that defied gravity, and seeing none of it. An Illuser I didn't know came with my meals. He told me his name was Reftim and he was carefully neutral when he spoke to me. He was a small rotund man, with rounded features, a puffball nose and the face of a market joke-teller, but I sensed his antipathy and did not make the mistake of equating his jovial looks with his character. However, he was polite enough and, in answer to my first question, he told me Brand was also confined to his room. I asked him to tell Temellin I must see him and he promised to pass on the message.

But Temellin didn't come.

Later in the day, Reftim did bring Aemid to see me.

She looked wretched. Her face was swollen, her eyes reddened. I wanted to hug her, comfort her, but my sense of betrayal stopped me. She should have had faith in me.

'I'm sorry,' she said. Her eyes were fixed on the floor. 'I couldn't let you betray my land.'

'Our land,' I amended. 'I wasn't going to. You should have known me better.'

She met my gaze then, and her expression hardened. 'I did. That's the trouble. I saw what you became. You became like him. Gayed. You even had the same look in your eyes, the look of someone who doesn't care what happens to others as long as you reach your goal.' She took a deep breath. 'I know it's my fault. And I deserve punishment. I think this must be it – to see you here, imprisoned like this. To know that the little girl who so bravely hid her cabochon from them because her mother told her to ... To see her become the woman I see now, trapped here for the rest of her life. All because I allowed it to happen. I failed you. I'm sorry, Ligea. I'm so, so sorry.'

She started crying and turned from me. Reftim led her through the ward and out of the room. I averted my face so he wouldn't see the tears welling up in my own eyes. She was right. I had tried so hard to be like Gayed. And I had promised her I wouldn't pose as a Kardi, only to break that promise without a second thought? That was the person I had become.

The next day, I asked to see Korden. He came, bringing all his dislike and distrust with him, none of which he bothered to conceal. 'Well?' he asked without preamble, but I could see that the room startled him. In addition to the wall drawings, one corner now contained a floating set of multicoloured bubbles, each the size of a man's fist and full of moving pictures portraying an insane world of animals that became people, people who became flowers, stars that talked and similar absurdities.

'Several things,' I said. 'You can be as arbitrary as you like with me, but Brand deserves better. A fair hearing. After all, anything else smacks too much of Tyrans, does it not?'

'In matters of treason, it is the will of the Mirager that prevails,' he said stiffly.

'Brand can hardly be said to have committed treason. He is not Kardi,' I snapped. 'You know Brand cannot lie to you. See to it the Mirager is fair. It is your duty as one of the Magoroth, surely.'

'What else?'

'I would like to know my fate.'

'Most of the Magor are pressing for your execution. But we Magoroth have voted to allow the Mirager to take the ultimate decision by himself. You are his sister, after all. Besides, you are – unfortunately – his heir, which means it is difficult to subject you to the ordinary processes of Magor law anyway. Although there are many who feel we shouldn't bother with niceties like that.'

'I would like to see him.'

'He does not want to see you.'

'Do I get no opportunity to defend myself?'

'That is also the Mirager's decision.'

'Rough justice, eh?'

His lips tightened, but he said nothing.

I breathed in, deeply. I had made up my mind. It was time to make irrevocable my decision on whether I was Tyranian or Kardi. Time to bring an end to lies, to deceit, to keeping my options open. And yet, it was so hard to say the next words, to discard publicly the values of a lifetime and replace them with other principles. Ligea Gayed was difficult to kill.

'Korden,' I began, 'when I was still in Tyrans I heard of a plan to attack the Mirage from the west. The legion known as the Stalwarts was to be sent across the Alps—'

He laughed and his scorn swirled around him. 'What is this, some kind of joke? Next, you'll be telling me they intend to bring their gorclaks across the peaks. The mountains are impassable.'

'The plan is a serious one. Taking into account the difficulties of the terrain, the amount of preparation involved, and considering the seasons, I estimate the forces will arrive in less than three months' time. A whole legion; three thousand on foot perhaps, and another seven hundred mounted Stalwarts, on gorclak.'

'Don't be ridiculous. No such force could ever cross the Alps!'

'Your parents' generation underestimated Tyrans. Don't make the same mistake. Especially not of the Stalwarts.' I frowned, baffled by the intensity of his disbelief. 'You know the truth when you hear it. Why, then, should you doubt me?'

He remained contemptuous and angry. 'Believe me, we have talked about little else lately. We have come to the conclusion that you must be able to do what we cannot: hide a lie. How else could you have walked among us concealing your identity so cleverly? Temellin even slept with you without sensing your duplicity! You are an enormous danger to us. You represent something we always felt was impossible: a liar in our midst.'

I stared at him, suddenly aware of another emotion, inadequately concealed, lingering around him. Korden was in a state of shock.

I tried to explain. 'I didn't lie to any of you. I just didn't tell all the story. There's a difference. You can see that, can't you?'

But he couldn't. The Magor not only didn't lie, they didn't try to deceive. And the ordinary Kardi, awed by the reputation of the Magor, would never have tried, either. What I had done was unthinkable, and it had left them reeling. Their only explanation was that I was able to conceal lies; therefore nothing I said could be automatically believed.

He said finally, 'I can't possibly imagine what you hope to gain by telling this tale about the Stalwarts.'

'Tell Temellin. And tell him I must see him.'

'I'll tell him. But don't wait up.'

He turned on his heel and left.

Temellin did not come to see me until the next day. He was not alone; Brand was with him.

Brand entered first, his expression as unreadable as ever. He didn't speak, but he came up to me and raised the back of his hand to my cheek in an intimate gesture of caring far more moving than any kiss would have been. I looked away from him to Temellin. I sensed a tinge of shame and uncertainty about the Mirager as he watched the two of us.

He did not greet me. He said flatly, 'You wanted to see me?' and then walked across the room, avoiding eight or nine fish swimming around in an expanse of apparently unconfined water at head-height, to stand with his back to the hole in the wall.

From where I stood he was a silhouette, rigid and forbidding. He continued, 'You have an unlikely tale about a Stalwart invasion of the Mirage. I asked Aemid what she knew about it. She said, not unexpectedly, that she had never heard of it. So now I'm going to ask Brand, because if there is such a thing planned, I'm sure you would have told him. Tell me what you know about it, Brand – and remember I can detect lies.'

Brand looked at me helplessly, his anger at Temellin growing.

I intervened. 'He knows nothing.'

'She didn't tell me everything. Only those things where she thought my advice would be useful,' Brand said.

Temellin looked unconvinced. 'That's not what Aemid says. She says Ligea always asked your advice.' He sighed. 'You're loyal, I'll say that for you, Brand. What I can't understand is *why*. She'd put a slave collar around your neck again the moment she had the chance.'

'Ligea freed me before we ever came to the Mirage. She has paid me for every year of my service to her or to her father. I give my loyalty to her because she is worthy of it, not because I am ordered to do so. In fact, she has been asking me to leave her, to seek a life of my own.'

Temellin looked at him, astonished. 'Then why didn't you?'

'I didn't want to leave, that's why. And I'm glad I didn't. Ligea's damned lucky she didn't die in the dining hall with your sodding sword in her heart – how could you do that to a woman who gave you all the love she had to give? She would have died for you half a dozen times over, but you couldn't trust her, could you?' His voice was so thick with contempt he could scarcely speak. 'When I think of the way she felt about you—'

'It seems she has fooled you just as she fooled us.'

'Ligea and I were brought up together. There's nothing I

don't know about the way she thinks. She was raised by men who tried to twist her into a cold-blooded instrument of their revenge. They tried, but they didn't succeed, because she could never quite reconcile what they tried to make of her with what she knew herself to be. They tried to sharpen her into a ruthless killer; instead, she made torture obsolete in the Cages of Tyr. How could you have loved her, and not sensed her capacity for loving?'

'You're the one who is mole-blind—'

Brand shook his head, his stare in Temellin's direction unforgiving. 'I remember the day I arrived at General Gayed's house in Tyr. He'd just bought me, cheap, at a slave auction. I was twelve years old, a dirty, skinny, ill-fed boy who had spent two whole years on auction blocks, being passed from one foul slave dealer to another across the Exaltarchy. I'd been beaten, starved and abused in ways you probably haven't even heard of. My parents were dead, my home and my inheritance stolen from me, my body used.'

He turned away from Temellin, apparently to look at the fish. I doubt he really saw them, though. 'I remember seeing Ligea for the first time. I think Gayed had bought me as a sort of joke, to see what she'd do with me. I was hardly a quality slave. He'd got me from the docks in Tyr where they sell the dross of the slave trade. Most girls brought up the way Ligea was would have scorned me, sent me to be the middenboy in the stables. She looked me over and I could see her anger growing. But she wasn't angry at me, or even at her father.

'"Who beat you like that?" she asked. It was a hard question to answer – I'd been beaten so many times – but I gave her the name of the slaver who'd inflicted the last and most vicious beating. I never spoke of it again, and neither did she, but ten years later, when she had the means to do so, she had that man banned from the slave trade and his assets impounded by the State for tax evasion.

'She was ten years old when she saw me for the first time. She could have seen the dirt, the sullen face, the ugliness of an undernourished body – but she didn't. She saw only the abuse. And hated it.

'I was her slave for eighteen years before she freed me. I never felt less than her friend, for all that she maintained the conventions of a slave-owner relationship. I know that as a compeer she's killed people, condemned others to a life-time in the Cages of Tyr, but I've never known her to be less than fair, or to harm anyone who wasn't a criminal. Her special abilities saved as many people from torture or wrongful imprisonment or execution as condemned them to such.'

He looked across at Temellin. 'But what's the use in talking to you – you've made up your mind, haven't you? Condemned her on the word of your bitch-wife and a prematurely old nurse who hadn't the spine to tell her charge the truth about herself when she was a child. You aren't fit to lead a nation, Temellin. Even with all your powers you still don't recognise the truth when the smell of it is in your nostrils. Vortexdamn you, you had everything I would have given the world for, and you tried to kill her. If I were free, I'd run a sword through your innards sooner than I'd look on your face again.' He turned his back and went to stand by the door, his dismissal of his jailer as rudely abrupt as he knew how to make it.

And Temellin accepted the dismissal. He called someone to come and escort the Altani back to his room.

I hoped Brand understood the look I gave him as he left. It was the only way I had to say thank you. He'd been my slave, and he could still defend me. I had never been so humbled.

*   *   *

It was hard to be alone with Temellin.

I opted to keep the conversation away from the personal and said, 'The Stalwarts *are* coming. And that's the truth. You are supposed to be able to distinguish a lie when you hear it.'

'*Can* I, though, with you? If Brand had known about them, I would have believed you. But he didn't. And why, if you had changed your loyalties, did you not tell me of this invasion before? You would take an oath to serve Kardiastan, and yet you wouldn't mention an intended attack on the country; worse still, on this part of it – the Mirage? Everything that you've done, Shirin, begs to make me wonder about your honesty. It begs me to wonder if you can do what others can't, and disguise your lies in the same way we can all hide our emotions.' He sounded rational and unemotional, but I could feel his contempt. And his pain. 'There was one other person who deceived us with his lies. We don't know who it was, but we do know it was one of us. A Magoroth. We trusted, because we didn't believe we could be deceived. And he brought Tyranian legionnaires into the Shimmer Feast, and killed our parents, yours and mine, and all our cousins, all the babies in the nursery and our whole way of life. I can never risk that happening again. *Never.*'

His resolution, as hard as the iron in his voice, was thick in the air about him, but so was his underlying horror. He believed he had come close to another such abomination occurring because of me. *And he was right.* I had come to the Mirage with the intention to betray them all. And what then? Would I have stood by and watched while the legionnaires killed babies, and thought it a job well done? Dear Goddess, what had I been?

I ripped away all the covers from my inner mind, let him sense whatever he wanted, bared myself to him as I had never done to anyone before. Even so, the words did not come easily.

'Temel, I was too ashamed to tell you the truth. Ashamed of what I had been. Ashamed of the role I played in strengthening the Exaltarchy. And I was afraid you would despise me, reject me. I was going to tell you eventually – I just wanted you all to know me better first. It was what I wanted to tell you about, the day you arrived back from Sandmurram. I knew I could not delay any longer.' Everything I said sounded weak to my ears. Ridiculous. I had been a Brotherhood Compeer, and here I was describing the doubts and frailties more appropriate to an adolescent girl. Yet it was the truth. It was just that loving him had rendered me an idiot.

He snorted. 'You knew you couldn't delay because you were afraid Pinar might find out about you in Madrinya. Perhaps you even guessed she had gone there expressly to investigate you.'

'Perhaps. I was a coward, Temellin. I didn't really want you to know, so I kept on postponing the telling.'

He put his head to one side and looked at me. 'Do you know,' he said finally, 'I have a great deal of trouble believing that. If there was ever anything that impressed me, it was – is – your courage.'

'There are different kinds of fear, Temellin. I was afraid of losing your respect. Perhaps I was even afraid of having made the wrong choice. As long as I didn't tell you about the Stalwarts, I could always change my mind . . . and betray you to Tyrans. I knew I loved you – loved you as a lover. But it was hard for me to believe in this love of mine for you. I was brought up to believe love was a weakness I must never allow. I was taught that to feel too much was a failing, not a virtue. It was even harder for me to acknowledge this respect I was learning for much that was Kardi; it went against everything I had ever been. You want the absolute truth? I had made my choice. I made it before I took the oath, and when I swore to uphold the Covenant, I meant it, but it wasn't until I stood there in the dining room and knew you were going to kill me that I was certain I had made the *right* choice. In that moment, I knew it didn't matter if I died – what mattered was *you*, and what you believed in. For the first time in my life, I cared more about someone else than I cared about myself.'

He looked down at the floor. 'I wish I could believe you. But I can't; on your own admission you were lying to us when we first met, and I had no inkling of it. Not even when I lay with you. You were very clever. No one I know could hide so much when cabochon to cabochon. Your lies are impossible to detect. How can I ever believe what you say now?'

'But, Temel, I *didn't* lie to you! I never lied to you. I just – just didn't tell you the whole truth. I let you jump to conclusions. There's a difference. Temellin, please – look into me now. You must be able to sense my truth.'

'How can I be sure? I doubt everything now! I doubt every relationship I've ever had because of what you have done. I even look at my friends with suspicion, and wonder if they deceive me as you did. I look at Korden, and wonder if one day he'll stab me in the back because he wants to be the Mirager. I look at my wife and wonder if I dare tell her my secrets. You've made me doubt myself. Doubt my fitness to lead this land and these people.'

We stared at each other. I choked on the lump in my throat, aware of the damage I had done. Useless to say I hadn't meant it.

He continued, 'And as for this supposed invasion over the Alps, Aemid says you have a lover among the Stalwarts. Someone you have been bedding for years. She says anything you knew about the Stalwarts would have come from him, so if there was an invasion, he would probably be part of it. But she also says you would never betray this man; you are too close. She says you would never deliberately endanger his life.'

'Do you think that comes easily to me?' I asked and allowed him to feel my bitterness. 'I had to make a choice between Kardiastan and Tyrans, and I made it. Either way a man . . . a man I care about is endangered. I chose you and Kardiastan rather than Favonius and Tyrans. I stand by that choice, although if Favonius dies, his death will haunt me. He is a brave man, and he has been a good friend.'

'Betrayal comes easy to you, it seems.'

I drew a sharp breath at the hurt in that. 'You can't have it both ways, Temellin. Either I am betraying you or I am betraying Favonius. It can't be both. To one of you I am true. To you – my brother.' I stood up and went to go to him, but he held up his hands as if to fend off my approach and I stopped. 'You still don't believe me, do you? Not a word of it—'

'No,' he said sadly. 'I don't believe you. You're my sister, and just the thought of what was done to you rasps my soul. The bastards took a child and corrupted her. That was the little Shirin I remember. They bent her and used her and probably laughed at her behind her back while they did it. But all that doesn't make me trust you now. I can't see anything of her in you. She was sweet and trusting and kind.' He folded his arms, his whole stance one of rejection. 'And now I am left with a puzzling question. Just why do you want us to believe in this Stalwart invasion?'

I didn't answer. What could I have said?

'There must be a good reason. It's a diversion of some sort, isn't it? You want us to worry about the wrong place, or the wrong kind of danger. What is it the Brotherhood really has planned for us, Legata? I've heard enough about them to know they are masters of deviousness, of deception, of plots and counterplots. And this, I know, must be one such. You're General Gayed's daughter and Rathrox Ligatan's apprentice, and Aemid says she believes you were sent here at the express order of Exaltarch Bator Korbus. All three men were once humiliated at the hands of Kardiastan. You came as the lance blade of their revenge, Shirin. Did they know when they took you that you were my sister? They did, didn't they! Were you to gain the trust of us all, then kill me and take over as Mirager? Is that what you are trying to hide from us with this fanciful tale of the Stalwarts crossing the Alps, a tale you conveniently tell only when your main deception is uncovered?'

I still didn't speak; I couldn't think of any words to convince him of the truth.

A fleeting look of anguish crossed his face. 'Ah, Shirin, Shirin – it hurts so much to look at you, to see what they made of you. It could so easily have been . . . different. When Solad sent the Ten to the Mirage, I cried because they didn't include you. "Can't you make it eleven?" I asked. Shirin, we shouldn't be standing here like this, as enemies. We should be husband and wife with children playing at our feet. You've lived among us, you've seen what sort of people we are – can't you be one of us now?' He must have known the question was ridiculous. It was exactly what I did want, and exactly what his disbelief wouldn't allow him to grant.

I said, 'No matter what I said, you'd still doubt me. The truth remains the same. I'm not your enemy, Temellin. Not any more.'

The look he gave me then was poignant in its sadness. 'I suppose I shouldn't blame you for what you are. As a child I was taken to the Mirage; you were taken to Tyrans. Had it been the other way around, who is to say what might have been? And you're right, of course; no matter what you said, I would have my doubts. So much of you is Tyranian. Worse still, you know too much. You have too much power and the potential for so much more. We cannot let you have your liberty, perhaps not ever. When I threw my sword at you, I acted in passion and it was an evil thing I did. I'm glad you had deliberately protected yourself against it, for cabochon knows, you are still my sister and I don't want your death. But in truth, perhaps it would have been kinder for you to have died then, for I doubt you can ever be freed.'

My heart wobbled absurdly; there were tears in his eyes.

'It wasn't deliberate,' I said, but I doubt he heard.

'I'm sorry, Shirin. I'm sorrier than I can say – for everything. I wish – I wish things could have been different.'

'They could be, if you believed me. Never mind. When the Stalwarts attack, perhaps you'll think again.' *If it's not too late for all of us. Too late for the Mirage.*

'If there's anything you need, ask. I will see that you receive anything within reason to make your imprisonment more comfortable.'

'Oh, go away, Temellin. Imprisonment cannot be anything but uncomfortable, even when the Mirage does its best to entertain me. Watch out for the fish,' I added as he turned abruptly to leave me.

After he had gone I sat down shakily, all my emotions spilling free once I was alone.

Two nights later, Pinar came.

She came late, long after I had fallen asleep and she came silently, yet I was attuned to the malignancy of the emotional aura surrounding her. I woke the moment she stepped into the room. 'What do you want, Pinar?' I asked.

She did not answer. She raised her left hand and sent a narrow beam of light around the room from her cabochon. When it illuminated the candle on the desk under the window, she let it linger a moment and the candle flamed. By its light she began a circuit of the room, investigating the fish in their water, the bubbles and their pictures, the wall paintings, the bathroom. By the time she had finished, I had flung on a shawl and was sprawled casually in the room's only chair.

She came to stand before me, sword sheathed, hands on her hips. 'What is the meaning of all this?' she asked. 'Why do the Mirage Makers do this for you?'

I shrugged. 'Perhaps to compensate for my wrongful imprisonment?'

'Temellin should have killed you. You are dangerous to us somehow—'

I made a gesture of weariness. 'Pinar, don't be moondaft. Soon you'll be convincing yourself I really did try to kill you and not the other way around.'

'What I did was justified. You are still a danger to us. And just as bad, having to imprison you here like this is devastating Temellin. He is tortured by guilt. Guilt! As if he has anything to be guilty about! I've tried to tell him we'd all be better off if you were dead, but he won't listen.'

I raised an eyebrow, the mockery a cover to my own pain. 'Poor Pinar, only a few weeks married, and already your husband ignores your suggestions?'

The tight expression on her face reminded me of Rathrox when he was planning revenge on someone who had slighted him.

The feeling remained, even when she'd gone. For the first time in my adult life, I had no control over my own destiny. I'd never felt so helpless and frustrated. So *powerless*. I doubt if anyone could have devised a more effective form of revenge than this one.

The next morning, as usual, Illuser-reftim brought my breakfast and left it on the desk. Normally he gave a swift look around to see what changes had been wrought during the night; this time he didn't seem interested. There wasn't anything new anyway, nor had anything been taken away. The fish were still swimming in their unconfined waters and occasionally one would poke its nose out into the air before withdrawing into the safety of its element. Reftim ignored them, ducked his head in my direction without looking at me, either, and left the room as quickly as he could.

Worried by his behaviour, I went to the desk and sat down. Fresh bread, a glass of juice, a pot of hot herbal tea, smoked fish, fresh fruit. My normal breakfast. I stared at it without appetite.

I jabbed my knife into the fish, more in a gesture of disgust at my situation than with any intent of eating it. And smelled something that didn't seem quite right: a faint whiff of unpleasantness. It was vaguely familiar and, a moment later, I knew why: it reminded me of the Ravage.

I stared at the fish; it looked normal. I opened up my palm and passed my left hand over the meal without believing anything would come of such a gesture, yet as I looked, I saw a writhing black mass appear in the middle of the fish. In revulsion I flung the tray and all its contents away from me, smashing them from the desk onto the floor.

Some time later, Reftim returned to clear away the tray. His face glistened with sweat and his initial step into the room, even before his glance took in the empty desk and the food on the floor, was the palsied movement of an old man. Then he paled, the colour draining from his plump face so fast I thought he would faint. His guilt was obvious, but I knew he was not the initiator. I stood leaning against the door, waiting while he wordlessly cleaned up the mess. When he had finished and was on his way out with the tray, I did not move and he was forced to stop in front of me.

'In all my years working for the Brotherhood, I never poisoned anyone,' I said.

The colour returned to his face as rapidly as it had left it. 'Magoria—' he began, but his shame strangled any further words in the back of his throat.

'Do you think the Mirager would approve?'

He did not reply.

I knew I had no hope of him reporting the attempt, not when he himself was involved. 'Tell Pinar she will have to do better than that,' I said and stood aside to let him pass.

Once he had gone, I crossed the room to the desk and hit the desktop with the flat of my right hand, all my repressed anger and frustration surfacing. My helplessness was suffocating me. I plunged away from the desk, forgot the uncontained water and splashed into it, sending fish flying about the room.

'Vortex*damn* you!' I shouted, venting my rage on the Mirage Makers. 'Do you think a poisoned baby is going to do you any good? Why don't you find some way of getting me out of this? Or at least send me something useful, like a – a – a book!'

For a moment I continued to stand, hands clenched by my sides, and then calm prevailed.

I bent to pick up the fish flopping on the floor and stuffed them back into what was left of the water.

CHAPTER TWENTY-TWO

The morning after the poisoning attempt, I didn't have to look far to see what changes had occurred during the night. The fish and all the other useless additions to the decor had gone. Instead, the room was lined from ceiling to floor with book-shelves, each shelf packed with vellum-bound volumes and scrolls.

I had never seen such a collection outside of the Public Library in Tyr; it was rare for even the most scholarly of indi-viduals to have more than three or four treasured volumes. Copying a book cost money and not many people could afford them.

I rolled off my pallet and ran my eye along the roughly tooled spines of the closest shelf: all were written in Kardi. The first book was a compendium on Kardi freshwater fish, with illus-trations. The next was a tome consisting mainly of dates and figures and, as far as I could make out, it detailed the heights and times of the coastal tides of Kardiastan for their entire five-year cycle. The next was a philosophical work, with a title I couldn't understand, written by a past Mirager; something, I thought, about the morality of using supernatural powers on people who had none. The trouble was this: I was by no means at ease with written Kardi. I'd had little opportunity to study it.

Well, I certainly had both the time and the opportunity now. Quietly I thanked the Mirage Makers for their extravagant answer to my request, and in the days following I began to go through the books, sorting them out into those of no conceivable interest, such as the tide timetable, and those I would like to read. I did wonder if I'd be allowed to keep the library, but if Reftim reported it, no one did anything about it. It didn't take me long to realise the lack of interest was just as well. Had the Magor known of the treasure I now possessed, they would surely have separated me from it, for among the books were twenty-two volumes dealing with the power of the Magor.

Twenty-two volumes written by Magoroth, dating prior to the Tyranian invasion – some of them more than five hundred years prior – written as manuals for students, each dealing with different aspects of Magor art. Some of what was written there I already knew, but the rest took my breath away as I began to realise the possible extent of Magor powers. A fully trained Magoroth could call up a localised windstorm strong enough to flatten a shleth; he could conserve air in the body and walk under water or mimic death; he could shut off pain and not feel; he could produce light, abort a baby, kill a person or start a fire – all with his cabochon. He could hear a whisper spoken two hundred paces away or see acutely enough to note the twinkle in a windhover's eye as it drifted the skies.

Abort a baby.

It was easy. I could abort someone else's, or my own, simply by laying the cabochon on my lower abdomen and conjuring the right words in the right way.

I learned the words. I studied the texts to make sure different books outlined the same method, and they did. No latent maternal instinct arose to usurp my normal indifference to the thought of motherhood. No concern for an unborn child, scarcely started along the path of its life, came to overwhelm my sense of self-preservation. This was going to be so easy. I could live. I could stop being haunted by the knowledge I might die with the child ripped from my womb, sacrificed against my will in order to fulfil a bargain I'd had no say in.

I laid my hand in the correct place, and opened my mouth to say the words – *and couldn't do it.*

I, who'd slid a knife into several people during my years as a compeer and then walked away without a qualm, couldn't kill the life growing in me. It wasn't the Mirage Makers who stopped me. It was the thought that this was Temellin's child, and I couldn't kill his son.

The next morning when I awoke, I thought about that. I thought of all Brand had said about the woman I had been. And after breakfast, I turned to the books, skimming through volume after volume, looking for references to the Ravage. Most authors who mentioned it subscribed to the theory that it was a disease. The Mirage Makers, the theory went, were living beings and as such were prone to infection, just as humans were. The Ravage was a disease or an infection like gangrene or a suppurating abscess. The creatures inside the Ravage were the animals that lived inside such infection. One writer even postulated that little creatures lived inside our infections too, but we couldn't see them because they were small, just as no one would be able to see what was in the Ravage if it were scaled down in size. Needless to say, I didn't give any credit to that idea.

In the past, the Magoroth had attempted to cure the sores in the same way as they might try to cure an abscess or gangrene, by cleaning them out and washing the wound left in the land. It hadn't worked. None of the texts had mentioned the kind of hallucination I had suffered. No one seemed to have been attacked with such intense personal hatred as I had been.

I continued to explore the books, my hunt fuelled by a desperation only partially choked down to a manageable level. And finally I found a writer who had another theory. Perhaps, he wrote, the Ravage was caused by the evil of the creatures within, rather than the other way around. The creatures were evil, ergo, the effect they had was also evil. The author offered no evidence to back his idea, and I wasn't sure I agreed with him, either.

I knew the things I'd seen in the Ravage weren't true creatures. They weren't like insects or worms. I'd *felt* them as much as seen them, and I'd never before felt anything that wasn't human. The emotions of normal animals were as closed to me as they were to anyone else. I knew a growling dog or a spitting cat was angry when I saw and heard them, not because I sensed the rage. I puzzled over this, even wondering if the Ravage creatures were some form of deformed human.

In the end, I decided the hatred of the Ravage beasts for me, and the Mirage Makers' need of a child, were linked. At a guess, the Mirage Makers believed a Magoroth child who became a Mirage Maker would make them strong enough to win the ongoing battle with the Ravage. The Ravage wanted me dead *because they wanted to stop the Mirage Makers getting hold of my child.*

I had to be careful, or I was going to die, killed by the Ravage. Or by the Magoroth, to settle Solad's murderous bargain with the Mirage Makers. And I couldn't expect the Mirage Makers to help me.

I sighed. My future was looking increasingly grim.

I couldn't risk telling Temellin about the baby. If Pinar got to hear of it, and if she knew the nature of Solad's bargain, she'd be lobbying the others to sacrifice me and my son. I knew how strongly the Magor felt about the covenant between themselves and the Mirage Makers. I knew they would want to uphold any new agreement Solad had made. Without it, there would eventually be no Mirage Makers.

And who better to supply the child than a Tyranian compeer they didn't trust? Which left the question: would Temellin sanction my killing, even if I were unwilling? There had been a time when he wouldn't have contemplated it. But now? He wouldn't like it, but if he were under pressure from the others? Perhaps he now despised me enough to do it without a qualm. The difficult part would be to offer his own son . . .

As soon as he found out I was pregnant, he would have to order my death. He really didn't have any choice. Without the Mirage Makers' support, there would be no Magor – and I was expendable. One supposedly traitorous woman's life in exchange for a whole way of life and the health of the land. It was a bargain.

If I had been truly Kardi, brought up a Magoria, believing in the greater good of my fellow Magoroth, perhaps I would have made the sacrifice gladly. But I wasn't. Underneath I was still Ligea, and she was the kind of person who'd go to her death kicking and screaming every inch of the way . . .

The powerlessness of my existence gnawed at me. Imprisonment, I found, was something not taken too kindly by even the remnants of Ligea, Brotherhood Compeer. It wasn't the feeling of confinement that tortured, although that was bad enough. It was the feeling I had no influence over anyone, and even less over my own future. I could die one night, unexpectedly, if the Ravage came, and I could do nothing about it. I wanted to talk to someone about it. But there was no one. I considered mentioning it to Reftim, the miasma of his antipathy followed him into the room with every visit. He would have seen me dead without hesitation, and his attitude was doubtless a reflection of every Magor in the Maze. I was so Goddessdamned *lonely*.

I turned back to my studies of Magor magic, as recounted in the books.

And found out how Temellin had escaped the might of Tyrans. An imprisoned Magoroth of skill could use his cabochon to burn through the iron of manacles, produce pain in people bathed in its light, or raise a temporary ward between his skin and the blows rained on him. The one thing Temellin couldn't have done was make smoke appear out of nowhere. Anything like that would have been an illusion – a mirage – and mirages were banned to the Magor. Ciceron, the officer in charge of the execution, must have been right: something had been sprinkled on the wood of the execution pyre beforehand. Which meant, not surprisingly, that others had helped Temellin to escape.

Of more surprise to me was the discovery that the Magor could enhance their hearing if they wished. My true identity could have been discovered much earlier if Temellin or Pinar or one of the other Magor had listened in on my conversations with Brand. But they hadn't. Evidently, strong Magor distaste for invading another's privacy prevented such an action, although I suspected that where Pinar was concerned, it was perhaps more likely she just hadn't listened at the right times.

The days of my incarceration began to fly past. I hunched over the books, reading and rereading, then practising what I learned. Garis had already shown me much that was helpful; even so, I made mistakes. After three days of trying to light a candle from a distance, as Pinar had done, I finally produced a beam of light, set fire to my desk and crumbled part of the wall. My next attempt melted the candle to an unusable lump of wax and shattered the holder to powder. Fortunately, I improved with time. Even more luckily, the Mirage Makers repaired the damage before Reftim entered my room again.

I learned how to draw a ward of a simple kind around myself with my cabochon. It would not prevent a skilled Magor from entering that space, but it ensured I would always know when they did. It meant I could not be surprised by an intruder while I was asleep.

Nor could I be poisoned. It was comforting to have in writing what I had already assumed to be true: the passing of my cabochon over food or water would always betray a poison into displaying itself. However, no one tried poison again; all food brought to me was just as it should have been.

Unhappily, a ward drawn with swords, such as the one imprisoning me, could not be broken by the person who was the object of it. The door to my room remained unlocked. Anyone else could come and go through it, but if I tried, I walked into a barrier as solid as gorclak horn.

The first month of my imprisonment passed, then the second. The life within me continued to grow; I was aware of it even though it was still too early for it to make its presence felt with discernible movements. I made no move to tell Temellin. I didn't want to give the Magoroth the excuse to kill me.

Temellin never came near me anyway. Sometimes I wondered if he knew just how solitary my confinement was, and if he did know, whether he cared. I yearned to hear from him – a word, some expression of concern or interest, *something*, but day after day passed in silence. When I was feeling especially low, it seemed as if the world out there had forgotten my existence and I was doomed to live as a sort of peripheral being, someone who could never enter the mainstream of life where things happened, and who was therefore only half alive.

For someone who had loved power, who had once loved to make things happen, it was a bitter situation.

When Caleh finally came to see me, with messages of support from Brand, it was all I could do to stop myself from crying in gratitude at her presence. Although she had received permission to see me, she was obviously uneasy, uncertain of how much she should tell me. Brand, she said, was well and asking me not to worry about him; Temellin was also well, but was becoming known for his bad temper. 'He doesn't know what to do about you,' she said sagely, 'and people are saying the thought of your imprisonment preys on him. Ah, Magoria, Brand tells me you truly wanted to serve Kardiastan, and I believe him. He is too shrewd to be deceived.' She shook her head in sorrow as she left, saying, 'I don't know how all this is going to end.'

I didn't know, either.

The only other person I had any real contact with was Reftim and he rarely spoke. He was polite, and perhaps his silence was more my fault; he always answered if I spoke to him first. Most of the time, though, he wouldn't even meet my eyes and I guessed – I hoped – he was bitterly ashamed of his part in the attempt to poison me. I wondered sometimes if he had deliberately told no one of my library as a way of compensating me; I found it hard to believe Pinar would have tolerated my having access to all those books, had she been aware of them.

One other person who did have contact with me – of an oblique kind – was Garis. After the first two or three days of my imprisonment he sent me a bunch of flowers via Reftim, and continued to do so every few days. There was never any note or message, but I was touched. I hoped it meant he was not convinced of my utter perfidy.

Two days after Caleh's visit, I noted Reftim was upset, so I asked what was the matter, saying, 'Surely it can't be all that bad, can it? You look as if your father-in-law has moved into your bedroom!'

He looked at me with distressed eyes that seemed out of place in his clown-like face. 'The Ravage has come to the city,' he said. 'It swallowed up several of the houses on the south side during the night, just like that.' He clicked his fingers in illustration. 'Four families disappeared.'

I remembered what the howdah-shleth driver had said to me, about the Ravage being so close. *One day we'll wake up to find a swathe of it destroying the Maze like legionnaires on the rampage.*

Sickened and frightened, I turned away.

And so the days passed. I exercised rigorously, I ate, I slept and every other minute of every day was spent either reading, or exerting my will on that delicate curve of golden stone in my palm, inveigling it to do my bidding – without reducing everything in its path, myself included, to a heap of ashes.

And then came the shock: the thrilling, breath-robbing, devastating shock.

I was seated at my desk, browsing through a book entitled *The Mirager: His Powers and Responsibilities*, when I came across it, the passage that made a mockery of everything Zerise had said about Sarana and Shirin and me. A passage that took away one pain, only to replace it with another, just as tearing. A passage that changed everything.

On the death of the ruling Mirager (or Miragerin), I read, *the dead ruler's heir will walk the Shiver Barrens and be given a Mirager's sword. If they already have a sword, they will exchange it.*

At the same time, this new Mirager or Miragerin will be given the conjurations that will bestow cabochons on the newborn. This information is given only to the ruling Mirager or Miragerin, and is not bestowed on any other Magoroth; nor is any other sword capable of bestowing cabochons. For this reason, the ruling Mirager or Miragerin should take special care of their sword. No other will ever be given to them . . .

My first thought was one of protest: but this is wrong. I had been given the conjurations under the Shiver Barrens. I knew how to bestow a cabochon; the Mirage Makers had shown me in the vision. Presumably my sword was capable of producing the gems. Yet Temellin was the Mirager.

I sat there, thoughts tumbling through my head, and the truth came, a crushing avalanche of knowledge roaring into my consciousness in a single wave, too much to absorb all at once.

This information is given only to the ruling Mirager or Miragerin – I looked up from the book. The Miragerin. Goddess, that was *Sarana*, not Shirin.

The Mirage Makers had told me, implanting the knowledge through the indelible clarity of one of their visions, but I hadn't seen it. My own memories had told me, but I hadn't thought them through.

. . . nor is any other sword capable of bestowing cabochons.

The behaviour of the Magoroth had told me, but I had forgotten. Only now did I recall the reverence with which they had treated Temellin's newly recovered sword. Garis had told me, but I had missed the significance of what he'd said: 'Until Temellin grew up a bit, no newborn Magor children received their cabochons.' Temellin had told me, but I hadn't realised: 'You don't know it, love, but you've just saved my life—' Sweet Melete, if I had not returned his sword to him, he would have had to kill himself so that someone else would become the Mirager – and receive a new Mirager's sword.

Dear Goddess, I was Sarana, daughter of Solad and Wendia; I was Miragerin of Kardiastan; I was the little girl in the shleth howdah who had watched her mother jump out to her death at the hands of the legionnaires led by General Gayed of Tyr.

I was the girl who had become a pawn of Tyrans, a hostage who had enslaved a nation.

PART FOUR

SARANA

CHAPTER TWENTY-THREE

I stood at my window looking down on the street below. I had been drawn there by the jingling of a shleth harness and the chatter of voices, to find the road filled with a line of mounted Magor and pack animals, all heading out of the city. There were those of gold cabochon rank, as well as Illusos, Theuros and ordinary Kardis, all of them heavily armed.

I raised my cabochon to my ear and listened, trying to gain some clue as to what was happening. In the confusion of sound it was hard to hear individual conversation, even with my enhanced hearing, and the sort of remarks I did pick up were of little value; things like: 'Your girth needs loosening, Jaset,' or 'Did Bethely give you a hearty farewell last night, Mooris? It could be a while before you see her again!'

My eyes searched for and found Temellin: he had pulled his mount to the side and was watching those who rode past. His ivory full-sleeved shirt and rusty brown trousers were crumpled, as though he'd been sleeping in his clothes, or had simply lost interest in his appearance. The scarlet slash of his cloth belt and the blood-red of his bolero didn't quite match; his hair was longer than usual and more unruly than ever.

The moment my gaze found him, he looked up to see me,

and I wondered if he had deliberately stopped where he had just for that purpose.

I brought my cabochon up to my face, close to my eyes, and concentrated. The stone, which I now kept uncovered by skin, began to glow faintly and I used the light bathing my eyes to enhance my vision. Temellin sprang into clarity as though he were close enough to touch. He looked thin and tired; nothing of his laughter was visible on his face any more. The brown eyes regarded me thoughtfully, the mouth was tight.

My body hungered, my heart grieved, the sight of him lacerated me. Temellin. My cousin. I could have bedded him without guilt, if he would have had me. Well, perhaps not quite without guilt. What my blood-father had done to save me had left me with a burden that would last forever.

Tears came to my eyes and Temellin blurred back into a distant figure mounted on his shleth. I opened up my palm and flattened it against the glass of the window in a gesture of greeting and farewell. I thought I saw him begin to raise a hand in acknowledgement, but the gesture died half made and he turned away, urging his mount along with the others.

I sat by the window looking down the road for a long while after it was empty of people. The Mirage Makers created a flock of pink flamingos for me to look at, and then – perhaps because the birds looked a little lost standing on the cobblestone road – added a marshy pond with waterlilies. None of it eased my torment.

I had finally thought it all through: a story of betrayal and tragedy that started when I was a child and wasn't finished yet because I was the one who held the endings, and I didn't know which one to write into Kardiastan's history. I may have thought it all through, but I still didn't know what to do.

It had all started because a woman took her daughter away

from the child's father. Magoria-wendia removed Sarana from the palace because she thought the Mirager-solad was ruining the child with his lavish spoiling. I could even remember some of the arguments now, the incomprehensible shouting matches between two much-loved parents, arguments so shattering to a child not quite three. Far distant memories: *running, barefoot, across polished agate floors into my father's arms. Adoring him, feeling safe and loved in his strong clasp . . .*

And somewhere on the journey to another city, Magoria-wendia's party had been ambushed and wiped out – with the exception of that same child, Sarana, heir to her father's Mirager sword. She fell into the hands of General Gayed and Rathrox Ligatan, who knew exactly what they had, and were prepared to use her in ways Solad could never have envisioned. *My mother, jumping out of the howdah, sword in hand, leaving me in the care of my Theura nurse, while she battled to save us – and died . . .*

Sarana, the beloved daughter of an obsessed father, a man so crazed by the thought of what they would do to her if he didn't obey them, he was prepared to betray the rest of his family, his fellow Magor, his country: prepared to raise wards around the annual Shimmer Feast so no one sensed the trap closing in on them, prepared to lower those same wards at the crucial moment to turn the trap into an extermination.

Solad's supposed discovery and identification of his daughter's body, his return with her already shroud-wrapped in his howdah, her burial griefs – all playacting to conceal the kidnapping, to hide the existence of a hostage he would do anything to save. The scale of his treachery was breathtaking. I even wondered if he'd killed another child in order to have a body to wrap.

Of course Solad knew what was going to happen at the Shimmer Feast: he had arranged it. And some shred of remaining good sense or conscience made him send away ten Magoroth children to build the core of a new leadership. Just ten of them, with a few teachers; not enough to be missed by the Tyranians. The calculated cruelty of his decisions – take Temellin, but leave his sister Shirin; abandon the babies to their fate. Did his conscience bother him, my father? Did he think I was worth all those slaughtered that day? A whole nation enslaved? Did he really think the vestiges of future hope he seeded by sending the Ten away was enough to atone for his crime?

My Mirager father had sold his honour for his daughter. Temellin's parents and his sister Shirin, and Goddess knows how many Magoroth had died – *to keep me alive*. Kardiastan was enslaved because of *me*. Temellin and the others of the Ten were brought up in exile because of me.

Because of me. Sarana. Solad's heir. The rightful Miragerin. Miragerin-sarana. Me.

It was the only explanation that made any sense.

My memories all fitted; I'd seen Wendia jumping out of a howdah into battle. If I'd been Shirin, I would never have been sitting in a tiny curtained room that swayed just before my mother was killed. I would never have seen her rip off her skirting to fight. Shirin's mother had been attending the Shimmer Feast and would have been shot down with the others, far from the nursery.

There was more evidence, too, once I started to think things over. The Mirage Makers had said, *You are the Miragerin*, not, *You are the Miragerin-shirin*. And now I had the book to tell me they would never have given Shirin the cabochon-making conjurations. Sarana was another matter. When Sarana had disappeared from Kardiastan, they must have thought her dead, so they bestowed the Mirager's sword on her heir: her cousin Temellin. Once they had seen Ligea Gayed, they had realised Sarana was far from dead and they had tried to make up for their past mistake.

I'd been so blind. I was the one with the memories of what had happened in the ambush; I should have known those memories didn't fit with what Zerise told me of Shirin. I should have realised much earlier about the significance of the Mirager's sword. Temellin and the Mágor had been so upset by its loss, so relieved at its return. Why, even the ordinary Kardis had cheered to see it again. I had seen the reverent way the Magoroth had touched it back in Madrinya; I'd heard Temellin say to Korden, 'At least you can stop worrying about that baby of yours.' I'd been told the first thing Temellin did when he returned to the Mirage City with the sword was to bestow cabochons – which would not have been necessary if other Magor or other swords could have performed that task in the year the Mirager's sword had been missing – yet I'd still blithely gone on thinking there was nothing special about my knowledge, about *my* sword.

And then that casually uttered but infinitely tragic, 'Ah. You don't know it, beautiful one, but you've just saved my life.' Temellin had thought there wasn't going to be another Mirager's sword until he died, and without one there would never be a new generation of Magor. So some time before he'd met me, he'd decided to die.

The cold-blooded courage of that decision pierced me. I remembered his reluctance to ask if I really did have his sword; he'd been so concerned about what my answer would be that he hadn't been able to frame the question.

I remembered the strange reaction of Korden when he'd seen with his own eyes Temellin's sword safely returned: the odd mixture of relief and guilt. Part of Korden desperately wanted to be Mirager, but not over Temellin's body. In his heart he believed he'd be a better Mirager, but he'd been terrified

Temellin was going to suicide, and he had feared the guilt that would have consumed him as a consequence.

I understood Korden better now that I was burdened with the guilt of my own past.

I wondered at my own blindness ... The compeer in me had been granted enough evidence to unravel the tale long ago, but this hadn't been a crime I could solve objectively, distancing myself from the players; this had been my life.

And most of all, it was hard to acknowledge that for much of that life I, independent, manipulative, power-hungry Ligea Gayed, had danced to another's direction. I'd been betrayed by the two men I called father. Mocked by the man I'd called my mentor. I'd been manipulated, a poor senseless marionette jerked on the end of strings held by my enemies.

One good thing came out of my new understanding of who I was. I knew now that my son had been fathered by my cousin, not by my brother.

When Reftim brought in my lunch later that day, I asked abruptly, 'Where were they all going?'

'I don't know that I should answer that,' he said, his plump cheeks flushing to match the colour of his bobble nose.

'Then let me speak to someone who can. Who's in charge now the Mirager has gone?'

'The Miragerin-consort.'

'Oh. Well, I hardly want to see her. Who else of the Magoroth is still here?'

'Garis didn't leave. Nor did Gretha.'

Gretha was Korden's wife and a little calculation told me she was expecting another child any time. 'I'll see Garis,' I said.

'I'll tell him you want to,' Reftim replied, making it clear he doubted Garis would come.

He was wrong; Garis came barely half an hour later. He

paused in the doorway and we stared at one another, both looking for the right words to say. He was doing his best to shield his emotions, but Garis tended to leak things at the best of times. I'd felt his curiosity even before the door opened.

'Well met, Garis. What have you done to yourself?' I asked, indicating the sling he wore around a heavily bandaged left arm.

'Broke a bone,' he said briefly. 'Came off my shleth yesterday like a damned fool.'

'And you so proud of your riding skills!'

He gave a reluctant grin, and for a moment he was his usual cheerful self. 'Don't rub it in – everyone else has. The Mirage chose to grow a tree right in front of my mount just when I was taking a drink from my waterskin; hardly my fault. Those wretched Mirage Makers! I could almost believe they wanted me to miss out on all the fun.' He gazed around with interest. 'I was told your room was prone to changes, but I didn't hear about the books.' He walked over to have a look; it did not escape my notice that he'd made no attempt to touch my cabochon in greeting, and I doubted the snub had anything to do with his injury. He ran a finger along the spines of a row of volumes, reading the titles. 'They're all in Kardi! Did you know you're breaking Tyranian law? It's one of the new promulgations of the Exaltarchy: the Kardi language is now barbaric and unlawful. They have been destroying our written works for years, of course, but now they want to make it illegal even to *speak* our own language in any public venue.'

'I didn't know that,' I said, 'about not speaking Kardi, I mean. But there's a great deal I don't know, Garis. I haven't spoken to anyone except Illuser-reftim – and Caleh very briefly – for two months, and Reftim never says anything anyway. Why has everyone left?'

He looked up sharply, shedding his concern. 'Did Temellin never come?'

'Only once. Right at the beginning.'

'Ah. I did wonder. Cabochon, you must have been lonely. I would have come if you'd asked for me.'

'That might have been unwise on your part. I am hardly the city's most beloved guest at the moment. I did appreciate your sending the flowers, though; that was a kind thought.'

His emotions blanked over. 'Flowers? What flowers?'

I stared. 'You haven't been sending me flowers?' I indicated the vase on my desk. That day the petals of each flower reassembled themselves every few minutes, so that the flower arrangement was different every time I looked.

He shook his head. 'I'm sorry – I didn't think of it. I wish I had.'

'Reftim told me they came from you.'

'I didn't even know about them. I bet I know who did send them, though.'

'Do you think so?' I was doubtful, yet wanting to believe.

'Who else?'

I thought immediately of Pinar, some trick of hers, but had to dismiss that idea: the flowers were harmless and perfectly ordinary, insofar as the Mirage's flowers were ever ordinary. Who indeed. Yet he hadn't wanted me to know they came from him . . . I pushed the thought away before it could hurt me with the other memories it would bring. 'Garis, did you believe me when I said Brand had told the truth – that I had changed, and given my loyalties to Kardiastan?'

He looked away to take a book down from the shelf. 'Perhaps. I don't know. I can sense your truth, but Temellin says you can lie and make it seem like the truth.'

'No. I can't. I never lied. I just omitted to tell the whole story, and let people jump to the wrong conclusions. It was deliberate, of course, but it does make a difference. It means you can trust what I *do* say.'

'I've never been convinced you were wholly as Tyranian as Pinar or Korden said. Anyway,' he added, his expression suddenly mischievous and admiring, 'if you did come here with the idea of betraying us all, I can only salute you. It was a gloriously brave, wonderfully insane thing to do.'

I chuckled. 'It was rather involuntary, if you'll remember. Events sort of overtook me.'

He wasn't listening. He had just read the title of the book he was holding, and his attention was now back on the books on the same shelf. 'Mirageless soul! Shirin, do you know what these books are?'

'Old Magor texts.'

'But so many of these were destroyed in the palace fire following the invasion – they haven't been in existence for twenty-five years! I've heard about them, but I never *dreamed* I'd actually ever see any of them.'

'Ah. I suppose the Mirage must have remembered them.'

'Sweet cabochon – you've been *reading* these?'

'Certainly. I've had plenty of time to perfect my Kardi reading skills.'

He looked at me in consternation. 'Shirin, was that wise? Surely you must realise the more you know of Magor powers, the more reluctant Temellin will be to ever let you go.'

'He has already told me he will never release me, so what difference does it make?'

'If Pinar hears about this, she'll have a new argument for your death. She's already quite boring on the subject.'

I snorted. 'So much for cousinly love. She has, in fact, made two attempts on my life as well.'

His look was guarded, but his seeping emotions communicated his disbelief.

'You haven't answered my question: where has everyone gone?'

He considered. 'I don't suppose it matters if I tell you. Temellin is moving against Tyrans. We have had word fresh troops have been landing at one of the southern ports. Temel believes them to be reinforcements, not replacement troops. It seems Tyrans is going to try to wipe out all Kardi opposition; Temellin wants to ensure the reverse. This is to be a full-scale war, Shirin.'

I felt physically ill. 'Goddessdamn! Garis, those troops are not reinforcements; they are diversionary. Did you hear about what I told Korden and Temellin concerning the Stalwarts?'

'Yes,' he said carefully. 'But – well, Shirin, we all found it very hard to believe. Once Temellin heard about these new landings, he decided your talk of the Alps crossing was an attempt to divert our attention away from the south.'

'Oh, Vortexdamn him! That idiot!' I sank down into the chair. 'Garis, things are even worse than I thought they would be – and I'm a fool too. I should have done more to convince Temellin. It's just that I didn't envisage this diversion. I didn't know of it.'

'It's not possible for the legions to cross the Alps.'

'Has anyone ever tried from here?'

'No. Why should they?'

'Then how do you know what it is like? The Stalwarts would have sent someone to reconnoitre before they made the decision to attack from there; they must know it is possible. And Temellin has left the Mirage defenceless. I'm surprised he even left you and Pinar behind,' I added disgustedly.

'Well, I broke my arm. But I'm going after them as soon as it's mended, which should only be a week or two.'

'Why did Pinar stay behind?'

'Um, well . . .' He hesitated, flushing. 'She's pregnant. Not by very long, of course, but she's not that young, and she carries the next Mirager. Temellin wouldn't let her ride with them.'

Illogically, that hurt. I pushed the pain away; I didn't have time for it. And then the thought came, uninvited: another baby. Another woman who could die instead of me . . . I pushed that thought away too. I would think about it later. 'Garis, I want you to free me so I can deal with the Stalwarts.'

'Shirin – you know I can't do that.' There wasn't another chair, so he flung himself down on my pallet and began to pluck at the threads of my quilt.

'You must. First I'm going to tell you the whole truth about myself . . . about how and why I became a Compeer of the Brotherhood. Then I want you to go and get Aemid – how is she, by the way? Reftim said she was better.'

'She is. She says she feels ten years younger. Apparently her heart was weak and some of the Magor have been practising their healing skills on her. But still, she doesn't look happy. She doesn't say much to anyone, either.'

'And Brand?'

'He's fine. He was bored out of his mind at first, but then Temellin gave permission for him to go to the practice rooms for weapons training – under strict supervision and warding. I don't think Temellin intends for his imprisonment to be permanent. I go and see him in his room sometimes, and so do some of the others. He made a lot of friends while he was training with the troops, you know; he is well liked. Caleh asked to be allowed to sleep with him, so he has company on his pallet as well.'

I gave a wry smile. Trust Brand.

'Garis, I want you to take Aemid to Brand and question him about me, with Aemid there, so she can confirm what he says about my past. Ask him, too, about Pinar's first attempt on my life. Ask Reftim about the second; I think he may tell you. He feels guilty about it, I know. Once you have done all that, perhaps you may be more willing to believe me. But first let me tell you about myself, about how I ever got mixed up with the Brotherhood in the first place.'

He glanced at me warily, as if wondering what trick I was up to now.

I licked dry lips. 'It's not an easy story to tell. It was Brand who prodded me into seeing the truth. Even then, I didn't want to believe what was so painful. I was *used*, Garis. I've been used all my life, and by the men I most wanted to please.

'I don't really remember my early life in Kardiastan, but I do remember being terrified and among strangers and knowing my mother was dead. Then this man came and he treated me kindly. I thought he was very handsome. He said he would take me home and look after me, and he did. Eventually he took me back to his home in Tyr and gave me everything I wanted and taught me to call him Pater. I worshipped him. His wife ignored me, but I had Aemid to care for me, so I didn't mind.

'I grew up thinking I was lucky to have such a wonderful father. I didn't see all that much of him, but he was a busy and important man and everyone said he spent too much time with me anyway. All the while I thought it was because he loved me. Do you know how much children can deceive themselves, Garis? When they really want to believe something is true?'

It was a rhetorical question, so he didn't answer, but his interest was stirred and his gaze was fixed unwaveringly on my face.

I continued, 'But I was different from other children: I had a cabochon to tell me who was a liar and who wasn't. When I was very young I didn't understand what it was saying, but later I did – and you know what I did then? I deliberately shut it off whenever I was with my father. I blocked it out. I told myself that was the polite thing to do. I became so good at it that it became automatic: whenever Gayed spoke to me, I had no feelings of truth or falsehood, no feelings of his mood or his emotions. Clever little Ligea, who needed to think herself loved . . . Goddess, what a baby I was!

'Brand saw through Gayed right away. He hinted at things back then, until I made it quite clear I wouldn't listen to such insinuations.

'When I was sixteen, all my friends were thinking of marriage, but Gayed was saying things like: "My little girl is not going to be like those silly friends of hers who think of nothing but pretty clothes and jewels and revels, is she? She's better than that. She's going to be like her father. She's going to serve the empire." And I swallowed it all. I thought it was marvellous he wanted me to take the place of the son he'd never had. I thought I was special.' I wondered if I were leaking anything of what I felt then. Bitterness, rage, hurt – it was all there, still passionately felt. Ashamed of my lack of restraint, I tried to hide it and continued on.

'Because I was female, I couldn't become a legionnaire or a statesman or a trailmaster or a trademaster, so that only left the semi-secret cabal of the Brotherhood. I was proud to join. Rathrox took me under his wing, almost unheard of for a novice, and taught me. Because I had special abilities, I proved to be good at my job.'

By this time, Garis was no longer lounging on my pallet. He was sitting up, chin propped on his good hand and arm, listening intensely. His tawny eyes sparkled; he always did like adventures. I went on: 'Brand tried to tell me what I ought to have known all along: they were laughing at me. Neither of us could have known the whole story, though. They intended to turn one of the Kardi highborn into a pawn of Tyrans, into a compeer whose duty it was to root out the traitors to Tyrans. It was a deliberate joke on the part of the three of them: Gayed, Rathrox, and the Exaltarch, Bator Korbus. A private way they had of revenging themselves for the defeats they suffered while taking Kardiastan.

'Eventually I saw what Brand had been trying to show me for years. Eventually I added up all those times when I'd been given a clue, but had chosen to ignore it.

'Gayed is dead now, killed in a campaign. In a way, I had the last laugh on him without him ever knowing it. Ordinarily, his wife, Salacia would have inherited everything, but she died before he did, while he was on that last campaign. Under the laws of adoption, everything came to me. I'm sure it's not what he intended, but he hadn't made a will to say otherwise. He was the sort of man who believed in auguries, you see, and his augur had told him he would live to be an old man and would die on his pallet.

'Looking back, I think he hated me. I think he and Rathrox always planned for me to be sent to Kardiastan. They made sure I spoke Kardi, and spoke it well. It was some sort of terrible revenge their twisted minds devised; to use me against the land of my birth. They knew exactly who I was. They'd always known.'

Much of Rathrox's protestations of the Brotherhood's ignorance of things Kardi had been evasions. He'd always known I was Solad's daughter and, after Solad's death, the true ruler of Kardiastan. He'd known just who 'Mir Ager' was. No wonder Bator Korbus had laughed. This time the bitter rage I felt made Garis blink; I'd not bothered to conceal it. I did not, however, explain that I believed myself to be Solad and Wendia's daughter, not Ebelar and Niloufar's. I hadn't yet decided what to do with that knowledge.

Garis, frowning, went to stand by the window.

'I was very good at my job, Garis,' I said, speaking to his back. 'And they knew it. Rathrox, Korbus, they thought I had a good chance of bringing a Mir Ager, who was causing them all the trouble, to the stake for burning – whether he was the same one they'd caught in Sandmurram or not. I suspect once I was successful, once Temellin was dead, they had every intention of making it public just who had brought him in. One of the Kardi elite, a Magoria, would now be the rightful ruler of Kardiastan. Imagine the terrible blow that would have been to the Magor. Imagine the confusion of the ordinary Kardi. The knowledge would have shattered resistance.'

'They were going to make *you* the Mirager?'

'I believe so.'

I felt his nausea, but he didn't say anything, and he still had his back to me.

I went on, 'I've had my eyes opened, finally. I can see their evil now. More than that, I can see the truth about Tyrans now that I've been able to compare it to something else. There are many wonderful things about Tyranian culture and civilisation, but they don't make up for the Exaltarchy's lack of humanity. Garis, there's no way I would ever serve Tyrans again. If I had the chance, I would see Rathrox and the Exaltarch dead by my hand.' It was only once I'd said the words that the truth of them gripped me, tearing my breath away until I had to drag in air. They were *true*. I wanted to kill the two men who had – with Gayed – made a mockery of my life, who had tried to pattern me to their damnable mould. The desire for revenge – no, not just for revenge: for *justice* – was a hard ball in my stomach.

I had finished, but Garis, still rigidly turned away and skeining out a whole tangle of emotions, didn't move or speak. I had no idea whether he believed me or not.

*   *   *

When Garis entered my room for the second time that day, after he had spoken to Brand and Aemid, it was almost dark outside. The flamingos and the pond had gone; all that remained were some forlorn-looking lily pads draped over the cobblestones.

'Well?' I asked.

'Well, I'm willing to concede Pinar misled us about the first murder attempt, and that she tried to poison you. As for the rest, I can see Brand believes in your innocence, but I've always known that anyway. He's told me often enough. And then, it's just as clear Aemid doesn't.'

'Aemid is shot through with guilt; she had the care of one of the Magor and instead of bringing me up with a knowledge of my country and my heritage, she told me nothing. She has to believe I am still Tyranian at heart. Otherwise she would not be able to live with what she has done to me.'

'Shirin – I want to believe in your change of heart. But I can't accept it merely because you and Brand say it happened. I'm sorry. What if you actually do have the ability to hide your lies?'

Exasperated, I asked, 'Tell me, Garis, after you ride off and leave me to the tender care of my dear cousin, do you really expect to see me alive again?'

He looked uncomfortable and painfully out of his depth. 'I know what she did was awful, but she's not usually like that. I can hardly believe it – Mirage damn it, I wish Temellin was here! I suppose I can lend you your sword for a while so you can ward Pinar out—'

'Pinar has fitted her cabochon to my sword hilt.'

'Oh?' His discomfort deepened. 'Well,' he suggested at last, not sounding very hopeful, 'I can try a warding spell against her with my sword—'

'How long would that last once you left? Can't you free me instead?'

'No.'

I cursed silently. 'I hoped it wouldn't come to this, but if there's no other way—' I rose from my chair and went to take a book from the bookcase. 'Have you asked yourself why the Mirage Makers have given me so much help?'

'Well, yes. Temellin also wondered and he didn't know about the books. Shirin, we thought so many of these volumes were lost to us. Do you know what a treasure you have here? Any one of us would have sold our swords for them!'

'Perhaps the Mirage Makers would have produced them for you if they had known you wanted them. Garis, I don't think they understand us easily, at least not unless they use the medium of the song of the Shiver Barrens. There's something strange about that song ... but that's another matter for another time. I have the feeling the Mirage Makers do their best to oblige; it's just that they're not human and don't know what humans *want*. They like quite different things from us, and the things that are of use to them, we don't know how to use. I had eight or so fish in water just hanging in the centre of the room; possibly they would have solved all my problems if I'd known what to do with them. I asked for books, but even then they didn't know *which* books I'd want, so they gave me everything they could, from a treatise on how to cure diarrhoea in shleths to navigational maps of the Kardi coast. As soon as they found something I could use, like the bathroom or the books, they left them. The other things all disappeared in time, to be replaced by something else.

'As for why they take such special care with me, well, I think they know I am important to their own future. They do not approve of my imprisonment, Garis. They may have deliberately made your shleth throw you in the hope you'd be hurt enough to have to stay behind, just so I wouldn't be left alone here with the likes of Pinar and Reftim.'

He was horrified. 'They wouldn't have done that, would they? Shiverdamn, I wish Temellin were here. Perhaps I should ride after him. I don't know what to do, Shirin. I can't take all you say on trust.'

'No. Never mind.' I held up the book I had taken from the shelf. 'This provides an answer to your problem of trust. Read the fourth chapter tonight, Garis, and come back tomorrow morning – and if you value my life at all, don't tell Pinar anything.'

When he returned in the morning, Garis looked unhappier than ever. In his good hand, he was holding the book out from him as if he would have liked to have thrown it away. He was also carrying my sword thrust through the loop of his sling. 'I can't,' he blurted out to me the moment I opened the door to him. 'You can't. What if—?'

I waved a hand in dismissal. 'Don't you trust the Magor who wrote the book?'

'How do we know this volume is actually what he wrote? There may be mistakes in the copying. Or the Mirage Makers may have changed it.'

'I've found no other mistakes in anything I've read or tried. Garis, this renewal of vows is for a Magor who is believed to have broken the Covenant. You all believe I have done just that. It is right, therefore, that I should be tested in this way. If I am false, then it kills me. If I am true, I survive. I don't have a problem with that. Why should you? I do know the Stalwarts are coming, and soon – and that unless someone stops them, they will conquer the Mirage. Have you thought about what that means? All the Magoroth children, your future, are right here, in this city. Remembering the Shimmer Festival, what do you think the legionnaires' orders will be concerning children? And the Kardis who have escaped slavery will be faced with a Tyranian army. Who is there to protect them? Who did Temellin leave behind, anyway?'

Garis licked his lips uncertainly. 'Pinar, Gretha, me. A few of the older Theuros and Illusos, people like Illuser-reftim. That's all. Even Zerise went with them.'

'That's all? Dear Goddess! Garis, *think*! How do you imagine I feel being trapped in this room? I will do anything, anything, to be free, even risk death.'

'Shirin, if you are doing this because you think I will relent rather than let you undergo this trial by sword, you are mistaken. I will not stay your hand at the last minute.'

'Have faith, Garis. Haven't you always been told it is impossible for a Magor to be harmed by their own sword?'

'Yes, but no one has actually proved it impossible by driving the blade into their own heart,' he said miserably. 'At least, not as far as I know. There is a ritual that involves driving your blade into the palm of your hand, but the *heart*? We also know that if someone else turns your sword against you, they die. Horribly. Your sword kills them . . . There could be a paradox here.'

'That's irrelevant,' I said. 'We are not talking about someone else doing this to me. I'm going to do it to myself.'

He still looked unhappy as he added, 'The sword may divert, just the way it did when Temellin flung his at you.'

He was so agitated he didn't even notice I had stripped to the waist. I said, 'I'm not going to give it that chance. My sword, Garis.'

'I – I should tell you, I fitted my cabochon to the hilt.'

I chuckled. 'Wise lad. But I wasn't thinking of turning it against you.'

'I can't risk anything,' he said wretchedly. 'I'm sorry.'

'It's perfectly all right.' I took up the sword and fitted it to my hand. It sprang into light joyously, as if recognising its owner; I welcomed the feel of it. Just to hold it made me feel younger, stronger, more powerful.

I thought it was just as well Magor swords were short, otherwise what was required of me would have been physically impossible. I placed the tip of the blade on my chest and prepared to drive it into my heart, wondering – with surprising calm – if my blood would fill up the hollow of the blade through the open tip.

'No!' The word exploded out of him, making me pause. 'It's all right, Shirin. I'll believe you—'

I shook my head with a smile. 'No, you won't. Not really. It has to be done this way, Garis.' I eased the sword towards me, feeling it slip upwards between my ribs. I had studied the diagram in the book carefully, and took care to avoid the sternum and the lung. Still the sword resisted me, protesting the path I sent it on. Blood trickled down the blade. I applied more pressure and knew it had entered my heart. In confirmation, the sword flamed blue, crackling and sparking. Pain flared, impossibly intense, and I had to divert some cabochon power to reduce it to a manageable level. Even so, moans escaped my throat, beyond my control. My vision changed; everything became tinged with red, without other colour.

Garis held the book up, so I could read the required words. I saw he was crying, tortured by his inability to do more to help me, worried we were doing the wrong thing.

I repeated the vow of the Covenant aloud, and followed it with the caveat that would kill me if I lied: '*In the name of my Magoroth sword and in the name of the Magoroth blood that runs in my veins, in the name of the heart's blood that I spill, may I die here and now if my intentions are not to fulfil my vow, or may I die in the future at the moment I am foresworn.*' I looked up at Garis through a red haze.

'That's enough, Shirin! Please, withdraw your sword.'

I pulled the hilt back. A little blood followed the withdrawal of the blade, which had filled with gold light. The blue light faded and then the gold as I laid the weapon down. I was still standing, but weakness dragged at me. Garis pushed me into a chair and took up the washbowl and towel I had ready. Gently he washed the blood away, his hands trembling as he did so. 'Are you all right?' he asked in an agony of apprehension.

'I think so.' I felt weak. My vision was still distorted and pain still rippled through my chest, but I thought it was the pain of healing, not of death.

'I would never have forgiven myself if something had happened to you.'

'Yes, you would have,' I said, with an attempt at a smile. 'If I'd died it would have been because I intended to betray Kardiastan, and you would have felt satisfaction.'

'I don't think so.' He was staring at my skin where the blade had entered; not only was there no more blood, but there was no recent cut, either. The only mark, where earlier there had been nothing, was a white sword-shaped scar, perfect in detail. I stared at it, fascinated. Garis touched it gently with his fingers in awed reverence. 'I have heard of this,' he whispered.

'What is it?'

'I always thought it a legend, a story. It is said that anyone who bears the shape of a Magor sword on their body is especially holy.'

'*Holy?* Garis, you have to be joking! If there is one thing I am not, it's holy! Goddess knows—'

'Oh, not holy in the religious sense. Holy to us, to the Magor, in that such a person is special, of importance in our history, to our land.'

My hand went involuntarily to my womb and I felt the blood drain from my face. 'Don't say any more. I don't want to hear it.'

He suddenly realised where he had placed his fingers, and drew back, blushing furiously. I pulled on my blouse and, still weak, went to lie on my pallet. 'Will you let me out of here, Garis?'

'Yes. Yes, of course. I can bring down the wards. Now, if you like. But what ought we to do, Shirin? Shall I have someone ride after Temellin? Ought I to go myself? He may not believe anyone else. I'm not even sure he'll believe me.'

'No. Let him go on. Let him face the legions in Kardiastan. Someone must. I shall deal with the Stalwarts myself.'

He looked at me in confusion. 'But we need more people – you yourself said that! They are the *Stalwarts*. Even I've heard of them.'

'I think I can do it, if I plan carefully. I am stronger in Magor power now. I shall have their trust, remember. And they don't know what they face.'

'But won't it be – well, especially difficult for you? Because of this Favonius?'

'That is why I must do it. I would like to save him. I know I must try. But what of Pinar? She will never let you release me.'

'Mirage damn it! I had forgotten her. Shirin, what we did was foolish; we should have had witnesses. Others who could testify to your truth—'

'Too late now. I don't think I could go through that again. Anyway, Pinar wouldn't believe anything good about me no matter what she saw or heard. Listen, Garis, break the wards tonight, immediately after Reftim has taken away the dinner dishes. Arrange shleths and food – all that I'll need. By the time anyone knows I am gone, I will be well away. There's no need for you to be implicated. Let them wonder how I did it.'

'But you can't go alone!'

'Well, I was wondering if you'd also release Brand.'

'Oh. Um, good idea. But I shall come with you as well.'

'Still don't trust me, Garis?'

'It's not that. It's just that I want to be in on this too.'

'And what about your arm?'

'Damn the arm. I can still use my cabochon. Can't I come?'

'Temellin wouldn't let you ride out disabled, and therefore I won't, either. Sorry.'

'You may need help—'

'Trust me. Garis, I have worked for two whole months with these texts here. And I have come to believe that my powers are special, just as Temellin's are. True, I haven't really had enough time, but I will manage. And now, can you fetch Brand to me without anyone knowing?'

Only when I saw Brand again did I realise how much I had missed him. He knelt by my pallet where I lay, and took hold of my hand, squeezing it so tight I almost cried out – but there was no denying the surge of gladness I felt.

'I've missed you,' he said.

'And I you. Has Garis told you he's setting us free?'

'Yes. I might have known you'd find a way to do it. In fact, I'm surprised it took you so confoundedly long.' I pulled a face and hit him. He laughed. 'What now?' he asked.

'I'm going back to Tyrans, but first I have something to do.'

I explained about the Stalwarts, concluding with the words, 'So, I want to stop their invasion, without – I hope – killing Favonius.'

'Just like that?'

'Just like that. Believe me, Brand, I have the power now.'

'And you want me to go with you?'

'I'd like you to. But you are a free man, remember.'

'You want me to help you save your Tyranian lover and then have me watch while you go back to his arms and I lose you all over again?'

'I was never yours to lose, Brand,' I said tartly. 'And no, I'll never go back to Favonius. I can't. If I belong to anybody at all, it is Temellin. But perhaps I'm not cut out for – for a partnership with anyone. I like my independence too much.'

'You're mad. A week or so in a man's arms and you'd condemn yourself to a lifetime of celibacy when he turns out to be your brother and marries someone else? That's crazy! Just because I love you, but can't have you, doesn't mean I deny myself the pleasures of a friendship and, er, other things, with another woman.'

'So I've noticed. But you haven't given me your answer: will you come to the Alps with me?'

He threw up his hands in capitulation. 'Ocrastes help me, yes, I'll come. But one of these days I'll either have you in my arms – or I'll break free of your spell and leave you.'

We both wrote letters before we left; Brand's was for Caleh, mine for Temellin. It was the hardest thing I'd ever had to write; it didn't say one-quarter of what I wanted to tell him, and it certainly didn't come close to telling him all the truth.

Temellin, I began, *by the time you read this, I shall be gone – out of your life, and out of Kardiastan – probably forever. I'm sorry I have brought you grief. Ironic, isn't it? It was originally my intention to bring about your death; now I worry because I have caused you pain . . . but perhaps you won't believe that.*

I go to stop the Stalwarts – yes, they do come, whether you believe in them or not. I hope it won't come to a fight, but if it does, I have every intention of winning and none of dying. You see, I am carrying your child. Your son.

Nonetheless, it is not my intention to stay in Kardiastan. I will go on to Tyrans where I will bear the child and there I shall stay. I will send the boy to you so he can receive his cabochon. And I shall keep all your Magor secrets, never fear.

I suppose there is a chance I shall not live long enough to bear

this child. The Mirage Makers showed me what it is they want
from the Magoroth. I believe you know to what I refer. I will
fight such a fate for myself and our child, but should I lose, then
so be it.

I don't regret a thing. At first I told myself all I felt was lust,
soon quenched, but we know differently, don't we? Even when
you meant to kill me, we both knew how much we loved.

Full life, Tem.

Your Shirin

Just before we left, I gave the letter to Garis, who looked at
me uncertainly and said, 'I wish I could be sure you're doing
the right thing.' He gave a wry smile. 'Impossible, I know. But
how will you know what part of the Alps the Stalwarts will
cross? You may miss them.'

'I won't miss them. The Mirage Makers will see to that,' I
said with certainty. I swung myself up onto one of the shleths
he had procured for us. 'Full life, Garis.'

He nodded unhappily and stood watching while Brand and
I rode out of the Mirage City.

This time there was no cheering.

CHAPTER TWENTY-FOUR

'This place gives me the spine-crawls,' Brand said, looking around uneasily. 'It's so unnatural.'

I shrugged. 'It's a mirage. I find it . . . entertaining.' Enjoying the view from the back of my shleth, I saw a landscape of green and blue boulders, of bushes scurrying along trying to hide behind one another like frightened furry animals, of pink and white lakes hovering in the distance, of tree blossoms tinkling in song or birds wafting past in perfumed flight or insects floating along streams in flower-petal boats.

Occasionally we saw something more commonplace: a Kardi with a cartload of fruit on his way into the city, or a field of grain being hoed and weeded by people who waved as we rode by – sights that wouldn't have been out of place in a Kardi vale or along a Tyranian river, except they were set against a mauve sky studded with candleholders.

Brand regarded it all sourly. He indicated the grey and white brick paving we were following. 'And you think this road will lead us directly to the Stalwarts?'

'If the Mirage Makers have already seen the invaders, I think they will supply us with the path to the place of their intrusion. I could be wrong, I suppose. Let me check . . .' Several women were digging pottery clay from a small pit beside the road. I pulled up beside them and asked them how long the paving had been there.

'Ah, about ten minutes,' one of them said matter-of-factly, using a clay-smeared arm to push her hair away from her face, with interesting results. 'Nice one, isn't it? I hope it stays. It'll be much more convenient for us. The old road was much further east.'

I raised an eyebrow at Brand. 'Ten minutes. I'd say it was made for us, wouldn't you?'

Brand remarked it was convenient to be on such good terms with the Mirage Makers. As we rode on, he added, with less flippancy, 'You think we're being followed, don't you? You're not pressing these poor beasts of ours merely out of your eagerness to meet the Stalwarts.' The shleths were at that moment only ambling at a walk, but that was just because they needed the respite; they had been pushed hard for three days now. His animal reached back with a feeding arm to scratch absentmindedly at an itch, and connected with Brand's sandal instead. He knocked the offending limb away in annoyance.

I said, 'There is a possibility Pinar might take it into her head to come after us. I'm hoping Garis can persuade her not to; that's really why I wanted him to stay in the city.'

'But if he doesn't tell her where we've gone, surely she won't know where to find us.'

'Yes, she will. She has a certain, um, affinity with me, Brand. She has put her cabochon into the hollow on my sword hilt; that gives her some advantages, including the ability to follow the traces my sword leaves behind it as it passes, or so I have read. And no,' I added, forestalling his next suggestion, 'I can't leave the sword behind. I need it.'

He frowned uncertainly, not liking the nature of the conversation, but persisting nonetheless. 'If these Mirage Makers can help us, then can't they hinder her? Stop her from following us? Couldn't they throw a lake across the landscape between her and us, or something?'

'I'm sure they could. But I'm not sure they will. She is Magor, so presumably the Mirage Makers think of her as an ally. There may be other considerations as well.'

He sighed. 'Ligea, I think you ought to tell me everything you know instead of just hinting at things. It is *very* irritating.'

I tried not to feel exasperated. His persistence was edging me towards the thing that had been skipping around the fringes of my mind for weeks; something I had been doing my unsuccessful best to stave off because I didn't want to think about it. I said, 'I'm not being deliberately obscure, Brand. It's just that I don't really *know* anything. I only guess. All those weeks we were imprisoned, I had time to do a lot of thinking. And I had access to a great many books about Kardiastan and the Magor. And then I have what the Mirage Makers have told me more directly . . .'

'And?'

I pointed at a black patch scoring a hillside with darkness. 'You've seen those diseased areas?'

'Of course. They are – foul.'

'Yes. Evil. I have come to believe they are a sort of physical manifestation of things we usually think of as abstracts: things like cruelty and hate. Just as a mirage can have solidity here, so can evil have a physical reality. Those patches are slowly and surely destroying the Mirage. But I think the Mirage Makers know a way to make themselves strong enough to resist. I think they believe an infusion of humanity, of Magoroth humanity, will provide them with what they now lack.'

'Dubious reasoning,' he objected. 'Surely humanity is more usually known for committing evil than for combating it.'

'Perhaps those who are capable of committing evil are also the best at fighting it, for just that reason. And there are those who do combat it, especially among the Magor.' There was another hole in my reasoning, though, one that was harder to plug. I could be right about the nature of the Ravage, but where did it come from in the first place? Ravage patches predated the arrival of the Ten in the Mirage . . .

'What do you mean by an infusion anyway?'

'The Mirage Makers need a life. A Magoroth life to grow inside the Mirage, to become one of them, one of the immortal entities that comprise the Mirage. At least, that's what I have come to understand.'

He interrupted. 'Yes, I remember. I was there when Temellin told us.'

'Years ago, the then Mirager – a man called Solad – made some sort of bargain with the Mirage Makers.

'That debt has yet to be paid. I think he promised them a Magoroth life, a living, unborn child, in exchange for shelter inside the Mirage for the Magor fleeing the invasion. They want a child to become one of them. A child who, when his mind is grown, will provide them with the strength to destroy the Ravage. I suppose I could be wrong in this, but I don't think so.' *And I believe the Ravage hates me so much because it knows I am bearing such a child . . .*

He was silent for a while, absorbing all I had said with a growing horror. His mount, sensing his inattention, stopped, forcing me to pull up as well. 'Sweet Elysium,' he said finally, his voice hardly more than an appalled whisper. 'Are you saying you think these Mirage Makers want *your* child, your unborn baby?'

'Not exactly. I think they want – need – *a* Magoroth child, any such child. I think they believe the most, er, appropriate would be one sired by Temellin. It is, after all, the ruler who has the responsibility for Solad's decisions and promises.' I could have added: and what better than a child from the womb of Solad's daughter, Kardiastan's *truly* legitimate ruler?

He stared at me, appalled, 'You – you think they're going to kill you to rip the child out of your womb?'

I shook my head. 'Under the terms of a covenant made way, way back with the Magor, the Mirage Makers are prohibited from the deliberate killing of humans. If the Mirage Makers could still kill, then I wouldn't be needing to ride all this way to halt an invasion. The Mirage would do it instead – drown the legionnaires in a lake or drop them into a gorge or something. I have been hoping they may be able to hinder the advance of the Stalwarts without actually hurting them, but I'm not sure enough of that to leave it up to them. You see, the Mirage Makers are not human. They sometimes don't understand just what is useful – or conversely, what is of a hindrance to us.' My mount reached out to groom Brand's animal with its feeding arms. I thwarted its intention by urging it into a walk once more.

Brand hurried his beast after me. 'What about the Shiver Barrens? They kill enough people—'

'The Barrens are not the Mirage. The Barrens are a natural physical phenomenon caused by the heating and cooling of a certain kind of desert sand. The Mirage Makers use the Barrens as a barrier, that's all.' I paused, remembering. 'When I was inside the Shiver Barrens, under the sands, I thought I caught a glimpse of the Mirage Makers; now I think what I saw was a mere projection. Another mirage, if you like, with no substance. The reality of the Mirage Makers *is* the Mirage, just what you see around you now – nothing else. This is the closest they get to having a body, a physical being.'

He swallowed. 'You went inside the Barrens? Ocrastes' balls!' He made a helpless gesture with his hand. 'It seems I may as well have been asleep for all I have understood about what has been happening since we came to this place!' He gave me an uneasy look. 'Ligea, there is surely no way to remove a child from its mother's womb without killing the mother.'

'Not that I know of. However, my feeling is that the Mirage Makers take an intense interest in me because – because of my son. They might not kill me, but they might not save me, either; they may even have an interest in seeing Pinar catch up with us . . .'

'So that *she* can kill you on their behalf?' For a moment he was speechless, searching for the right words to express his outrage. Then he exploded. 'Goddess *damn* them! They are a sly, shifty piece of worm-ridden *dirt!*'

'I wouldn't insult them too much, my hasty Altani friend. Their understanding might be a little unconventional, but I suspect they do hear every word we say. I could add, too, that Pinar's death might serve the Mirage Makers just as well. She also carries Temellin's child.'

He was further incensed; this time – illogically – with Temellin. 'That bastard. Vortexdamn it, Ligea, what do you see in that frigging whoreson? Never mind, don't answer that. I don't want to hear. And if Pinar's death would suit the Mirage Makers just as well as yours, why don't you let her catch up with you, always supposing she is following us, and kill her off? She's no loss to the world, not even to Temellin. The woman's a murdering vixen.'

'Yes, she is. She's also well on the way to madness.'

He blinked. 'You sound almost sympathetic!'

'I wouldn't put it quite so strongly. I do pity her, though. Her instincts with regard to me were good, yet no matter what she did, she couldn't get rid of me. Her husband loves me still. However, if I had to choose between the two of us, yes, I'd kill her if I could, and it wouldn't particularly worry me to do so. Unfortunately, in any confrontation between Pinar and me, *I* would probably be the one to end up dead. Pinar is a Magoria with years of experience and training, and my sword can't be used against her. She, however, can kill me from across a room with hers. If she'd really put her mind to it, I'd already be just so many bones scattered in the soil of the Mirage. So far she has been hampered by a need not to be associated with my death – but out here, with me an escaped prisoner – who will blame her?'

'I still have my own sword. Hardly a patch on yours, I know, but why don't we lay a trap for her? Kill her before she has a chance to get you?'

'She's a Magoroth, Brand. She has the power to sense the position of people around her. An ambush is not going to work.'

He stared at me, aghast. He had finally absorbed the magnitude of the danger I was in. 'Does she know about this child business?' he asked.

'I haven't the faintest idea. I doubt she knows I'm pregnant.'

'And Temellin?'

'He knows about the bargain, yes. But I never did tell him I was pregnant.'

I had never seen Brand so enraged. 'He got two women pregnant at the same time, *knowing* one of them may have to be killed to save the Mirage and the Magor?'

'That's an oversimplification of the situation, and you know it.'

'The situation *stinks*, Ligea, and so does Temellin.'

I ignored that and said instead, 'You may as well know another thing I've found out, which no one else realises. I'm not Shirin. I'm not Temellin's sister. I'm his cousin, Sarana. Solad's daughter.'

His grip slackened on the reins and his shleth halted again. I felt his bewilderment. 'But didn't Temellin tell us she was—' He gaped. 'You're the rightful—?'

'Miragerin. Yes.'

He rolled his eyes upwards. 'Elysium save me. Ligea, all this stuff – it's unreal. Magic swords and Mirage Makers and dancing sands, I don't know how to deal with it.' He sighed and added, 'And if you are the Miragerin, why in all Acheron's mists are you thinking of leaving Kardiastan?'

'What difference does being the Miragerin make? In Magor eyes, I would still be a traitor. Worse still, the daughter of a traitor. I can't explain who I am without revealing the extent of Solad's treachery. He's the one who betrayed Kardiastan. I'm the daughter of a man who sold his country and his people into slavery and humiliation and subjection – just to save *me*. They would never accept me, and I can't say I blame them.'

I shook my head at the accumulation of bewildering irony. 'I revered Gayed, and have found him since to be a man who feigned affection for me so I would become the instrument of his revenge. I know now why Salacia was complacent about my presence. She knew, and revelled in the joke. And now, when I discover the lie and replace Gayed with my real father, what do I find? A man who loved me so much, he didn't care how many people died and how many others suffered just to keep me alive. My life was bought with a pile of corpses and a tide of suffering that's lasted a generation.'

I turned to Brand, and the shleth took advantage of my inattention to start pulling leaves from a nearby bush with its fingers. 'I could atone by giving up my life and my child, but I'm damned if I'll do that willingly. It's just not in me. But I *can* try to stop the Stalwarts. And my only chance to do that is to stay ahead of Pinar if she is indeed following me. Or hope Garis manages to delay her.'

He was thoughtful. 'Once the Kardis find out you were telling the truth about the Stalwarts, they will forgive much. Especially if you turn the legionnaires back. You could return to the Mirage City. They can hardly blame you for what Solad did. You could claim your rightful place as their Miragerin.'

'No.'

He looked at me shrewdly. 'You're doing this for *him*. Denying your chance to have the kind of power you've always wanted, because it would be at his expense.' For once I felt his emotions, and they were such a contradictory mix I couldn't decide exactly what dominated. There was certainly plenty of rage, but I suspected most of that was directed at Temellin.

'So what if I am?'

'By the Goddess, you've changed!' He shook his head in a sort of bemused wonder and then drawled, 'Do you realise that in a couple of months you have managed to change your name three times? Ligea – Derya – Shirin – Sarana. Aren't you overdoing things a bit, my dear?'

As usual he managed to drag a reluctant chuckle out of me. I said, 'Let's gallop again. I really don't want to confront Pinar.' I slapped a hand down on the neck of my mount and, startled, it leapt away up the track.

As I rode, I wondered if Brand was right. I wasn't sure I was as altruistic as he thought. True, I didn't want to come to the position of ruler at Temellin's expense, any more than Korden had. To strip the man I loved of everything he had been raised to believe was rightfully his would be to castrate him, to take away his reason for living. I loved him too much to do that to him. But there was a selfishness in my reluctance too. Once Temellin found out I hadn't lied about the Stalwarts, there was always the possibility we could get together again, that he might forgive me my deception. I could tell him I had decided that being closely related to him didn't matter after all . . . I was never one to close doors behind me if it were possible to leave them ajar.

On the other hand, if I took away Temellin's mandate to

rule, I would be slamming a door and probably locking it as well, because part of him would never be able to forgive me.

Besides, I wasn't convinced I wanted to be Miragerin anyway. What joy would there be in ruling a country that didn't want me? Especially when the seed of a much better idea was already rattling around in my thoughts . . .

That evening, when we pulled up to water our shleths at a roadside pond, Brand said, 'We have to stop, Ligea. These beasts are ready to drop and I'm not much better. Vortex only knows how you feel.'

'Don't coddle me, Brand.' I smiled at him. 'That's one sin you've never been guilty of yet, so don't you dare start now just because I'm having a baby. But I agree with you: we'll stop here for the night. There's plenty of grazing and water.' I slid off my mount and started to unsaddle.

I had just finished hobbling my beast when a startled exclamation from Brand had me whirling, with my sword already halfway out of its scabbard. In the moments it had taken me to attend to the shleth, a building had appeared beside the pond. It was a solid structure of grey stone, three storeys high with several turrets and some pine trees on the roof.

'Where in the name of the Goddess did that come from?' Brand asked in consternation.

'I imagine that's a gift from the Mirage Makers for tired travellers,' I replied, amused.

He gaped. 'Isn't it a mite, um, *large* for the two of us?'

'I suspect the Mirage Makers have always been a little confused about the needs of humans. You only have to look at the Mirage City to see that.' I picked up my saddlebags. 'Shall we see if they have thought to supply any furniture? The idea of a pallet is very tempting.' I rubbed my buttocks ruefully. 'Two months in prison doesn't do much good to muscles.'

There were pallets, an abundance of them. There was also a surfeit of more trivial objects that weren't of the slightest use: toys, candelabra (but no candles), a spinning wheel, a small boat, enough saddlery to outfit a legion. Brand shook his head in bewilderment. 'Mad,' he muttered. 'Quite, quite mad.' He turned his attention to preparing a meal, while I went outside to ward the building. I could not keep Pinar out, but I could fix it so I would be warned the moment the Miragerin-consort entered, if indeed she came at all.

Later that night, it was the breaking of that ward that woke me, sending a searing pain through my hand from my cabochon. The stone had flared and was still glowing its alarm. Quickly I crossed to Brand on the other side of the room and shook him awake. 'Someone's here,' I murmured.

I raised the cabochon to my ear, listened – and my heart sagged within me. It was Pinar.

CHAPTER TWENTY-FIVE

Pinar was not alone; Garis was with her.

Brand wanted to sneak away immediately, but I disabused him of the notion such a feat was possible. 'She already senses me,' I said. 'We move from here, and she'll know. My only chance is to talk, to try to show her—'

'*Talk?* Are you crazy? That woman is beyond reason!'

I turned from him, strapping on my sword, knowing the truth of his words, fearing I was going to die.

'You can't do this! Will you risk your life so casually?' he raged at me. '*His* son—?'

'The child will not die. He will live forever.'

'As what? As some creature that is not human? Without body, without soul?' He shuddered. 'I would not wish such a fate on my worst enemy, Ligea.'

'Who are we to say it would not be a better existence than the one we live? We have no concept of what it's like to be a Mirage Maker, Brand. My son might save this land, might save these entities that are the Mirage, and the bond between Magor and Mirage Makers will be strengthened. Do you think I *want* to do this?'

'And what of you? Vortex, Ligea, *what of you?*'

I turned back to him. I wanted to scream at him, to say: I

want her dead! Of course I do! I want her child sacrificed, not mine, not me! Oh, Goddess, Brand, I don't want to die – I just don't know how to save myself . . .

Instead, I said, 'What of me? Perhaps this way of dying will give my life some meaning. And Garis could see that my son goes to the Mirage Makers. Tell him, Brand, if I don't have the chance. And as for the Stalwarts, do what you can to persuade the Magor they are coming.'

He was incredulous. 'Is this really you, Ligea? I never thought I'd ever listen to words of defeat from your lips. Fight the bitch!' He took up his unsheathed sword.

'Keep out of this, Brand,' I warned. 'You cannot fight anyone of the Magor. She will not harm you if you stay out of it.'

'And what sort of a man do you think I will be if I stand aside and let the woman I love be killed, and then allow her body to be mutilated?' he asked, enraged.

I had no time to reply. The door opened and Garis stepped into the room. His arm was no longer in a sling, its recovery hastened, I assumed, by the Magor ability to aid healing. He was followed by Pinar. The Magoria's sword was already drawn and glowing, adding to the light I had coaxed out of my cabo-chon.

Garis spoke first, anxiously apologetic. 'Sorry, Shirin. I couldn't stop her.'

'What do you intend, Pinar?' I asked quietly. 'I'm sure Garis has told you of the way my honesty was tested—'

'A fraud!' she snapped. 'He's a child, easily deceived by sleight of hand. And who's to say the text was accurate anyway? I've never heard of such a test!'

Garis opened his mouth to make an indignant retort, but I stepped in first. 'I'll undergo the test again, if that will help you believe the truth.' Even as I spoke, I knew Pinar would never acknowledge the truth, no matter how large it was written. I turned to Garis, although I knew it was useless to ask for his help. He would never be able to bring himself to raise a hand against Pinar, one of the original Ten and the consort of his Mirager. I said merely, 'If I die here, Garis, it will be up to you to stop the Stalwarts. And there will be another task for you that Brand will explain.'

He gave a strangled gurgle. 'Die? No one is going to die! Pinar just wants to take you back.'

Brand was scathing. 'Look at her, you mash-brained witling! Does she look like someone about to act as an escort to the woman she considers her worst enemy?'

Garis took one look at Pinar's face and said, 'Miragerin, please think. Temellin will never forgive you if you harm Shirin—'

'He's never forgiven me anyway,' she said venomously, 'for not *being* her. She's won against me every time. Even when she was warded, she went on winning. Well, this is one time *I'm* going to win. And this will be the time that counts.'

'Murder me, and not only will you have to explain my death to Temellin,' I said, 'but you will have to explain why you also killed his son. I, too, am bearing his child, Pinar. Would you kill your child's brother?' I was gambling that she didn't know about the details of Solad's bargain, but it was a stupidity anyway; an appeal to a woman who was beyond appeal, a woman whose mind was so fettered with jealousy nothing mattered except vengeance.

Even as I spoke, I knew I had lost. I didn't need Brand's wince, and his agonised, 'Mistake, love, mistake,' to tell me.

Rage boiled inside the Miragerin-consort. Her sword flared to white brilliance, spilling out of the blade.

'Pinar!' Garis cried, his anguish swamping us all, but it was Brand who moved to fling himself at her. He hit her with the impetus of his forward rush and knocked her off-balance. The beam of power she had been about to direct at me hit the ceiling, crumbling wood to splinters, and showering us all with wood-dust. Garis shoved Brand aside and tugged at Pinar's arm, shaking her. 'Pinar, for Magor's sake, don't—'

'Leave me be!' she shouted, heaving him out of her way. She made a wild shot at me and I ducked and rolled. Several stones were blasted from the wall and fell to the ground outside.

Brand, blinking in the glare from Pinar's weapon, launched himself at her from behind. In a fury, she slashed back with her sword, narrowly missing Garis. Brand flung himself flat as power poured from the end of her blade and cut a smoking swathe through walls and ceiling. Garis was hit by falling stone. He sagged as he fought his dizziness, then succumbed and fell unconscious. While Pinar was distracted with the others, I heaved a piece of stonework at her head. More by luck than skill, it connected and she collapsed, blood trickling down from a temple wound.

I drew my sword, then remembered its uselessness against her and dropped it to the floor where it still glowed – together with hers – to light the room. I focused my power into my cabochon instead and prepared it to kill.

There was nothing beautiful about the Miragerin-consort as she lay there in the broken remains of stone and wood. Her hair was tangled and sprinkled with dust, her face older than her years, the skin dry and slack. I felt once more the stirrings of pity. Pinar would have been a different woman had Temellin loved her . . . I raised my left palm and directed it at her throat. She had no defences against me; a small flare of power and she would be dead. I could give her child to the Mirage Makers, make myself safe.

Yet I paused.

'Do it,' Brand said, pulling himself to his feet. 'She's already stirring.'

I whispered, 'She's Temellin's wife—'

'Turd take it, Ligea, since when have you been squeamish? Kill the woman and put her out of her madness and pain, because if you don't, she'll have you and the Mirage will have your son.' He turned, looking for his sword.

He was right, and I knew it. Yet I couldn't do it. I couldn't kill her.

I don't know just what kept me from murder. She was Temellin's wife, she was pregnant, she was one of the Ten orphaned and exiled because of my father's obsession for me, she was my cousin, she carried the child of a man I loved, my son's sibling – they were all reasons enough to stay my hand.

'Vortexdamn you! If you can't, I certainly can.' Brand groped around in the rubble for his sword, pulling it out from under some crumbled stone. It was slightly bent, but that hardly mattered. I was still hesitating, for the first time in my life unable to act decisively when a death was called for, unable to kill quickly and cleanly and without conscience.

And then Pinar grabbed her sword and erupted up from the floor, swinging first at Brand. Taken utterly by surprise, he was felled by a flash of light and crashed back with his astonishment written in every line of his face, already beyond thought by the time his body hit the floor. Then his surprise and shock blinked out of existence.

I couldn't sense him. *I couldn't sense him.*

I sent forth my cabochon power in protest and Pinar was hurled backwards, hitting the wall behind her with a clunking thud. Yet there was no change in her expression or her alertness. She smiled, warded herself and pointed her Magor sword at the centre of my chest.

She said, 'I have you now.' Brittle words of promise and I didn't even notice.

Brand . . . *Please, not Brand.* It wasn't possible. Yet that was his body there on the floor. Could any normal man take the brunt of a bolt from a Magor sword and live?

My fault. I had broken every rule I ever learned about surviving a brawl and now my closest friend was dead. Because of my foolishness, my misplaced compassion. Another body to bury under my bloodied doorstep . . . What's her unborn child to you, anyway? What about *your* unborn child?

Grief such as I had never known submerged me. Oh, Goddess, cabochon, *Brand*! The only true friend I'd ever had. Who had never doubted me, all through the years.

The hot pain of loss seared; unspilled tears turned to fury.

I called up the whirlwind, the storm. It came tinged with the potency of my anger and swept into the room, tearing at us all. I centred it on Pinar, trying to wrench the sword from her hand. A flash of energy and light shot from her blade and met the wind in a whirl of gold and light and swirling rage. Power was flung out in random bolts, shattering more stones and shredding room furnishings. I myself was lashed with it, my clothes torn, my skin blasted with grit. Across the room Pinar screamed at me, but the wind brushed aside the words unheard.

Another bolt flared outwards in my direction. I raised my cabochon against it and the power of the two met, clashing in a maelstrom of spitting wrath and sparks. The strength of the sword was greater, and I felt my hold over the wind falter. Pinar's wards protected her; my own – poor weak things made using a cabochon, not a sword – could have been cobwebs spun to impede the thrust of a gorclak charge for all the good they did. No ward I could raise would offer me a defence against her sword.

The whirlwind was now full of colour and spinning with misdirected power, a horrifying storm of destruction, yet still Pinar could keep it at bay and have her sword pour out its stream of puissance. I staggered behind the ineffective barriers of the wind and cabochon, feeling my strength slip away as Pinar's power battered me, rammed me against the wall, pierced me with splinters of pain. I knew I could not withstand much more.

I concentrated on the whirlwind, tightening its circles, forcing it faster and faster into a smaller and smaller area until it was just a blur of dust and energy hardly the size of a man's arm. I quenched my pain – it was a distraction I could do without – and coaxed the twist of air to do my bidding. And Pinar, alarmed, swung at it—

Her sword passed out of the protection of her warded area. Too late, she knew her mistake. The wind plucked up the weapon, and whirled it away through the air.

But I had no more strength. I released my hold on the wind and it spat out in all directions, random and wild. The air was filled with grit and dust and spluttering power. I did not see what happened to Pinar's sword. I fell to my knees, the last of my strength gone. And the more experienced Pinar was far from exhausted.

She came across to me, scooping her blade up out of the wreckage of the room, grinning her triumph. 'You fool, Shirin,' she said. 'Did you think you could withstand a Magoria of my expertise when you didn't even have a Magor sword you could use against me? I will have your life and that of your child. It will be *my* son who is heir to Kardiastan, not yours.'

There was no hesitation in her. She laid the tip of her sword to my chest and thrust down hard.

I toppled onto my back, the sword pinning me to the floor. I felt the path of the blade as a swathe of pain as it pierced me. I knew the way it took: straight into my heart . . . I wanted to weep at the waste, at the futility of my struggle, at the fate of my son. I thought of Temellin and longed to tell him how much I cared.

I felt my power drain from my cabochon – not outwards, but inwards, into my blood. I felt the rush of it through my body until it met the power of the sword blade, united with it in joyous recognition ... and for a moment, in my befuddlement, nothing made sense.

'Die, you Tyranian vermin,' Pinar said. 'You and your bastard.'

I saw the world with renewed clarity and felt unexpected grief. 'Pinar,' I said, my voice surprisingly calm and clear. 'Pinar ... what have you done?'

'I've killed you, Ligea.'

'I am Kardi ...'

'With a Tyranian soul.'

'I am sorry ...'

'I'm not.'

'Pinar ... you don't realise ... Your child will not die. I swear it to you ... he will be a Mirage Maker.'

She was mocking. 'What do you dream of now? You are dying, Ligea!' Then her hand – still on the hilt of the sword – began to shake and the shaking was carried over into her body.

I said in gentle pity, 'You ... hold ... my sword in your hand, Pinar.'

She looked down in disbelief.

'You picked up the wrong blade. You have tried to turn a Magor sword against its owner.'

'No!' The word ripped out of her, but the horror on her face said she recognised the truth. 'You'll die! The sword entered you—'

'You gave it no chance to change direction.' I shuddered, remembering Temellin's weapon hurtling towards me.

Pinar struggled to release the blade, but her hand seemed welded to the hilt. She pulled and the blade slid free, renewing my pain.

Her shaking was so severe, she could not stand. Her knees bent under her and she slipped to a kneeling position. Her eyes were wide with the fear of death, echoing her raw emotion bleeding out into the air. 'Shirin – help me. Help . . .'

'Pinar . . . I don't know how.' It was true. My sword drained her of life because she had dared to use it against me. Only at her death would it release its hold on her. I crawled over to her side. 'But I have made you a promise and I will keep it: your child won't die. He will live . . . and he will save the Mirage.'

But Pinar was past hearing. She fought against the sword, tearing at it with her right hand, raking her own flesh into bleeding tatters in her desperation to free herself, beating the hilt on the floor to break the clasp of her left hand, screaming her panic and anger and disbelief. With a howl of terror she rolled across the floor to where her own sword still lay, snatched it up and tried to bring it down on her left wrist.

She was turning her own blade against herself, forgetting even now that a weapon could not harm its owner. The sword refused to sever her hand, and jerked out of her grip instead. In its place she seized on a hunk of stone debris and used it to batter at the glowing blade she still held. A flash of light, a smell of seared flesh. She gave a scream of pure agony. I looked down at my cabochon. Still a flicker of colour there. I coaxed back the power until the stone was glowing again. I thought, briefly, of using it to cut off her hand, the one clutching my sword. I doubted it would save her life – hadn't someone told me removing a cabochon meant death? I thought about it, then thought of Brand, and sent the fire of my cabochon to sink deep into her chest. The screaming was sheared off as life ceased and she collapsed.

I wanted to rest. I wanted to give my body time to heal. I wanted to give my mind time to accept what had happened. I wanted to give myself time to recover from the shock. I wanted time to forget the look on Pinar's face.

I wanted time to grieve for Brand. To feel the pain, the guilt, the precious love that wasn't the right love.

Brand . . .

I was not given time.

I heard something in my mind, ordering me, not doubting my obedience. It did not come as a surprise, but it was unwelcome nonetheless. *Now*, it said, but not in words. In concepts. In pictures. In emotions. At a guess, without the song of the Shiver Barrens, the Mirage Makers found communication difficult.

Action. Offer. Time. Consequences. I interpreted, hoping I understood: *With your own sword. We shall guide your hand. Hurry, or the child will die.*

I untied Pinar's clothing, my fingers clumsy with distaste. Then I took up my sword from where it now lay free of Pinar's grip, placed the tip to the bared skin and waited. I could have sworn I felt a hand, as chill as spring water, close over mine and press down. The edge of the blade opened up a gash from navel to pubic hair. My eyes were blurred with unshed tears as I saw the womb displayed before the blood ran and covered it. I reached in with a hand to lift the organ out, cutting it away from the body that had sheltered it. Then I felt my cabochon encircle the child inside, swaddling him with protective power to keep him safe.

I held Temellin's son nestled in my palm and my tears spilled over. He was so tiny.

'*What in the name of the Magor are you doing?*'

I looked up, startled.

Garis was pushing himself away from the floor, his eyes wide with shock and revulsion. 'What abomination have you committed? You – you – *numen*! Sweet cabochon, Pinar was right! Oh, Mirage damn my wretched soul, *what have I done?*'

I looked at him in silence, my own distress overwhelming

me. I wanted to speak, to explain, to erase the horror on his face, but he had started to fade away. I looked at him in puzzlement as he lost solidity, then any semblance to reality. He had disappeared and so had Brand and Pinar and the wreckage of the room. I was standing in total blackness, swathed in it.

I looked down at my precious burden, feeling its life, not seeing it, but knowing it was there.

Well? I asked. *What now?*

CHAPTER TWENTY-SIX

As I stood there, the floor still solid beneath my feet; in a black-ness so thick I could feel it, that last sight of Garis calling the light into his sword and looking at me in horror was etched into my brain, along with the detailed image of the remains of the room. The wooden ceiling sagging in smoking tatters. The floor, gouged and pitted, littered with stone rubble and dust. Holes large enough to walk through gaping in the walls. Piles of splintered wood scattered around the walls. Brand lying against one wall, rolled there by the forces Pinar and I had unleashed, his deep red-brown hair with its copper flash dusted with dirt, his body half buried under broken wood and a tattered something that may or may not have once been a pallet. One arm outstretched towards me as if in rebuke.

His death hurt me so much I couldn't even consider it true. He *couldn't* have died. Not *Brand*.

Nearby lay the Miragerin-consort. The expression on her face, caught in the rictus of death, was one of utter terror. Her eyes bulged, her mouth gaped open in a silent, endless scream. Her left hand was scarified into bloodied pulp, her arm burned and charred to the elbow. A burn on her chest revealed the manner of her death, unmistakably the mark of a cabochon! And then the worst – the thing that horrified Garis so much

– the bared, violated body; the gash where something had been ripped out . . .

Garis standing there, so young and so hurt I wanted to take him in my arms and tell him it all wasn't as bad as he thought.

But I couldn't. I was rooted to the spot, rendered first dumb and then horrifically blind with only the memory of his face before me. The blackness was so total I felt the air itself had turned to pitch. It was a relief to inhale and realise I could still breathe. To realise I was still alive.

A moment later, all my fears dropped away like shed skin. I was swaddled in love, a gentle flooding emotion quite unlike anything I had ever felt before. A totally unselfish love accepting me exactly the way I was, requiring nothing of me except my existence. A united love of many individuals . . .

And inside my head, those wordless ideas: Time. Patience. I waited.

And realised I could still hear what was happening in the room.

Comfort followed hard after the love, soothing me, attempting to take away my grief, but every sound I heard was a slash of painful memory. Someone retching. A rustle of movement. Then a groan, partly of pain, partly of anguish.

Then a voice. 'Brand?' Garis's voice. 'Brand? Oh, Ravage hells—'

I could no longer see or sense emotion, but I was hearing everything as if I were still standing there in that room watching. Thumps and scrapes: Garis flinging off the debris to uncover Brand's body. An intake of breath at what he found, followed by sounds of unidentifiable movement. I tried to shut it out, not to hear. To concentrate on what was happening to me.

I was still standing motionless, Temellin's son in my hands. The blackness was just as solid. The love was still there, unquestioning and total, the comfort doing its best to trickle through me, to find and fill all those crevices where grief lurked and hurt. The burden I carried felt marginally lighter.

Then Garis's voice again, coming out of the darkness like an arrow of light. 'Come on, Brand, fight it, you great lunk. You can't die yet – I won't let you.'

Tears came, but I couldn't wipe them away. I still couldn't sense Brand. Garis I could feel, but not Brand. Didn't that mean he was dead? Oh, Goddess, tell me that just means he was unconscious. Tell me I was wrong . . .

It wasn't the Goddess who replied; it was the Mirage Makers. Concept: Death. Image: Brand. Concept: Negation. *He was not dead, not yet.* But then I heard the sob in Garis's voice, the despair and exhaustion. And I couldn't help. I couldn't lend my healing to his, I couldn't move. Brand still might die while I stood invisible and helpless just a pace or two away, yet so far off I could have been in another world.

Time passed so slowly.

I should have tired, but the darkness seemed to support me. My arms did not ache even as the hours passed. The Mirage Makers did not speak, but neither did their love falter. Almost indiscernibly the thing I carried lost its reality, lightened in my hands, to become less substantial, until I held a wraith, a being created from nothing more substantial than mist or sunlight.

Occasionally I heard Garis make a movement from the other side of the darkness, but I could not identify his actions. I had no proof Brand was alive – until I heard his voice.

Weak, hardly more than a whisper. 'Garis?' It could have been the final mutter of a dying man; I had no way of knowing.

Garis's reply: 'Yes, it's me.'

'What are you doing?'

'Healing a great gash in your belly. Lie back and let it happen.'

A moment's silence, then Brand again. 'Pinar did it. Where's Ligea?'

'Who? Oh, Shirin. I don't know. I think she's all right.' His bitterness speared me. 'Pinar is dead.'

And still more silence, like the blankness of death.

It was several more hours before either of them spoke again. Then it was Brand's voice I heard, stronger now, no longer the voice of a dying man. My heart rejoiced, but the saner part of me wondered how it was possible. His hold on life had surely been as tenuous as a last solitary thistledown resisting the tug of the wind. And Garis was hardly an experienced healer. How then had he saved someone so close to death? It didn't seem to make sense.

I heard Brand ask Garis, 'Did you see what happened?'

'No. I was knocked out. But Shirin was alive at the end of it all. Then she, er, sort of disappeared.' He kept his fear tightly clutched within, yet I felt it anyway. 'I don't know where she went. I can sense her, though. It's strange; it's as if she is close by, but also somehow remote at the same time.' The sound of water being poured, then a pause. 'How do you feel now?'

'Stronger. I don't suppose you're going to say it, but I know I was near death then, and you brought me back. I am in your debt.' Another pause. 'Shall we bury her?'

'Cabochon knows how I am ever going to tell Temellin this—' Garis sounded sick and his voice faded. 'I shall ride after him today. He must be told.' I felt the ragged edges of his despair.

'And the Stalwarts?'

'I no longer believe in them, Brand. Or in her. Somehow she distorted what should have been true. She has power, but it is not like ours. It is tainted.'

'No.'

They were silent for a time. Two men agreeing to disagree.

'And you, what will you do?' Garis asked him.

'Wait here for her. She will be back.'

'You witless Altani ass! She doesn't deserve anyone's loyalty.'

'Because she killed Pinar? Come on, Garis, what else could she have done? Pinar was the one who attacked her. I almost died because Ligea hesitated to kill her. That's when Pinar did this to me.'

More silence.

Then Brand's: 'Let's get her buried.'

'Are you sure you're strong enough?'

'A five-year-old could probably flatten me with a cooked turnip, though I think I can help you carry a body. I don't know what you did, Garis, but it was nothing short of miraculous. You don't look so chirpy yourself, come to think of it.'

'All power has its price. That five-year-old would only need half a turnip to knock me into next week . . .'

I listened to them leave the room, and relief brought my tears back.

A little later, I was aware of a change in the darkness around me, a thickening. My hands seemed empty. Concepts in my head: Completion. Appreciation. *It is done. We thank you.* A hand – a mirage of substance rather than vision? – took mine and clasped it. I felt a flood of gratitude, not from one but from a host of individuals, each giving me their blessing through that one hand. Then there seemed to be a movement in the darkness and I felt what might have been lips against my cheek, a kiss as light and as soft as the brush of a falling snowflake. An illusion, of course. Their attempt at a human gesture.

I was once again standing in the room, blinking in sunlight.

I was desperately weak. I had to clutch the wall to support myself as I made my way downstairs, reeling from step to step like a wood-possum drunk on fermented fruit. Then, just as

I reached the outside door, I heard Brand say, 'You're going immediately?'

I stopped, leaning against the wall. I could see the two of them through the gap of the half-open door. Garis was holding the bridle of a shleth and Brand, stripped to the waist, was seated on a boulder nearby. An ugly wound ploughed raw and fresh across his stomach. Behind him, a mound – not there the night before – was covered with flowers, living ones: the Mirage Makers paying homage to the mother of their newest companion.

But it was Brand who held my attention. He was ... changed. I reached out, trying to touch his mind, to gauge his emotions. As always, he shielded himself, yet still I felt he was different. He reminded me of someone. A moment later, I had it. He reminded me of a Magor child. He had the same faint hint of undeveloped Magorness as such children had before they learned control of their cabochons.

And that was surely impossible.

Garis nodded in answer to Brand's question. 'Are you sure you won't come with me?'

'I'm sure. Garis, I don't know what you're thinking, but whatever it is, you're doing Ligea – Shirin – an injustice. Why don't you wait until she returns? She can explain—'

'There can be no explanation that would justify what she did. None.' He knew I was there, of course. He must have sensed my presence. He wanted me to hear.

'There is, you know. She told me—'

'And you believe everything she says, don't you? You're even more gullible than I was! She hated Pinar because Pinar had Temellin, so she slaughtered her. She's a dangerous killer. I don't want to see her, Brand, because if I do I will try to fry her and probably end up dead myself. She murdered Pinar; she'd make crow bait out of me. I'd give a lot to know how she managed to fade out of that room, though,' he added thoughtfully as his anger died. 'She must have learned from those Magor books.'

Garis shook his head in an expression of sorrow and went to fetch his saddlebags from where they lay on the ground nearby. He looked little more than a boy. His charm and his good looks, the curling lashes and the unusual tawny eyes – they all accentuated his youth rather than his maturity. He had performed a miracle that would have taxed a strong man, but for all that, he was vulnerable. Garis would carry the mental scars of this day just as long as Brand would carry the physical ones.

'Garis—' Brand said.

Garis cut him short. 'Don't bother, Brand. You're even worse than Temellin! The woman has made a fool of you. Of us all. At least Temellin knew enough to ward her. Vortex only knows how I am going to tell him what my foolishness has wrought here. How do you tell a man you were responsible for the death of his wife?' He mounted his animal. 'Full life, Brand.'

'Full life, Garis.' Brand touched the rough scarring at his waist. 'I hope I can repay you one day.'

'You can repay me by putting your blade through her.' The youth wheeled his mount and rode back up the track.

Brand watched him go.

I stepped out into the sunlight. 'Not a very happy farewell,' I said. 'He's going to torment himself with his foolishness and his supposed cowardice all the way to Temellin.'

He spun around in shock. He stared, taking in my exhaustion, the dirt and blood still streaking my clothing and hands. 'Ligea . . .' His voice was gentle with concern.

'I thought I had killed you with my foolishness.' I held out a hand to him. 'Can you forgive me?'

He took my hand, supporting me. And I felt again that faint

whisper of undeveloped Magorness. He said, 'It is always better to err on the side of compassion.'

'Is it? Pity can be as big an error as hate. I have loved Temellin with a passion I'll never find again, but you have been my closest friend; I do not know that I could have gone on living, knowing I had caused your death.'

He was moved; I felt the trickle of his unconcealed emotion. 'It was not you who brought me to the edge of death; it was Pinar. And Garis was able to save me.'

'How? How in all the mists of Acheron did he do it?'

He looked uncomfortable. 'He didn't have the power himself, so he cut out Pinar's cabochon. It powdered and he put the powder in my wound. He told me just then he got the idea from some old tale of a Magor who committed suicide by removing his cabochon and giving it to save a friend he had mortally wounded in an argument.' He shivered, not liking anything to do with powers he didn't understand. 'It seems to have done the trick.' That explained his sudden attainment of a faint Magor's aura, and I blessed Garis for his inspiration.

'Garis says time will eliminate it from my system and I'll be as good as new. But you – where have you been, Ligea? I was worried.'

I shook my head. 'I don't know. Here, but not here. Knowing the love of the Mirage Makers, giving them the child . . .'

He glanced around, every line of his body an eloquent expression of his unease. 'Are they separate . . . minds?' Poor Brand. How he hated this!

I nodded. 'I think so, although perhaps not in the sense we think of separation. There are many entities and each has a separate . . . personality, but there can be no dissension between them because they are all part of the same whole: the Mirage. Do I make sense?'

'I think it is sick. They are each trapped, prisoners in one body—'

'No, it is not like that. It is wonderful. They are a unity.'

'And the child? You have delivered Temellin's son to these – these creatures?'

'Yes. He is part of them now. In this –' I touched a flower on a bush near me. The glitter from its petals stuck to my hand and I brushed it to the ground in a shower of silver '– or in that. He is already all around us. He has been received with love, such great love: something larger, more perfect than we can ever know, and it is our loss.'

Brand said flatly, 'He will go mad.'

I shook my head. 'No. He will never miss what he has not known. His mind will grow, his personality will develop just as it would have done had he been born in the normal way. He was part of his mother; now he is part of the Mirage. He will never know what it is to be a separate creature, so how can he miss it?' I remembered the pain the Ravage gave to the Mirage and shivered. I had delivered Temellin's son to be a part of that pain until such time as he was old enough to bring an end to the suffering. Goddess, what if he died in there? What if he couldn't cure the illness of the Mirage anyway? What if he lived in constant pain for the rest of eternity?

My breathing quickened, my heart thumped. Temellin's son . . . it could have been mine. *Don't think about all that could go wrong. Don't think.*

I continued, 'I was surrounded by such love, such caring. Perhaps I should have spoken to Garis, told him to tell Temellin it went well.'

'I didn't know whether I should say anything about the baby, about why you did it, or not. In the end, I didn't.'

'He probably wouldn't have believed you anyway. And Temellin will, I think, know what I have done once Garis says what he saw.' I looked down at my hands. They were red with dried blood. 'Pinar's . . .' I said and added, puzzled: 'Ah, Goddess, Brand, why do I feel as though I killed part of myself? I hated her. I shouldn't feel this way . . .'

I staggered against him and he caught me, holding me with gentle tenderness. 'You are ill.'

'I don't think so, but I must rest. A few days . . . I've over-extended my use of power.'

'Vortexdamn it, Ligea! I loathe this stuff. Look at you! You are as weak as an unweaned kitten.'

'Are you still with me, Brand?'

He sighed, then nodded. 'So far.' But even as he said the words I sensed an unease inside him: a strange reluctance which I couldn't put a name to, but which fingered me with sorrow.

It was three days before I was strong enough to ride on, before I had renewed enough of what my battle with Pinar had taken from me. I was still Magor-weak, but my body at least was sufficiently strong to continue the journey.

That third morning, when I came down the stairs carrying my saddlebags, I knew something was wrong even before I stepped outside. I could smell it. The stink of the Ravage, that vicious hate for me, personally mine – it hung in the air like the stench of sewerage in the Snarls of Tyr on a hot day.

Pinar's grave had disappeared. In its place, another foul green-black sore. The Ravage had evidently searched for the source of its doom-bringer, traced her – and found her already dead. It had erupted in a baffled magma of rage, swallowed her remains and grave into a new seething inflammation in the skin of its host. Now I felt its delight in its consumption of dead flesh; I felt its rejoicing in the silent agony of the Mirage Makers.

I could feel it casting around for me, the one who had brought its doom into the weave of the Mirage. It was a disease in search of a victim, an assassin in search of its supposed nemesis: in search of me. Damn them to Acheron's deepest hell, I hadn't solved my problem at all.

Brand looked over my shoulder at the place where the grave had been. 'Ah,' he said, in that thoughtful way of his. 'I think perhaps you were right, Ligea. About the reason for the Mirage Makers wanting a Magor baby, I mean. I don't think the Ravage liked what happened one little bit.'

CHAPTER TWENTY-SEVEN

Brand and I sat on our shleths at the top of an escarpment and looked across at the Alps. Neither of us had ever seen anything like these mountains before. Ragged peaks scarified the sky, ploughs to snag and shred the wisps of clouds forming there. Mountainsides plunged down, sheer-walled, into shadowed canyons. Snow whipped away from crests in wind-blasted flurries. A landscape of extremes, ruggedly beautiful or grimly forbidding, scenery to be enjoyed – or a barrier to be conquered.

'They crossed those?' Brand asked. 'On gorclaks? By all that's holy, how was it possible?'

'Vortex knows. Yet they are here.' I looked down on the narrow alluvial plain below me. Unlike the Alps, the plains were clearly still part of the Mirage. The grass glittered with silver as if it had been sprinkled with mica; the wind played across it to make waves. Grass crests broke in splatters of silver only to swell, whole again, a moment later. I scarcely noticed. I was gazing at the legionnaire camp erected on the plains, next to the snow-fed river dividing Mirage from alpine foothills. I now had no problem using my enhanced sight to scan the army camp; I may have been thinner than before, but otherwise I'd recovered the strength drained from me several weeks earlier. 'Holy Goddess,' I whispered. 'Favonius said a legion – three thousand men or more.'

'There's not three thousand there, surely.'

'There's not *half* that number. Vortex, but they are battered, Brand. Some are barely hobbling. Frostbite perhaps? They seem to have most of their gorclaks, though. But where are the camp followers? The support people? These are all soldiers!' I could see no proper kitchen tents set up, no blacksmith's travelling forge, no store, no slaves. I shook my head. 'They have had a hard time, and yet they are here.'

'Can you see Favonius?' Brand could not make out any detail at all, but he no longer questioned my ability to do so.

'Not from this distance. Let's ride down.'

He was surprised. 'Just like that?'

'Just like that.' I set my shleth at the slope.

'Ocrastes' balls, are you *sure*, Ligea?'

I grinned at him. I was beginning to feel like my old self again.

There were guards, of course. We were challenged long before we reached the camp, but I spoke to them and one deferentially escorted us to the verandahed tent of the commanding officer, Legate Kilmar. There we dismounted and waited while Kilmar was informed of our arrival. A moment later, we were ushered inside.

The interior had none of the usual luxury of an officer's tent. There was no furniture, just a few cushions and saddle pelts on the floor. The Legate lounged back on some of these, a goblet in one hand and the remains of a meal spread out on a pelt in front of him. He was a man of fifty, thick and muscular and tough-skinned, his face rough and scarred by a lifetime of campaigns. One of his ankles was bandaged; blood seeped through.

Behind him and to one side stood Favonius, his blue eyes

startled, the slant of his nose accentuated by the increased lean-
ness of his face. His tunic was ragged, his cuirass and greaves
scored, but apart from that he appeared unhurt. Military
protocol permitted him nothing more than a suggestion of a
smile in my direction, but his amazement, his tender regard,
the quick climb of his desire were all as obvious to me as if
he'd shouted them to the world. I nodded slightly, then ignored
him, turning all my attention to the Legate.

'Legate Kilmar? I am Legata Ligea Gayed, Compeer of the
Brotherhood.' I did not introduce Brand; to the Legate, a free
Altani could never have been anything more than a minor
servant. Brand remained by the entrance with his hands
clasped behind his back and his face expressionless. Favonius
stared at his bare neck and gave a wondering frown.

'Greetings, Legata,' the Legate said. 'It is indeed an honour
to receive you. You will please forgive my reluctance to rise.
As you can see, I had a slight mishap – a rockfall.' He dismissed
the injury with a wave. 'Please be seated. Can I offer you a
meal?'

'I have not long eaten,' I said politely. 'A drink would not
go amiss, however.'

The Legate nodded to Favonius, who poured some wine
from a skin. It had been well watered down and splashed pinkly
into a dented goblet. Legionnaires were not known for the
moderation of their drinking habits; I could only assume they
were low on supplies. 'You know the Tribune, I believe?' he
asked.

'I've had the pleasure. Well met, Tribune Favonius.'

'Well met indeed, Legata. It seems you found a way to cross
the Shiver Barrens after all?'

'And you found a way to cross the Alps. Not without cost,
though, I think.'

The Legate grimaced. 'There was an avalanche. Those at the

back of the column were cut off. More than two thousand men are behind us somewhere, together with the camp followers, most of our supplies and our support slaves. It will take them weeks to clear the route. And that will mean they will have to send back for more supplies before they can join us.' He looked at his foot ruefully. 'There have also been injuries. And deaths. But even a weakened Stalwart legion is better than a legion of ordinary men. We have our gorclaks and our weapons; that's all we need. We can pillage on our way across the Mirage.'

'Perhaps. But you have a bare quarter of a legion, I think. Will you allow me to look at your injury, Legate? I have some experience with doctoring.'

'I would be grateful.' His face tautened, belying his words. He knew any unwrapping of his bandages would hurt him. 'Neither of our physicians made it this far,' he added.

'Get some clean bandages from our pack, Brand,' I said and knelt beside the Legate. I began to unwind the bloodied cloth.

'What brought you here, Legata?' Kilmar asked, gripping his leg above the knee in a valiant effort not to show his pain.

'A warning. You must not proceed. I have come to tell you there is no question of victory here: you must turn back.'

The Legate gave a harsh laugh. 'Legata, I'm certain I couldn't persuade my men to cross the Alps again! Besides, the Stalwarts do not turn back, especially when they have not yet seen the enemy.'

'You will see them, and soon. This is a war you cannot win. Legate, the Kardi people of the Mirage make a practice of sorcery. Proceed and the death that awaits you, all of you, is the death of nightmares.'

'*Sorcery?* Legata, since when has the Brotherhood believed in sorcery?'

'Since we have come to Kardiastan. You've heard stories, I feel sure. Legate, have you ever known the information of the

Brotherhood to be false in concept? A detail here and there, perhaps, but always the basis is correct. Ah, you have broken some bones, I think. Can I have that wineskin, Tribune? I need to wash away some of the infection in the wound.'

Favonius handed over the wine and I continued the conversation where I had left off. 'The Brotherhood does not make mistakes in major matters and it is as Brotherhood Compeer that I tell you, categorically, if you do not turn back you and your men will die almost to a man, killed by the sorcery of the Kardi and their numina.'

I sensed his scepticism and sighed inwardly. This was going to be just as difficult as I had thought it might be. 'The strangeness of this land can hardly have escaped your notice. Have you had a look at the sky?' I gestured with my hand towards the open tent flap. The sky was blue that day and the candleholders had gone, but it was still crazed with lines like the imperfections through a block of ice. 'And haven't you noticed that the grass glitters with silver and hums in the wind?'

'We've noticed.' The Legate shrugged. '"A stranger's tongue tells strange tales." Every land is different.'

'Your foot should be completely immobilised. And the flesh wound itself should be exposed to the air as much as possible—'

He looked down at his feet in surprise. 'It has stopped hurting. What did you do?'

'Just a small manipulation to make the bones lie better,' I said vaguely. 'Legate, about your return to Tyrans—'

It was almost evening before I emerged from the tent. I was a little drunk, although not as drunk as the Legate had intended, thanks to the watering of the wine. Unfortunately, I had not convinced him he ought to turn back. He had ended by being patronising, treating me as if I were a hysterical woman, an attitude as exasperatingly hard to deal with as it was irrational.

Brand put a hand out to steady me when I lurched slightly. 'Weren't you tempted to use that on the sanctimonious bastard?' he asked, nodding at my left hand. The cabochon was not visible: I still wore my riding gloves.

I pulled a face. 'Almost, almost. Brand, make our camp on the other side of the gorclak lines, will you? Away from everyone else. Sorry I can't help you, but it wouldn't look right.'

He almost laughed. 'Ah, you've come a long way, haven't you, my love?'

I let him enjoy his mockery.

He added amiably, 'But don't worry about me; you go and snuggle up to Favonius. Been a while since you've had a man, hasn't it?'

I gritted my teeth. 'May you disappear into the Vortex, Brand.' I turned away to greet Favonius, who had just come out of the tent.

The Tribune grasped my hands and raised them to his lips. 'Goddess, Ligea, the sight of you is drink to a thirsting man! You've lost weight!' He touched my face with roughened fingers. 'You've been through a lot. By all that's holy, how did you get here?'

'Ah, it's a boring story. I'm sure you have much more to tell. But everything I said in there was true. Favo, you must persuade the Legate to turn back. If you proceed the Stalwarts will suffer a defeat here so devastating, there will *be* no Stalwarts any more.'

'Goddessdamn, Ligea, can't you think of anything else? Come to my tent and I'll take your mind off sorcery and put it on something much more interesting.'

I shook my head. 'No, Favonius; not any more. That's over.'

He was incredulous. 'Over? What do you mean, over? You

ride across the Shiver Barrens, cross this place called the Mirage, all to warn me of the danger, and you say it's over?'

I nodded, wondering why his arrogant certainty that I had done all this for him surprised me. I had always known his faults, as well as his strengths, after all. 'I'm sorry. But that's the way it is.'

He gazed at me, face blank. Then he looked after Brand in disbelief. The emotion that followed the realisation was unpleasant. 'It's him, isn't it? I couldn't believe my eyes when I saw he wasn't wearing his slave collar. You've taken up with your own Altani slave! Goddessdamn, Ligea, to think I never used to believe those rumours about you. Where's your pride? You're a citizen of Tyrans, a Legata! He's an Altani barbarian – and a *slave*. Or he was last time I saw him.'

'Don't be tiresome, Favonius,' I said, my voice tight with warning. 'Brand is a friend, a slave no longer. Please bear that in mind next time you refer to him. He is not – and never has been – my lover. However, you are right about one thing: there is someone else. Who it is doesn't matter. I'm sorry.'

The arm he had put around my shoulders had long since slipped away. Rather than see the hurt in his eyes, I turned and walked after Brand.

That night I dined with Favonius and the other tribunes. I told them stories, mostly completely untrue, of Kardi magic powers. I exaggerated and coloured and lied; anything to have them turn back. But they had been through something close to the Vortex of Death on the mountains. They had struggled and survived; faced with a fight against mere Kardis, they felt invincible. The thought of a return across the Alps, where the enemy – nature, an avalanche, the weather – was more obvious, brought them far more dread than any prospect of meeting a Kardi army.

'We are going to wipe those bastards off the face of the

earth!' one of the tribunes boasted. 'Every man and boy in the Mirage, right down to those in swaddling clothes.'

'Are those your orders?' I asked. 'Children as well?'

'That's right! If they have anything dangling between their legs, they're dead meat. Women too, if they have gemstones in their palms. Dunno what that means, m'self, but those are the orders. Direct from the Exaltarch, we heard.' He grinned at me, ignoring a furious stare from Favonius. 'You'd better hang onto Favo here, Domina, cos you're going to find it hard to meet another male in the whole of the Mirage in a month or so!'

The latter part of the evening was unbearable. The men teased both me and Favonius, making me the butt of increasingly coarse jokes, envying him his luck, wondering aloud just what it was about Favonius that had brought his woman across a hostile land to his arms. I tried to freeze them into politeness, in vain. Here, in this remote part of the Exaltarchy, to these men who had endured so much, being the daughter of a general or a compeer of the feared Brotherhood meant nothing. I read their reckless contempt for me and fumed. And I grieved; it was clear my friendship with Favonius was not going to survive the end of our physical relationship. There had been a time when he would not have tolerated my being subjected to such jokes, but I had hurt his pride and his bitterness showed. He grew more and more sullen as the evening wore on.

I conquered my anger and left. Behind me I could hear the laughter of the officers as they asked Favonius why he didn't follow.

I didn't go to my pallet in the tent Brand had rigged away from the main camp. Instead, I sat outside the tent flap on a patch of sand and stared at my cabochon, calling up its power. Brand watched me wordlessly. I concentrated, bringing forth the wind from nothing, turning it, whirling it, calling it across the plain towards me. The gorclaks heard it and stirred uneasily. Brand rose and went to check the tethers of the two shleths where they grazed by the river.

When the wind neared me, I unsheathed my sword, brought the blade to a blaze of light and touched it to the whirlwind. The swirl became more than just movement and sound; it was visible now, a giant gyre of sparking, flaming light, brilliant beyond imagining.

I dropped the sword and concentrated on the cabochon again. Slowly the fiery spout began to move.

It spun towards the main camp, taking in the gorclak lines on the way. It didn't touch the animals: it was not necessary. In desperate fear they broke their tethers and thundered away, trampling their terror-crazed path through the camp.

Everyone was awake now. Those who had not heard the first whine of the wind certainly did not miss the screams of the animals or the shouts of panic from those men who saw the whirlwind or who were run down by the maddened gorclaks.

I enhanced my hearing and eyesight, my finely focused concentration steering the column of whirling air to where it would do the maximum damage to property and the least harm to people. I could not forget that I had once admired these men; that I had once considered them my allies.

Tents flared into flame, cooking fires and pots and saddlery and weapons were whirled up to join the vortex as I systematically destroyed half the camp. I was careful to make its path quite symmetrical; I didn't want anyone thinking this was some sort of natural phenomenon. It had to appear quite deliberate. Once I decided I had done enough damage, I sent the whole maelstrom vertically up into the sky above the camp. There I released my hold on it so it exploded outwards, shooting off in all directions, a vast dissipation of colour and brilliance and fury and noise.

The quiet following the rain of debris was unnatural. Then, a minute or two later, black ash – all that remained of what had been burnt – began to drift down out of the sky in silent witness to the cataclysm.

'That was spectacular,' Brand remarked dryly. 'Is that just the opening act, or is there more to follow?'

I muffled a laugh. 'That's all for tonight.' The colour in my cabochon had dimmed, and fatigue was dragging at the corners of my mind.

Someone was running over the grass towards us. Quickly I sheathed and hid my sword and pulled my leather glove on over my left hand. It was Favonius. He stopped a little distance away, taking in my relaxed posture and the presence of Brand. 'Are you all right, Legata?' he asked stiffly. 'I saw it pass this way—'

'It didn't touch me. That was your warning, Favonius. You must turn back.'

'That – that thing came from them? From Kardis and their numina?'

I nodded.

He looked around uneasily, frowning. 'Where are they?'

'Not here. Miles away probably. But they see you. This was just the beginning. Next time it will be more than just a warning – there will be deaths.'

'There already have been,' he said savagely. 'One of the legionnaires jumped into the river in a panic. He couldn't swim. At least one person was hit by falling debris and killed, maybe more. And I saw a man trampled by a gorclak; I don't know whether he died. And there are tens injured!' He was still looking at me, his eyes flaring with suspicion. 'How do you *know* where these Kardis are and what they will do? And how in Vortex did *you* find us anyway?'

'They sent me. To warn you. They don't want unnecessary deaths.'

'*They* sent you? The Kardis? *You*, a Legata Compeer? To take a message like some slave? Vortex, Ligea, you've changed since I knew you in Tyr! There was a time when you would have sent them to a lifetime in the Cages and joked about it, not carried their messages.'

'This is not Tyrans, Favo. This is Kardiastan. I have no power over these people – they control numina with sorcerous power.'

Fear battled disbelief. 'They have *ensorcelled* you?'

'No, no. I came of my own free will. To warn you. Tyrans has no way of defeating the people of the Mirage. If you try, you will all die. A wise man shoulders his pack and takes his leave when he meets his match and here the Stalwarts have met something they cannot conquer. Persuade the Legate to turn back, Favo.'

He made a gesture of helplessness. 'Surely you can see how it is? We won't be turning back. We *can't*. Not when we have come so far and have so little to show for it. We haven't even met the enemy in battle, how can we justify a retreat? We have our pride!'

'You have just met the enemy. And pride won't save you. It will kill you.'

'Yes,' he said bleakly. 'Perhaps. So be it.' He glanced at Brand and then back again. 'And perhaps it won't worry you all that much, either.' He turned towards the camp, shouting orders as he went.

I entered the tent.

'Well, it doesn't seem as though your whirlwind accomplished much, does it?' Brand asked, following me. 'Except the death of a couple of legionnaires.'

I looked across at him, wondering what he was thinking. 'I find that the easier it is to kill, the more reluctant I am to do so, and the harder it is to live with when I have done it.' I pulled off my glove and looked down at my left palm. 'Life was a lot easier when I was a compeer and had no scruples.' I raised my eyes to his. 'Two dead, Brand, just like that. Maybe more. But they had orders to kill babies . . .'

He nodded, understanding. As I staggered with fatigue and weakness, he came to me wordlessly and held me in his arms. I took comfort from his closeness and stood within the circle of his love, drawing courage from his friendship. Then, sensing that this time my proximity was not a torment to him, I drew back a little, in wonder. 'I thought – I thought you were the only one who hadn't changed.'

'What do you mean?'

I stepped away from him and went to sit down on my pallet, my arms resting on propped knees. 'Everyone has altered so much. Including myself. I don't think like a Brotherhood Compeer any more—'

'Goddess be thanked!'

'Perhaps. But I was happier when a compeer was all I was. I was arrogant, cruel even, but at least I was never as uncertain and muddled and miserable as I am now.' I dropped my head down onto my arms. 'And I'm not the only one. Look at Aemid. She's changed. She's free, among her own people in her own land, yet she's racked with guilt. She'll feel even worse once she realises that I haven't betrayed Kardiastan, but Tyrans. And what about Favonius? He wanted to marry me once, and now he looks at me and I can see him thinking, "She's a Kardi, a barbarian. How could I ever have loved her?" He despises me, Brand. I felt his emotions, and I didn't know him! Faced with something he cannot fight, he has reverted to a primitive sort of hate for anyone or anything different from him.' I shuddered. 'Everyone I have touched has changed. Almost as though I contaminate. Do you remember how much Temellin used to laugh? And Garis; he was always so cheerful and resilient – so mischievous! Was that the same youth who left us to go to Temellin? Even Pinar changed. She might always have been jealous, but she wasn't mad at the beginning.'

He knelt beside me, and touched my hair gently. 'I'm not unhappy. Or despising. Or mad, either.'

'No, but you have changed nonetheless. Your passion for me has dulled. Do – do you *fear* me, Brand?'

He laughed, an unforced chuckle of amusement. 'No. No, I could never fear you. Not even when I was a slave, and you were that arrogant bitch, hanging on Gayed's every word. I always knew what was inside you, Ligea. I always knew there was more compassion there than cruelty or indifference. And now that compassion rather than arrogance rules you, I think I love you even more than I did then.'

For a moment I was silent, half hearing what he had not said. 'But?' I asked finally.

He chuckled again, wryly this time. 'There's always a "but", isn't there? At least where you and I are concerned.' He gave a gesture of surrender. 'All those years of being your slave, I never once felt I was not your equal, Ligea. I *knew* we were equals. I knew I was anyone's equal, for all that I wore a slave collar. I thought one day it would be possible you'd come to love me as I loved you. I thought it could happen, even when you talked of mere friendship. Until these last few weeks. Then I began to realise I *wasn't* your equal. That I never will be. That you are not for me.' He took up my left hand. The cabochon, quiescent, was just a rounded gem in my palm. He touched it with a finger. 'Because of this. I don't fear you, Ligea, but part of me is in awe of you.'

He raised his eyes to my face. 'I should be devastated – all those years of loving you wasted because you are unobtainable after all.'

'But?'

'But I find I'm just resigned. That desperate passion: it is part of my past. I shall always love you, but not quite the same way. Not any more. You are Magor and you are not for me. I can go forward now. You suggested once I go to Altan, that I help free it from Tyrans, do you remember? I thought the idea ridiculous. Now I'm not so sure. I have become a soldier and find I have some talent for the life. I have found I can lead men, and do it well. So, I shall go back to Altan and try my luck.'

I grinned at him, my depression lifting. 'I'm glad. So very glad. Although I shall miss you more than I can possibly say.'

He returned the grin, but our mutual mood of complacent self-congratulation was short-lived. We had been sitting side by side on the pallet but a sudden heave underneath us sent us both sprawling.

'What the—?' Brand began, but words failed him as he struggled up. We were in the middle of a softly padded pallet the size of a small room. The tent was gone. In its place was a large hall containing a fireplace, complete with a fire, and a table cluttered with objects as diverse as a loaf of bread and a weathervane. Beyond the table, a startled bird ruffled its black feathers and tried to maintain its perch on a pump handle. There was no pump to go with it.

I began to laugh.

'Vortex take it, woman,' Brand growled. 'It's not funny – this damn land will be the death of me! One day my heart will simply not survive the arrival of one of these mirages!'

I continued to giggle helplessly.

'You'd better give some thought to what your Stalwart friends are going to think about this,' he said sourly.

I stifled my laughter. 'I imagine they will get a shock. Never mind, I shall go outside and ward the place; then they won't be able to disturb us.' I picked up my sword and, still chuckling, looked around for a door. Fortunately, there was one.

Favonius arrived before I had finished, and other legionnaires began to gather as well, just to stare at the building, until he sent them on their way with shouted orders. When they had gone, he waved an agitated hand at the structure behind me. 'What is this? Where did it come from? Why can't we enter?'

'This world doesn't work the same way as Tyrans, Favo.'

'Did *you* do this?'

I stared at him in unfeigned surprise. 'Come now, Favo, when have I ever been able to conjure a building out of nothing?' What had prompted him to say that? I stirred uneasily, and remembered their orders. *Kill all women with gemstones in the middle of their hands.* That had come from Bator Korbus and Rathrox, of course, with their memories of the early invasions and the Magoroth victories.

I put my left hand behind me and changed the subject. 'Tell me, did you inform the Legate of what I said earlier tonight?'

'I did. We are not retreating.'

'That's a mistake. You had better prepare yourself for more trouble.'

'Damn it, Ligea, just whose side are you on here? Give us some help! What can we do to combat this kind of sorcery?'

'I came here to offer you the only kind of help I can give you: good advice. This is a war you can't win. Turn back.'

'There must be *something* we can do to – to defend ourselves. Counter-spells perhaps . . .' He looked as if he couldn't quite believe what he was saying.

'There is nothing.'

'I don't understand you. You're acting as if your loyalties are to Kardiastan, not Tyrans. Tell us, at least, how to cross the Shiver Barrens. Then – win or lose – we won't have to cross those Vortex-scoured Alps again.'

'Favo, I can't tell you that.' It would have opened up the Mirage to attack from Tyranian troops in Kardiastan.

'Why not? You must have done it, or you wouldn't be here.'

When I didn't reply, he shouted at me. 'What's happened to you? You're behaving like a traitor, Ligea Gayed! A traitor to your country, to the memory of your father! You help us, or there'll be a report about you on the Magister Officii's desk the minute I'm in a position to have it there.'

For a moment we stood staring at each other, both aware there had been another fundamental change in our relationship, a change that had gone too far to ever be reversed.

And he wasn't finished yet, either. 'I should have known not to get involved with a Kardi barbarian,' he said and his viciousness went straight to my inner core of uncertainties. 'You're shit, Ligea, and you're the colour of shit. You always did have the vulgarity of an ill-bred barbarian. What highborn woman of Tyr consorts with the Brotherhood? What real Domina makes friends of her slaves? You never did have any class! And you geld a man. I only ever took up with you because I thought it would do my career good to be seen with a general's daughter but, by Ocrastes' balls, it's been a hard grind to bed such an ugly, castrating whore.'

Then he turned on his heel and walked away.

I felt his hate, I experienced it. I dragged in breath as hurt ripped through my chest.

No, Favonius, no. Don't end it like this. We were friends . . .

He'd loved me once, as much as he was capable of loving. He said so often enough, and my ears knew the truth when it was spoken. Even the words he'd just used were no more than a skimming of surface validity obscured by a twist of bitter lies. Why, then, did it hurt me so much? My insides cramped.

The colour of shit. Ugly.

When I re-entered the building a few minutes later, it was

to find Brand leaning elegantly against the mantelpiece to one side of the fireplace, sipping a glass of wine. 'Well,' he said, 'at least they got something right this time. This is very good wine.' He held out a glass to me. 'Bet it tastes better than that pink stuff you were drinking earlier on. Rather nice glassware, too. Beautifully cut.'

I came across to take it. 'Mmm. Just what I need. A drink, a warm fire, a soft bed—' I raised my glass in a toast, but then didn't drink. I was suddenly stilled, my own words a revelation to me. Moments passed with neither of us speaking.

'I was never meant to be celibate,' I said finally.

'Why now?' The words blurted out of him; he was caught by surprise.

'Because now we are friends. Because now you will be able to walk away afterwards.' *Because Temellin's gone from my life and I need comfort. Because I need reassurance that I am not an ugly, castrating whore . . .*

He nodded thoughtfully. 'In some things, my Magor friend, you were wiser than I. You were right – there was a time when this would have been a disaster.' He reached out, took my wine and put the two glasses down on the table. 'But not now.' He took me into his arms and bent his head towards my lips. 'Now,' he murmured, 'this is exactly right.'

CHAPTER TWENTY-EIGHT

When I looked out of the door the next morning, it was to see the legionnaires trying to restore what was left of the camp to some kind of order, and herding stray gorclaks back to the tether lines. They were carefully avoiding passing near – or even looking at – a jet of water shooting up out of the grass of the plains just behind the camp. The water fell to the ground in rainbowed droplets, each a musical note singing like the plucked strings of a harp. A flock of purple ducks preened nearby, ruffling their feathers and their ribbons in obvious enjoyment of the shower.

Inside, Brand was poking around among the things on the table, looking for something to eat. The black bird had abandoned its perch on the pump handle and was now on the mantelpiece, flat on its back with its feet up in the air. Its bright red eyes regarded Brand's investigations with interest.

I pushed away my guilt and smiled at Brand fondly. I had wondered if his lovemaking would disappoint me. I had wondered, now I knew what the touch of a lover's cabochon could achieve, if I were doomed to dissatisfaction without it, but I hadn't been disappointed. The lovemaking might have lacked the physical intensity of what I had found with Temellin, it might have lacked the sheen that comes with the consummation of a different kind of love, but it had been satisfying nonetheless. Especially satisfying, after I'd seen how happy it had made Brand. That had surprised me; I had not realised giving someone else so much delight could have made *me* so happy.

When I thought about Favonius, my emotions were darker. He'd tainted something inside me that had once been good. He'd turned a pleasant past into a bitter memory, and the sadness clung in my thoughts like rot. And he'd severed more than he'd known. He'd cut the last strand of my ties to the belief that I was truly a citizen of Tyrans. Oh, I still had the paper somewhere, but if someone like Favonius could call me a shit-skinned barbarian and mean it, then what was such citizenship worth?

I wasn't a Tyranian about to go home. I was a Kardi going to a foreign land with murder in my heart.

Brand finished his investigation of the table with a sigh. 'Pickled fish,' he said, 'stale bread and some kind of sour – very sour – fruit. I was hoping for something of a similar standard to the wine.' He held out what looked to be an orange plum to the bird. Without getting up, the bird took it in one foot and proceeded to shred it and swallow the pieces, sour or not, with evident enjoyment.

'The Mirage Makers getting it wrong again,' I said with a shrug of incomprehension. 'I ate our own food.' I looked back over my shoulder, out of the open door to where the legionnaires struggled to repair the camp. 'They won't leave Kardiastan. I'll have to offer some more inducements, I'm afraid.'

Brand looked up quickly. 'What are you planning this time?' His ambivalent tone was enough to tell me he found any talk of my power both fascinating and repellent. It interested him, but he did not like it. 'You're still drained. You'll exhaust yourself.'

I shrugged. 'Can't be helped. I won't let them ride on into

the Mirage, Brand. I can't. Only the Magoroth have the kind of power that could take on the Stalwarts, and the only Magoroth left in the Maze is Gretha, and she must be within a baby's kick of birthing her eleventh child. But it's more than that, too; if the legionnaires ride on into the Mirage, in the end they will have to face Temellin and the Magor somewhere. And the Magor would defeat them. Only by sending the Stalwarts back across the Alps can I save them.' I gave a half-laugh. 'Sometimes I don't know what I want, Brand. With one hand I would tumble the Exaltarchy if I could, even while I stretch out the other hand to help the Exaltarch's finest legionnaires.'

'I'm worried about you; you are still so weak.'

'I'll wait until tonight. I might feel stronger by then. I thought of trying to destroy as many of their weapons as I can. After all, what damage can an army do if it has nothing to fight with?' I gave him a wan, joyless smile and went to lie down. At least, I thought, it was days since we'd seen any sign of the Ravage. One less thing to worry about. Or was it? Perhaps it was watching, biding its time. Mostly, though, I was just too tired to spare it a thought.

The legionnaires spent their time mending tents and replenishing supplies. The purple ducks found their way into cooking pots, minus decorative ribbons, and so did a great many rabbit-like creatures scuttling around in the grass. Only when the camp had settled into sleep that night did I turn once more to my cabochon.

Once again I moved the air, this time creating eddies to sweep the ground, catching up dust and grit. I moved this warmer air from the plains down to the riverside, cooling it along the ice-cold waters of the river, where the moisture in it became mist, then fog; a thick suffocating blanket of moisture and dust. I rolled it across what was left of the camp – there were fewer tents now – and settled it there.

'Time to go,' I said softly to Brand. 'Let's get this over and done with.'

He squinted into the fog. 'How? I can't see a thing.'

'I can sense where people are, and who they are,' I reminded him. 'And I can enhance my hearing too, if necessary. Come.' I led him past the fog-clad sentries, unseen and undetected, into the heart of the camp.

I ignored the tents and aimed for those legionnaires lying on the ground, wrapped tight in whatever blankets or pelts they had, their heads covered to escape the damp. I moved from one sleeping bundle to the next, seeking out the weaponry that lay close at hand to each legionnaire: swords, lances, spears, arrows. A short burst of cold light from my cabochon and the metals melted, rendering the weapons useless. Whenever I sensed someone was awake I avoided them. It hardly mattered; I didn't have the power to destroy every weapon they had. My aim was not to leave them entirely defenceless, but to reduce their fighting potential to a degree sufficient to force them to turn back.

By the time we had circled through most of the sleeping men, I was leaning against Brand and staggering. The flash from my palm had become a mere gleam, the results less spectacular. 'It's time to go,' Brand whispered.

I could have used the power in my sword to continue, but it was less subtle and already people were awakening. We could hear agitated cries from the other side of the camp. I nodded my acquiescence.

'Which way is out?' he asked. The fog was as thick as ever and he had no idea where we were.

I pointed in the correct direction. 'Goddess, Brand, I am so tired . . .' I drooped against him, and in my fatigue, my powers failed me. I was not aware of Favonius's approach until he had actually loomed up out of the fog, close enough to touch.

His enraged voice lashed at me through my tiredness. 'I knew it! It is you!' He seized my left hand and looked at my palm. The golden glow of the uncovered cabochon was just visible. He flung my arm away in a gesture of distaste. 'I knew it had to be something to do with that lump of yours; it's you who has sorcerous powers! Well, there's no way the Stalwarts will retreat before one person, and a woman at that. Go to the Goddess, Ligea—'

His sword was out and aimed at my throat before I could move. But he had forgotten Brand, forgotten Brand wasn't a slave, forgotten Brand had never had the slave mentality that would have stopped him from ever threatening a legionnaire. He moved just as quickly as Favonius, and the knife he held rested at the Tribune's throat long before Favonius's sword pricked at my neck. I stepped out of reach.

'Lower your weapon very carefully,' Brand said evenly, 'or you die right here and now. And don't doubt it, Favonius.'

It was the insolent use of Favo's given name, an unthinkable liberty for a slave or even a servant, that convinced the Tribune of Brand's sincerity, more than the threat or his tone. Favonius dropped his sword point and stood still, shocked. 'I'll see you dead for this, thrall,' he said at last, his anger so strong I could taste it in the back of my throat.

'But not now, I think,' Brand replied, his voice full of quiet menace. He did not move his knife. 'What shall I do with him, Ligea?'

I straightened, almost too tired to care what he did. 'Let him go. I shall deal with him.' This time I used my sword.

Brand stepped back. Instantly, Favonius raised his sword, only to find the blade of it was no longer useable. It was a travesty of a weapon, a tangle of knobbed metal. His jaw sagged.

He took a deep breath and regained his equilibrium with a

supreme effort of will. 'You can't think we will retreat before any barbarian scum, let alone one of their bitches.'

'Why not? Think of it this way, Favo: if you are right, then they sent only one, their newest, most inexperienced recruit, to stop the Stalwarts. Go on, and you'll face the whole population of the Mirage. They will turn you all to dust.'

'How do we know others even exist?'

'You've heard enough tales to know they do. Think back, Favo. I'm sure you've heard stories about the early conquest of Kardiastan. I'm equally certain you've heard more recent stories from your fellow officers about what happens in this land.'

He paled at that and strove to understand. 'I don't know you any more. And I don't understand, Ligea. *Why?* Was it all a sham, right from the beginning? Were you always a Kardi barbarian at heart, bent on betrayal? You seemed so – so *loyal* to Tyrans. What happened? Did they ensorcel you?'

'I grew up. I learned what Tyrans really is. A behemoth, Favonius, that crushes the weak beneath it. A giant beast without compassion or understanding. Melete's heart, you came here with orders to kill babies! Is that what the Stalwarts are all about? Well, this servant of the behemoth doesn't serve any more.'

'I don't understand. I'll never understand how you could change so.'

I nodded. 'I never expected you to. Go back across the Alps, Favonius. It's your only chance.' I waved a hand around me to encompass the camp. 'You don't have enough weapons to fight with any more.' I used my sword again. The shaft of light caught him on the temple and he dropped where he stood.

'Have you killed him?' Brand asked. He didn't sound particularly upset at the thought.

I gave a low laugh. 'Brand, the way I feel at the moment, I couldn't kill an ant if I crushed it between my fingers. Although it might be wiser if I ended his life here and now. He meant what he said about seeing you dead one day.'

He wasn't perturbed. 'Our paths are not likely to cross too often.'

I lingered for a moment longer, gazing down on Favonius's prostrate body, and wondered if I did him a disservice by leaving him alive. His career was finished after this fiasco, for a start, and the Stalwarts were all he'd ever had. Or perhaps I was just looking for a reason to kill him and satisfy the panic in me, the deep unease that told me not killing Favonius would be as large a mistake as not killing Pinar when she'd lain unconscious at my feet.

I was right, of course.

If only I had done it.

If only.

Brand touched me on the shoulder. 'Let's get out of here.'

We heard shouts of consternation. The bellow of an officer, as loud and as inflamed as a male gorclak's challenge call, penetrated the fog. And the opportunity was lost. Brand put his arm around me and pulled me away. 'Quick! Which direction?' he asked.

When I awoke in the morning, Brand was cooking at the fireplace. 'Smells good,' I said. Fatigue tugged at me; even rolling over to face him was an effort.

'I had some luck hunting this morning,' he said, adding laconically, 'Duck. At least I think it was. It did have a hairy tail like a cat, though.'

'How did you get back in through the ward?'

'You forgot to renew it last night.'

'Oh, Goddess . . .'

'No harm done. I kept watch. And I didn't have to go far away to find the duck, either.'

'What are the legionnaires doing?'

'Packing up to go. The fog has gone. They've been sifting through the remains of the camp to see what they can salvage. Some of the men have been off hunting – they are short of food now. I've seen Favonius from a distance; he seems to have recovered. The Legate wanted to see you again. I told the messenger you were ill. I hinted you were ensorcelled. He – the Legate – sent back the advice that you ought to move out of the building. He says you're welcome to join them on their retreat across the mountains. Ligea, why in all Acheron's mists didn't Favonius tell everyone he believes you were responsible for what happened last night?'

'I told you he wouldn't.' I had reassured Brand of that the night before, but he hadn't quite believed me.

'How did you know he wouldn't?'

'I know Favonius. How could he tell anyone? Everyone knows he and I have been lovers for years. How can he tell his comrades-at-arms he was bedding something capable of sorcery all that time and never knew it? His pride won't let him say a word. Pride has always been Favonius's weakness. Pride and the arrogance of the younger son who made it on his own.' He brought across a plate of food to me. 'Goddess, this looks good, Brand. And I'm so hungry. There's nothing like a spot of sorcery to increase the appetite!'

By midmorning the Stalwarts were on their way.

There was nothing proud about them now. Many of them still had their gorclaks, but there was little else of value for them to take back over the Alps. Their food would be whatever they could hunt or forage on the way, their only shelters the caves they could find, their only warmth the fur cloaks they wore. Many of them were going to die, and they knew it.

I also knew it and part of me grieved.

Brand and I stood by the river and watched them ride past. The men rode without speaking, many of them making the evil-avert sign as they passed the building the Mirage had built. The Legate reined in when he came level with me. 'Legata.' He inclined his head in greeting. 'You look ill. Your servant told me you were sick.'

'I am recovering, fortunately.'

'Do you wish to ride with us?'

I shook my head. 'I have no mandate to return to Tyrans.'

'Tribune Favonius tells me you refuse to give us the information of how to cross the Shiver Barrens. Is that true?'

I nodded.

'Why is that?'

'If you sought to return to the coast that way, you would all fall to sorcery, without exception. There is no other way back to Tyrans for you but this one.' I nodded to the mountains.

'By your silence you ensure that we have no choice. Yet it is not the task of the Brotherhood to make decisions on behalf of legionnaires. You exceed your authority. Do you persist in withholding the information?'

'I do.'

He sat there looking at me in silence for a long minute. From his emotions, I had a fair idea of what he was thinking. He wondered if he could force me at sword point to tell him what he wanted to know.

I stared back. 'I'm a Compeer of the Brotherhood, Legate. You know my reputation.'

He nodded, resigned. A compeer would die rather than talk under torture. Or they'd give the wrong information. And then he'd have to face the wrath of the Magister Officii. He said, 'I shall be making a complaint to the Brotherhood about your lack of cooperation.'

'That is your privilege.'

He nodded curtly and rode on.

I said quietly to Brand, 'Rathrox will make animal mash out of him if he starts talking about what the Brotherhood should and should not do.'

Favonius was one of the last to ride by and he, too, halted his mount in front of me. His face twisted unpleasantly. 'I told no one here of what you are, but I will make you a promise, Ligea. The Brotherhood will be told all I know when I return to Tyr. If you dare to show your face again within any civilised portion of the Exaltarchy, you will have to deal with them. And if I ever hear of your return, I shall ride after you personally. You may be clever with that gem in your hand, but I doubt even you are immune to an arrow in the back.'

I was overwhelmed by a need to explain, to try to eradicate that expression of vicious hate on his face. 'Favonius—' I began, not knowing what I was going to say, but he didn't let me finish anyway.

'There is nothing – nothing! – that you could say to excuse what you have done.' He waved savagely at the line of men now fording the shallowest reach of the river. 'How many of them do you think will be alive when we reach Tyrans? Without shelter, food supplies, weapons?'

'A great many more than would have ultimately survived an incursion into the Mirage.' I didn't know whether that was true or not, but I wanted him to believe it.

'But at least they would have died in a fight, with swords in their hands! They would have fallen with honour, not perished slowly of cold and hunger and fatigue.'

'With *honour*? Is there honour in killing children, Favo? Anyway, what does honour matter to the dead? Some of you will survive this way.'

'Goddess, you understand nothing. Nothing! We are the

Stalwarts—' He choked on the words, his anger silencing him. He jerked the reins brutally to swing his mount away from me, then dug in his heels and plunged the beast down the riverbank.

Brand glanced at me. I stood, shoulders slumped, in a posture of defeat rather than triumph. My face felt pinched; I knew I looked older, and ill.

'There would have been no honour in what they would have done to the Kardis and the Mirage,' he said gently.

'No. None.'

He took hold of me and began to help me back towards the building. I could hardly walk. 'Will he really go to the Brotherhood, do you think?' he asked.

'Oh yes. Pride won't let him tell his fellow Stalwarts about me, but it won't stop him telling the Brotherhood. It is necessary for his self-esteem that he does so. He must exact his revenge at being bested by a woman, bested by someone he once trusted. Wouldn't you do that if you walked his road?'

He laughed. 'I have my pride, but it doesn't need to be fed by revenge. And as long as I have done my best within the limits of my knowledge and abilities, my pride remains intact. To be bested under those circumstances is not to be shamed. Just as it is no shame to the slave to be enslaved.'

'But to stay enslaved?'

He was still smiling. 'That was my choice. No one would have kept me a slave for very long if it hadn't been my wish. But I think I begin to understand your lack of interest in me as a man up until recently. It had nothing to do with being a "brother", did it? It had more to do with being just a shade contemptuous of a man who allowed himself to be a slave.'

I looked away, shamefaced. 'Perhaps. You are a remarkable man, Brand, and I was both insensitive and blind.'

He nodded in amicable agreement. 'And I was undoubtedly

a little stupid. I should have made things clearer long ago. Instead, I waited, and you fell in love with another man.'

'That would have happened eventually anyway.'

'Because you are both Magor? Yes, you are right. Too bad for me. And now let us change the subject – is what Favonius said true? *Are* you vulnerable to an arrow in the back?'

'Oh yes. Although I should be able to sense the approach of an assassin.'

'So, are you going to return to Tyrans?'

'Yes. We must get to Tyr before they do. I have to sell my property and secure my money before Favonius or the Legate talks to the Brotherhood and that bastard Rathrox Ligatan has my assets impounded.' I smiled without mirth. 'Otherwise you'll be claiming what is yours from empty coffers, my friend. You will have nothing to get you back to Altan. And I will have nothing to give my son when he is born.'

He made a gesture of dismissal. 'Better you forget your money. Stay here, Ligea. Explain to Temellin. Now that you have turned back the Stalwarts, he will know where your loyalty lies.'

I gave a hollow laugh. 'Ah, I fear I have done my work too well, Brand. Where is the proof the Stalwarts were ever here?'

He turned to point at the remains of the camp, only to have the gesture die half made. Behind us the grass of the plains rippled in the breeze unburnt, unmarked. The discarded weapons and broken gear had vanished. Even the legionnaire graves had been smoothed over, wiped away as if they had never existed.

'Goddessdamn.'

'As you say.'

'So what will we do? We can't cross the Alps—'

'No, I know. It would take too long. We will ride south to the edge of the Mirage, cross the Shiver Barrens there, and so on to the coast. To a place called Ordensa. It's a fishing village near the border. We'll ask a fisherman to take us to Tyr.'

'And he'll do it, just like that? A Kardi, sailing to Tyrans of his own free will?'

I raised my palm to show him my cabochon. 'I am still a Magoria. Any Kardi would be glad to serve me? We had reached the building, and he opened the door for me. I collapsed gratefully onto my pallet. 'We'll stay here a couple of days so I can rest. Then we'll ride south. Right now, all I want to do is sleep.'

CHAPTER TWENTY-NINE

Dusk came early to that part of the plains in the shadow of the mountains, but the twilight was long. Brand and I ate our evening meal sitting on the stoop in the half-light, then – still tired as a result of my use of my cabochon and sword against the Stalwarts four days earlier – I went to my pallet. Brand was pottering around, stoking up the fire, repairing a broken harness, feeding the red-eyed bird. We were intending to make an early start on our ride south to Ordensa the next morning.

I watched him and wondered at the newness of what I felt. A sort of fond affection, something more than what there had been, something less than what I knew was possible. There was no trace of Magorness about him now, and the scar on his stomach was fading. His lovemaking had become a joy to me, smoothing away some of the ache of Temellin's absence. We both knew it would end sooner or later, but the thought worried neither of us. It was something we had for now, it was precious to both of us, but not so absorbing that we would not be able to walk away from it when the time came.

I watched him, and knew he was trying to find the right words to tell me something. I said, 'You still think I should go to him, don't you?'

He looked up, relieved I had been the one to bring up the

subject. 'You belong in Kardiastan, Ligea. Look, if you want, I can go to Tyr, alone. You still have your seal and your papers on you. I can carry your instructions to Tyr, with your seal on them. I can pick up what you owe me, I can arrange to have your money transferred here, anything you like.'

I shook my head. 'No. As soon as I'm able, we'll ride for Ordensa – and Tyr.'

'But what of Temellin? Sooner or later he must find out what you have done to the Stalwarts, surely, and then he'll want you – and your son – here, if you'll forgive him for his distrust.'

'Forgive him? I never did blame him!' I turned from him so he could not see my face. 'He will have his son when the time comes.'

'And do you think he will sit quietly in Kardiastan and let you ride away? He's not that sort of man, Ligea. He'll follow you.'

'He can't leave Kardiastan. He is their Mirager, Brand. He is needed here. Anyway, they are about to take on Tyrans. They are about to begin the disintegration of the Exaltarchy; he has more to do than worry about me.' I added for good measure, 'Just as you will have, when you continue the process in Altan one day. And I, too – when I do my part, in Tyrans.' Perhaps I'd be able to forget Temellin in the process, and expiate some of the guilt I felt. Guilt at what I had been, guilt at the evil Solad had done to save me. I had perfected the art of persuading others to betrayal, when betrayal had been the basis of my life, had I but known it.

Brand radiated worry. Quite deliberately, of course. 'In Tyrans, you will be alone. Condemned, if they catch you. Stay here. Here at least you'll have power, position. In Tyrans you would be forever on the run, always hiding. Rathrox Ligatan will have your head on a stake at Tyr's main gate if ever he catches up with you.'

I turned back to him, smiling. 'No power, Brand?' I raised my hand and showed him my cabochon. It had already regained much of its colour. 'What of this? What of my Magor sword? I have all the power I need.'

He opened his mouth and then closed it again. Finally he said carefully, 'Er, may I ask just what you are planning?'

'Well, I'd like to have a hand in seeing Rathrox Ligatan gets what's due to him. At one time I would have liked to be Magister Officii, but not now. Why should I aim so low? And what better way of ending slavery, of helping Kardiastan – or even your Altan for that matter – than being the rooster at the top of the midden rather than one halfway down?' It was an idea I had been playing with for some time now, and it had been growing more and more attractive as time went by.

Brand stared, puzzled. Then his jaw dropped. 'Sweet Goddess!'

I arched an eyebrow at him. 'Have I finally managed to penetrate that inhuman calm of yours, my Altani friend?'

'The *Exaltarch*? You want to be the *Exaltarch*?'

'And why not?'

He continued to stare. Then laughter bubbled up from inside him. He slapped his thigh and roared. I had never heard Brand laugh quite like that before. I waited patiently until the gasping whoops reduced themselves, via more manageable guffaws, to the occasional chuckle.

'When you've *quite* finished—' I said.

He gave a final laugh. 'Ah, Ligea, you are really something. The compeer who was a general's daughter might be long gone, but for all that, there's still some of that old Ligea – indomitable, irrepressible Ligea – in this new one. And she's much more likeable.'

'You think I'm being ridiculous.'

He thought about that and then shook his head. 'No. No,

I don't. If you say you're going to be Exaltarch, then that's just what you will be. If you say you're going to break the Empire into a thousand pieces, then I'll believe that too. I just wish I could be there to see Ligatan's face when you wave that sword of yours under his skinny nose.'

We both smiled at the thought.

It was Brand who splintered the moment. 'I must go and start the packing while there's still a bit of light in the sky,' he said. He picked up the saddlebags and strolled out.

I lay back on the pallet, planning. There should be a way to preserve the best of the Exaltarchy while doing away with this whole idea of enslaved or tributary states. A loose trade federation, perhaps, with some kind of voluntary tax to maintain peacekeeping forces and tradeways. Yes, that might be possible. The hard thing would be to change an economy and a culture dependent on slave labour . . .

I drowsed while I waited for him, enjoying my laziness. And was jerked back to alertness by a sound. A rumbling, a deep-throated thundering, a growl, as if the ground itself were venting its rage. My head jerked up in shock, just in time to feel the pallet beneath me take on a life of its own. First it twisted, then it slewed sideways, humping up at the same time so that I had to grab hold of it to avoid being tumbled onto the floor. I was more puzzled than frightened; I thought it was another trick of the Mirage Makers − until something black flapped by my head, giving out frantic kitten-mews of terror. The red-eyed bird the Mirage Makers had supplied with the house. It wouldn't have been frightened of a change wrought by its makers.

I leapt to my feet, sword already in my hand and flaming into light − and gagged on my horror. A foul stench soured the air around me.

The Ravage.

The floor of the room between me and the door dissolved into writhing blackish slime. The far wall was already crumbling into the foulness, sliding stone by stone under the surface scum. The flagstones beneath the pallet heaved and cracked. The pinions of the black bird scraped my face as it swooped towards the broken wall on its way out; I envied it its wings. I knew I had only moments before the floor disintegrated and plunged me into the corruption of the Ravage.

I whirled, pointing my weapon at the wall closest to me. I sent the power forth to smash against the stones, praying they would give before the onslaught and provide a way to escape. The Mirage was on my side: a hole appeared that was more like a window and far too symmetrical to be wholly the result of my sword-bolt. Even as the floor disappeared from beneath my feet, I pulled myself up into the gap. The wall was thick and there was plenty of room to sit comfortably. I had no intention of lingering, however, and went to jump down on the other side.

And stopped myself just in time.

There was no ground there. Even in the near-darkness I could see that for twenty paces on the other side of the wall there was only the heaving surface of the Ravage. Shock blanched me.

I looked down. By the light of my sword I could see the monsters thrashing in the depths, swelling with obscene triumph as they tried to reach me with their slavering muzzles. I screamed then: Brand's name.

His voice came back to me out of the darkness, surprisingly calm. 'I'm here. I see you. I'm getting a rope.'

I directed a beam of light his way and found him kneeling at the edge of the Ravage, rummaging through a saddlebag with desperate haste. Behind me the roof of the building toppled, dragging much of the wall I was crouched on with it. Somewhere inside my head I heard a scream of pain that was not mine. The stones I knelt on shifted slightly; narrow cracks opened up under me. A battle, the like of which I could only guess at, raged beneath the wall. And the Mirage Makers were losing.

'Hurry!' I cried, unable to keep the panic out of my voice. This was one time when there was no pleasure in the excitement. A stone tumbled, and I heard the glugging plop it made as it hit the surface of the Ravage and was sucked under.

'I have it,' Brand said. 'Listen, Ligea. I'm saddling up a shleth and attaching one end of the rope to the saddle horn. I'll throw the other end to you. Tie it to the wall, as high as you can. That should give it some height. Then you'll have to come across hand over hand as best you can.'

'Yes.' The word was a croak, not my voice at all. I reached up with my sword and used its power to punch a hole through the wall above my head. Rock dust showered me. Somewhere to my right several more stones fell into the Ravage. Behind me the rest of the building had disappeared; my part of the wall was all that remained. I began to shake.

My brief hope that the Mirage Makers would help – build a bridge for me perhaps – had long since died. They were already doing all they could just to maintain this section of the wall so I might live a little longer. I felt their agony and thought of Pinar's son.

Inside my womb my own baby stirred, making itself felt for the first time. My concern for him was real and compelling – and a revelation. Perhaps there was something of the mother in me after all, but I had no time to think about it.

'Are you ready?' Brand asked.

'Ready.'

The rope sailed across the blackness and I caught it easily. Goddess be thanked for Brand. I threaded the rope through the hole and tied it fast.

'When you're ready,' Brand said.

A portion from the end of the wall tumbled and the rest trembled. I thrust my sword through my belt and seized the rope in both hands. At his end, Brand urged his shleth forward to keep the rope taut, but even so I found my bare toes skimming the surface of the Ravage. I hoisted my feet up and began to swing my way across the horror.

More stones fell, from both ends of the wall this time. The remaining portion was only five or six paces long now. Along the rope I could feel the way the stones shivered.

Something scraped against my leg, drawing blood. I looked down. A green scaled arm, stick-thin and dribbling slime, had reached up to me, raking me with razored claws. It gripped my ankle, digging in viciously, pulling me down towards an open gape of curved teeth and serrated jaw waiting just below the surface. My forward movement was halted.

I let myself hang by one arm and aimed my cabochon at the creature's body, bringing the gem to light, then changing light to burning coldfire. The golden stream hit the surface of the Ravage and dissipated in a spatter of molten sparks, none of which seemed to harm the thing holding me. In terror, I kicked at it with my free foot, but my bare toes connected only ineffectually with its snout and I ripped my sole open on its serrations. Moreover, the movement made me bounce, dipping me towards the surface simmering below.

'*Sod you*,' I told it and drew my sword. I slashed down, severing the creature's limb at the wrist. The clawed portion remained fastened to my ankle; the rest of the arm fell away into a roiling whirl of blood and slime.

I gagged, forced myself to return the fouled sword to my belt, then swung my legs up to lock my ankles over the rope.

'Ligea.' Brand's anguish hit me. '*The wall—!*'

I was already moving, still slung below the rope, but I was

only halfway across. At Brand's warning I looked back. The wall was heaving as the last of its foundations dissolved into the corruption. Cracks ripped through the stonework; blocks toppled.

I felt the triumph of the Ravage. I was not going to make it.

Snarling my frustration, I reached once more for my sword and slashed my connection to the wall.

Brand's howl of warning echoed in the air as I hit the surface of the Ravage. My actions were instinctive. I twisted the rope slack around my right wrist. My sword was fitted into my left hand, my cabochon in its place ... The blade flared into a blaze of gold, bathing me in its light as I was sucked into the fester. I was still screaming the conjurations of self-warding as I was dragged under.

And even while I cried out the words, I knew the limitations of their value. Any movement of mine would negate such warding: the wards might still stand, but I wouldn't be inside them ...

And so it was. First there was shock: the disbelief of a body struck by more agony than it was possible for a human being to bear. I was on fire. My skin screamed out its pain; my inner organs shrivelled with their burning; anguish tore my mind, shattering my knowledge of myself. My hands spasmed, tightening my hold on both sword and rope. My body convulsed, twisting me into a foetal travesty. I felt the core of my being, my soul, was touched by the Vortex of the Dead. I diverted as much power as I could to keep the pain at bay.

I slowed my heartbeat, slowed my breathing. I had to use power to push fluid away from my face in order to breathe at all. My sword still flamed to stave off the creatures homing in on me. Through blurred, uncomprehending eyes I saw them: twisted bodies of organic dross, twisted intelligences thriving on my suffering, watchful eyes shining with carnal glee. The beam of power from my blade sputtered ineffectually. Still, they were wary of it. Or perhaps it was the wards that held them off.

I looked upwards. As a fish might see a fisherman on the edge of a lake, I saw Brand: a dark, distorted figure, looking down. The light of my sword glowed beneath the surface, illuminating my agony for him. He was shouting to me, but the words were lost and I didn't have the strength left to enhance my hearing.

A moment later, I started to move and knew he was urging his shleth forward to pull me out. Slowly I began to roll through the foulness towards the edge. Yet as the rope dragged me one way, the Ravage sucked me down another, until I felt I was being torn in two.

It was well Brand did not understand how much pain he was bringing to me. Wave after wave of agony became a blaze that left my mind shrieking. I tried to build new wards. I tried to control my body's need for air. I tried to keep the power of my cabochon alive.

Around me the predators saw their prey being drawn away from them. They snarled and jostled, swooped down on me with claws and fangs bared, only to be turned away at the last moment by the force still glowing in my sword. The Ravage churned. And the blaze of my sword was dimming even as my body approached the edge and safety. The creatures closed in, crowing their anticipation.

One of them, its knobbed skin criss-crossed with sores, tore at my blouse with decayed yellow teeth and bit into my breast, fastening itself to me to suck my blood. In mind-blowing terror, I beat at it with my sword, but there was no strength there, nothing left to fight with. The curled mouth-parts of an obese worm ripped a piece out of my cheek and passed the flesh into its mouth. I was being eaten alive . . .

I wanted to scream and scream and scream.

But somewhere inside me I knew if I did, if I opened my mouth, the Ravage would enter my throat, burning, corrupting and killing. I kept my lips clamped closed.

Brand's roar of rage reached me, but meant little. I felt I was slipping away. I could see and hear, but movement was beyond me. The Ravage had long since seeped through the remains of my warding; the creatures were now stronger than the power of my sword; the pain was more than I could bear.

I had come to the end of my endurance. I capitulated.

Beyond feeling, I let the rope slip free.

CHAPTER THIRTY

Brand howled his anguish once more and plunged his arm into the putrescence, groping blindly in the poison, refusing to feel the acid agony shrivelling his arm to irreparably cripple him. He managed to touch me, but his fingers slithered on my slime-covered skin, couldn't grasp me as I slid away from him. His weakened fingers skidded over my breast, my neck and the torn side of my face. I couldn't do anything to help him. I scarcely comprehended what he risked in his attempt to save me. Then, as I slipped away, he hooked fingers into the limb of the beast sucking at my breast and pulled it from me.

I fell to the bottom of the foulness, came in contact with the rock beneath the sore, felt myself enclosed in a cocoon of safety. The pain didn't disappear – there were too many raw and torn patches for that – but the agony reduced itself to a manageable level. Better still, I felt the comfort and love of the Mirage Makers. Rationality returned.

They piled concepts into my head, pictures, feelings. Concept: Time. Need. *We can keep you safe here, but you cannot stay. You will soon need air. You must have help.* They offered me nothing more than a temporary security.

I said, *There is no one.*

That was when I saw Temellin in my head, his image startlingly clear.

Temellin? What could he have to do with this? *He is too far away. I do not know where he is.*

The next picture was of an embryo, and the urge I felt was a desperate desire to follow the child.

Follow the child? I assumed they referred to Pinar's son, and despaired. What kind of advice was that? I was doomed . . .

Another picture: this one showed me driving my sword tip into my cabochon. Garis had said something about that, hadn't he? But someone else had told me that if you cracked your cabochon, your life leaked away. None of this made sense! I beat down the panic once more.

I asked, remarkably calm, *You wish me to die?*

Emotion: Exasperation.

I don't know what you mean! Panic crept back, nibbling away the edges of my sanity.

They tried again: images of Temellin, of an unborn child, of a sword in my cabochon.

But for these beings, language was constricting, not liberating. Away from the Shiver Barrens, unable to use the sands, without a human form, how could they use words?

And yet they found a way. They used the only things available: the creatures of the Ravage. Goddess knows what pain it cost them, but the Mirage Makers forced the deformed jaws of those monsters to articulate laboriously formed words, spoken words, that I could hear.

'Shadow self. Your shade.' A grinding, scraping Ravage voice. Four words that chilled my soul.

And then, 'Release your essensa.'

I knew that word. Someone had said something once . . . Aemid? Temellin? *The legions can never kill our essensa. All living things have a life-force we call the essensa.* And the word had been in one of the books I'd read, too, but I couldn't remember the context.

'Put your sword through your cabochon. You will not die. We want to save you.' Kind words uttered in ugly rasping sounds, sentiments at variance with vicious teeth and foul breath and gleeful eyes.

Irresolute, I dithered. Perhaps I was wrong. Perhaps it wasn't the Mirage Makers who spoke. And if it were them, I should still question their motives.

But I was dazed and in pain and tired of the struggle. I looked down at my hand, surprised to see I still clutched my sword. I swapped it to my right hand and looked at my cabochon. Barely any colour remained; my power was almost gone. A shade? It was the best offer I had. The only offer.

Weakly, I placed the tip of the blade on the cabochon and pressed. Feeble the movement might have been, but the blade split the cabochon and drove through my hand to pin it to the rock beneath. There was no pain. I released the sword hilt, but the weapon stayed upright, quivering.

A moment later, the Ravage and its vile creatures disappeared. I was clothed in blackness. All I could see was the faint glowing outline of my sword. A mist began to form where blade met cabochon, seeping out of me, at first formless and indistinct, then becoming a bubble of vapour, mist-white against the black background. I looked into it and saw the shape there: a baby, still incomplete and embryonic – *my* son, not Pinar's. My son . . . and Temellin's. There was a whisper in the darkness, or perhaps it was in my head: *Follow him.*

I said, *I don't know how.* Yet even as I said the words, I floated free of my body, pulled by a mother's ties to her flesh and blood. *Goddess,* I thought, *the shade that came into my bedroom in Sandmurram. This is what it was. Jahan. It had been*

Jahan. No wonder I had thought him familiar when we'd first met in Madrinya.

The bubble drifted away into the utter desolation of the blackness, beckoning me with its longing.

I looked down at myself and saw my translucent form: naked, torn, defiled with sores and smirched with corruption. At my feet my body lay, solid, clothed in tatters, equally ravaged.

Free of pain, I drifted away, following my son through the darkness to his father.

And found him on the southernmost Rake. It was dawn there, and the camp was just about to settle into sleep for the day. Part of my rational mind puzzled over that – surely they should have been further away, somewhere deep in Kardiastan by now. Yet, there they all were: Temellin's small army, and Temellin himself. He stood on the edge of the rock, watching the red light of the sunrise wake the Shiver Barrens. He didn't see me at first. I opened my mouth to speak – and found I had no capacity for speech. I went to touch him, but my hand passed right through his body.

His eyes widened as he focused on the movement and realised it had form. '*Derya?*'

His use of that name, the one he had known me by when we had been lovers, brought forth a rush of tenderness for him. I nodded.

He, however, was appalled. 'Are you – are you *dead?*'

I heard the dread in his voice and his concern warmed me. I shook my head. He stretched out a hand to touch me, but it passed through my image as though I were not there.

Then he saw the floating bubble that was the shadow self of our son, and looked at it with equal incomprehension. In the dim predawn light, I doubt he realised what it was. He looked back at me. 'You can hear me.'

I nodded again and I held out my left hand to him, indicating the split cabochon.

'You know how to release your essensa? Who taught you that? And *why*? It's dangerous! You are not yet Magor-strong enough to do such a thing without risk.'

Helpless to explain, I just stood. My thoughts were muddled, not fully my own.

He took a deep breath, striving to find sense in what was happening. 'Forgive me, Shirin, for what I did. For not trusting. I have your letter.' Finding no words to tell me how he felt, he made a helpless gesture with one hand. 'What can I say? I want you – and the baby.' He ran fingers through unruly hair. 'Garis told me everything. He was a fool not to go on believing you. Korden and I are on our way back to the Mirage City with half our force. In case you weren't able—' The words almost choked him. 'Is – is the Mirage City in danger, Shirin? Is that why you have come in this form? To warn us?'

I shook my head, and he slumped with relief. He sat down at the edge of the rock, but his eyes never left my face. 'I've failed you all,' he said. 'I let my personal prejudices, my mistrust of you – I let them override my wisdom. Did you stop them, the Stalwarts?'

I nodded.

'How can I – we – ever thank you?' He heaved in a breath, trying to find the right words for what he wanted to say next. 'About Pinar; I know what you did. And I thank you – for saving my son.' He paused, his face white and strained. 'I've often wondered if I could have saved Miasa's child, if I had ripped my daughter from her mother's womb at her death, if I had given that baby to the Mirage ... When we all knew Miasa was dying, I broached the subject with her, thinking it could give her some comfort to know I might be able to save the baby. But she was appalled. She forbade it, again and again. She made me swear. The child was hers too; it was her body . . . I couldn't do it to her.' His voice trailed away and he was silent.

'I think I was wrong,' he said at last, looking away from me to the Shiver Barrens. 'With that decision I condemned the Mirage – the Mirage Makers – to further years of pain and desecration. Now it seems someone else had the strength and the determination to do what I could not.' His grief and guilt were palpable and I longed to take him into my arms. 'I should have told you. I should have told Pinar.'

I nodded, and meant it. It had been more than just a mistake; it had been *wrong*.

Brand would certainly agree with that, I thought. What's more, if he ever met Temellin again, he would doubtless tell him so, at length.

He went on, 'I had no right to keep the nature of the bargain a secret. I've known it since I was ten years old, you know. I've had to live with it since then. Never knowing what to do about it. But . . . I was always afraid someone would sacrifice themselves. How could I face Korden, for example, if it were his wife? I didn't know what to do. So I kept it to myself. I thought maybe the Mirage Makers would solve the problem themselves, somehow . . . That it would never come to this. I failed my people, Shirin. I failed my Miasa's child. I failed the Mirage Makers.'

Goddess, I thought, appalled. Realising for the first time what it must have been like for him. A child, growing up with that knowledge, not knowing who to tell. Not knowing what to do about it. Knowing that somewhere in his future he had to sanction a murder.

'Pinar,' he said, after a long pause. 'She was thoroughly irrational where you were concerned. Cabochon knows, that at least was clear enough to me. She poured out her bitterness day after day, carried it to our pallet at night.' He raised tormented eyes to me. 'My fault, I fear. I couldn't give her the love she needed to be a happy woman. You have that. You always will. And she knew it. You can't tell lies to a Magor woman. Shirin, we can work this out – is that why you came?'

The sun's rays reached us at last and by its light he saw my ravaged skin. His gasping '*Derya—!*' tore at me. He stretched out a disbelieving hand towards the wound on my face, but then withdrew it, remembering I had no substance. 'The Ravage . . .'

I nodded again.

He swore, words I didn't know, and turned from me, shouting, his voice harsh in the windless silence of the Rake. Within moments they were there: Korden, Zerise, Garis and tens of others of the Illusos and Theuros.

'Ravage sores,' Korden said with certainty, his eyes hostile. He wouldn't forgive me Pinar's death in a hurry.

'That's her essensa,' Zerise said, her scarred face thrown into stark relief by the coming light of day. 'The other is her child.' She brushed back an untidy hank of grey hair.

'But he – he is still in her womb, surely,' Temellin protested, finally understanding the floating globe.

'The Mirage Makers must be involved, and who knows what the Mirage Makers are capable of? But she needs help, Mirager.'

This last was said with so much reluctance I found it hard to nod my agreement. I could already feel myself fading.

'Can she hear us?' asked Garis. His emotions yearned at me, full of guilt and shame, asking for my forgiveness. I pitied him; I recognised all the signs of an overdeveloped conscience playing havoc with someone who failed his own high standards. Garis was finding it hard to live with himself.

'Yes,' the Illusa replied. 'But her essensa has no strength, no substance.'

Temellin cut her short. 'I want to get to her. I am going to follow her back.'

Zerise's razored features jabbed at me even as she looked at him. 'She is close to death wherever she is. Act wisely, Mirager. Kardiastan relies on *you* for its future.' Her emphasis nagged at me, telling me something, but I had no inclination to think about it just then.

'No, wait—' Korden interrupted. 'Temel, *think*! If you go as an essensa, how will you be able to help her if you have no substance?'

'My cabochon will retain its powers. Some of them, anyway. Garis, get my sword.'

'What can you do for her that she can't do for herself? She has her own cabochon! She's dying, Temel. There's nothing you can do. But if you go, you may not come back. There's always a chance the essensa may lose its hold on reality – forget it has a body to go back to. And if it delays too long, the body dies.'

'I've done it before,' he pointed out, his voice tight with irritation. 'And so did Jahan, when we needed a spy after I'd lost my sword.'

I wanted to laugh at the irony. If Jahan had glimpsed me that night in the Prefect's villa in Sandmurram, my whole charade as Derya would have been doomed from the start.

'It was dangerous then, and it's dangerous now,' Korden said. 'You shouldn't risk yourself.'

Temellin looked back at me as Garis returned and handed him his sword. 'There's not much a person can do as an essensa, but if you are ill with the effects of Ravage sores, I can help to heal you.'

But Korden still wasn't about to give up. 'If you must help her, send someone else.'

'This is my child. They are both my responsibility.'

'This is the woman who killed your wife,' Korden said, 'who killed one of the Ten.'

Temellin turned on him, almost vicious. 'This is the woman who went to save your family, Korden, when our foolishness left the Mirage City undefended and our future – our children – in jeopardy. And you'd better hope she did succeed against the Stalwarts, as she says she has, because if she has failed, there's little hope we'll get there before the legionnaires do.' He pointed to the sword-shaped mark on my breast. 'Look at that, Korden, and tell me she's not worth saving.'

Illusa-zerise laid a hand on Korden's arm. 'He is your Mirager, Magori,' she said, resigned.

'He's also my cousin – my friend! I can't let him kill himself for this – this – Tyranian traitor!'

'Magoria-shirin is your cousin too.' The words came not from Temellin, but from Garis. 'And she is Kardi. Don't make the same mistake I did, Magori.' He blushed miserably, embarrassed perhaps by his temerity, perhaps by the memory of his unjustified suspicions of me.

But Temellin was done with talking. He sat and pressed his sword down onto his cabochon. As mine had done, it split and the sword went on into his hand. He lay back down on the rock.

Zerise cried, 'Fah-Ke-Cabochon-rez!' and the words were taken up by all standing there, even Korden.

A mistiness gathered around his cabochon, a fog that grew and took on form as it swelled, pouring out of the palm. It wavered, gained definition and then steadied: Temellin, naked and visible, but with an unreality about his figure. The face lacked expression, the body moved with a stately smoothness that seemed unreal. The skin was waxy smooth, the eyes unblinking.

The Temellin lying on the red rocks of the Rake was as motionless as death.

I turned to our son and the blackness closed in on me once more.

CHAPTER THIRTY-ONE

I was back in my body, back with the pain, in desperate need of air. And so very, very tired. It was tough even to keep my eyes open. I wanted to slip away ... I managed – just – to wrench the sword point from my cabochon. The gem closed up behind the blade, leaving the surface unblemished.

Temellin stood rigid and taut a few paces away. His cabochon glowed gold, casting an eerie light on his sweat-glazed skin and the knotted muscles of his body. The fluid ooze of the Ravage did not seem to touch him; he had enclosed himself within a warded space, perhaps more out of distaste for his surroundings than any real need. The corruption of the Ravage could not hurt an essensa. Nor could its creatures; they swam in frustrated circles, tails flicking angrily, spines and claws and talons extended.

Temellin gave them a cursory glance as though he were dismissing them from his calculations. I knew better; he paid them no attention because he didn't need to just then – but he knew exactly how dangerous they would be to me the moment I left the cocoon of safety the Mirage Makers had built for me.

He looked up at Brand and made a throwing gesture with his hand, following it with a mime of rope pulling. Seconds later, a length of rope curled out over the Ravage, rested for a moment on the surface scum, then began to sink, slowly, through the muck. Ignored by the swimming beasts, it finally landed several paces from where I lay.

I didn't know what good it would do. I was too weak to move, too close to suffocation to do more than lie as still as possible. And Temellin couldn't touch or hold anything.

I underestimated him. He may not have been able to pick up the rope, but with his cabochon powers he could call up a wind, and he could penetrate the ward the Mirage Makers had placed around me. It was hardly a gale he created, but it was sufficient to stir the viscidity of the Ravage, to create a flow. The Ravage resisted, but it was Temellin who prevailed. The rope wavered forward on the flux, inched into my cocoon of protection and then under the curve of my ankle. It took longer to coax the flow upwards so the rope snaked around my foot, then over itself to make a knot.

Finally it was done.

Temellin looked at me in compassion, then nodded to Brand.

And I was back in the Ravage, back in the agony, back in the midst of the beasts. A battle boiled around me, with Temellin at the centre of it. Gold fire sizzled in rotting flesh, globules of molten fire spattered and burned. A worm-shaped creature disintegrated in a gush of pus; another melted. Something tangled momentarily in my hair before a beam of light seared a hole through its body and, threshing in pain, it dropped away into the depths. I was drenched with the decay of evil. I swam in bloodied slime and green rot . . .

Then I was free, cradled in Brand's arms. I let go and faded into the nothingness beyond me.

*   *   *

When I woke, I didn't open my eyes. I wanted to test the world little by little, one sense at a time, in case it was better not to wake at all.

Touch first. I was warm. I was wrapped up in something that prickled roughly, and the heat from a fire warmed one side of my body. More intimately, joints and muscles protested; my skin felt raw enough to have been exposed to the Shiver Barrens for a day or two; my cheek ached. A tentative fingering of my face told me I had an indentation there that would be permanent. I'd been scarred.

Next, hearing. The crackle of the fire, the far-off sound of river water over stones, and the nearby rustle of someone moving quietly. I had the idea it had been a voice that had awoken me. They were all pleasant sounds.

And pleasant smells too: the sweet scent of cooking remba rhizomes mixed with barbecued meat. Brand had been hunting again. There was also a whiff of shleth, a little too strong an aroma for my taste, as though I'd been snuggled up to one in my sleep.

Next, I tried my cabochon sensing powers – nothing. They were far too weak.

I opened my eyes.

Temellin's essensa hovered at my side; Brand was by the fire. Neither of them was looking at me. Brand was gazing at Temellin belligerently, which seemed odd, considering the essensa was now much more ethereal than it had been. In such a form, the Mirager was hardly somebody to raise Brand's ire. But irate he was. He said, 'Do you know what hell she went through thinking she would be the one to supply the Mirage with what it needed? She thought *she* was the one who was going to die, Temellin – all those weeks of imprisonment she thought she was doomed – and all you could do was turn your back. Ocrastes damn you, was it her fault she was taken by Tyrans as a child?'

I had evidently woken in the middle of what must surely have been a one-sided argument. I moved restlessly, and they both swung towards me. 'He knows it, Brand,' I said. 'Leave it be, eh?'

He stared at me, expressionless, then shrugged and turned away.

I looked back at Temellin. 'You are weakening. You must go back. Now.' I hesitated, not wanting to say goodbye, because any farewell would seem too final. In the end, I settled for: 'I'll miss you.' It sounded banal and quite inadequate.

He nodded, but made no move to go.

'Tem – I'm fine. You've healed the worst – the rest will improve with time. And the baby is fine too.' He still didn't move. What was it Brand had said? *He's not that sort of man—*

He was blackmailing me. And I wasn't foolish enough to call his bluff. I capitulated, as he guessed I would, and threw up my hands. 'All right, all right! We intend to ride south, to Ordensa, to arrange a passage for Tyr. But I'll wait for you there first. It's a small place, isn't it? You'll find me. I'll wait two weeks; no longer. But, Tem, it will just be to say goodbye. We have to be in Tyr ahead of Favonius and the Stalwarts, because I need time to settle my affairs before Rathrox moves in and seizes my property.'

He smiled, a smile of angry triumph, and then he was gone, fading out within a second.

Brand sighed. 'One day you'll have to tell me about the Magor and shades. But not now. I feel as if I've had enough unpleasant surprises to last several lifetimes. Are you hungry?'

'Ravenous.' I tried to struggle up, but pain in my chest made me wince. 'By all that's holy, how did I manage to crack a rib?'

Brand looked guilty. 'Er, well that was me, actually. You didn't seem to be breathing when we got you out, and I couldn't feel your heart, so I sort of, um, thumped you to get things started again, while Temellin did whatever it is you people do with that cabochon thing.'

I groaned and bit off the ungracious complaint I was tempted to utter; instead, I managed to sound grateful as I thanked him. He helped me to sit up and I looked around.

We had left the Mirage. We were in the foothills somewhere, near a stream, and I was safe from the Ravage. Our shleths were grazing nearby; those scarifying peaks of the Alps towered beyond. It all looked peaceful. And normal.

I glanced down at the blanket covering me and identified the source of the strong smell of shleth. '*Saddle*cloths?'

He gave a dismissive wave of the hand. 'Our cloaks went down with the building. Fortunately there were a few odds and ends still in the saddlebags, including your purse and a change of clothing. 'Fraid that's all we've got.'

'My sword. What happened to my sword?'

'It's safe. You held on to it. You dropped the rope – but not your sword.' He snorted. 'Typical bloody-mindedness.'

I managed a smile, as he had hoped I would. 'Watch who you insult, you Altani barbarian. And tell me what happened.'

'You've been out for a full day. Temellin healed you. Mostly, anyhow. I guess a broken rib takes time to grow back properly.'

I looked at my cabochon. The gem really was whole again, without any sign of a crack or cut, although it was colourless. My hand touched my cheek, not wanting to remember.

He cleared his throat. He could have offered all kinds of platitudes to console. Instead, he said, 'It's noticeable. And not pretty. It's red and puckered. The colour will fade with time. It won't matter to him any more than it matters to me. Don't worry about it.'

'I don't.'

He heard the catch in my voice. 'What is it? The baby?'

'He's fine. It wasn't the baby I was thinking of – it was you.'

'What about me?'

'I'm not blind, Brand. What's wrong with your arm?'

'I had to haul you out somehow.' He swallowed. 'It's not so very terrible.'

I reached up to run my fingers down his left arm from shoulder to wrist. The arm was withered, without muscle or strength, a pitiful parody of what it had been.

I asked, 'Why didn't he heal you too?'

'All his efforts had to go to you. You were so close to death. And it took all the strength he had. I don't begrudge the way he used his power, Ligea, and neither should you.'

I said sadly, 'I can't heal it now, Brand. It is too late. And I'm too weak anyway.'

He gave another shrug. 'I guessed as much. It doesn't matter. It gives me no pain, and I still have some use of my fingers. It's just there's not much strength there any more. Neither of us has come through this unscathed – but we are still here.'

I took his hand in mine. 'Dear friend. How much I owe you.'

He gave a smile. 'Maybe I'll claim the debt one day – from the next Exaltarch of Tyrans.'

He would, too, the Altani bastard. I grinned at him.

CHAPTER THIRTY-TWO

The small fishing boat was tied up to the jetty in Ordensa and the owner was sitting in the open area at the back of his vessel, strengthening the stitching in a sail. He was an old man, dressed in shabby work clothes spangled with fish scales. A cloth cap pulled over his head protected a bald patch from a hot sun. His toughened hands and scarred fingers manipulated the curved bone of the sailmaker's needle and the stiff hide of the sail with a confidence born of long experience.

He was so intent on his job he didn't notice someone had stopped beside the boat and was looking down on him – but I did. I was seated in the cabin, and from where I sat I could see the newcomer's feet and sandals. I didn't need to see more; my sensing powers told me exactly who it was.

The fisherman finally looked up, and surprise stilled his fingers.

The expected voice: gentle yet authoritative – and so well loved. 'Bitran of the *Platterfish*?'

The fisherman nodded. 'That's me. And this here is the *Platterfish*. Best boat on the coast, even though we are bound for Tyr next trip.'

The man squatted down at the edge of the wharf so that he came into my view. He was thinner than he had been, but his brown eyes – so like mine – tilted at the corners and his hair, as usual, was in disarray. He said, 'I believe there is someone here I want to see, Bitran.'

Bitran gave me an uncertain glance, and I nodded. He gestured at the companionway. 'The Magoria is in there.'

Temellin took a coin from his purse. 'Go and buy yourself a drink, Bitran. In fact, buy several.' He swung himself down into the boat and walked across to the top of the companionway.

'That was very high-handed of you, Tem,' I said. 'It *is* his boat.'

He was looking down at me, but with the sunlight behind him, I couldn't see his face. He said, 'I wish I dared to be just as high-handed with you. Derya, *why*? Why do you feel you have to leave?' He came down the steps, ducking his head to avoid the low beams. The cabin was tiny and with both of us standing, we were only half a pace apart, yet he didn't touch me. 'Where's Brand?'

'Delivering our shleths to the man who's agreed to buy them. He won't be back for several hours. I *have* to go, Tem. You know why. I don't think sisters should marry brothers.'

His face took on a look of stubborn resistance and genuine bafflement. 'You could still stay. And we're having a child. I love you, Derya. I want you around. I want my son. Derya, for pity's sake – I have lost two of my children, don't let me lose the third. Please.'

'You won't lose him! I will send him to you. Or better still, you send someone to pick him up.'

His surprise, and his paradoxical hurt, filled the cabin. 'You'd give him up, just like that?'

I feigned indifference, hiding the truth in the way I phrased the next sentence. 'I don't think I'm cut out to be much of a mother.' Perhaps I wasn't, but when I thought of this growing life, tenderness seeped into my heart. Treachery from within.

Is this how Wendia once felt about me? And Aemid? Wendia died knowing she had failed to protect her daughter, and that must have been a terrible way to end one's conscious moments. And Aemid lived, knowing she had failed me. Perhaps I was only just now beginning to understand her anguish. And I was about to fail my son as a mother too . . .

Melete give me strength.

I knew I couldn't keep him, this boy of ours. He was Kardiastan's heir. I had a flash of memory: my hands soaked in Pinar's blood, her son cupped in my palms. Why was my life studded with separations of children from their mothers? My son would never know me. That gnawing at my insides, it was painful.

'But why must you go at all?' Temellin asked. The emotion he allowed me to feel was more puzzlement than anger. 'Is it because you haven't forgiven me for my disbelief?'

'No. Goddess knows, I gave you grounds enough to disbelieve! But I do have reasons for leaving Kardiastan. Half a dozen of them.'

'I don't need half a dozen. I need just one that makes sense to me. And – and the one you did have is not valid. This brother-sister thing. Derya—' He stood straighter, made an effort to be more in command of himself. 'I'll give you a reason to stay, the best I can think of. You aren't Shirin. You aren't my sister. We were wrong. You are Sarana, my cousin, Miragerin of Kardiastan.'

I went cold all over. *He knew!* And then: *He loves me enough to tell me?* Goddess, I didn't deserve that. I swallowed. 'How did you find out?'

His smile quirked with irony. 'You told me in your letter. When you hinted that the Mirage Makers mentioned to you their need of an unborn child. I couldn't believe they would give that information to Shirin. They hadn't given it to Korden when he walked the Shiver Barrens, and at that time he was my heir, so why would they give it to you? I tried to tell myself it was because you were bearing my child, but somehow it just didn't seem right. Especially when, in the end, it was Pinar's son who became a Mirage Maker. So I started to think about things. I remembered what you said about your memories of your childhood in Kardiastan, and suddenly it seemed more of a description of a fight involving a howdah. And then I went to Zerise again. I pestered her, and finally she admitted she was uneasy about you being Shirin. It seems you have Sarana's eyes.'

I waited for him to go on, to tell me how Solad had made a traitor of himself, but he said nothing, to spare me the pain, perhaps. He must have worked it out, of course. Maybe he'd always suspected it; Solad was the one who had sent the ten Magoroth children away, after all.

I stared at him, emotions suppressed, stomach churning. Was he truly willing to sacrifice all he was, all he had – for *me*? Sweet Elysium, *he was prepared to trust me with his land*! With his people.

This was what it was to love.

Something fundamental inside me shifted position, grinding into me with deep-felt, intense pain. I knew myself inadequate, less than he was. I loved, but my love was a damaged thing, torn by so many betrayals, folded and put away and ignored until now, when I wanted to take it out again and shake it free – only to find it flawed and tattered, creased with memories of where it had been, of what had been done to it, of the pain it had caused.

He touched my shattered cheek with the back of his hand. 'You are beautiful,' he said, and perhaps I was to him.

My eyes filled with tears. He took me in his arms, holding

me gently, shielding his feelings, as if afraid the strength of his passion would frighten me away. 'Stay,' he said. 'Be our Miragerin.'

'Tem,' I said, 'I couldn't take away from you what you are! You *are* the Mirager of Kardiastan. More than that, you are the ruler everyone wants; not me. I'm not the person for this land.'

'You want power. I know you do.'

'But not this way.'

'When you walked the Shiver Barrens, what were you told? Did they show you a Mirager bestowing cabochons? Did they tell you the conjurations for it?'

I nodded.

'Then you were given a Mirager's sword. And a mandate to rule. You just didn't realise what you had been told.' He pulled back a little so he could see my face. 'Derya, you are the rightful Mirager, not I.'

'I don't want it.'

He saw something in my expression I hadn't known was there. He exclaimed, bewildered, 'You – you knew all along! That's why you are leaving, isn't it? Damn it, you make me so *ashamed*. I didn't trust you, and all along you knew what you could have had.'

I interrupted. 'Not all along. And I'm no saintly handmaiden to the gods, either, Tem.' Just a better person than I once was. I'd felt the claws and teeth of evil in my flesh, and the horror of it was still with me. In the creatures of the Ravage, I'd glimpsed the soul of what I had once nearly become, and I hadn't liked it. I wanted to be better than that, better than I had been – but there were limits to how much one could change in a single lifetime.

I said, with brutal honesty, 'I'm doing this for myself as much as for you. I don't *want* to rule Kardiastan. I'm not the person for the job: you are. The Mirage Makers may have given me the sword, but they haven't taken yours away. You still have a mandate to rule.'

He absorbed that, feeling my truth. And said, 'We could rule jointly. As husband and wife. How much better if Kardiastan had two Mirager swords! I almost wrecked everything when I lost mine.'

'You were going to kill yourself, weren't you? I saw the relief in your eyes, but I didn't recognise it for what it was. You were going to sacrifice yourself for your land because you'd lost your sword, and now, in a way, you want to do it all over again. For me. Well, I won't let it happen.'

'It's not a sacrifice! Not if we rule jointly. We need never fear the loss of a sword again. We'd have two! And you would stop me making so many mistakes. The only person I've ever been able to rely on is Korden – but I don't see eye to eye with him on so many things. Derya, I've been so damned *lonely*.'

With that, he almost persuaded me. Almost. But something else prevailed. Commonsense? Selfishness? 'Tem, Tem – it wouldn't work. Think about it for a minute, the practicalities. We'd end up hating one another. It's one thing to make a sacrifice, it's quite another to live with the results. We want the same things, you and I, but neither of us is big enough to share them. And I'd never be accepted by most of the Magoroth. I killed one of the Ten, for a start!' Every word was the truth, and every word was a destruction of desire, a slash across the dream of a future. 'I bet you and Korden had yet another argument when you told him you were coming here to see me. Especially when you should be off fighting the legions.'

His anger stirred, a remnant ember glowing in the cold ashes of the rage that had once led him to fling his sword at me. 'You can't turn me down because of Korden!'

'No. Tem, I'm – I'm going to Tyrans. I'll work for Kardiastan there; I'm going to bring down the Exaltarch from within. I'm going to halt the slavery.'

'That's ridiculous! I can't let you go.'

'Tem, you can't keep me here against my will.'

We stared at each other, and I felt the ember flicker as his anger burned brighter. 'Skies above,' he said, 'have you thought how dangerous it will be for you in Tyrans? Once the Stalwarts return to Tyr, the Brotherhood will be looking for you. And you would take our child into such danger?'

'It's no safer for me in Kardiastan. Less so, in fact, because I can't stay in the Mirage, because of the Ravage. It will be years before Pinar's son is strong enough to help the other Mirage Makers get rid of it. And even here, outside of the Mirage – well, the Tyranians must be scouring the streets looking for Ligea by now, and that's just when they think I'm on their side. You aren't going to take back your land overnight. You'll have to fight the legions every inch of the way, and there are still so few of you. I'd be no safer here than in Tyrans.'

'We need you, Derya. We need your Magoroth strength. I need you.' His voice shook. The ember of anger was a glowing coal now; I could feel its heat. 'You still haven't given me a reason I can accept.'

'Tem, I have something to do in Tyr. Something I need to do. Until I have, I shan't be able to live at peace. I love you more than I can say, but I don't want to stay here.'

'There's something you're not telling me.' His shrewd brown eyes narrowed. 'What is it – guilt? You've guessed—?'

'About Solad? Yes. Had you realised he was the traitor before all this happened?'

'I wondered. I always wondered. It seemed so . . . convenient that he sent the Ten to safety just before the massacres. And as I was growing up I heard people say he was not acting normally after the death of his wife and daughter. And then

Zerise told me long ago that Solad had his sword with him that night of the Shimmer Feast. She saw him kill legionnaires with it. But it was forbidden to bring swords into the hall, so that was strange too.' He scowled. 'A salve to his twisted conscience, I suppose. As if taking a few Tyranian soldiers with him could make up for what he did.'

'I've been unlucky in my fathers, haven't I? And I do feel I owe Kardiastan something because of that. But even that's not what drives me. It's more personal than that.' I took a deep breath. 'It's a need to do something about what was done to me. They *wronged* me, Temellin. Gayed, Rathrox Ligatan and Bator Korbus. They murdered my true mother in front of my eyes.' That golden woman, splattered with crimson. She died under the swords of Gayed's men while I watched, too young to understand what I saw. 'They turned my true father into a traitor and made him commit a crime, the immensity of which I can't even begin to imagine. They twisted him until there was no way out but to join those he betrayed in death.' That laughing, loving man holding out his arms for me while I ran barefoot, across an agate floor, towards his embrace. 'They enslaved my people. They took me from what was left of my family, to raise me themselves. I was only a child when they began a deliberate plan to . . . deform me. They deprived me of everything that was mine, and distorted my life into something that was foul. And as they did it, as they watched me grow up, they mocked me.'

I met his eyes, begging him to understand. 'Then they threw me back into the arena, intending *me* to finish what they had begun. To have me kill my own people. My own cousin, the Mirager. What they did was evil. Vile, by anyone's standards. And they almost succeeded. They shouldn't be allowed to triumph. Do you understand?'

He nodded. 'Yes. Of course I do.' He cupped my face,

touching me gently, belying the ever-present anger. 'But you can fight them here. We can defeat them here.'

'Perhaps. But it won't bring me the satisfaction I crave. Bator Korbus would still occupy the Exaltarch's seat in Tyr, and Rathrox Ligatan would still run the Brotherhood. Every year there would be another attempt on your borders. They would blockade your ports, sink your fishing fleet. Your whole rule will be one of battle and invasion. Is that what you want? Continually having to breed more Magoroth to throw against an enemy who can draw on resources all the way from here to the Western Reaches? Is that what I would be delivering our son to?'

The ember of anger flared, to unite with his scorn. 'I have an army. And I have fifty Magoroth swords behind me. You have no one except Brand, and you think you can make a difference in Tyrans? You think you can help us by being in Tyr – one lone woman against the Exaltarch? Are you *mad*?'

'I won't be one lone woman for very long, Temellin. For every two citizens of Tyrans, there is a slave.'

His breath caught as he considered the enormity of what I planned to do, and the fire of his anger seared. I think he knew then that I needed justice for myself more than I needed him. More than I needed his son. How could such knowledge not hurt him? He was willing to sacrifice all he was for me, and I rejected that offering. Worse, the sacrifice I made, of my own chance at happiness, was made not for him, nor for our son – but for myself. I needed to bring down the men who had wronged me. I needed to obliterate the system that had made it possible. And I was willing to pay heavily.

He stepped away from me, but in the confines of that cabin there wasn't far he could go. I was so aware of the rage flaming through him.

'Yes,' he said. 'That is a reason I understand. There was a

time when I burned with a similar passion for revenge. I grew out of it. Perhaps you're even right, we could become two reed monkeys fighting over the same stretch of rushes if you stayed, but I doubt it. I think what we had would have helped us rise above such pettiness.'

What we had. I heard the past tense and lowered my head so he wouldn't see the anguish in my eyes. 'I want justice. Not revenge.'

He snorted. 'Justice, revenge, whatever you call it. You will find out one day just how high the price you are going to pay really is.'

'I already know.'

'No. You haven't the faintest idea.' His scorn was obliterating, wiping my words away.

And, of course, he was right. I thought I knew, but I really had no idea at all . . .

If I had known, I would never have started.

By now his anger and his love and his hurt were so inextricably mixed, it was hard for him to pull them apart and for me to recognise them. When he showed me the way he felt, it was an assault on my senses, driving breath from my lungs. I turned away from him, leaning against the hull, resting my forehead against the boards. The cabin was awash with too much emotion.

There was a long silence until both of us had more control.

'Will you ever come back?' he asked finally.

'Yes, yes, of course.' I turned to face him. 'To see you – to see you both. And one day I shall come as Exaltarch, as the ruler of a State coming to visit a fellow monarch and his son.'

He stared, disbelieving. 'You're out of your mind! The *Exaltarch*? Cabochon, Derya—! How can you even *envisage* that? With a ragtag army of slaves more used to wielding a scythe or a pickaxe or a broom, against the empire's finest legionnaires?

That's insane! And stupid. And it's not like you to be stupid.'

'I spent a lot of time warded in a room with no one to talk to, day after day. I did a lot of thinking about this. I have no intention of being stupid.'

There was another long silence. I could almost feel him dampening down his rage, smothering the flame, depriving it of fuel. It was still there, though, smouldering in some dark, deep recess of his soul. It always would be. What I was doing to him was just another form of betrayal and I was uniquely placed to know how much fury betrayal generates. Goddess, I thought, we are becoming experts at hurting one another.

Then his lips twitched, but there was more sardonic appreciation than amusement in the result. 'Sarana – you always were a little devil. I used to hate playing with you. Who'd have thought that would change so much?' He gave a laugh, half rueful, half bitter. 'Or maybe nothing's changed. You used to make me cry then, too. Ah, Derya – no, Sarana – fate played a nasty trick on us.'

'Do I go with your blessing then, Tem?'

He shook his head. '*Blessing?* Never! But I don't know how to stop you.'

'No. That's because there *is* no way.' I let him feel the truth of that.

He threw up his hands in resignation. 'So when do you leave Ordensa?'

'We were just waiting for you to arrive. We'll sail tomorrow morning.'

He put his head on one side, regarding me with eyes that had lost their laughter and a gaze that hungered. 'I'm not your brother any more. Is that going to make any difference to how you spend the next few hours?'

I swear my heart stopped beating. 'Ah, yes. Um, it certainly could do.'

We both knew this time would be different. Our need was there, but the joyous sparkle had gone, and we both doubted we'd ever get it back.

But we still loved, oh, yes; only it was such a dark, grieving love.

Glenda Larke is an Australian who now lives in Malaysia, where she works on the two great loves of her life: writing fantasy and the conservation of rainforest avifauna. She has also lived in Tunisia and Austria, and has at different times in her life worked as a housemaid, library assistant, school teacher, university tutor, medical correspondence course editor, field ornithologist and designer of nature interpretive centres. Along the way she has taught English to students as diverse as Korean kindergarten kids and Japanese teenagers living in Malaysia, Viennese adults in Australia and engineering students in Tunis. If she has any spare time (which is not often), she goes bird watching; if she has any spare cash (not nearly often enough), she visits her daughters in Scotland and Virginia and her family in Western Australia. Visit the official Glenda Larke website at www.glendalarke.com

Find out more about Glenda Larke and other Orbit authors by registering for the free monthly newsletter at www.orbitbooks.net